NOIR
BOOK TWO

*The Illumination Paradox*

*Jacqueline Garlick*

This is a work of fiction. Names, characters, organizations, places, events, and incidents are either products of the author's imagination or are used fictitiously.



Published by Skyscape, New York

www.apub.com

Amazon, the Amazon logo, and Skyscape are trademarks of Amazon.com, Inc., or its affiliates.

ISBN-13: 9781503944565
ISBN-10: 1503944565

Cover design by Kevin C. W. Wong & Mae I Design and Photography

Printed in the United States of America

*For my son Seth, who has tasted the color purple.*

*And for my mother, Milly, who recently passed away after spending eight long years trapped inside her own Madhouse Brink, trying desperately to escape through the memory-robbing doors.*

*May she at last be reunited with her long-lost Urlick, who I'm convinced is up there busily wooing her all over again, on the off chance she has forgotten him. Kiss Dad for me, will you, Mom?*

# Prologue

***Flossie***

Grey, wraithlike bodies twist and turn through the mist—swooping, chanting, cackling. Their white-eyed faces ignite terror in my galumphing heart.

*The Infirmed.* Eyelet wasn't bluffing.

I swing at them and attempt to run, but atrophied fingers sink deep into my skin. They drag me to the forest floor and anchor me there with the weight of twenty Brigsmen. *"No!"* I scream and wrench my head. *"Eeeeyeleeeet!"* I shout after her.

"T'ain't no use screamin'. T'ain't nobody left alive out 'ere to save yuh." The bloodshot eyes of a ghoul appear in front of me, bulging from inside a levitating head. His irises burn, white flames inside silver candles. I try to look away, but I can't. His skin is parchment-paper-thin, transparent in places, flaking and torn in others, showing layer upon layer beneath—but no blood. I scream at the thought of it. He claps a bony hand to my mouth. The bloodless veins in his arms have risen to the surface and hardened, shining like twisted silver bars. He must be on the verge, about to Turn. He'll need to feed again to complete the process.

"No!" I thrash and squirm.

"T'ain't no use struggling, either." He grins, producing yellow fangs for teeth. "It's over for yuh now." He laughs, and I gag on the stench of his rotting-corpse breath. Bits of his nose and ears fall away, dropping to my chest.

I shudder and buckle.

"Relax." He hovers closer. "It'll be easier that way. *At least—for me!*" He laughs again as I scream out. He breathes his toxic mist into my mouth. It tastes of cyanide silver, tinged with arsenic. I try to spit it out. The world around me tilts and shifts. I'm acutely aware of every nerve in my body jumping. Bile rises up from my gut and pools in my throat. I twist and fight, or at least I think I'm fighting.

The creature swirls in behind me with lash-like speed, sinking his fangs into the back of my skull, popping them first through the skin—then penetrating the bone. I cringe and cry out under the force. Others ghouls swoop above me, filling the air with demonic chants. Their howling reverberates off the trees and through my bones. Slowly I feel my marrow evaporating.

The creature begins to feed. His venom coils through me, paralyzing my muscles and numbing my thoughts. *I can't stop him. I can't stop him . . .* my arms drop at my sides.

Then, just as quickly as he started, he stops.

A strange light glows above his head. There's a violent, crackling crash. Whips of green lightning snap.

A seam rends the sky, and another world is revealed behind it.

Or at least I think one is.

A beautiful world, beyond our own . . .

White clouds, blue sky, yellow sun . . .

It is glorious. Simply glorious.

But it doesn't last.

The forest falls dark again, save for the eerily green glow of the light hovering just above the treetops. What is this? What's happening?

I long to turn my head to see.

A deafening boom shocks the forest floor beneath us. The earth rolls violently at my back. I'm tossed around inside the movement like a tiny ship in a tumultuous sea. Hurriedly the ghoul extracts his fangs from my head, prying them loose with a hollow *thwock, thwock.* I wince, feeling a rush of pain from the release of his venom, as the earth rolls again. All around me, apparitions rise, looking like moth-eaten curtains fleeing to the sky.

They're leaving. They're abandoning me. Why?

Something very bad must be happening.

"Wait!" I force myself into a sit, clawing after the cloaks of still-spiraling apparitions scattering to the trees. "Wait! Don't leave me here!"

They churn away into a cloud of dust, leaving me alone in the rocking forest.

Noise, I reason. They hate noise. That must have been it?

Or is it light they hate?

Either way, it doesn't matter. They've gone. *I'm saved!*

Reaching up, I tentatively explore the wounds on the back of my head, a thin veil of blood trickling down my neck, and I faint.

*

A gun goes off and I launch upright, eyes wobbling. The sound of carriage tack jangles. Hooves stomp the dirt. Gunshots again. The shots are coming from the clearing.

Someone's here! They've come for me, to save my life—or what's left of it.

I've got to get to the edge of the forest, quick!

I grab for my skirts and bobble to a stand, with a great sight-bending *whoosh*. Head throbbing, I turn with the intention of running but fall instead, against the jagged bark of the tree. I grip its girth, my brain sloshing around in its cavity. *My heavens*, what is this? I reach up to steady my head, but it takes several moments before my brain anchors into place again. *Good Lord*, what's happened to me?

I look down and gasp, realizing the problem—or at least one of them: I'm no longer in possession of feet. They're gone, completely gone, replaced by a mass of curling vapour that spreads out from under my dress in all directions. Tentacles now drift across the forest floor where feet used to be. Tentacles, like those of a sea creature. There must be eight of them, if not ten. A fearful, high-pitched noise escapes me, of which I'm not proud.

I hike my skirts higher, realizing my legs are gone, too. All the way up to my knees. "*Good God*," I squeak. "The Turning has begun."

I clap a hand to my forehead and it slides on through. Lord have mercy, I've lost half my head.

Slowly I grope the ground, tentacles floundering in a sad attempt at movement, but movement eludes me. I whimper, hearing the voices in the clearing again, growing distant. "No, please wait for me!" I hover above the earth—half in this world, half in another . . . a world I know nothing of. I'm unsure what to do. My spit tastes of copper. A metallic tingle burns at the back of my throat. I retch, and the spit falls through my hand.

"Oh, Lord!" I holler. This has to be fixed. Quickly. But how?

A lightning-like current jerks through me, causing my whole body to intermittently twitch, like a short-circuiting machine. All at once, my muscles tense and then go slack. Thoughts misfire in my head. Sparks fly. I'm robbed of sight. I zap and buzz and then fizzle out. My eyes waggle side to side. At last they settle back in their sockets, and my sight is restored. *Thankfully*. Plumes of smoke puff from the ends of my hair and fingertips as the malfunction peters out.

They stink and sizzle. I stink and sizzle. *I'm sizzling.*

*Good Lord in Heaven*, what's happened to me?

I gasp, fearing I may faint, when all at once I'm struck by the feeling of being lost, or having been lost, or losing . . . Who am I? I look down at my hand and see it's fading.

Oh, good God!

I clench my eyes shut and try to remember, why am I here? Who's done this to me? The thought is blurry. I have to fight hard to make it come around.

*Eyelet.* That's who.

Pulling the scarf from my neck, I reach down and create a tourniquet, tying it tight around the tops of the tentacles to keep the venom from spreading, and grab a rock from the ground. I use it to attack the problem at the source, gouging the sharpest end into the wound on my head. I cringe, flinging the festering guts to the ground. *How vile.* I turn my eyes away. I should not have to be doing this!

I clean the wound out the best I can, then reach for the slough spruce, packing the remaining hole up tight. There. That should be better. *I hope.*

Another gunshot shakes the forest. I start off, and my body catches and misfires again. Teeth chatter in the not-so-distant trees. Red eyes glint. *Criminals*, my mind registers. That's all I need. Haven't I been through enough today?

I grab my chest and whirl around, and, to my surprise, the sudden rotation causes my body to float several metres. Oh my! I gulp, leaning back against a tree, my stomach leaping, my heart—*or what's left of it*—aflutter. Something deep inside me ignites. All my fears of immobility are dashed. My feet may be gone, but the rest of my body still works.

*The perfect vehicle for revenge . . .*

I grin, lurching forward, craning my neck out, then thrusting my hips shakily, drifting over the forest floor like a new skater across an icy pond. Slowly, I will myself toward the voices. Leaves crackle beneath the ruffle of my skirts. Twigs catch and drag. I repeat the motion over and over, slowly increasing my agility and speed—*not to mention my grace and poise*—until at last it's as though I'm flying.

I've always wanted to fly.

Pungent Vapours pour through the trees, curling about my waist, and I panic. I open my mouth to scream—until I realize I've nothing to fear. The Vapours are having no effect on me. *This is troubling.*

I must be further gone than I thought.

Add *this* to my growing list of terrifying concerns. I twist my fingers, lobbing another one off.

*I've got to hurry, if there's any chance to save myself at all.*

I've got to get to the clearing. I burst forward, making short order of the journey, tucking in behind the trunk of a tree at the clearing's edge, and draw my tentacles in underneath me. Best not spring myself on them all at once.

I brush my hair from my eyes, hoping it stays, primping what is left of the bun I so painstakingly stacked this morning. Or was that yesterday? I adjust it over the gaping hole in the back of my head to hide what's happened, then peek out around the bark of the tree. A plume of ash-choked dust rises from the centre of where the Core once stood.

*The Core.* Good God, what happened there?

Orange flames lick the sky, bolting up from the earth in a circle. All the tops of nearby trees are charred. It's as if the Vapours have just moved through the area again, but they haven't. Have they?

Amid the flying soot and whirling dust a pair of Brigsmen appear, hauling a bedraggled and badly beaten, black-faced Urlick. *Urlick!* My heart sails ahead of me, though I am stationary. Despite everything that's happened, he still has that effect on me.

*Oh, Urlick, rest assured our connection will never cease.*

My eyes follow their tracks to the very brink of the belching ravine at the back of the property. Embers? I scowl. Good Lord. He didn't try to escape to Embers, did he?

Urlick struggles with the Brigsmen as they lead him through the wreckage of the Core. His eyes are blackened and his skin is cut. Good God, he looks like he's tangled with a tiger. He turns, and I also notice his arms have been burned.

My heart pangs to see him hurting; a warm rush of dedication pulses through me. I yearn to race after him, to fall at his feet and confess my true love. But then again, I already did that and he didn't give a *shite.*

I close my eyes and see us as we once were, *pre-Eyelet days*: Urlick sitting across the parlour table, gazing up at me during lessons—the special way he used to crimp up his lips whenever he couldn't solve a problem.

That *damned* Eyelet, she's ruined everything.

"I've done nothing!" Urlick's voice reverberates in the trees. The Brigsmen slap his belly up against the side of a paddy wagon parked at the edge of the woods. He struggles as they try to stuff him inside. "You have no proof—"

"We've proof enough to put yuh in the slammer," one Brigsman hisses. "And once we've found his body, we'll 'ave enough to see yuh 'ung."

"Body?" I gulp. My eyes scan the premises. My brain slowly works out the math. Eyelet was after me, and I left him with . . . *uuuuh-hhh* . . . "Daddy?" I feel my face go slack. My gaze swings to Urlick. "Oh, good God, he didn't. Did he?"

"Please, you don't understand," Urlick pleads, staggering, his hands now tied at his back. "I can assure you, I'm of more use to you alive than dead!" He writhes against his restraints. "I know things! Important things! Things that could save our world!"

*Things that could save our world?* What does that mean? Wait a minute . . . I whirl around. He's right. His mind is brilliant. After all, he was the one who came up with the cure for Eyelet, wasn't he? The serum that combats the ill effects of her father's so-called *miracle* machine. The antidote . . . *the glorious antidote* . . . that my father was willing to give up his life for!

I arch a brow. That was Urlick. *Wasn't it?*

I search my memory for the answer, but it appears my thoughts are still foggy on that.

At any rate, if anyone can come up with a way to save me—*to slay the demon that now lurks within me*—it'd be Urlick! I can't let them kill him!

I need him more than ever now!

*"Stop!"* I spring from my hiding place among the trees, drifting out into the clearing.

The Brigsmen whirl around. "Ghoul!" one shouts.

I turn, then turn back, realizing he means me. In the meantime, he's raised his steamrifle and squeezed off a round. A hot ball of metal slices through the air. It drives a hole clean through my chest. I gasp, falling back, choking, bringing a slow hand to the hole. No blood trickles through my fingers. No guts fall to the ground. Instead a gentle wisp of steam curls from the bullet hole's rim, quickly sewn over by pulses of gentle vapour.

I raise my chin and narrow my eyes at the Brigsman.

He gulps and scrambles for the wagon, stuffing Urlick into the back. The other slams the door shut, locks it, then rushes to his seat at the mount. Both Brigsmen vault up.

*"No!"* I shout as one gathers up the reins and brings them down hard over the gas-masked horse's back. The horse whinnies and leaps forward, and the paddy wagon bolts up the road.

"Wait!" I propel myself after them. "Wait! Don't leave me!" I reach for the wagon, but my hand drags through. "But I need him more than you do!"

I fly after the coach, but my awkward undulation is no match for the speed of horse and wagon. "Blast it!" I swear and fall back.

I sag against the bark of a tree. "What'll I do now?"

I sniff, surprised that my eyes produce tears, and wipe them away, looking out across the bleary forest.

Something's glowing. An eerie green light pulses up from over the back edge of the Brink.

I jerk toward it, through the ruins of the Core to the crest of the belching black ravine I've come to fear so greatly over the years. Extending a mare's tail of a hand down over the side, I grin, as what's left of my fingers meets up with a cool length of chain.

*It can't be . . .*

I gasp and fall back, yanking the treasure loose from the nasty, smoking mire. The black-and-emerald-beaded chain pops free of the root where it's been ensnared, wrapping around my bluing palm. A glass-vial pendant dangles from its end. It pulses green with light. I stare at it, astonished.

*"It is . . ."* I whisper. *"The vial with the antidote."*

# Part One

# One

***Urlick***

The old stone jug smells like a bad day at sea. But then again, this *is* a prison. I wince and roll over in bed, tracking the culprit with my nose: the overflowing chamber pot under my cellmate's bed. The one he filled around midnight, and has managed to snore his way through the stench of, ever since.

I roll back, stuff straw into the flour bag that serves as my pillow, and bring it down over my head in a desperate attempt to blot out the fumes.

*Good Lord, what has that brute eaten?*

A sharp clank of keys against the iron lock has me surfacing. The guard with the bent nose and the yeasty breath peers in through the bars. "You there." He points a plump finger at me. "Time to move."

"Move?" My spittle forms a ball in my throat. Fear jags through my blood. I throw back the covers. "I was told I'd have five days in here before—" I stop short of stating the obvious, the fact that I'm to be dipped in a vat of boiling wax for the murder of Smrt, possibly even drawn and quartered and hung on display—without trial or a jury of my peers.

*Justice at its finest.*

"Yeah, well, tell it to the warden," the guard says. "I was just told to come get'chu. Not my business what for." He shows his teeth. Most of which are missing. Boozy breath seeps in through the rusty bars.

Turbines clank, gears grind, the lock rolls slowly open. Chains rattle like tin snakes through the bars as he drops them to the floor. "Let's go." The guard jerks his head to one side.

My stink-dumping cellmate wakes. He pops an eye open and laughs at me. "I say yuh make 'em come in an get'chu." He twists a tight fist into his palm.

"No thanks." I stand and tuck my flour-sack pillow under my arm. "I'll go peacefully." I'd rather not dance another round with Mr. Filed-His-Teeth-Into-Spikes over there, even if it does mean a chance to overthrow the guard. I'm still nursing black eyes from the last whupping the brute gave me. I don't fancy going to the gallows a battered wreck.

Besides, I'm relieved to be leaving his chamber pot behind.

"Ah-ah-ah," the guard tsks and signals for me to drop the pillow. "Won't be needin' that where yer goin'."

I stare at him, confused.

Mr. Spike-Toothed throws his head back into a hearty laugh. "I know wheres that tis," he sings.

"Move," the guard says without expression.

I toss the pillow away and take a step. My eyes fall to my overcoat, lying rumpled on the floor. I swoop to pick it up, but the brute beats me to it.

"Won't be needin' this, either." He rubs the sleeve against his filthy beard, sporting a sharp-toothed smile. My mind flashes back to the gadgets hidden in the seams of the lining. I'm going to need those if there's any chance of me getting out of here.

I lunge for the coat, and the brute flings it back.

"Get movin'!" the guard barks.

I glare into my cellmate's eyes. "I'll be back for that," I say, trying to sound a lot more confident than I really am. Truth be known, I doubt I'll see it again.

Shuffling toward the door, my feet in chains, I glance back at the window where I last heard from Eyelet. I wonder where she is. It's been two days since Pan brought me her Ladybird message and I returned one.

There's been no word since.

My heart sears at the thought of having to tell her I've lost the vial, the one thing that was truly important in all this. I'll just have to get it back. We've no other choice. But first I need to get out of here.

A smile comes to my lips, remembering Pan pecking on the noggin of my cellmate to keep him busy as I hurriedly contrived the message to send back to Eyelet, stamping out the words and rewrapping the foil around the cylinder as fast as I could. We both took equal beatings for that. But it was worth it.

Pan's a tough old creature, she is.

I rather admire that bird.

"What are you smilin' about?" The guard sneers. He grabs my arm and flings me out of the cell, cuffing me and slamming the cell door shut behind. The lock tumbles into place before my cellmate has had the chance to get his smelly arse out of bed.

"Better luck next time," I say.

The guard pushes me down a long, narrow corridor. My heart picks up speed as we round the corner. "Where are we going? There are no cells past here." He says nothing, just flings open a door to a set of stairs and shoves me down them in the dark. The soles of our boots echo noisily off the walls as we spiral down the steel-tread steps.

"Where are you taking me?" I glance back over my shoulder.

The guard won't answer. It's as if he's made of stone.

With every step, I get further away from Eyelet ever being able to find me.

If she's able to make it here at all.

I go cold at the thought of never seeing her again. Never being able to look into her eyes and tell her just how much I love her. Hot tears press at my lids. I flip my hair from my face and blink hard, trying to clear the sensation, as we reach the room at the bottom of the stairs.

It's dark and smells of rotting worms and musky dirt. The floor is gritty beneath my feet. Cold water drops from the ceiling, down my neck. "What is this? Where are we?" My heart jumps when I realize where he could be leading me. This could be it. The end. My throat closes off, parched.

The guard flings open a heavy wooden door across from the stairs. It creaks back madly. The sound drums up my spine. I brace myself, expecting to be blinded by the shock of twilight. Instead, darkness consumes me like a blanket thrown over my head.

"In here." The guard casts me through the door and down a short corridor, then shoves me into a hole. I smack my head on something hard and fall to the stone floor. I struggle to stand, hitting my head again on the room's low ceiling, and end up on my backside. "What is this place? Where am I?"

"Purgatory." The guard reaches up, and through the wisps of my shadowy vision I see him pull a chain. An iron gate falls to the ground in front of me, its poker-sharp ends driving deep into the stone floor. They would have impaled my feet had I not pulled them in.

"They say you 'ad a visitor up there." The guard breathes through the bars. The smell of his breath makes me gag. "Brought you some sort of fancy message." He loops chains around the metal gate and secures them with a lock. "We'll see how yuh fare down 'ere in the 'ole. Ain't nobody lasted more than three days in solitary. But then again, they tell me you's *special*." The guard triggers another lock. Turbines grind and shunt, and then there's silence. "We'll see 'ow special yuh are."

My heart seizes, hearing him step away.

"Wait! You can't just leave me here? Not like this!" I raise my arms behind my back, hands still in chains.

"Sorry, mate, orders."

The guard's boots turn, twisting on the grime-topped stones. He slams the thick wooden door behind him as he exits, and the room gets even darker, as if dunked in a well of ink.

I slide on my shoulder down the wall to the floor, listening to his footsteps fade with each loop of stairs he climbs until he reaches the top. A door groans open, then swings shut. A lock drops with a clank. The hole I'm in falls eerily silent. I rest my head against the cold stone wall, press my face between the rusty iron bars of my new fortress, and shiver.

"Oh, Eyelet, if you're able, please come quick."

# *Two*

***Eyelet***

I stumble through the weeds, struggling to take in enough air to keep me going. The mask I found in the wreckage at the Core is severely damaged and had less than half a tank of oxygen. I've been travelling long stints without wearing it, trying to conserve the air that's left, but the Vapours are becoming too overwhelming, too thick to ignore, their stench too explicit, and I've had to resort to wearing the mask continuously.

"How much farther!" I shout to the sky, forgetting that I sent Pan on ahead. I thought it best, if I became delirious under the power of the Vapours—which I'm seriously starting to consider might happen—that at least Pan make it to the Compound to tell the others and hopefully send someone out to retrieve me.

I bend at the waist, gasping, trying to slow my breathing, reminding myself that air is scarce. I have to stop gulping the supply. I check the gauge: less than an eighth left. I need to make it to the Compound soon, or I'll never make it.

My mind runs briefly over the idea of the Infirmed, and my heart jerks in my chest. Flashbacks of their previous attacks mingle with new fears of them materializing again, and my knees turn to syrup. I twist my head in both directions, thinking I see their swarthy bodies in the mist—imagining I hear their chants.

I suck in a deep breath. "I can't let this get the better of me." I bring my hands to my forehead, cradling it. The pungent odour of the Vapours has caused a migraine.

I've got to stop this worry *now*. I've got to think of Urlick. I've got to survive, so I can get to him. I look up into the swirling, darkening mist pouring out like a storm before me. *I cannot die.*

I pull Urlick's Dyechrometer from my pocket and check for heartbeats, pleased when it registers only my own. That's enough to settle my mind for now and at least slow my chequered breathing, though my heart still gallops at victory pace. I dip my hand back into my pocket and pull out another of Urlick's priceless inventions. His tie stud. I found it in the dirt, along the edge of the ridge of the Core, its tiny chain clinging to a weed. He must have lost it in his struggle with Smrt.

My mind shifts briefly to the scene.

My stomach aches at the thought of Urlick being dragged away.

*Don't worry, I'm coming.*

As with everything of Urlick's, I assumed that the tie stud was not simply what it seemed, but a clever disguise for something else—something far more foreboding. A bit of fiddling unlocked its hidden purpose. *I was right.* It's a compass of sorts, where true north is, instead, the true direction of the Compound, as verified by Pan from above. It was only after this discovery that Pan agreed to leave me and go on ahead, content that I couldn't get lost. *No matter where you are, you can find the way home*, I imagine Urlick saying as he shows it to me, wondering if he dropped it on purpose for me to find.

I shake off the idea, thinking it silly. He had no idea what was going to happen back there. No idea I'd be left alone in the woods. I think of him and wonder if he's thinking of me. I wonder if he's all right? If he's warm. Hungry. If he's still . . . I swallow down the word, not willing to give the thought life, and push on through the woods.

"It won't be long now." I wipe the face of the stud pin clean of mist and check my direction, hearing the hose on the oxygen tank slur and hiccup in search of air.

"It can't be."

*

I pick up my step, trudging on through tangled weeds, trusting in the compass, praying that this is one of Urlick's gadgets that actually works. Breathing heavy, I reach for the oxygen mask, realizing it's run out of air long ago. I lower my head and try to slow my heaving. I have to be getting close.

Lifting my gaze toward the horizon, *hopeful*, I spot something through a small tear in the fog. It's stony and round. I rush toward it. The circular turret of my old bedroom at the Compound crests through wafting streams of broken cloud cover. Its window gapes at me; its light beckons me home. I'm almost there! It's not close by any means, but it's not far away, either.

Exhausted, I start to run. My feet flop around beneath me like rubber. My woozy, oxygen-deprived head spins, wreaking havoc with my vision. Closing in on the last few metres, I stop and squint, focusing on the Guardian lock system next to the entrance. I've never been so elated to see a door in my life! Its activation button blinks red in the white glow of the day. "*At last.* I've made it!"

I hike up my skirts and race at the door, stumbling the final few steps to the back stoop. Collapsing, I bang wildly on the door's smooth steel surface as I drain down the front of it, into a heap on the pallet porch, too weak to stand again. "Please." I pound the heel of my hand into it weakly. "Please, someone, hear me . . ."

Pan appears in the sky, squawking and circling overhead. "Help me," I mouth to her.

She swoops in, diving beak-first at the kitchen's window, then the parlour's, and back again, repeatedly. "Stop!" I shout at her. "It's no use! You're going to kill yourself!"

She ignores me and throws herself at the window again. A short alarm sounds. My eyes snap up. The Guardian system above my head deactivates. The lock on the door tumbles. It springs and the heavy door creaks open, drawn back by an iron lung. A curl of Vapour seeps through as I try to pull myself to my feet.

I crawl forward, the alarm pulsing, threshold beating red with light. I grab the handle and drag myself the rest of the way through.

Once inside, I push the door closed, sucking in deep breaths of filtered air as I fall back against the inside of the door, closing out the Vapours once and for all.

Cleansing steam coils up from the vents at my feet, filling the tiny alcove I sit in with its sharp Creolin scent. I take in deep breaths, feeling the steam's healing powers restore strength to my muscles and lungs.

I can't believe I'm thinking this, but I'm so glad to be back at the Compound.

Flustered footsteps fill the adjacent corridor. I stand, collecting myself, when suddenly Iris is upon me, her arms round my neck, squeezing me as tight as she can. We fall back against the wall inside her hearty hug.

"What's all this?" I cough and choke, my lungs still purging Vapours. But Iris doesn't pull away—instead she squeezes me harder. "Iris," I say, peeling her off me. "Oh, my goodness." I catch my breath.

As I pull back, I see tears trickling down her cheeks.

"Iris." I pull her to me. "Oh, my." I pet her head and allow her to sob on my shoulder, tears starting in my own eyes.

"She was afraid you was never comin' back, mum," C.L. says, creeping out from the shadows of the stairway. He flashes me a welcoming toothless grin, and I smile, happy to see him in the shaky aether lamplight overhead.

"I must admit, I wasn't sure I'd be back myself." I squeeze Iris a little tighter.

"At any rate, you're *'ere* now," C.L. says. "And yer a merry sight, I must say." He drops his head. He reaches up with a toe and guides a tear from his cheek, and a soggy lump forms in my throat. How little time I've spent with these people, and yet, how much room they've made for me in their hearts.

Outside of family, that's never happened before.

"Any word from Urlick?" I say, on the off chance he's been able to get them a message.

C.L.'s head droops. His smile erases, replaced with a wobbling lip of gloom. Iris pulls back from my shoulder, fear in her eyes.

"He will be back," I say. "Don't you worry." I cup Iris's cheeks, thumbing away her tears. "You have my word on that. Nothing's going to happen to him. Not as long as I live and breathe."

She half grins through her tear-filled eyes, as if she'd like to believe.

"I'm afraid it might be out of your power, mum." C.L. raises his head, a look of defeat in his eyes.

"Why is that?"

His lip quivers as he folds his feet. "We've gotten word. They've shortened his sentence. He's to be dipped in less than seventy-two hours."

"That's just three days."

"Yes."

"It'll take a full day, maybe more, just to cross the woods."

C.L.'s eyes grow watery as he stares at me.

"That's a Sunday. They never perform dippings on the Sabbath."

"Perhaps they've made an exception." C.L. hangs his head.

His words gnaw through me like a dull arrowhead.

My thoughts shift to Urlick sitting there in the stone jug, facing his end, feeling helpless, not knowing if help is coming for him. Those piercing pink eyes of his brimming with tears as he stares out between the bars. I close my own eyes, imagining us in a kiss. The kiss we'll share when he's free. I long to taste his mouth on mine again, feel the dart of his soft peppermint tongue brush against my own. To feel the strength of his warm, muscled arms envelop me. I can't imagine a world without that. I won't imagine one.

"Well, then," I say, sucking in a brave, jagged breath. "I guess we'd better get on with the plan, hadn't we?" I release Iris from my grasp.

Something lands with a thud at my knees, knocking me slightly off balance. I fall back, seeing a pair of tiny white hands clutching the sides of my skirts. Fiery red curls cascade down the back of a ruffled emerald dress.

"Hello, Miss Cordelia," I say, petting her head.

She looks up, her big brown eyes sparkling with tears.

"I thought you were dead," she whispers. Her voice is small and weak, as if saying the words louder might make them come true.

"A popular consensus round here," I jest, floating my gaze around the circle. Iris and C.L. grin. I bend at the knees. "Go on, now," I say, wiping the tears from her round pink cheeks. "Would I go and leave you alone in this world, after we'd only just met? What kind of a new friend would that make me?"

Cordelia looks up with a smile, and I take her tiny face in my hands. "I want you to promise me something. Can you do that?" She nods her curly head. I lean forward as if sharing a secret only with her. "I want you to promise me you'll never think that way again. All right?"

She nods.

"Thoughts are power, you know. They control the universe." I dart my eye up. "Whatever we dwell on, will come to be. So we must try *hard* never to think negative thoughts. Only positive ones. Do you understand me?"

She nods with a grin.

"Good." I bounce the tip of my finger off the end of her nose. "Besides," I bring her in for a quick hug. "Our loved ones never die as long as we keep them alive in our hearts." I pull her back. "You know that, right?"

She shakes her crimson head and sucks in her quivering lip.

"Well, it's true. It has to be. My father told me that, once." I stare off at nothing for a brief moment then bend forward, planting a determined kiss on Cordelia's worried forehead. "Now you know, don't forget it." I smile, and snap to a stand.

"Is Bertie with you?" she says in a soggy voice.

The look in her eyes shreds my heart. I hesitate before speaking. "I'm sorry, sweetie." I run a hand through her hair. I shudder, recalling the vision of Bertie, the glorious winged hydrocycle, lying charred among the ashes of the Core. "I'm afraid he didn't make it."

Her brown eyes brim with tears.

"Now, now." I bend and pull her in. "Remember what I just told you?"

She gulps her feelings back.

"As long as we keep Bertie alive in our hearts, he'll always be with us."

She sniffs.

"I'll tell you what," I whisper in her ear. "When Urlick gets home, we'll build another Bertie, in his honour—Bertie Junior, we'll call him. How does that sound? And we'll start with these." I pull back, digging Bertie's scorched headlights from my pocket and laying them in her hand. She looks down and smiles.

"About that," C.L. interrupts. "Not to throw a damper on the party, but 'ave you given any thought to *'ow* you'll *get* back into Brethren without the *'elp* of Bertie?"

"I was rather hoping maybe you and Iris had a plan." I stand, my voice lilting.

Iris chews her lip, looks away. C.L. diverts his eyes.

"Well, then." I take in another laboured breath, rolling my hands. "We'll need to find some other way into town, won't we?" I turn away, my mind a flurry of thoughts—none of them viable. I pace, tapping my lips. "Some alternate form of transportation." I think aloud. "Some way to breach the gates of Brethren without using the ground." I turn and my eyes catch on something glinting on Cordelia's chest, hanging on a chain round her neck. *Iris's sister Ida's locket.* That's it.

I bend, hinging at the waist, and take it in my hand. I brush a thumb over the etching of an angel wing on the locket's front, a wry smile warming on my lips.

"We'll use Clementine," I say.

"Clementine?" C.L. staggers. "But you'll be spotted on *'orse* for sure."

"On an ordinary horse, perhaps . . ." I swing around. "But not the kind I have in mind."

"I beg your pardon, mum?"

"Do you have some parchment and some ink handy?" I roll up my sleeves.

"Likely," C.L. says.

Iris races off to find what I need, returning quickly, passing me a pen while C.L. sets up the inkwell.

"What are you thinking, mum?" C.L. says.

"I'm thinking Urlick's not the only one who can make something fly."

Cordelia claps.

I stretch the roll of parchment out over a table at the end of the hallway, dunk the nib in the well, and start to draw. C.L. and Iris stand at my shoulder, hovering. A furious speed overcomes me.

"An armoured *'orse,* mum." C.L. smiles as he examines my strokes. "You planning on storming the city in a Trojan?"

"Better than that." I add the finishing touches. "Have you ever heard of Pegasus?" I drop the pen and spin the paper around, stretching the drawing out for them all to see. "Now imagine Pegasus in an armoured suit and a set of mechanical raven wings."

"Oh, my . . ." C.L.'s jaw falls open.

Iris gasps.

Cordelia jumps up and down.

"We'll have to hurry, though," I say, turning back. "As you've mentioned, we don't have much time." I run my fingers over the drawing on the table again. "But I figure together we'll be able to finish the armour and wings by late tonight." I turn to C.L. "And then we can leave late tomorrow morning. I know it's rather tight, but it's the best we can do—"

"We?" C.L. swallows.

"Well, I was kind of hoping you'd come with me." I wring my hands. "I'll need a wingman, and I hear you're the best." I smile at him, remembering Urlick, how much he respected C.L.'s loyalty.

"Very well, then." C.L.'s eyes grow big. "Consider it done." He salutes me. "Anything for you, mum."

"Good." I take in a breath. "And Iris, you'll stay here with Cordelia in case, by the grace of God"—I cross my chest—"Urlick comes back on his own?"

She nods.

"If we need you, we'll call for you. Otherwise, you'll man the post. You, too, Cordelia." She grins. "Now"—I rub my hands together—"we should probably get started." I turn.

"Aren't you forgetting something?" C.L. says.

"What?"

"Once you're back in Brethren, 'ow are you going to disguise 'oo you are? We 'aven't any masks left. And they take at least three days to make new ones."

"Good point." I sag, defeated. "No use to the masks, anyway. We've already been made out." C.L.'s right. I'll be arrested the second I set foot in Brethren. "Wanted" posters of me hang everywhere. Even the Northerners will be looking for me by now. I hug my waist. I can't just waltz in as myself, now, can I? "We'll have to create some sort of diversion." I pace. "Elsewise, I'll be picked up immediately." I turn to C.L and sigh. "I'm afraid this is not going to be easy."

"Well, nothing worth doing ever is, mum," he says, scratching his head with his toes, then looks up with a devilish light in his eyes. "Unless . . ."

"What? What is it?"

"I think I just might know some people who'll *'elp*, mum."

"You do?"

C.L.'s eyes light up. He dips a toe into his waistcoat pocket and pulls out a weathered advertisement. A poster board of sorts. He unfolds it and stretches it out over the table, pressing down the seams as he goes, revealing a full-colour illustration of a travelling freak show. The faces of five or more tortured individuals peer up from the page, staring out from behind the bars of the cages of a train. The one to the far left looks suspiciously like . . .

*C.L.* "Oh, my God." I bring a hand to my mouth.

"I know, mum." His eyes flash. "But they's *good* people, I know they is . . . If only we was able to commandeer the freak train on its way into Brethren, they'd be more than 'appy to 'elp us free Urlick."

"What are you trying to say?"

"The freak show's due to arrive in Brethren in two days' time. All we 'ave to do is commandeer the train 'ere in these woods"—he points to a remote part of the forest on the map—"then ride the train into the city—"

"You're suggesting we shanghai the travelling freak show, and then what? Tie up its master?" My voice squeaks.

"I prefer we kill him, but sure, we can do it your way."

"Have you lost your *mind*?"

"Can you think of a better diversion?"

I let out a breath and roll my eyes. "No, I suppose I can't."

# Three

***Flossie***

A cackle in the trees behind me has my head swinging around. The edges of my body blur as I twist. Something swoops past me, howling, and I catch my breath. Chants trickle through the trees.

"Oh, *no*, not again." I clutch my translucent hand to my chest, feeling the steady beat of my still—*thankfully*—human heart.

And I want to keep it that way.

I stare into the cloud cover, spotting the beginnings of coiling grey mist, and suck in a quick breath. With the speed of a lash I spin around, stuffing the pendant down the top of my corset between my breasts, and rise into the sky above the ravine, arms spread out to my sides, head thrown back, in an attempt to look ominous.

The chants grow louder, the voices shrill. Swooping, swarthy bodies close in.

I open my eyes to find myself completely surrounded—by hundreds of blinking, glaring, white-eyed Infirmed.

I gasp, feeling the pull of air inside what's left of my rib cage. It crackles under the weight of my breath. "What?" I say, realizing they've gone silent.

They've fallen to their knees in front of me.

"You've come," one of the ghouls breathes, her eyes stretched open—the shimmering light inside them quavering as she homes in on my chest.

"Look!" another says and falls to his knees. "It is her!" His torn mouth falls open.

The other ghoul's head twists around.

He points a decayed and shaky finger in my direction, and they bow their heads.

I track his gaze to the bleating light hidden in the bodice of my outfit.

"It's her! It's really her!" another cries on a winded breath. "The messiah!"

"Messiah?" My system short-circuits, rendering me blind for a second, and then slowly my sight returns. But the picture before my eyes isn't any different. What on earth is going on here? I stare down at the crowd of kneeling, worshiping Infirmed before me. I tremble.

"The holy one," another says, and they break out into chants. Only the chanting this time is more like a prayerful moan.

My eyes widen. I drop my gaze to the pulsing light of the pendant, tucked down inside my corset, nestled low between my breasts. The whole front of my attire is aglow in its eerie, angelic light. They must think . . .

*They do think.*

"She's come to save us all!" they chant. "To restore us to our former states!"

To what? My chin snaps up, bathed in the vial's ghoulish, green glow. I swallow, staring out at their gape-mouthed faces, their fangs glinting in the flickering beams of twilight. And then a mad thought comes over me.

A wicked, wicked, mad, mad thought.

"Yes," I say slowly on a breath that straightens my back. "I am she. And I have come to save you all!"

They rise to their feet in a collective cheer.

"But first!" I raise my hands to quiet them. "You must do something for me."

"Anything! Anything, Messiah!"

"You must protect me!" I shout, narrowing my eyes. "You must promise me, from this day forward, I will come to no harm!"

"Never, Messiah! Never!"

"At the hands of yourselves, or anyone else!"

They cross their hearts and lower their heads. "You have our solemn promise!"

"You solemnly swear to protect me from all that is evil in these woods!"

"Yes, Madame Priestess." They nod their heads.

"And to serve me, and only me, whatever my request."

"Yes, Madame Priestess. *We solemnly swear!* Whatever you want!"

My heart races with my newfound power. "Be warned." I clench my teeth and jut my chin toward the crowd, delighting in how they cower backward. I stare hard at them and lower my voice. "He who crosses me will never be restored, but will instead face the wrath of Embers!" I point to the belching quagmire at my back.

"We won't," they gasp. "We'll worship only you!"

They bow their heads in prayer again.

"Very well, then," I smirk, smoothing my skirts, surging with the power of my new appointment and confident in the fact that I'll be rightfully restored and long gone before they discover I've lied and taken advantage of them to save my own soul. I lift my palms to the heavens, look out adoringly at my new disciples, and smile. "The sooner we get to what I need, the sooner you'll get what you want."

"What is it that you want, Madame Priestess?"

The white rays of their eyes fall on me.

Flashes of the fight I had with Eyelet in the forest suddenly come back to me like bits of broken film. The answer to the question of why I'm here. The journals. The vial. The argument she had with me. Her hands, pushing me into the Infirmed.

The father I lost.

The admirer she stole.

The life she took from me . . .

I lift my chin high and address the crowd. "I need your help to destroy an enemy, and bring back into the fold another who has gone astray."

# Four

***Urlick***

A spider picks its way across my face and I flick my head with such madness I nearly snap my own neck. I swallow hard, tip my chin back, and close my eyes, working to slow my heartbeat, taking measured breaths and letting them ease back out again. If I'm to survive this misery, I need to keep my wits about me. No more of this imagining terrifying illusions in the dark. All this darkness is playing havoc with my mind—being immersed in it, twenty-four hours solid, day after day.

My mind drifts to Eyelet—the only vision that keeps me going. She stands before me wearing a devious, crackling smile. Those creamy caramel eyes of hers burn with such depth, a whole world is revealed behind their glass. A secret world I've only begun to explore. Oh, Lord, I hope I have the chance to continue.

I allow myself to smile, remembering the taste of her kiss—a long, slow drink of peppermint tea swirled with honey.

I wonder where she is. What's become of her?

Does she know what's become of me?

The thought presses in that I might never see her again, and every muscle in my body tenses. I shake it off. *No!* I must not allow such thoughts. I turn away from her image and shudder in the cold.

The damp darkness of the hole has burrowed straight into the marrow of my bones. Without blanket or pillow, I cannot escape its clutches. And the stone walls and floor provide little comfort. Near as I can figure, it's been about two days since the guard stuffed me in this hellhole and left. Maybe three, I don't know.

Days and nights pass the same in this darkness.

I've had no food or water. They've left me a wooden pail in the corner for defecating, though that seems futile, considering I'm chained. I'm growing more and more shaky as the hours tick on. I wince, licking my parched and peeling lips, feeling dizziness pour over me. I need water. I need it now.

I can't go on without it.

Pinching my eyes shut, I clench my teeth as another wave of hunger pains passes through me. At least the growl in my stomach reminds me I'm still alive. The ongoing deprivation of food has caused my mind to drift in and out of reality. I've begun to hallucinate—horrible images, of me strung up on the pegs, vat of wax bubbling beneath my feet. The pictures play out so real in my head I feel the heat, hear the caw of the raven, and the bubble bursts.

I push the image away and I see Eyelet again, this time in a field of bluebells racing toward me. An impossibility, I know, as we've never seen a field of bluebells in our lifetimes except for in a book, but I see it clear as a Vapourless day—and then it's gone. Replaced by an image of her hanging next to me, rope around her snapped neck, creaking as she swings.

*"Stop it!"* I scream and crack my head against the wall.

My rage echoes in the tiny room, bouncing off the stone until at last the room falls hushed again, save for the sound of something trickling overhead.

I wrench up my chin and perk my ears. Is this just another hallucination?

I swallow, using the sound as a baseline of truth in my ears, when I hear the noise again. *Water.* It's seeping in from above, drizzling down the wall. But which wall?

I fling myself forward, up onto my knees, turning my head back and forth. I'm too weak to stand, not that I could—at my height I have to hunch. So instead, I roll onto my backside and use my heels, digging them in against the jagged stone floor, and propel myself backward toward the wall I think the sound is coming from.

I know when I've reached it as I clunk my head. My hair feels wet at the nape. The trickle of water grows louder, and I realize I'm there. I've found it. Water rolls down the wall at my back, puddling around me on the floor.

I sit up, trembling. The shock of the water's polar presence chills my skin. I try to lean forward and arch like an animal to drink from the puddle, but it's no use, I can't get low enough to reach it. Pressing my cheek to the stone wall, I attempt to lap it up as it trickles down, but the water hugs the curves of the wall too tightly, I cannot draw it into my mouth.

*"Please!"* I whisper. *"For the love of God, please . . ."*

I jut my neck out farther—then realize it might not be safe to drink the water at all.

If the stones are made of lime, which I strongly suspect they are, it'll only hasten my dehydration—dry the flesh to my bones. But if I don't try to drink it . . . *then* . . . I'm destined to die anyway. So, what choice do I have?

I think of Eyelet on her way, risking her life, to rescue me. I can't let her risk her life to save a corpse.

Leaning in, I smell the rock, feeling its chalky texture against my cheek. It has to be limestone, what else would it be? This whole area is coated in it. Unless . . .

*Slag stone.* The remnants left over when they excavate limestone from the quarry. They'd never use precious limestone to build the foundation of a prison.

I press my nose to the seam and draw in its fragrance. It reeks of worms and earth and salty sand. *Sand!* I hunker closer. Not limestone! Sand!

Rolling my tongue, I reach out, meeting the slow trickle of water running in the seam. Its cool elixir sparkles like liquid gold as it funnels down my throat, quenching my thirst, filling the parched cracks in my lips, and soothing swollen sores. "Thank God!" I lick the stones again. "Thank God for this!"

# *Five*

***Eyelet***

Sadness draws like a curtain around me as I work to dismantle Urlick's lovely mechanical flowers—but we need the metal for the wings. I promise myself I'll help Urlick re-create each and every one of these once he's safely home.

As well as replicate Bertie.

I sigh and wipe a stray lock of hair from my eyes, drinking in the bareness of Urlick's laboratory, now that the flowers and Bertie are gone. Everything is gone. There's so much empty space. The basement looks more ominous than ever. Flickering gaslights dance the walls, haunting reminders of Urlick's absence. *Oh*, how I miss him.

"That should just about do it," C.L. shouts over the hiss of Urlick's lamplight-slash-welding-torch. He retracts the headlight and steers the kerosene burner away from his face, aglow in its diminishing flame. "Now for the mechanical bits."

"I'm just about there." I whirl around, astonished by the amount of work he's accomplished already. A set of giant flower petals forms the basis of the new Pegasus wings. They rest, draped across wooden sawhorses set metres apart, their span filling most of the centre of Urlick's forbidden laboratory. Several more petals lean against the structure, waiting their turn to be applied.

"Not bad, eh?" C.L. flips up his welding mask and smiles. "Should look spectacular when I'm done."

"No, not bad at all." I step closer, dragging a hand over its scalloped edges. He's curled the outer tufts this way and that, to catch the wind's currents. "Amazing." I admire the nickel-plated air flaps and horizontal stabilizer, grinning at his choice to use the flower's stamen as a winglet.

"I think this might make a good rudder, whadya think?" He holds up a piece of the flower's broken stem.

"I think that'll be excellent," I say. "But don't forget, Clementine's going to be doing most of the work. So we needn't worry too much about balance."

"Yeah." C.L. scratches his head with a greasy toe. "'Ow *is* that going to work? Exactly?"

I lift up the pair of odd-looking leather knee socks and adjoining straps, like a racehorse might wear. "We suit Clementine up in these fancy new horse socks I've been constructing." I wag them in the air. "When she gallops, the socks will pull on these straps, here"—I tug—"creating tension, which in turn rotates the bicycle-wheel chain assembly under here." I point to the undercarriage of the saddle. "The turning wheel then activates these accordion folds, which crank the wings up and down, and she'll be flying in the air . . . hopefully. The tough part's going to be getting her off the ground." I frown at the assembly. "Not sure how we're going to make that happen. It's going to take a good bit of luck and a whole lot of wind. Or a whole lot of momentum."

"I'm thinkin' a generous 'elpin' of all three," C.L. adds.

"At any rate, I've designed the socks to slip over her hooves, up her fetlocks to her knees, where they'll tighten with a twist of this clasp."

I demonstrate on my arm. I turn the notch, and the material sucks in and shrinks, pinching rather nastily. "That way they won't come off, no matter how hard she kicks." I look up, release the tension cord. "The good bit is keeping her galloping in the air."

"'Ow are you gonna get 'er to do that, mum?"

I turn, swinging back around with an armoured metal facepiece attached to a halter, mounted with an extendable fishing rod dangling a carrot from the end of its line. "What do you think?"

C.L. laughs. "Well, carrots are 'er favourite."

"Yeah. I figure this way she'll have something to focus on, should she become afraid, you know, midair . . . midway through the forest." I gulp.

Just thinking about it gives me the shivers. At least with Bertie we could switch on the engine to control him. Not so with Clementine.

"I think it's brilliant," C.L. says. "Absolutely brilliant. A mite smarter than what I woulda done, I'll tell yuh that! Urlick would be so proud." He smiles his tooth-spare smile. "I can see now why Urlick did a turn for yuh. Beautiful and smart. What more can a chap ask for?"

I blush and then it fades.

"I've made a breast-and-belly plate of armour for her, too." I turn, lifting another piece of Clementine's gear to show him. "Just in case, *you know*, someone was to shoot upward." I tap my knuckles on its undercarriage. It clangs hollow and loud.

C.L. tottles over and knocks it himself. "Again, brilliant."

I spin around and back. "And I made a little something for each of us, as well." I hand him his ensemble—a helmet, chinstrap, breastplate, and back protector, and a pair of scaled metal leggings. "I stretched the breastplate and back protector out a bit longer than normal, you know, to cover the spleen and the kidneys. Oh, and instead of a shirt, I made you this to wear underneath." I hand him his chain-mail sleeveless shirt.

"My, yuh've thought of everything."

"I would have made you gloves for your feet, but—"

"This is perfect." C.L. stops me short. "Are we done, then?" he says, having a look around.

"We just might be," I say.

Evening is upon us. The room is dark, save for the flicker of the gaslight sconces that line the room. A faint cone of light seeps down from the tunnel that leads to the main house above the retractable mechanical stairs.

"I'll 'urry and finish with this," he says, raising the broken metal flower stem in his hand. "Apply the rest of the feathers and secure the bone straps, and then I'd say we can leave at first light."

I wipe my greasy hands on my apron and take a big breath. "Yes, I suppose we can." I stare off across the room, thinking of Urlick sitting in his cell, waiting to be rescued. And then the thought presses in on me that he might not be there when we arrive . . . but rather hanging, strung up in the gallows, ravens circling, already succumbed to his fate, as my mother had . . . when I arrived . . . too late.

My shoulders hunch.

"What is it?" C.L. says.

"Nothing."

I turn my back, thinking about what I just demanded of Cordelia.

*I will not give the thought air.*

I pick up the socks and finish knotting the ties, using the handheld steam-powered stud-rivet to force grommets through the material. The crunch of the metal ring chewing through the flesh of the leather brings back memories of the woods—the gnashing teeth of hungry criminals and the whooping howls of lunatic spirits. Fear balls up in my throat. As I fell through the door of the Compound yesterday, I swore I'd never willingly return to the woods again. But in order to save Urlick, there'll be no avoiding it. In my heart I know that. I bite my lip to keep it from trembling, and I lean again on the rivet plunger, intent on keeping my mind on the positive.

"Yuh sure yer all right?" C.L. lowers his chin and tries to catch my gaze.

I snap my head up. "Yes, I'm fine."

I set the last grommet, rub the remainder of the grease off my hands, and manage a smile. "I'll go see about gas masks."

God knows we're going to need them.

I dart for the mechanical stairs and leap to the landing, activate the button on the handrail, and brace myself as it rises. I'm not even sure we have enough oxygen packs left in cold storage to make it to Brethren, and we certainly won't be stopping at Mercantile to purchase more. Not with every Brigsman in the county searching for me.

I swallow. Not to mention the ticking clock on Urlick's life.

The stairs creakily retract back up to the top of the room, toward the entrance to the main tunnel halls. The mechanism jerks, squeaking to a stop against the lip of the opening, revealing the darkness of the caverns beyond. I exit, swipe a torch from the sidewall, about to duck out into the passageway that leads to the kitchen, when I hear Iris scream.

"What is it?" C.L.'s head snaps up.

"Iris," I confirm. "Something's wrong!"

C.L. drops the lamplight torch and starts running.

I trigger the switch to lower the mechanical stairs for C.L., then rocket out into the corridor alone, bolting the few feet to the sealed vault-like door that stands between here and the main house. Triggering the lock, I push through the surge of steam that follows, race the length of the dark stone passageways back to the main house, up the back stairs, taking them two at a time up, and burst for the kitchen. C.L. bolts past me at the last second, beating me through the door. He flies to a stop next to Iris in the middle of the room.

"It's Cordelia!" he turns to me, shouting. "She's not breathing!"

I scramble over. Cordelia lies at Iris's feet. Her skin is blue.

"What happened?" I fall to my knees beside the two of them.

*An episode*, Iris signs. *But worse than ever before.*

"Oh, good God!" I drop my mouth over Cordelia's, forcing puffs of air into her chest. It rises temporarily, then falls again the second I stop. Locking my fingers, I leap forward, pumping her chest with my palms. I drop my ear to her mouth, hearing a weak release of air. "Quickly," I say, "Iris, take my place. Keep doing exactly what I've done."

I rise to my feet and run.

"Wait! Where are you going?" C.L. calls after me as I scramble down the back stairs, into the corridors beneath the house.

"I'll be right back!" I say, leaping into a run, the clap of my boots echoing off the walls of the underground cavern. "Just keep doing as I said!"

I get to the forks and turn toward the terrarium room. Hurtling down the corridor, I throw back the doors.

A pulse of steam coats me, rendering me damp from head to toe. I push through the heat and white mist, through the trees to the sycamore at the back of the room. *Where is it? Where were they?* Frantically I bat back the leaves of the ground foliage, searching. *Ginseng. Fennel. Hawthorn.* I clip through them. *Think, where was it?*

I turn, and the elephant-ear-like petals of the giant hostas catch my eye. The delicate leaves of *Chemodendryum charcoalreous* peek out from under their skirts. *There it is! It was close to the* charcoalreous*!* I rush forward and fall to my knees at the plant's base, lifting the leaves of the ones around it and tearing others. *The scent. The scent. I'll know the scent when I smell it.* I lower my head and breathe deep. At first I smell nothing but sheep shite and dirt, and then . . .

My nose finds it: a sharp, musky scent, like the vinegar-mustard poultices my mother used to mix for my chest when I was young and sick—only this one's gone rancid. *That's it!* My gaze locks on to the spidery plant with fluffy, oak-shaped leaves growing in a spiral around the stems of a heavy hosta, in a living circular staircase. I bat the big dog-ear hostas aside, snatch a handful of greyish-white leaves, and curl them into my palm.

Funny, I remember them being darker than this, a greyish-brown. I stare down at them, my heart pounding, and within seconds they begin to crumple and turn colour, affirming what I remember. "These are right." I leap to my feet and race to the door.

*Please, Lord, don't let me be too late . . .*

Bolting back through the kitchen door, I dash over the threshold a sweaty mess, my dress clinging to me. Perspiration rims my hair.

"Where have you been?" C.L. turns and scowls at me, his chin wagging.

"To get these!" I hold out my hand.

His pupils flash at the sight of the leaves. He didn't know I knew about the terrarium room, neither of them did. The shock on their faces confirms that.

I drop to my knees beside Cordelia and wave the withering leaves past her face . . . but nothing. She doesn't respond. My already-galloping heart races up my throat. If this is just a severe seizure, the leaves should have done something. Perhaps I've taken too long. Perhaps she's too far into the seizure. If she is, just smelling the leaves won't bring her out of it. I've got to get them into her system—*into her bloodstream*—quickly.

"Go and get more of these!" I bark at Iris, tipping Cordelia's head back and blowing into her mouth, taking over her duties.

Iris sits back and stares at me, bewildered.

"From the garden!" I shout, threading my fingers and pouncing on Cordelia's chest, pumping up and down briskly. "Hurry!"

Iris jolts into motion.

"It's near the *Chemodendryum charcoalreous* plant," I shout after her. "At the back of the room under the hosta leaves! They're grey and white in colour before you pick them!"

Iris's shoes hit the stairs at incredible speed.

"Boil some water." I turn my head toward C.L. "And find me some woodworm and aloini tincture—"

"But that has belladonna and strychni—"

"I'm well aware what it has in it! Now, just go!" I'm going to do something I've never done before. I'm going to draw Cordelia's blood out and infuse it with serum, and then send it back in her body to battle the attack right in her veins. The strychnine should shock her pulmonary system while the belladonna opens up her airways—if it doesn't stop her heart first. Belladonna is known to make the heart race at inhuman speeds and, if overdosed, can be a killer. It's risky, I know, but I don't know what else to do to stop it. "Don't look at me like that," I say to a still-stunned-looking C.L. "I know you know where to find them!"

C.L. closes his gaping mouth and sets off for the stairs, clearing two at a time, heading off to the forbidden laboratory of Urlick's father.

"It's going to be all right, Cordelia," I say between breaths. "Everything's going to be all right."

*I hope . . .*

Iris appears in the doorway behind me, three different plants in her hands, roots and all. She's yanked them right out of the ground. She looks frazzled, her hair unpinned, holding the plants out in front of her like a frightened child. "That one," I say, nodding at the fuzzy, dreary-grey plant in her left hand.

She drops the others and runs at the sink.

I keep pumping Cordelia's chest. "Chop it very fine, *very* fine, then put it in the boiling pot of water on the stove." She pulls out a knife.

C.L. slides into the room, woodworm and aloini in a sling round his neck, medical jars clinking. "Two parts woodworm. One part aloini," I instruct. "But not until after the water's come to a full boil!"

"Isn't it going to scald her?"

"Yes, that's why you're going to cool it down afterward. Iris, get the ice block!" I turn to her. Iris flies at the icebox, leaving C.L. to man the pot. He nods in my direction and then scoots over, setting the bottles down atop the cupboard, using his foot to dip a wooden spoon into the water and stir it. Bubbles swelter to the top and burst.

"Now," I say, and he tosses the potions in. Wafts of offensive smoke rise. Iris drops the ice block from its hooks on the woodwork, next to the stove, and wields the leaves up and over C.L.'s head, dropping them in clumps into the pot.

"Stir," I shout. *"And quickly!"*

Cordelia's pulse is slowing.

Iris and C.L. grab wooden spoons and turn the water over, moving their faces out of the way of the tiny grey heaves of smoke.

Cordelia still hasn't moved. Despite my efforts, her breath has still not come back. She is less blue than when I first arrived in the kitchen, but she is still blue. "Come on," I say, pounding her chest. "Come on, Cor. Work with me, Cordelia! Work with me!"

"It's no use, mum." C.L.'s shoulders fall. He looks across the room at the clock. "It's been too much time."

"Don't say that!" I snap. Ice water puddles around us. "It's not over until I say it's over." I slam my fists down on her chest again.

"It's been nearly five minutes now, mum." C.L. looks at me through glossy eyes.

"It's not too late," I say, and I pound again. "Do we have a syringe?"

"I dunno, mum."

"Go FIND ONE!" I push air into Cordelia's mouth again. "Come on, little mite. Take a breath . . ."

C.L. returns seconds later holding a brass syringe in his toes.

In school, we practiced suspending the breath of frogs for up to ten minutes with diriethoxy ethane and then successfully bringing them back with a jolt of woodworm and aloini. Here's hoping things work like that with humans. I swallow, feeling the press of fear drive the last of the oxygen from my lungs.

*Please, Lord, let it work like that.*

I added the leaves to the concoction because I knew what they did for me. If what's happened to Cordelia is the result of the most severe episode she's ever experienced, the potency of a whole plant should hopefully release it. I've honestly no idea if any of this will work. But what else am I to do? What I'm doing is not working!

"Fill it up!" I shout. "With the contents of the pot! Then run it under cold water to cool it!" C.L. rushes to fill the syringe, and Iris jumps in, dunking it in a pot of ice water before she passes it to me.

I take the syringe in my hand, trembling, as I contemplate where best to inject it. *The thigh—we used the thigh in the frog.* "Close your eyes!" I shout to C.L. I pull up Cordelia's skirts and yank down her stocking.

Iris brings her apron to her mouth to stifle her scream as I jab the syringe into the muscle of Cordelia's thigh. The potion sizzles and it gurgles out the sides of the thin pin. I feel a swell of sick sneak up my windpipe. I close my eyes and pray what I've done will be of some assistance.

Cordelia sputters and starts to shake. Her heart picks up speed. I hold her wrist in my hand, counting her pulse, panicking, my own heart galloping in my throat.

"Mum!" C.L. shakes my eyes open.

Cordelia's limbs twist, then start to gyrate. She heaves in a healthy gulp of air.

"More," I say. "I need more leaves!"

Iris tosses me the leftover leaves I'd brought up originally. I crumple them in my hand to get them to weep, and then wave the leaves under Cordelia's nose.

She coughs and sputters and gasps, sucking in a deep breath. Her eyes spring open. "Eyelet?" she says weakly.

Iris squeals and falls to her knees, hugging first Cordelia, then me.

"You've done it, mum! You've done it!" C.L. claps my back, nearly knocking me over.

*I have done it.* I can't believe it. I draw in a breath.

The biggest most grateful breath ever.

I feel a slight twinge of silver coming on and slip a leaf into my own mouth . . .

# *Six*

***Urlick***

I wake to the sound of footsteps descending the staircase adjacent to the mud-and-stone coffin where I'm being held. Blood pumps in my ears. I take a sharp breath and hold it in, listening. It is not the thunderous slap of the guard boots against rails, but rather a gentle padding of bare feet, cautiously negotiating the treads of the looping staircase as if exploring unfamiliar territory . . . or trying hard not to be heard.

I right myself immediately, preparing for anything, my heart beating like a warrior's. My mind loops through scenarios of who it could be.

A guard. The warden. Death.

*Eyelet.* The thought comes over me. What's to become of Eyelet?

I close my eyes and her image appears before me, her posture serious, her expression stoic. There's a distant light in her eyes.

"What is it?" I say to her likeness. "What's the matter?"

Her mouth shrivels into a painful grimace and she throws out her arms, and just as I'm about to swallow her up in my embrace, she vanishes into a thin wisp of corkscrewing black smoke.

*No.* I gasp, leaping to my feet, swimming through the illusion in my mind. I try to catch hold of the spiraling tails of Vapours as they rise, but they're swiped from my grasp. "No!" I shout, shuffling after them. "You cannot have her! She is mine!" The Vapours flip and turn and laugh at me, engulfing her until every trace of her is gone. "No!" I fall to my knees, shaking the vision off. "That can't happen! It won't happen! She is coming for me! I will see her again! I will!" I lower my head. "Please, Lord, let me see her again . . ."

The footsteps in the hallway stop, as if my screaming has frightened them. A guard would never hesitate. I press my face through the bars. My heart balloons with hope.

"Eyelet?" I whisper, listening to the rise and fall of the intruder's ragged breath. "Is that you?"

There is no answer, only a feeble gasping. After a short hesitation, the sound of steps again, picking up pace, skittering softly across the narrow hallway between the landing of the stairs and the door that blocks the short hallway to my cell.

I hold my breath and squint my eyes as something struggles to throw back the heavy wooden door that separates the two rooms. The door creaks slowly open, letting in a vertical sliver of white light that blinds me temporarily—long enough that I cannot make out who is entering—before the door swings shut and the space falls to darkness again.

I suck in a breath and prepare for the worst, pressing my shoulder to the stone wall. *Eyelet would have answered me.*

Unsure feet pad toward me. Something jingles in a hand. Whoever it is strides up to my bars and stops, silent and trembling. The jingling object picks up speed.

"Who are you?" I snap, unnerved by the silence, my heart a thrumming ball of nervous fire in my chest. "Why are you here?"

Folds of cloth crinkle as whoever it is bends and drops something flat and metal to the stone floor with a spine-nipping clank. A small, exasperated breath escapes me when I realize it's food. The hearty waft of greased potatoes drifts up through the bars, causing me to salivate.

"Yer last supper, sir," a small voice says. It sounds like a boy. "I'm afraid the Jack Ketch 'as requested yer services, first light tomorrow." The voice falls.

"What day is this?" I push closer to the bars.

"Saturday, sir."

My heart sinks. "But I thought there were no dippings on Sundays?"

"There aren't, sir." The boy hesitates. "But the Jack Ketch ain't got 'angin' in mind for yuh—"

"Yes, I know." I stop him short of the gruesome details. I'd rather be surprised. Tarred and feathered. Drawn and quartered. Whatever it is, I don't want to know until it's upon me. It'll be easier to face it that way.

Besides, I'm still holding out hope that Eyelet will show.

Somehow.

"I'm afraid it's mostly potatoes, but I did score yuh a chunk o' sausage." The boy slides the tray of food toward me through a narrow slip at the base of my pen's bars. The bottom of the pan chafes slowly over the gritty stone.

"Thank you for that," I say and bend at the waist, lapping up a mouthful of potatoes like a dog, swallowing them slowly, knowing that if I eat too fast they'll just come back up. "Who are you, anyway?" I say in between mouthfuls.

"Sebastian." The boy crosses his legs to sit. "Sebastian Jacobs."

"You live round these parts?"

"No." He hesitates. "I'm from Gears."

"How did you end up here, then?"

"I'm in for thievin', sir." The boy sounds ashamed. His chin scratches the collar of his shirt. "I stole kippers from a smoking barrel on the outskirts of town." He goes on. "But I 'ad to. We was starvin'.

Me and me family, we were. Slipped under the fence from Gears and got caught on a wire on me way back."

"You're a labourer's son, then?"

"No, sir. I ain't got no father." His voice drops again.

There's a sadness to it that is all too familiar. It sits heavy in my throat. "So, because of that, they make you serve the food as punishment, is that it?"

"Yes, sir. They says I'm too young to stay in a cell with the others, so they house me in a cage in the kitchen and make me their scullery slave. It's not so bad, though." His voice perks up. "I get more freedoms than the rest of the prisoners. I serves the slop twice daily, both breakfast and dinner to all the inmates, and run errands for the guards and the churchman, and the Ruler. That way I gets to sneak about a bit. But if I's caught sneaking, they beats me, so I needs to be very careful."

"By churchman, do you mean the Clergy?"

"Yes, sir. He's in on everything goes on about 'ere. The jug's sat right next door to the parish. Sometimes they make me clean the manse for him. And do other things." His voice drops again and I sense his head does, too. Queasiness rises in me.

The boy's stomach growls. Loudly.

"Do they ever feed you?"

"Sometimes," the boy admits slowly.

"When's the last time you've eaten?" I swallow another mouthful of potatoes.

"'Bout four days back."

"Here." I shove the tray back in his direction with my nose. "Take this."

"But, sir—"

"Go on. Eat it. It'll just be wasted on me at this point."

The boy hesitates. "Yer sure?"

"Positive."

"Thank yuh, sir!" The boy snaps the pan to his mouth and lays into the potatoes. "Thank yuh so much!"

"You're welcome." I lean back from the bars, thinking. "You must overhear things, in your cage in the kitchen, is that right?"

"From time to time, yeah, sir. Why?"

"Is there a chance I could get you to listen for me?"

"Yuh expectin' some news?" The boy's voice lilts up.

"No, not particularly. But if there were news for me, I'd want to know what's said. In great detail. Can you do that for me? Listen intently and deliver me the message?"

"Certainly, sir. Listenin's me specialty. It's just that, I don't know what good it's gonna do at this point." He gulps down the potatoes in his mouth and changes the subject. "'Ere." He slurps up some tea and then pushes the cup between the bars at me, sloshing. "Yuh 'ave the rest."

"No, it's all right."

"I insist." He tips the cup toward me again, and tea sloshes on my knee. "Yuh'll be needin' somethin' to wash down those taters."

I feel a grin growing on his face through the darkness.

"So we're square, then?" he asks as I lean forward, groping with my lips between the bars, until at last I've found the rim of the cup he holds.

"We are," I say as he tips it up, shakily. I swallow fast and hard, until I've drained the cup, choking some. He left me a lot more than I expected. "Thanks," I say, pulling back and flicking the excess liquid from my upper lip with a shake of my head.

"This, too." The boy pushes a nub of bread up against my teeth.

I open my mouth and accept it, chewing slowly, letting the savory spices of the dark pumpernickel bread wallow on my tongue before I swallow.

The boy returns to enjoying the potatoes, then suddenly freezes. "Yuh won't tell nobody 'bout this, will yuh, sir? Me stealin' this food, I mean?"

"Who have I to tell?"

"Right."

I sense a smile. "Now hurry up and eat before someone catches you," I say.

The boy gulps down another mouthful of potatoes and scrapes the plate with his fork, grating hard around the edges of the circular pan, collecting every last drop. "I best be going now," he says as he jerks to a stand. "Before they starts to miss me." He picks up the empty cup and pan; they clank together in the darkness like lock and key. "It was very nice meeting you, Master—"

"Urlick. Urlick Babbit."

"I'd shake yer 'and, but—"

"I know."

The boy falls silent. "Until later, then . . . I mean—" He swallows it back.

"Don't worry about it."

He turns and starts away, feet slapping hard against the grimy stone floor as he rushes at the door, then slowly he turns back. "For what it's worth, I'm sorry this is 'appening to yuh," he says into the darkness.

"So am I," I say.

He pries open the heavy wooden blockade door and slinks between, and I slump back against the wall of my cell, listening to the door fall shut. Pieces of me break away, wishing it were *I* escaping this wretched hole.

*Oh, Eyelet, where are you?*

# *Seven*

***Eyelet***

*Be careful,* Iris signs, passing me a pack of supplies. I wave away the trolling brume that lingers between us. It's cold and dark outside, still freshly morning—as fresh a morning as we ever get. Dew clings to the sparse tufts of grass at our feet and moistens my hairline.

"We will," I say, patting the overstuffed duffel. Tins of kippers and beans slap together inside, along with the familiar clunk of gadgetry—weapons, of course. No one should ever enter the forest without them. I've learned that lesson well. I peek inside, seeing, among other things: a candlesnuffer alias mace ejector, a whip adapted with a morning-star end, and a miniature fire poker hiding a launchable serrated *shuriken*—like an arrowhead, only much more lethal. A pass with it could sever someone's head.

C.L. has his own pack, filled with God only knows what, from Urlick's private treasure trove in the basement.

Iris surprises me by leaning in close for a hug, during which she drops fresh-baked biscuits into my side jacket pocket. Like that's going to help.

I reach in, checking the pocket for the supply of leaves I wrapped in a hankie and stuffed in there earlier—leaves from the miracle plant in the terrarium room, the ones responsible for reviving Cordelia, and me, the last time.

I dig a little deeper, searching for the syringe. The one I filled with the last bits of Cordelia's medicine, just in case I fall into an episode and raw leaves don't work. Finding them both there, I'm satisfied and pull Iris closer. "Don't worry," I whisper in her ear. "Everything's going to be all right."

She drops back and hands me an Insectatron along with another instrument I don't recognize. It's long and thin, like a reed, but there's something in the middle, tucked inside it.

"What's this?"

"Blow dart," C.L. says, slipping past. He's balancing Clementine's armour on his shoulders, her face gear over his head.

"Just a plain old blow dart?" I raise a skeptical brow.

"Of course not." He dumps the face gear. "It's good for one hundred and seventy paces. Has a spring-loaded arm in the back end."

"You people and your odd figures." I tip it over, examining it. "Why can't you ever round up? What's wrong with two hundred? How on earth will I ever determine precisely one hundred and seventy paces in the heat of battle?"

"Look on the side of it," C.L. says.

I flip it over. There's a gauge—a bubble of glass with a dot of mercury inside it and a scale of numbers etched into the glass.

"The mercury rises until it fills the glass, the perfect distance—a quick look at it will tell you if you're in range," C.L. says.

"Well"—I look up—"doesn't Urlick just think of everything."

"Wasn't Urlick," C.L. chirps. "Iris made that."

"You?" I spin around to face her. She grins.

"The apple corer, too," C.L. says, suiting Clementine up in her armour.

"Well"—I pull Iris in for another quick hug—"it's always good to know we have a couple of assassins in the house." She smiles. "We'd better be off," I say to C.L., reaching out to my pile of armour. I slip the chest plate over my head and fasten the buckles on the sides. Pulling my chain-mail trousers up under my skirts, I go for my helmet before my gloves, then I check the skies.

"I'm worried about Pan," I say to Iris. "I haven't seen her since I got here." I squint, holding my hand to my eyes. "When you do, will you send her ahead to check on Urlick? And let her know we'll meet her in the city?"

Iris nods and helps me with my gloves, which I'm thankful for; chain-mail gloves are not the easiest to manoeuvre. I check the skies one more time and take my mount, swinging an awkwardly heavy leg over Clementine, landing with a clatter over her heavily armoured back. "Perhaps we'll see her along the way."

"Perhaps," C.L. adds.

"Now remember"—I look down to Iris, who's now helping C.L. with his gear—"give Cordelia a full tablespoon of that soup every four hours for two days. She should be fully recovered by then. If not, continue with the regimen. And keep us posted via Insectatron." She nods her head. "If it happens again, you know what to do, right? You saw what I did." Iris nods her head. "And kiss her for me, will you? Every day while I'm gone—"

"We have to go, mum," C.L. says as Iris helps hoist him up into the saddle behind me.

"I know."

I take up the reins, looking down into Iris's worried face. There's been no time to test-drive the wings, not with Cordelia's sudden illness. But if we don't go now, we'll never make it to the city's edge by end of day. The last thing we want is to be passing through the criminal woods in the thick of night. "You take good care of our little one, will you?" I stare into her eyes.

Iris nods, her eyes wet, her fingers trembling inside tightly clasped hands.

"Very well, then." I take a breath. "Let's be on our way, shall we?" I turn to C.L. and then dig my heels into Clementine's sides, sending her into a brisk trot. "Here goes nothing," I shout back to Iris, who's waving us off from the lawn. "Okay, girl," I lean and whisper in Clementine's ear. "Time to go fetch!"

I take up the mock fishing pole with wire and launch the carrot out over Clementine's head. Her eyes light up at the sight of it, and she bursts into a gallop when I throw out the reins. "That's it, girl, go get it!" I shout, nudging her on with my spurs. The wings drag at first and then, thankfully, start flapping. C.L. bobs along behind me as we pick up speed.

"We're not gonna make it!" he shouts.

We leave the clearing and head for the trees, and even I'm worried.

"We have to!" I shout back.

I flip the rod to the left, steering Clementine out over the ridge.

"Embers? Are yuh crazy?" C.L.'s voice squeaks.

I hold my breath as I lean forward, charging her onward, encouraging her to leap over the edge of the ravine. She hesitates, nearly dumping us both as she slams to a staggered stop before at last her hooves leave the earth. For a moment we hang suspended in midair, my heart suspended midthroat. Then, at last, the wings catch some wind and we pitch slowly upward, out of the clutches of Embers's dark and vile-smelling smoke.

"They work!" C.L. jumps up behind me. "They really work!"

"Of course they do!" I say, puffing with pride. "Thank goodness," I murmur under my breath. I whirl Clementine into a tight turn and head off over the forest.

*Here we come, Urlick. We'll be there before you know it.*

*And you'll be a free man.*

I can't wait to see him and run my finger through his crazy hair.

And kiss that ghostly face of his.
*Please, Lord, keep him safe.*

# Eight

***Eyelet***

The woods are incredibly eerie from the air. Their ominous breadth abounds for what seems like a galaxy. Nothing but treetops and belching, gurgling gullies, the festering scars left over from the rage of the last Vapours, all tied up in a foggy, Vapour-laced bow.

The clouds up here are thick as cotton, ranging from light grey to black. More than twice we hear the chatter of teeth filtering up through the trees, but I must admit, they are much less intimidating way up here than riding among them below.

The air up here is very thin but somehow less intoxicating. Strange, I never noticed it before when we were up in the balloon. But then again, I wasn't exactly coherent. And while we travelled aboard Bertie, Urlick refused to let us take any chances; we wore our masks the whole way—save for the moment I kissed him.

I close my eyes and relive the moment in my mind—the warmth of his lips, the taste of his tongue, edged in vanilla and peppermint tea. I breathe deep, remembering his scent—rosewood and cinnamon, with just a hint of sandalwood soap at his neck.

And to think I once feared him a monster.

Now I don't know what I'd do without him.

"How close are we?" I shout back over my shoulder to C.L.

He swings around, checking the Continental Positioning System—a sort of human thermomultiplier that Urlick was tinkering with just before we left the first time, a spin-off of his famed Dyechrometer that, instead of checking for feral heartbeats, uses the accumulation of body heat to determine the distance between major metropolises. Using population as an indicator, it is then able to calculate the distance between towns and cities.

C.L. detaches the cone-shaped gun from its holster at the back of the saddle and aims it ahead of us. The galvanometer needle fluctuates, ejecting a beam of white light through the fog. After much fussing and bleeping, the needle comes to rest on a number on the dial. "Seventeen," C.L. says.

"Seventeen more kilometres?"

"No. Seventeen heartbeats," C.L. shouts above the wind. "Which means we's either comin' up on the edge of the grand metropolis of Gears, or we's meetin' up with a large band of criminals." He swallows.

My heart takes a jerk in my chest at the thought of the latter. I check Clementine's oxygen-tank gauge. It's running low. We're going to have to stop soon to change it. I can't possibly change it on the fly. But I don't want to stop where there are criminals. "Is there any way to be sure?"

"No, mum, I'm afraid there's not."

My mind wanders over the oxygen supply we have with us. Three full tanks and four half-packs, "minis," to be used only in dire emergency, as they don't always perform. We'll need to conserve at least a tank and a half for the return trip. I was right about the supplies in the cupboard. They were dashedly low.

I wonder about pitching ourselves higher into the clouds—could we risk breathing the air up here without any masks? Then again, the altitude might get us, and we could well find ourselves quite literally falling right out of the sky.

I have no choice, I'll have to land soon, the border of Gears in sight or not.

I push Clementine on with my heels, feeling my stomach clench at the prospect. The Continental Positioning System clicks wildly, then remains silent for a stretch of time. Criminals—it must have been criminals, elsewise the machine would have kept bleeping as it registered more and more heartbeats. We fly in silence until the needle on Clementine's oxygen tank falls to zero, sounding a harsh alarm.

I sit back, clutching the reins tight in my hands, a knot forming in my stomach. Sweat slicks my palms.

"What now?" C.L. says.

"I dunno." I swallow. "She's got a quarter-pint reserve, maybe, before she's completely out."

Clementine gasps for air, her mask sucking in.

The Continental Positioning System groans, then starts bleeping at rapid-fire speed, *thank God.* Its register shows thirty, sixty, eighty-nine, one hundred three, one hundred fifty-seven heartbeats. A town, it's got to be a town. We must be over Gears. The knot in my stomach gives way. "You'd better shut it off now," I shout to C.L. "We're getting too close. Someone's going to see the light."

He fastens the gun back into the saddle as I coax Clementine down through the clouds. The air becomes instantly more difficult to process. Our air-mask gauges scream, lights flash. I start to cough until I'm gagging.

"You all right?" C.L. grabs me. I've fallen sideways in the saddle under the force of the cough.

"I'm fine," I say, coughing hard again.

But I'm not fine. Far from it, actually. I haven't been since Urlick and I crawled down into the ravine at the back of the forest, on our way to the Core. For some reason my lungs react to everything now: changes in atmosphere, pressure, air quality, everything . . .

Or at least I hope that's all it is.

I clear my throat hard again, force down the urge to cough, for C.L.'s sake—and my own sanity—my heartbeats faster than the ones coming in on the register, as treetops come into view. Chimneys, rooftops, smokestacks flutter past. I swing out wide, avoiding Gears altogether, flying instead back over the lightly forested range just before her city limits, where the freak-show caravan is likely to have bedded down for the night. The plan is to commandeer the train and ride it into Brethren, creating a big-enough and long-enough diversion to give me time to break into the old stone jug and save Urlick.

According to C.L., the freakmaster travels the main road into Gears, so his train draws enough attention to lure potential customers out of their homes. He'd never arrive in the streets at night, always at break of day, when the most people will be out and about. They held one afternoon show for the people of Gears, then moved on to the higher-paying customers of Brethren, passing through the checkpoint and setting up in Brethren's town square for an evening performance.

"Do you see any sign of them?" I ask C.L., reining Clementine back, her mask wheezing, low on air. I bring her around low enough to see the earth, but far enough up in the air to still be camouflaged by cloud cover. "Any sign of the train at all?"

C.L. squints. "No, mum," he huffs, sounding worried. "I was sure they'd be here by now."

"Don't worry," I say, taking another swing over the city's edge. "I'm sure they'll show." I ask Clementine for another turn. She gallantly obeys, winging off over the edge of the forest so we can check deeper into the woods. Her mask blows a gasket.

"We've got no choice!" I shout. "We're going down!"

"There!" C.L. spots something through a seam in the clouds. He jumps in his seat, nearly falling out of it, pointing. "Over there! The campfire. Set us down over there!"

I squint, spotting what he's excited about through the dashes of the cloud cover, but I'm not sure we can make it. "Over there, girl." I point, leaning out and peeling open the end of Clementine's mask. "Can you make it there?"

At the edge of the woods, next to the clearing, about three hundred metres away, sit the colourful cars of the freak train wound in a linked semicircle, like an illuminated rainbow, around the skirt of a glowing campfire.

Clementine sees it and pushes toward it, losing altitude, her breath coming out in frothy gasps. She snorts as we swoop down through the waning darkness. Morning is nearly upon us. We've flown all night. We land with a clattering thud about twenty metres from the scene.

*

Snores filter up into the sky from between cage bars. Next to the fire, the top-hat-wearing, full-girthed ringmaster sleeps. He has no idea what's about to happen. None of them do.

Neither do I, really.

C.L. slips down from the saddle into the mud with a clank. My boots make a soft thunk as well. Clementine snorts, and C.L. clamps a hand down over her muzzle, like she's the only one making noise.

"So what now?" I whisper, tucking in behind the cover of trees, leaving Clementine to root for grass.

C.L. follows, digging a length of rope and a hood out of her saddlebag before abandoning her.

"We attack 'im from behind," he whispers softly. "That way, when 'e's found 'ooded and bound and roped to a tree, 'e won't be able to report who did it to 'im."

"So that's the plan, then, we're going tie him up?"

"Unless you 'ave another." C.L. frowns.

"No. No, tying him up will be fine, I guess." I turn and bite my fingers.

"What's the matter?" C.L. whispers.

"It's just that . . ." I turn. "What if he's *not* found? What if we leave him here and he gets eaten by the criminals?"

"'Ow is that a problem?"

"Where you're coming from I suppose it's not, but for me." I twist my fingers. "I don't know whether I'll be able to sleep."

"Are yuh suggestin' we bring 'im with us?"

"Would that be possible?"

"No!" he snaps. He charges away across the open ground toward the train cars, hood and rope tossed over his shoulder.

"All right, all right"—I scramble after him, taking in breath—"what do you want me to do?"

He spins. "Keep an eye out while I 'og-tie the bastard," he says between his teeth. "No offense."

"None taken." I bolt forward, catching up to him again. "Then what?"

"Then—"

His sentence is cut short by the cock of a gun, the barrel pressed to the nape of his neck.

"Then I'll shoot you both and leave you for criminal brekkie," the ringmaster says. "Just as you'd planned for me."

I swallow and turn my head slowly. The ringmaster's eyes fall hard on me from over the top of the gun. They are small and cold and slitted. Filled with such meanness, their presence stings my soul. Thick-hooded brows shroud them. His forehead carries several scars. Telltale signs he's not immune to being accosted.

"Well, well, look what we 'ave 'ere." His gaze tugs through the holes in my chain-mail chemise. I look down and up, embarrassed. I pinch my collar shut, hot with the feeling of being violated.

He twirls one end of his glossy waxed moustache to a point matching the other, and winks at me. A swell of sickness rises in me. "'Oo's the girl?" he says through fat, chafed, and freckled lips.

"None of your business," C.L. snaps, gun still at his neck.

"Oh, come now. She cain't be with the likes of you," the ringmaster laughs. "So, hows about you tellin' me who you protecting 'ere? What's a little wanker like you doing with a slippery little sod like this?"

"Don't call her that!" C.L.'s head spins.

I stumble back, feeling faint, weak in the knees. What did he just call me?

"Whatchu gonna do about it, *'it* me?" The ringmaster pokes C.L. in the armpits with the end of his gun. "Wif these little stubs." He laughs and spins him around, shoving him toward the freak train. "Go on, get over there with the others, where you belong."

"No!" I shout, stepping in between them.

"*Oh*, she *can* speak." The ringmaster lowers his voice. "And she's a feisty one, too." He sashays toward me, wobbly smile pitching over his two remaining good teeth. Last night's dinner takes a turn in my stomach. "I like that."

The sleazy timbre of his voice crawls up my spine.

"Leave 'er alone!" C.L. shouts.

With a quick turn of his hips, he throws a leg into the air, clipping the ringmaster in the side of the chin with his heel. The ringmaster's jaw rocks to one side. The freaks in the train jump to their feet and cheer, wagons rocking left and right as they whoop and yelp and moan. I can't tell if they're for or against us. Their gruesome, moonlit faces press out between the bars.

"Look out!" C.L. shouts at me as the ringmaster's gun flies from his hand. It tumbles slowly through the air and hits the ground with a thump, dislodging a bullet I narrowly escape before it bounces erratically off Clementine's gear and buries itself in a tree trunk behind me. The speed of the bullet has clipped the curl that hangs next to my cheek. I stare as the freshly sheared tuft flutters to rest on the ground at my feet.

The ringmaster's head whips up, his eyes aglow with revenge. He lunges, snatching C.L. by the throat, lifting him slightly off the ground.

C.L. chokes and kicks. The ringmaster tightens his grip. "You dare to challenge *me*!" His eyes flash. "I should *whip* you for running off the way you did!" C.L. gags as the ringmaster locks on his windpipe. "In fact, I should kill you now I 'ave the chance!"

"Don't!" I hit him. "Let him go! Let him *go*!" I jump on his back.

C.L. fights, trying to reach the ground with his toes, wriggling and gurgling, the skin on his face turning blue. I pound the ringmaster's head from behind.

"Get *off me*!" He grabs for my knee and flings me aside.

I hit the ground hard and scramble to my feet, his hold still tight on C.L. Spying the gun on the ground, I stoop to get it, but the ringmaster kicks it away.

"Do you really think I'm that stupid?" he says in a low, scratchy voice, still strangling C.L. His gaze sweeps over my body. He ogles every slope and valley on the way down and up. "But perhaps I should reconsider." He hesitates, leering at C.L. and then back at me. "After all, you did bring me a lovely gift. It'd be rude of me not to open it."

His eyes meet my breasts, and I gag in my throat. I launch forward and spit in his face.

"You little—" He tosses C.L. aside and comes at me with the speed of a jaguar, twisting me into his arms. C.L. falls to the ground, gasping for air, his head connecting hard with a rock. "Now," the ringmaster says, his breath at the back of my neck. "I think it's time to unwrap me present." He reaches for me and I duck, slamming us both back up against a tree. Air pops from his lungs as he bounces off. I spring free.

"Leave me alone." I turn, grabbing a sharp piece of bark and holding it out like a knife. "Leave me alone, or you'll never open another present again!" I swing it low, trembling, my wrist injured in the fall.

"Don't make me laugh." The ringmaster's chin waggles.

He reaches for me again and I swing, connecting and gashing open his arm. My wrist throbs with pain.

The freaks' voices rise up. They ring their bars with their chains. My eyes dart wildly between them, the ringmaster, and C.L., out cold on the ground.

*Please get up, C.L.* Through wisps of fog I see blood on the rock near his head. *No, please, God, let him get up . . .*

The sound of the freaks' screeches in my ears.

Teeth chatter in the trees at my back.

"Don't make me do this," the freakmaster says, pulling a knife from his pocket.

My eyes stick on the blade.

I look again to C.L. as the freakmaster storms toward me, closing my back in on a tree. I need a weapon. I've got to find something. My head jerks around, my mind searching. Wait, *the dart. Iris's weapon.*

I grope my chain-mail pocket, searching for it.

I can't find it.

Have I lost it?

Where's the dart?

The ringmaster's eyes flash. He presses himself up against me, dirty bits stiff and poking at my thighs. All the muscles in my back tense. "'Ow's about we call a truce and have a little fun, eh?" I turn away. His breath smells of spirits and regurgitated sausage. I long to retch, but I hold it in. His teeth are yellow and tinged with brown.

He reaches up, running a grimy hand through my hair as I fumble through the folds of my armour, still searching for the dart, shaking.

"What'sa matter, love?" The ringmaster's sour breath sweeps the hollow of my neck. "Your first time?" His eyebrows lift. He drags a slow, calloused knuckle down the side of my cheek as my fingers close around the reed. I snap it up to my mouth, sucking back a huge breath, and blow hard, only to discover . . . it's empty.

"Whatchu gonna do"—the ringmaster smiles—"'histle me away?" Perversion flashes in his dirty, dark eyes. His stomach bounces jovially as he laughs and clutches me by the wrists.

Panic pulses through me like a drug as he pulls me away from the tree toward his lair, stopping to cup my chin and press his grimy mouth to mine. His rough lips grate my skin as I struggle to get away. He smells of grease and guts and unthinkable desire. *"Please."* I squirm and turn. "Please, don't do this!" I pound my damaged wrist against his chest. A quick rise of my knee and I've balled him square, but even that doesn't seem to affect him.

"A fighter." He moves in on me again, all lips and hands and rancid breath. "God knows I love a good fight."

I pound and scream around the seal of his mouth.

Clementine turns her head.

The freaks roar, rock their cages, and angrily strum the bars.

My heart floods into my ears.

Out the corner of my eye, I see something rising. A quick flash of metal whips the air. The ringmaster's head snaps forward, slapping hard against my chest bone. I fall back, screaming, splattered in his blood.

The freaks howl. They chant. They scream.

He melts to his knees on the ground in front of me, his head flopped at an awkward angle. His eyes are wide, entranced with shock, stuck in a forward gaze.

I cover my mouth with both hands and scream, flicking his blood from my fingers as he collapses dead over the tops of my boots.

At first I don't realize what's happened, and then it registers. Clementine stands, fetlock bent, blood dripping from her shoe, her long guilty face peering back at me from where the ringmaster lies face down in the dirt—unmoving.

# Nine

***Eyelet***

"C.L.!" I run to him, crouching to my knees by his side. "C.L., wake up, please!" I shake him. "We have to get out of here! Clementine's killed the ringmaster!"

The freaks cheer.

Frightened, I haul C.L.'s head up. "Oh, my God, you're bleeding." There's a sizable gash at the back of his skull from where he landed on the rock. Blood trickles through his hair. I tear a length from my petticoat to try to stop it.

"There's a first-aid kit in the caboose," a raspy voice says.

I look up and stare at the train. The freaks have fallen quiet, receded into the shadows of their pens. Or at least it appears so, because I cannot see them.

I look all around me, searching for the voice, but through the trolling fog I see nothing.

"The keys," the voice says. "You'll find them in his pocket." A snake-scaled human arm pokes out from between the bars, pointing in the dead ringmaster's direction. A clamp and chain dangle from its wrist, connected to the wall of its car. "On the inside of his breast pocket, in a secret zippered compartment," the voice adds.

I scramble to my feet, a little afraid, racing on shaky knees toward the ringmaster's lifeless body. Bending down, I unbutton his vest quickly and run my fingers along the inside of his garment. I try my best to avert my eyes from the bones protruding from his neck. The pocket is cool, a fine grade of silk, just as fine as my father used to wear. I drive away the thought and keep searching. My fingers soon find the compartment. I unzip it and find a large set of skeleton keys on a ring.

I yank them loose, nearly flinging them into the trees, I'm so nervous, and race for the caboose. The lock on the door clamours as I stuff key after key into it.

"It's the gold one," the voice says. "The kit is inside the bench to the right."

"How do you know all this?" I ask curtly into the darkness.

"Let's just say"—the voice hesitates—"every freak show needs a doctor, even if he travels in chains."

The air fills with the clank of chain links and shackles, as one by one the freaks gather up enough courage to reveal themselves. The whites of four sets of eyes peer out at me through the bars. Their haunting presence chills my skin. I rub down the goose bumps that grow on my arms and will my feet to move toward them. I know I need to get back to C.L. But I fear I'll need some help to revive him. And the plan always was to overthrow the master and befriend the freaks for their help. I swallow. I just expected C.L. would be the one befriending them, not I . . . alone. I gulp again. No time like the present to meet my future accomplices, I suppose.

I tread lightly, looking back over my shoulder at C.L. The same kind of turbulent fury whirls in my chest as it did the first time I laid eyes on him and Cordelia.

What am I fearing? C.L. once lived among them, and he's wonderful. A branch snaps beneath my feet and I jump. A tiny bolt of terror shoots through me.

*Honestly.* I shake it off. They're just people. I bite my lip. A burning cold shivers through my body. My mind drifts to my epilepsy. All the violent episodes I've endured through the years. Had I ever been caught having one of those, I, too, could have been forced to live behind bars.

This could just as easily have been my destiny.

The notion emboldens my step, and I move more confidently toward the cars. "Hello," I say into the darkness.

"You a friend of Crazy Legs?" says a set of blinking eyes.

"Yes. Are you?" I test the waters, trying hard not to tremble. The creature shifts to the front of the car, and I try not to react, failing, gasping and feeling instantly shameful, as I'm taken aback by the look of his skin—parched and dried as a drought-damaged riverbed, not a single hair on his head.

"Any friend of his is a friend of ours, right, group?" He speaks over his shoulder.

Three more creatures rumble in their cages.

"I'm Martin." He sticks a mummified-looking hand out between the bars. Chains rattle at his wrist.

I hesitate before taking it, not proud of myself, but I do, trying my best not to cringe, worried as I shake it that his hand may snap loose.

He wears only a loincloth, which has my eyes darting for something else to focus on. My cheeks flush red. His entire body looks as though the skin has baked in the sun for a thousand years. I can't help but think it must be painful to wear. He is missing a nose, and parts of his lips are broken off, as if from age or weather. He is like a corpse that's been pickled and dried and kept for centuries, but he can't be as old as his skin appears. I think about him being carted around and put up for show, and my heart bleeds for his pain.

He shakes my hand and his eyes shine, so youthful behind their yellowed lenses. "Pleased to meet you." He smiles, and I'm surprised to see he has teeth. Not many, but more than the ringmaster. "You have a kind heart," he says, and his eyes roll as if he's channeling that information from another world. He launches into a momentary dream state still in possession of my hand, and my heart flutters uneasily in my chest.

"Oh, come now." I chuckle nervously, not knowing what to make of his strange actions. "How can you say that, you don't even know me?"

"I don't have to." He awakens, and shifts his gaze back to me. "I can tell everything about a person by just looking in their eyes." He stares.

I pull my hand back, a little unnerved, fighting hard to disguise the discomfort that's swallowed me. "You can, can you?"

"Yes, and from what I see"—he smiles, his weathered lips splitting—"you're our destiny." His words come out low and slow.

A niggling feeling creeps down my neck, a spider of sorts, spun of his words. I move on to the next cage.

Crouched in the corner is a decrepit stump of a man. I stoop, trying to better align my face with what I think to be his. I've never seen such a troubled creature before.

He stretches his eyes up to the tops of his lids, struggling to peer out from beneath a frightening mountain of tumour. One eye is so awkwardly placed on his head, it appears to be an ear—and his ear, offset and sliding down the side of his head, does not align with the other. His other eye can barely be seen for another massive growth.

His arms are of different lengths. One is but a stub with a hand, his fingers gnarled into a permanent hook. He looks like something out of the monster comics—the kind the masters forbade us to read in school for fear we'd all have nightmares.

"M' name is Reeke," he says very slowly. I notice an abundance of teeth in his mouth, staggered and jumbled, more than a double set in the lower jaw alone. Foam forms when he talks, and drool drips from his lips. He's quick to steer the excess away with his knuckles, flushing.

He offers his hand to shake, then just as quickly draws it back, realizing his mistake. He wipes it clean on his clothing and tries again.

"Pleased to meet you, Reeke," I say, patting him on what I believe to be his shoulder. My heart aches for this urchin of a man. How could I have ever believed myself unfortunate when there are people who face conditions such as this in the world? How narrow-minded of me to think myself so cruelly afflicted.

I turn to the next. The Snakeman, obviously—I recognize him from C.L.'s poster, named for the grotesque and painful-looking condition of his spine. Contorted from stem to stern into an almost perfect S, he shuffles toward me, rocking side to side.

"Sadar," he says, offering me his hand. He has the most beautiful, smooth, brown-coloured skin with matching eyes, and snow-white hair. I take his hand and he grips mine shockingly firmly, shaking it with such enthusiasm my shoulder feels temporarily dislocated. His chains jingle against the bars and he talks over them. "Though some call me the Snakeman. Either way, it's me." He grins.

"Sadar? That's a fascinating name," I say. "What does it mean?"

"In my country, it means 'respected.'" His tongue catches on his teeth in that lyrical way immigrants from the East speak, bringing to mind the faraway pleasures of incense and spice.

"Well, that's irony, isn't it?"

He smiles, and I notice he hasn't let go of my hand yet. He closes his eyes and mutters something, as if performing some form of prayer. He tips back his head instead of bowing. I worry he may be a Cantationer—the real sort, the kind that should be dipped in wax. Perhaps he *should* be in this cage.

I'm about to pull away when his eyes pop back open.

Cantation ended.

He nods as he steps back with a slight fluttery wave of his hands, as if to say, *Don't worry, all is well.*

I can't help but recognize what the commoners of Brethren used to think about me. Judging me over something they didn't understand. How rapidly my heart has just beaten. How quickly my mind jumped to evil things . . . over nothing, really: a man with his eyes shut.

I swallow down my prejudice and move on to the last cage, my mind occupied with concern for C.L. The sign below the bars reads *Wanda the Werewolf Woman*. My skin ripples at the thought. "Hello," I say, looking deep into the cage. My heart thumps in my throat. Something stirs in the corner, and I extend a hand, praying I get it back, feeling immensely afraid. When she doesn't respond, I say it again. "Hello?"

"She doesn't speak," Sadar says.

"She has a tongue, doesn't she?" I whirl around, feeling slightly panicked.

"Yes. She just prefers not to use it. Ever since the fire."

"The fire?" My head jerks forward.

"Yes. We had a stunner a few years back. We were all performing at the time. Wanda was alone in the train. She got the fool notion to try to burn the excess hair from her skin with a candle. Only it didn't go as planned."

I cringe at the thought of it. "You mean she—"

"Went up in smoke, yes. The whole train did. Cost the freakmaster a bundle. And he was none too pleased about it, either. After the whipping, she never spoke again."

"He beat her?"

"He beat us all, miss."

My mouth falls open.

"Come on out, Wanda. It's all right." Sadar adds, "She's a friend."

A woman covered from head to toe in hair appears. Big brown eyes shine from under long, lanky black lashes. She strides only halfway up to the bars and raises an arm, trying to shield her hairy face from my sight as if she's ashamed for me to look on her. Every inch of her is covered in hair but her gaze.

My mind jumps to thoughts of the Illuminator. If we were to recover the small one, the one my father first made, perhaps it could be used to help her. In one of my father's early tests he rendered a kiwifruit completely bald, I remember, leaving it only minimally scarred. Perhaps it would work the same way on Wanda's skin? I sigh, my thoughts slipping from there to the dangers of the machine. My eyes grow warm with tears. I don't dare try to help her; I could kill her.

Wanda glances up at me briefly, then just as quickly away, and I feel the pang of her heavy heart in my chest. She saw my tears and thinks I'm pitying her. I'll have to make it up to her later. Right now, I turn back to C.L., still knocked out on the ground, the dead ringmaster beside him. I've got to get on with things. "Well, now that we've all become acquainted," I smile and say, "I could use a little help."

Martin sticks his head out between the bars and smiles. "Slip the keys in the locks, love, and we're at your service."

*

I creep along the line, releasing each from their cages, shaky fingers manipulating locks. Each exits their cage—all but Wanda.

"Here, let me." Sadar waddles down the row of cars, stopping outside the caboose, sliding the gold key into the lock. He twists it, and I'm relieved at the sound of turbines clunking. He unhinges the lock and throws back the door, and I'm overcome by the stench of mould. Moss grows on every surface inside, mushrooms in the corner. The wood of the train is clearly rotting away.

"Tell me no one sleeps in here."

"Just the freakmaster." Martin grins.

I throw an arm over my nose, hike up my skirts, and haul myself through the doors.

"There are smelling salts in a jar on the shelf above the bench," he says, reaching for the first-aid kit inside. Hinges creak as I throw the door open. Spiders flee down my arms. I shriek a small shriek and fling them off, grabbing for the jar, and hurl myself back out the doors. Sadar following quickly behind, I race back to C.L., pressing a wad of gauze to his head.

"Here, put pressure on this," I say to Martin, spinning open the jar of smelling salts. I wave the whole lot past C.L.'s nose, and his eyes spring open, wincing at the white light of the beginning of day.

"Oh, thank God," I say, bringing a hand to my chest.

"What's 'appened?" His body pops up. He makes a horrible face. "It smells like bottled dead-rat guts."

"It is," Sadar says.

I drop the bottle and gasp.

"It worked, didn't it?"

"What's 'appened? Where am I?" C.L. spins around.

"Whoa, whoa, whoa," I say slowly. He raises a foot to his head, discovering the gash. "We're in the forest." I take his foot. "We've come to overthrow the ringmaster, remember?"

C.L.'s mouth forms a confused-looking O. His eyes travel past me to the heap of the ringmaster on the ground. "I take it we've done so?" He blinks.

"I'm afraid we've done a little bit more than just *so*."

"Played it my way, did we?" C.L.'s O becomes a full-bodied grin. "And you were opposed to tying 'im up."

"Let me see that gash on your head." I pull him around, tenderly parting his hair. The bleeding's finally slowed, though the wound is much deeper than I first imagined. "You could do with some stitches, I'm afraid."

"Good thing we've a doctor in the house." Martin steps up. "Out of the way." He nudges me. "I won't be a minute. C.L., bite on this." He hands C.L. a towel. Martin sits and threads a needle, his eyes travelling to the freakmaster on the ground. "Then we'll have to figure out what to do with him."

# Ten

***Urlick***

The door at the top of the staircase crashes open and my heart crashes with it. I hold my breath, waiting for whoever it is to hit the stairs.

*Feet.* Bare ones. I think.

I scooch to the front of my cell, expecting the boy, though I'm unsure at this point, if it's him or not. My heart pumps in my ears at the thought of it being a guard, here to collect me for my scheduled demise.

I swallow and close my eyes, awaiting confirmation.

Whoever it is grunts, slinging back the massive slab door between the stairs and my cell, and I suck in a tight breath. Bare feet slap the stones, racing the final small distance between the door and my cell, and relief pours over me. *The boy, it's the boy.* My eyes spring open, my heartbeat slows.

He slides to his knees in front of me, gasping and breathless. "This come for yuh," he blurts, sticking his hand between the bars as if he hasn't the luxury of time he had before. "I figured it might be important." He drops a glinting object from his palm inside my cell. It drops to the floor a few centimetres from me. A metallic ticking sound activates, and it scurries toward me, limping through the darkness.

"I'm afraid yer old cellmate ripped off one of its legs before I could get to it, but it still seems to be operating all right."

The thing latches on to my trousers and crawls up my leg to my chest, coming to rest on my shoulder, tapping my cheek with a tiny claw. "The Insectatron." The creature coos. "*My Ladybird.* How did you get this? Where did you find it?"

"Your old cellmate 'ad it, sir. Claimed it just flew in through the bars, outta nowhere, yesterday. I 'eard 'im makin' up the story for the guards, as they was trying to take it from 'im. 'E was fightin' 'em off whilst trying to tear it apart, shoutin' somethin' 'bout it 'idin' a secret message inside its bum. 'E was shoutin' that 'e saw you readin' one from it the last time it come. The guards and 'im, they got into a tussle over it, and that's when I nabbed it from 'im and 'id it in me pocket until I's could manage to deliver it to yuh."

"My pocket watch." I breathe, staring past the boy's shadow. "It was in my coat. He must have it. The Ladybird is attracted to its magnets."

"I beg yer pardon, sir?" The boy swallows hard.

"Nothing." I turn toward his voice "Here, take it back." I shrug the bug from my shoulder. The bug topples to the floor.

"Excuse me, sir?"

"You heard me." I nudge the bug toward the bars with my kneecap. "I need you to tear the bug apart."

"Yuh wha—?"

"The bug. I want you to pull the pin from its rear."

The boy hesitates.

"Go on," I say. "Reach in and grab it. It won't bite." The boy extends his arm, grabbing the Ladybird up in his fingers, and pulls it back through the bars tentatively. The bug coos as he flips it over in his hand.

"Now grab hold of the pin at its end and yank it out," I tell him. "Can you feel it? Between its last hind legs, below its wings."

I hear the boy feeling around, small fingers grazing metal. Then, with determination, he locks on to the pin and grunts as he pulls it out. The gentle twang that follows tells me he's successfully released the inner spring pin. I smile, feeling a ray of relief spread over me. "Now, feel around inside, underneath the wings. They should be open. You'll find a little round cylinder there. Can you feel it?"

"Yeah."

"Remove it, carefully, by lifting up. But don't pull hard," I caution the boy. I hear a soft tug and the cylinder snaps free of its enclosure. My heart beats a little louder. "The cylinder is wrapped in a thin sheet of tin. Unwrap it slowly," I say.

A brush of tin follows, then metal unfurling. "Now quickly. Tell me what it says."

"Beggin' pardon, sir?" The boy's voice lilts up.

"The message on the tin sheet, it should be glowing, what does it say?" I lacquered the tin sheets with phosphorescent paint just in case I was ever to receive a message after second twilight, or deep in the woods . . . or in such a precarious situation. I silently congratulate myself for being such a forward thinker, and for making sure it worked before our last journey. It is working, isn't it?

"Tip it forward so I can see, quickly!"

The boy stretches out his arms. The tips of his fingers illuminate briefly. Next to them the message glows very faint, but still it glows.

HOLD TIGHT. PLAN IN PLACE. C.L. AND I
LEAVING ABOARD CLEMENTINE IN MORNING.
BE THERE BY NOON TOMORROW. UNTIL THEN.
LOVE FOREVER. EYELET

The message fades.

"Clementine?" My heart jerks tight in my chest. "They'll never make it through the woods on that old horse."

"Beg pardon agin, sir?"

"Nothing." I gasp at breath. "Has there been any other word? About my situation, I mean?"

"I'm sorry, sir. No change, I'm afraid. Is someone really tryin' to come and spring yuh loose before it 'appens?"

"Appears so, doesn't it?"

"Oh, my." The boy falls back on his haunches. "An honest-to-goodness prison break!"

"You must tell no one about this, do you promise?"

"I swear. Cross me 'eart."

A clatter of keys rings out near the door at the top of the stairs, and the boy sucks in a sharp breath. He bolts to his feet. "I'd better be goin', before they comes looking for me," he whispers, starting for the door, then slowing. He swings back. "If I agree to 'elp yuh escape, is there a chance yuh'd take me with yuh?"

In my mind I try to work out how that would be possible. I don't want to leave the boy, but I don't want him to get hurt. "No," I say, then quickly add, "but I can try to come back for you, I promise—"

"Please, sir, I'll do anything." His voice shakes.

In my heart I feel the tug of his pleading tone. I can't leave him. "All right," I say. "We'll find a way, but for now, get going before you get yourself caught."

"Right, sir!" The boy starts off again.

"Oh, and Sebastian?"

"Yeah?"

"Keep an eye on my old cell, will you? If anything out of the ordinary happens, or someone shows up, find a way to get them to me."

"I will, sir. Don't yuh worry."

*"Boy!"* a voice booms down the staircase.

"Comin'!" Sebastian shouts, bare feet grinding over the sandy stones as he squeezes through the crack in the heavy separation door and punts up the circular metal stairs.

In the clip of light that follows, I bring a hand to my eyes, blinded temporarily, then catch a short glimpse of my new partner—a waif of a thing, eight, maybe ten, dark hair, ringlets flying as he twists up the steps. He's dirty as a corpse and wears clothes two sizes too big. My pocket-watch chain dangles below his shirttail.

*Why, that little thief . . .*

The door thumps shut at the top of the stairs. I fall back against the damp, unforgiving stone wall of my cell, grimacing at pain that shoots up between my shoulders in my awkward position, my wrists still in chains behind my back. I close my eyes and think again of Eyelet astride Clementine on her way through the criminal-infested forest. How will she ever get past the checkpoint to Brethren without being arrested, let alone survive the Infirmed in between?

By the grace of God, if she does somehow manage to make it here . . .

*I hope I'm not already dead.*

# Eleven

***Eyelet***

"Are you sure about this?" I say and twist my hands, pushing the layer of fog along in front of me. Perspiration beads my brow. I've never known C.L. to be unreasonable, not even flighty, but this idea sounds preposterous—no, *insane.*

"There's no other way, mum." He strips the freakmaster of clothes. I let out a small peep and turn my eyes away. I don't want to catch sight of any of his still-stiff nasty bits. It's bad enough they touched my leg.

"Couldn't we just string him up in the woods"—I pace—"and let the criminals have him?"

"We could, but if 'e was ever found, we'd be facin' prison terms for murder." C.L. crosses his brows.

"But we didn't kill him, *technically.* Clementine did."

"Do yuh honestly think there's a court in the land that'll believe tha' one?" I hide my eyes as C.L. yanks the laces of the freakmaster's corset loose and relieves him of it. "Last time I checked, they wouldn't take the word of a 'orse."

I rub down the guilty goose bumps that have formed on my arms. C.L.'s right. Clementine certainly can't speak the truth, and no one's going to take the word of a wanted girl and her armless freak-show sidekick. No matter how many other freakish witnesses there are. I turn to the rest of them. We're in too deep now. I bite my nail. Precisely the reason I didn't want him killed. Precisely the reason I don't want to go on with this. "You're sure this'll work?" I say, turning back to C.L.

"Not to worry, miss." Martin steps in, holding out a blanket like a drape, shielding me from the body. "We've done this loads of times."

"*Loads* of times!" I gasp.

"Well—not *us* in particular." Martin corrects himself. "The freak-master did."

"The freakmaster dissolved people?" I say, pawing at the air for something to steady myself. C.L. has explained the logistics, but I'm still not able to wrap my head around what's happening.

"Only those who didn't pay their debts." Martin smiles. "Besides, I think it only befitting he goes out the same way as the man who taught him the trick."

*"What?"*

"He learned the trick from a passing magician. The only magician in the land who could really make his audience disappear, if you know what I mean." Martin grins.

"Out of the waaaay!" Sadar totters through the rolling fog toward us, two buckets of smoking, sloshing liquid in his hands. I rush to his rescue, plucking the buckets out of his grip, one on each side, and steady them before I move another pace. Their pungent, chloric odour bites at my nostrils and sears my lungs. I can't believe we're doing this, any of this. I slump slowly forward, gingerly plodding over the brittle grass, acid gurgling. What has happened to my life?

I place the buckets down at the head of the body and turn my eyes away. "Is this going to be enough?" I rub the sting from my hands. "Or will we need more?"

"Oh, it takes very little, miss," Sadar says.

"And you're sure it's going to work?" I look to C.L.

"Sure as I know me name is Ernest."

"There'll be no trace left of him?" I wipe the wet from my brow. "None whatsoever?"

"No, mum. We just give 'im a good douse with this drink from 'ead to toe and 'e'll be gone—bones and all." C.L. spouts a satisfied grin.

"*Wonderful*, that makes me feel *so much* better." I feel bile churn in my throat. I swallow it down, buck up, and pace. After all, what other choice is there? "Let's just do this and get it over with, shall we?" I fan my face.

"You all right, miss?" Reeke asks me gently.

"No, not really." I bat a swirl of dark forest fog away from me.

C.L. strips the corpse of its boots and tosses them aside with a thump, and I jump. I clutch my heart. Good God, I can't believe we're actually doing this.

But I suppose, he's already dead.

C.L. loosens the stitching and rids him of his pants, then finally his drawers. Holding them up, he inspects them carefully. "Me own pair's got a 'ole in 'em," he says with a smile.

"Of course." I gulp and turn my back to him. A proper woman would never know about the state of a gentleman's drawers. Then again, a proper woman would not be about to douse a corpse in flesh-eating chemicals, now, would she. I shut my eyes and count to ten, calming my breath. "Can we just get this done?" I exhale and thread my fingers together.

Teeth chatter in the trees.

I twist around and stare into the mist over my shoulder. Fingertips of branches poke through the grey trolling cotton. The noise comes again and I twist left and right. "We need to hurry," I say. "Or we'll all end up in a worse situation than he."

Something lets out a whoop, and my head spins in that direction. Red beams of light burn out through a rip in the fog, camouflaged inside the base of a log, then extinguish as fast as they lit.

"I've never heard them do that before." I turn back, staring at C.L. "I've heard them chatter and scream, but never whoop like that."

"Maybe it's not a criminal." His eyes get wide.

I stare again into the rolling grey landscape sprinkled with skeleton trees. "Maybe it's the Brigsmen. Signalling to each other."

The whoop goes off again.

"Hurry," I say. "The rest of you, back to the train with me." I scoot them along. "C.L., will you be all right to finish this job on your own?" I turn back to him.

"It'll be me pleasure, mum." He smiles big, taking the bucket up in his feet.

"All right, then"—I haul up my skirts and scan the steamy forest in front of us—"quickly, the rest of you. Follow me."

"Here, take these." Martin flings the freakmaster's clothes in my direction. I look down at them, bewildered. I don't want to touch them.

"At some point you'll need to put them on," he says to me.

*"What?"*

"'E's right," C.L. says. "We'll need a ringmaster to get through the checkpoint, for obvious reasons—"

"I understand that—but me?"

"Well, you don't expect *me* to pass as the master of this caravan, do you?" He holds up his stubs, as if he's thrown out his missing arms. "And certainly, none of the rest of us will do."

I look around at the motley crew of broken people who stand before me. He's right, I'm the only intact logical choice. I bring a hand to my mouth to cover the gasp that escapes me. Another whoop sounds at my back. The thought of putting on the freakmaster's clothing makes me want to retch. Weakly, I reach down to collect the clothes. They stink of booze and sweat and other unthinkable body odours. "Right," I gulp breathlessly.

A series of whoops slithers past us.

"We'd better get going. But what about you?" I say to C.L. over my shoulder.

"Don't worry 'bout me, I'll catch up."

"Clementine! What about Clementine!" I spin around.

"I've already de-armoured her and tied her to the train, miss," Reeke says. "The circus horses are ready, too."

Another hoot rises from the forest, and C.L.'s head jerks up. "Just get into those clothes and take the mount quickly. Get going, all of yuhs, please!"

I turn and race for the freak train, Wanda waving us on. Martin takes the reins temporarily and I dash into the caboose to change my clothing, holding my breath before ducking in. Wanda joins me, screening me with a blanket as I shuck off my corset and skirts, retching as I don the freakmaster's clothes, the crevices of the fabric still moist to the touch. A whip cracks and the train lurches forward, couplings clattering, and I wonder how I'll get to the front.

I roll my hair into a bun and plop the top hat on my head to hide it. "How do I look?" I turn to Wanda. She drops the blanket, nods.

"Thanks," I say. *"Whooooaaahhh!"* She wrenches me up onto her shoulders, unexpectedly hurtling me through the hole in the rooftop. The wind up there is violent. I clap a hand on my head to hold on to my hat. "What are we doing?" I shout to her. Wanda pops up beside me and points a big, hairy arm in the direction of the front car, revealing a walkway that travels the length of the rooftops, a sort of rope-and-swing bridge without the swing.

"Seriously?" I say to her, wind whipping in my ears. "You want me to walk that?"

She nods her head and points again.

"All right, all right." I stand, wobbling against the juggle of the cars, and cautiously creep down the narrow rooftop toward the front, placing my feet one in front of the other. More than once I grab for the railing, more than once disappointed by its fragility. "Good Lord in Heaven, have mercy." I clutch my heart, boots slipping on the metal rooftop, the horses now bolting at top speed.

Behind us, a splash.

Then the sizzle of acid eating flesh.

The sound worms through my ears, into my brain, over the howl of the wind, snapping my shoulder blades back.

# Twelve

***Eyelet***

"Where is he?" I crank my head round from the mount of the freak train, searching for signs of C.L. in the woods behind. I see nothing but fog and trees and lines of lingering Vapours. It's been that way for almost twenty minutes now.

I lift up my mask to get a better look.

"He'll be here, miss," Martin says, knocking my mask back into place. "You really shouldn't do that. I suspect that's why you have that cough of yours."

"You'd suspect incorrectly," I say, a little more curtly than intended, not wanting to get into my exposure to the machine, and the serum, and my worried suspicions about all of it. "C.L. said he'd be straight behind us." I turn round again.

"And he will be, miss." Martin grins. "He was fast enough to get away from this train once, surely he'll be fast enough to catch up to it today."

I know Martin's trying to comfort me, but I can tell by the look in his eyes he's worried, too. It's been fifteen long minutes since I heard the splash. I look down at my chrono-cuff. Twenty.

"What are you doing?" Martin objects.

I slow the horses down, guide them up a side road off the main one, and turn them around. "Waiting here until C.L. catches up," I say, throwing the brake once the horses have stopped.

"But we're less than half a kilometre from the checkpoint." Martin looks frantic.

"I know where we are," I snap at him again. "We'll be fine under this cover of wood." I look around, searching the trees for lights. I see nothing, though a small piece of me is worried, too. We can't sit here for long. But we can sit here for now. Time ticks, agonizingly slowly, my chrono-cuff the only heartbeat in the forest. "Maybe I should go back." I twist round again, scanning the road behind us for signs of C.L. "Dress Clementine and me in the armour and go back."

Martin lowers his head. "Don't be ridiculous. We're too close to the city for you to reveal that. One sighting of a winged horse and the whole plan is blown."

He has a point. I lower my chin. My mind leaps ahead to Urlick in his cell. If we don't reach him today, he'll face his fate first thing in the morning. That is, if they've stuck to their word, not holding dippings on the Sabbath. If they haven't, we're already too late. I shake the niggling thought from my mind. I don't know what the officials will do in Smrt's absence. *Oh, where is C.L.?* I close my eyes and imagine him back there in the woods, surrounded by criminals, their teeth bared, crowding in. *Please don't make me choose who to save, Lord. Please don't make me choose between the two of them.*

"It's almost second twilight, miss." Martin's voice pulls me back to the moment. "We need to make a decision. And quick." His eyes are kissed with a forlorn sadness. "We need to think of what's best for ourselves."

I fling myself around one more time and stare into the woods. The dashes of cloud cover reveal nothing. No sight of C.L. anywhere. Perhaps it's already too late.

"He would have wanted you to continue on, miss. He wouldn't want you to give up on the mission."

I turn round, gazing into the swollen, glassy eyes of one of C.L.'s dearest friends, feeling the bubble of hope I've been holding on to burst in my chest.

"You've got us now, miss. We won't let you down. Master Urlick, he's waiting."

I pray that it's true and that he's not already gone like C.L. Sorrow bunches in my throat.

Urlick will be sorry to learn that C.L. lost his life trying to save his, and even sorrier to find out I left C.L. behind. I don't know what to do. Something soft tears in my heart. We can't sit here any longer or I jeopardize the lives of all the rest. I reach up, steering a tear from my eye. "You're right," I say weakly, picking up the reins. "C.L. would have wanted us to save Urlick."

Martin nods his head. He hesitates as if saying a quick, silent prayer, then looks to me. "I'd better take my place behind the bars, now, miss. We can't be sailing through the checkpoint with me up here. You be all right up here alone?"

"I'll have to be, won't I?" I swallow hard.

Martin stands and hikes himself up onto the roof of the train car. "Remember, whistle twice if they ask if they can search. That'll give us time to fake the chains. And keep your hat down low over your eyes, and your hair under it. That way, they've less chance of figuring out you're female."

He jogs his way to the next car along the centre path on the roof, opens the trapdoor, and drops down into his cage below with a thud. There's a release of the bars, a creak of the hinge, then a whistle, signalling for me to go ahead. He's ready. Am I ready? No.

I take one last look into the forest through soggy eyes, dreading the thought of C.L. at the hands of the criminals. I never should have agreed to leave him there. I never should have gone ahead without him. I can only hope they kill him first and don't eat him alive.

I close my eyes and slap the reins down over the horses' backs. Two black Persian mares surge forward, hooves slopping over the mucky ground. I drop my head and start to cry softly to myself, knowing I'll have to straighten up in little time. I can't believe it's true. I can't believe I've lost C.L. After all the things that have happened.

I can't believe the void in my heart, for a man I barely knew.

"What's this mutiny!" I hear someone scream.

I twist my head round. The fog is too dense to make out anything. "C.L.?" I shout. "Is that you?" A wisp of blackish-grey smoke trundles past, twisting and sweeping over the landscape in front of me. Then, like smoke over fire, disturbed by wind, it bends and sweeps past me again.

"Careful, miss," Sadar hollers up from his train car. "Remember, the Infirmed can throw their voices."

"No," I say, slowing the horses to a crawl. "No, it's C.L. It's him." I stand, hand to my eyes, squinting, searching the clouds for any faint sign of a figure. Something howls, and my heart plunges to my knees. Perhaps Sadar is right. The Infirmed. They do prey on your deepest desires. I wave my hand through the cloud cover, not willing to give up on C.L. just yet. "Ernest, is it you?" I've never called him that before—but I figure if I do, he's sure to answer.

The black entity curls past me again. Out of the stream a face appears, white vapour through the curling, dark mist. The piercing eyes of a ghoul stare through me like burning fire. It bares teeth as sharp as pins.

"Oh, God! It's not him!" I fall back into my seat, bringing the reins down hard. The horses leap forward, apparitions whirling round my head. The horses spook and rear. I fight to get them down on the ground and moving. We shoot forward through the chanting mist, apparitions forming all around us.

"Wait!" I hear someone calling but don't look back. "Wait! Please, Eyelet, it's me!" It's a ruse. It's not true. The Infirmed are trying to fool me. I mustn't listen to them.

"Eyelet!" The voice calls again.

What's going on? What's happening? The spirits cackle. Is it really C.L.? My neck wrenches toward the sound.

"Eyelet, slow down!"

Feet hit the back platform of the caboose, scuttling up the rails to the roof.

"Eyelet!"

"C.L.?" I breathe, wanting so badly to turn, yet at the same time so, *so* afraid to. Apparitions swoop and dip in front of me, their voices taunting. I close my eyes tight and slap the reins harder. The horses jerk forward under the pressure.

"What's this?" A voice niggles its way into my ears. Something plops down beside me, its weight bouncing me on the bench. "Thought yuh could pull this caper off without me, did yuh?"

I pop open my eyes. C.L. sits beside me, looking a bit battered and bruised, sporting a toothless grin.

"Never!" I shout, throwing my arms round his neck.

# Thirteen

***Flossie***

"What do you mean, you couldn't catch her? You're ghouls, aren't you?" I whirl around on them, staring hard into the daunting silver faces. The Infirmed cower and hang their heads.

"We almost had her, miss, but then the train sped up and . . ."

"Train? What do you mean, train?" I vex my brows. "I sent you after a coach, not a train!"

The Infirmed's heads swing back and forth, their white eyes pinched and confused. "But you said you wanted the girl," one of them bravely speaks. "We thought you meant—"

"You found the girl? Where?" I swish toward them.

"Just outside the entrance bridge to Gears."

"Was he with her?"

"Who, miss?"

"The boy with the purple scars on his face, of course."

The Infirmed look to each other. "Theys was a lot of people there, but none with a raised purple scar, miss," says one.

"There *was* one without any arms," says another.

"C.L." I whirl around, agile now on my newfound appendages. "She must be travelling with him." I bite a nail and pace on my tentacles, in complete command. "They must be on their way to save him."

"Save who, miss?"

"Never mind!" I snap at the dimwitted lot that surrounds me. "We need to catch her before she reaches him. But however will we get into town?" I tap my withering chin.

"We can't, miss. We'll be sucked up by the scrubbers, or shredded in the screens."

"Unless . . ." I tighten my lips into a smile.

The Infirmed wince their paper-thin brows and stare at me.

"We need to stop that coach!" I swish toward them, shooting forward on creeping tentacles.

The Infirmed shake their heads. "But we just told you we tried, miss—"

"Not *that* coach! The OTHER ONE!" I shout so loudly their cloth-like bodies stretch back from their sterns. For a moment, they look like they've seen a ghost themselves.

"What coach is that?" one meekly asks once their hair and clothes have fallen back into position.

"The one with the woman in it! The woman who was just here!" I turn my back, rubbing what's left of my hands together. "It's time to strike a deal."

# Fourteen

***Eyelet***

We trundle over the bridge and through the gates of Gears at high speed, causing quite the commotion, townspeople staring as we whisk by, but there isn't much else I could do given the circumstances.

I daren't slow down.

Once we're inside the gates, I allow myself to turn around, basking in the warm glow of the apparitions' screams as they get caught up in the filtration web. It's shoddy at best, compared to the highly technological system of scrubbers and filters that guard Brethren's perimeter, but I sure am thankful it's there.

I draw the horses down to a brisk trot and veer off the main street onto a back one, with a plan to afford C.L. the chance to take his place in one of the cages along with the rest of the freaks before we attempt crossing into Brethren at the checkpoint on the opposite end of the city. I stop the train when I'm sure the street is clear, hands trembling, a ball of jumbled nerves wedged in my throat.

"What happened to you back there?" I whirl around on him, sitting upright next to me on the front bench seat. "We were worried sick."

"And well you should 'ave been," he says, real casual, like my eyes *aren't* bugging out of my head. "We was wrong about those whoops, they wasn't the Brigsmen at all." He cinches in close to me, his face just a breath from my own. "Theys was a gang of criminals," he whispers, looking around. "They ambushed me, they did, just as you pulled off. I barely 'ad time to drop the acid on the master before tryin' to get away. I could see the train cars driftin' up the road, but I couldn't get to yuh. They 'ad me surrounded, they did. But I fought me way through 'em, knockin' 'em down"—he jumps from the mount and dances around, showing me, flinging his legs in the air—"until finally a brainstorm come over me, and I dumped the second bucket of chemical over one of the criminal's 'eads. Once 'e disappeared, yuh shoulda seen the others vanish." C.L. rolls back on his heels in laughter. "Never seen anything move that quick!"

I laugh along with him, relieved by his story, though my mind skips on to thoughts of the freakmaster, and then my stomach balls up in a knot. Had C.L. enough time and potion to completely do away with him? I don't ask. I don't want to know that answer. I'm just glad to have C.L. back.

Surely, knowing C.L., he finished the job. Wouldn't he?

I shudder, hearing in my mind the slosh of the chemical being thrown.

C.L. hops down from the mount and rounds the train, hopping up onto a train car and then the rooftop. Shuttling along, he finds the trapdoor, throws it open with a foot, then lowers himself into place inside, behind bars. He drops the roof down over his head and whistles to me, signalling all clear, then shouts, "Wait!" His head pops back up through the rooftop again. "I almost forgot. Take this!" He passes something forward; raised arms from the cages bring it to the front.

"What is it?" I look at the piece of folded paper in my hand.

"A moustache."

"A what?" I peel the paper open and quiver.

"His moustache."

I gulp.

"I stripped it from 'im before, well . . . yuh know, for yuh to wear it."

"But I can't—"

"I knew yuh wouldn't take kindly to it, but there's no other way. Yuh've got to wear it—it's 'is signature trademark. Elsewise the guards at the post'll know yuh ain't 'im."

I look down at the wad of whiskers in my hand, fastened together in the centre with a lock of the master's hair, spirit gum dripping from its back.

"I lathered it up there for yuh. All you got to do is pop it on—"

"You want me to put this on my face," I say, still stunned by the revelation.

"Precisely." C.L. nods. "Yuh need to complete the look if yer to be believable." He says it like this happens every day.

I look down at my reflection in the chrono-cuff lens. C.L.'s right. As it stands, I look like a waif of a girl stuffed into big man's clothing, wearing a hat two sizes too large. I'm never going to be able to pull this off, moustache or not. A strike of panic stills my heart.

"Second thought, perhaps yuh'll need a bit of this, too." I turn to see C.L. holding a footful of straw. "If we stuff yuh in just the right places . . ."

My face sours. I don't fancy the idea of being stuffed, but then again, I don't fancy the idea of getting arrested, either, and I could use a little bulk.

"It'll just be for a few moments whilst we pass through the checkpoint." C.L. shrugs his shoulders. "'Ow bad can it be?"

*

The cart in line in front of me moves ahead. I guide the horses up between the rails of the checkpoint, next to the guard's hut. My heart is strumming as if it's being bowed by a violinist, playing Beethoven's Fifth. My hands feel like I've been shucking clams.

"Papers, please," the checkpoint guard says. He smalls his eyes and squints up at me as if there were sun. I feel the heat of his gaze warming the glue beneath my fake moustache. Or perhaps it's just the radiance of my own about-to-convulse, tremulous cheeks.

Papers? We hadn't thought of papers. Had we? I lower my voice and small my own eyes. "Papers?" I say loud enough for C.L. to hear me. "I, the master of this travelling caravan, have no need for papers. As a traveller, I pass through cities all the time."

I have no idea if that is true, but that's what I say, loudly, deeply, *manly.*

The guard gnaws on the wad of tobacco he had tucked in his cheek, and leans, draping an elbow over the side of my stage. "Travellers or not, I still need to know where the *lot of you* is from." He smiles up at me smartly.

"From?" I repeat.

"Yeah. From where do you all hail?"

"All over," I answer, shaking.

His eyes rake the bars of the cages stacked up behind me. "Sorry," he says. "Can't let you through without papers."

My heart moves from Beethoven's Fifth to his Fourth. I can't stop my upper lip from twitching.

C.L. coughs in the cage behind me. I reach back and he passes a slip of paper through the top of the bars. Slowly I unfold it, my eyes focusing in on a birth certificate. *Connie Lovell, born Ramshackle Follies Cove, August 1860.* I struggle to contain the bubble of laughter that brims up inside my chest at the thought of that brute of a man having borne the name Connie.

"Will this do?" I say, repressing my urge as I pass the guard the paper.

His eyes flash over the paper, then my hand. I pull it back, fearing my nails are too long and well kept to be a male's. Then again, with a name like Connie, it might not matter.

The corners of the guard's lips lift. He raises his gaze, scans the cages.

"And the rest of them are mongrels," he says, flashing another look at me.

"Property of the state, sold over to me," I say, knowing they won't need papers that way. "I don't bother awarding them names." I'm not very good at lying, and I'm afraid it's showing. My cheeks are burning. My breath is hard. The straw under my armpits is digging in the skin. The guard stiff-eyes me a moment longer.

Sweat beads stretch the length of my forehead. I move to erase them, and the straw pricks my back. A strange, scratchy heat blusters up my neck from inside the collar, heating my skin.

"What's that?" the guard says, pointing.

I reach up and touch a patch of what feels like raised hives. "I dunno," I say, lowering my voice again. "Probably just some bad meat."

"You look a little warm—you're not virused, are you?" The guard steers back from me, billy club in his hand.

"No," I stammer. My moustache gives way, shifting a titch on my face. I twist the other side of my lip up to compensate.

The guard stares at me hard. "What are you doing?"

"Noffin'," I answer, trying to hold my lip in place—straw prickling, hives bursting, resisting the urge to disrobe.

"What's that?" he points to the corner of my mouth.

I stick out my tongue, swiping in the rogue dab of spirit gum that's drizzled loose down my face. "Just a bit of last night's supper," I jest, swallowing the bitter stuff. "Not the best gruel I've ever eaten. But beggars can't be choosers on the road," I add, feeling my moustache shift again. I wrench up the other side of my lip. I'm smiling like a madman now.

The guard glances down at the paper again, giving me time to shove my moustache back into place. My heart swings like a neurotic pendulum hitting the sides of my chest. The symphony inside my ears turns into a concerto. I feel another hive burst in a place it never should.

"William, is it?" I wriggle, catching a glimpse of the guard's name tag. The guard looks down and then up. "You should know, these mongrels 'ere"—I jerk my thumb back at the freaks in their cages, feeling an unnatural breeze flirt with my upper lip—"'ave an appointment at the Royal Palace this afternoon." I talk faster. My moustache travels south again, and I stuff it back up and keep talking. "They's to perform for a royal occasion. A birthday," I offer stupidly. Something easily checked. My heart seizes in my chest. Why did I have to say *that*?

I square my shoulders, narrow my gaze, and try to look intimidating. "Should we be late"—I swallow—"I'm sure the officials'll be interested to know 'oo the culprit was 'oo 'eld us up." My eyes flick to his name tag and back at him. "Isn't that right, William?"

# *Fifteen*

***Eyelet***

I take a quick right turn after we clear the checkpoint, directing the team up an old dirt road along the back of town. The moustache drops in my lap.

"That was *brilliant*!" C.L. shouts, leaping up and down in his cage behind me. "Just *brilliant*!" He stops. "Wait. Where yuh going?" he adds as we glide past the windmills and scrubbers, into the woods at the edge of town.

"I can't bear it any longer!" I holler, pulling the horses to an abrupt halt inside the trees and jumping from the mount. Hives have now hatched all over my body. I feel like I'm roasting in a fire. I race for the trees, guilt gnawing at me for holding up the mission, but I can't go on like this. I've got to get these clothes off now. Right now. I run, kicking off the freakmaster's boots and peeling his jacket from my back.

"What's yuh doing?" C.L.'s voice squeals after me. "Yuh need that disguise!"

"I'm sorry!" I shout, ducking in behind a hedge. "But we'll have to think of something else!" I peel off the rest of the freakmaster's outfit piece by piece and toss it back over the hedge. I dance in a circle, ridding myself of the hive-inducing straw, plucking it loose from my armpits and underclothes, feeling instantly relieved. I'm swollen as if I'd been ingesting cricket balls, covered in raised, throbbing marks from head to toe. But at least now, with the straw gone, the throb is dulling.

"Something else?" C.L. appears on the opposite side of the hedge, sounding angry. "Oh my!" he gasps and steps back at the sight of the red, swollen hives on my neck.

"Oh, yes . . ." I glare. "Wanda!" I turn my eyes to her. "Would you be a doll and bring me my clothes?"

"What are we gonna do now?" C.L. paces.

"I don't know, but whatever it is, we need to hurry up." I accept my clothing from Wanda and quickly dress, grateful for her help with my corset laces, stepping out from behind my hedge-leaf dressing screen moments later. "Perhaps if we make one of you, out of two," I say.

"Make what of us?" C.L.'s eyes crinkle.

"You and you." I point to C.L. and Martin. "Sit." I shove C.L. down onto a rock and steer Martin in behind. "Martin, tuck up behind him, duck your head down onto his shoulders, and throw your legs into his lap."

"Do what?"

"Just humour me, please."

Martin crawls up onto the rock, wraps his legs around C.L.'s middle, and folds his chin to his chest.

"Now put your arms around C.L.'s front."

Martin extends his arms out around C.L.'s compact frame, completing him as a whole person for the first time ever.

"This might just work." I tap my chin and swoop in with the freakmaster's jacket.

"What do yuh mean, this might work?" C.L. frowns, looking down at Martin's hands on his knees.

"Hush," I say. "Martin, push your arms through here." I guide his hands through the armholes, then arrange the jacket over his back until he's almost completely disappeared. "You look a bit like you've got a hunchback, but I think it'll work." I button the jacket up over C.L.'s front and stand back to have a look. Together they look like one body. C.L.'s head, neck, chest, and legs, and Martin for arms.

"Now, if we glove Martin's hands . . ." I slip the gloves over his dried, mummified-looking fingers.

"This is ridiculous," C.L. objects. Martin pokes him in the eye, groping the air for the reins. "He can't possibly drive the cart like this!"

"Of course not. You're going to direct him—"

"I'm to pass through the streets of Brethren mumbling to me back, am I?" C.L.'s brows knit. "Surely no one will notice that?"

"Can you think of another way?" My hands pinch my hips.

"I can't breathe," Martin murmurs from behind.

"Oh, good grief!" I huff and loosen the collar.

"Perhaps if it were me?" Sadar offers. "I'm a little smaller. A little more compact." He waddles up and grins.

"No," I sigh. "C.L.'s right. This is not going to work." I clap my hand to my head and start to pace. We're wasting precious time.

"What, then?" C.L. says, peeling himself off the rock.

"I don't know." I shake my head. I sigh and turn, frustrated. My eyes fix on something across the clearing that takes my breath away.

"What is it? What's the matter?" C.L. says.

"Unless there was another way . . ." I start up the road.

"Wait! Where yuh going?" C.L. chases after me across to the other side, but I've already slipped through the doors of a building left ajar: a factory, out here in the middle of nowhere—a tin-roofed, sprawling factory. Black smoke belches from its chimney. Twisted iron gates surround its premises, just like the ones at the Academy. Beyond the door, something draws me in, glinting.

"It can't be." I stagger forward through the doors, into the dark, dingy room. "What is *that* doing here?"

"Eyelet?" C.L. appears at my back. "Eyelet, what are yuh doing? Oh, good Lord in Heaven," he gasps.

"It is . . ." I bring a hand to my chest. "It's really you!"

# Sixteen

***Eyelet***

A brass mechanical elephant stands before me, glinting gold in the dim factory light. I can't believe my eyes. *It's him. He's here.* The same elephant from my childhood. The carnival elephant.

I stand, blinking at him; memories of my father flood forward in my head. That last day we had together. Father's promise to join us at the carnival. My mother. The elephant. The dastardly flash on the horizon that changed everything.

I wade deeper and deeper into the dark, dusty cavern, my curiosity driving me on. I must know if he's real . . . or just a dream. I need to touch him.

I know we should be getting on to Brethren, but I need to know. How is this possible? Why is he here?

"What are you doing, mum?" C.L. appears in the doorway behind me, breathless, his brows are drawn like curtains over frantic eyes. "We 'aven't time for this!"

"I know," I snap. "It's just that—" I jog the last few steps, closing the space between the elephant and myself, selfish thoughts driving me onward. I raise a hand, suck in a tortured breath, and stroke the elephant's massive brass head. "It is you! You're real! You exist!" I nearly weep.

It's like a little piece of my history hasn't died. The last memories of my father pitch forward in my brain. For an instant it feels as if I'm seeing the elephant for the first time, and my father's still alive.

I wipe a tear from my eye and run my fingers over the elephant's jeweled toes, clearing away the film. "You're even more beautiful than I remember," I say, petting its ruby-crested tongue, my fingers dancing along rows of ivory teeth.

"We gotta go, mum," C.L. urges.

"Yes, I know, it's just—" I swing round, reluctant to leave but eager to reunite with Urlick, when something stirs at my back.

A skitter, like a rat—only larger.

My heart trips. I spin back round, arming myself with a stone from the dirt floor, bracing for confrontation.

There's a clatter of chains. Breath heaves in and out. My head swings in the direction of the corner. But I see nothing. And then everything.

In the gash of light that streaks the corner, a young man appears. He's about my age, perhaps a little older; his arms and legs are in chains, bolted to the wall behind him. "Oh, good Lord," I gasp.

He's filthy, dressed in rags, and doesn't wear any shoes. Hazel eyes peek out from under the trappings of dirty, wheat-coloured hair. It's in need of a good washing and a cut and a brush, but otherwise he looks quite civil. He lunges to one side and turns his face to the wall, as if embarrassed I've discovered him . . . or frightened of me.

"Don't come any farther!" He waves a threatening hand at me.

"Holy jumpin' . . ." C.L.'s eyes bug wide as he slides in beside me. "Come on, we'd better get outta of 'ere." He tugs at my arm with his toes.

"What do you mean, *get out of here*, we can't just leave him!"

C.L. gulps and rolls back on his heels. He looks over his shoulder, and I can tell he's worried about the others back in the freak train, about getting discovered, and foiling our mission, but there's just something about the cruelty of this situation my heart won't allow me to walk away from. Of all people C.L. should understand.

I look back at the captive. "He's right," he says, gritting his teeth. "You'd better get outta 'ere while the gettin's good." His voice is angry, plagued with a lisp.

"Do you have a name?" I say, ignoring his warning. "I'm Eyelet," I add, offering him a hand, which he doesn't take. "This is C.L. And you are?" I try again.

The young man hesitates then mumbles, "Masheck. Now *go*. Get outta 'ere." He jerks his head toward the open door. "*Leave* while yuh still can."

"Why are you here?" I stare at his chains, my curiosity a burning flame.

"Because of 'im." His gaze shifts to the elephant and back. "And yuh will be too, if yuh stay."

"What do you mean? What does your being here have to do with the elephant?"

"That big brass bull you was fawning over. Me father made 'im—"

"He did!" My heart leaps, and I can't help it, I shoot bravely forward. "Was your father the operator?" My heart sings. I'm pulled from the tension of the moment by some strange nostalgic thread.

"No." Masheck scowls and my heart sinks. "Me father is the one 'oo made the beast. Then he sold it. Then 'e drowned, and I wound up 'ere. They came for me shortly after 'is death. Stole me from me muvver, they did. I was just twelve, then. I'm nineteen now." He shifts his eyes from me and hangs his head.

"I don't understand," I gasp. "How could anybody do such a thing?"

"Because *they* can." He looks up at me.

"Who's they?"

"The people from the Commonwealth. The Ruler's henchmen."

A cold shock shivers through me remembering the eye-patched man who worked for Smrt. "But why did they choose you?" I say.

"I used to 'elp me father build things in 'is shop before 'e died. Near as I can figure, that's why they come for me. To force me to work for them. To build them things."

"Like what?"

His eyes fix on something beyond, in the next room. I follow his gaze through the archway of the adjoining warehouse. "Go a'ead, 'ave a look." He tips his head.

I take a step in that direction and C.L. yanks me back, his toes clinging to my sleeve. "I'm not sure we should do this, mum." His eyes are round as bottle-bottoms.

"Then don't. Stay here." I tug loose, and stagger to a stop in the doorway. "Oh, good Lord," the words escape me. My heart triple beats. My hands snap to my face.

Past the stream of dim light cast by the factory's windows, stands an army of massive grey, steel mechanical elephants, lined up side by side, row upon row, as far as the eye can see. They're positively monstrous. Twice the height of a fire-pump station. With shoulder spans as wide as eagles.

"Jolly Jehoshaphat." C.L. jolts to a stop beside me, his maw drawn open wide. "There must be a hundred of them."

"One hundred and thirty-seven, to be exact." Masheck's voice sneaks up behind us.

"What *are* they?" I whirl around.

"Killing machines," Masheck answers, and his eyes flash in a weird way, like he hasn't just said the most terrifying thing ever spoken. What was I thinking wanting to save this boy? C.L. was right. We *should* be going. I drop a hand to my floundering heart. For a moment I forget how to breathe. "For whom did you make them?"

"The Ruler of course." Masheck lowers his head and his voice. "Who else does anyone make anything for."

What need would the Ruler of the Commonwealth have for these? What on earth could be their purpose? Unlike their carnival-elephant predecessor, these are *not* enchanting . . . in their thorn-covered coats of armour and spike-lined helmets, with bayonet-embossed blankets, and guns for tusks.

"They's as big as bloody whales, they is." C.L. turns to me. "Are those steam-fuselage machine guns inside their tusks?" He turns to Masheck.

"Aye," Masheck answers. "And they've steam torches for tongues to breathe fire, as well."

Both C.L. and I swallow hard. The very idea of those things snap my spine straight. A cold chill rustles up my vertebrae. "Machine guns?" I repeat, weakly, the meaning still escaping me.

"A sort of jacked-up steamrifle of sorts," C.L. clarifies. "Capable of shootin' consecutive bullets at rapid speed, in a matter of just a few seconds."

"And you made these?" I turn on Masheck, my gaze bullet hard.

Masheck lowers his chin and turns his face away. "The first one was a knock-off of me father's original plans. The factory workers made the rest."

I blink at him, astonished.

"It's not like I wanted to make 'em." His head swings back, his lips are quivering. "I was forced to do it, I was. At first, I thought 'e was just gonna be a novelty, y'know, somethin' to show off at the carnival, like the brass one. Then they 'ad me add real guns and I knew something was amiss. Then they started makin' others, and it became clear what was 'appenin' . . ." His eyes grow teary. "There wasn't anything I could do to stop 'em. I tried, believe me, I tried. I tried to get away. But it's useless." He rattles his chains. "And they'll never let me go. They say I know too much. That the only way I'm leavin' now is in a pine box. They'll kill yuh, too, if they catch yuh 'ere!" His voice shoots up, trembles. "Yuh should go. *Now*! Trust me!"

Before I can answer, the door we came through whirs open in a rickety swish across the track at our back. It crashes into the sidewall, causing me to jump. Three strangers rush in.

C.L. reacts, bolting for cover behind the elephant. I turn to follow, when a hand clamps down on my shoulder, and drags me back. I whirl around, breathless, looking up into a gruesome scar that travels the length of the Brigsman's face. Satisfaction glints in his eyes. A wicked smile tugs at his mouth.

"Well, well, well." The silhouette of a full-figured woman appears behind him. Bottle-bottom sized lens distort a set of bulging stone-grey eyes. A nest of frazzled hair streams out in coils from the sides of her head. *Rapture. Professor Penelope Rapture. It can't be.* "My, my, my. What have we here?" The hair from the mole on her lip wriggles as she speaks. Her mouth twists up into a crooked smile. She stalks around me, holding out the horsewhip in her hand. The brittle sound of its bending leather rasps in my ears.

Her eyes flit toward Masheck, trying his best to stay hidden. "You do have a fetish for the pathetic ones, don't you?" she says to me, rising a mocking brow, and I long to spit in her face.

"What are you doing here? Why have you come?" She snaps up close, her bugged eyes searching. "How did you find this place?"

When I don't answer, she slaps me hard with her hand.

My head jolts to one side.

"Answer me!" Her slate-grey eyes flatten.

The young man gasps behind me.

"I didn't mean to. I stumbled on it." I raise a hand to my stinging face.

"What have you done? What have you told her?" She turns on Masheck.

"Nothin', I swear." He shakes his head.

*"Liar!"* She cracks the horsewhip, splitting open Masheck's cheek. Blood squirts through his fingers.

"Don't, please," I gasp and lunge forward, as she raises the whip again. "He's telling you the truth! He's told me nothing!"

"Liars. Both of you." She turns, training her whip on him again.

"It's the truth. I stumbled in accidentally. He knows nothing."

"Very well." Her voice softens. "I guess we'll call it trespassing, then."

"Trespassing?" I scowl. "I just told you my being here is a mistake."

"Yes." She drags the tip of the whip beneath my chin. "The worst you've ever made. A wanted fugitive caught trespassing on the Ruler's private property, no less."

"What?"

"I own this factory." She darts toward me. "Along with all the rest of Brethren. Now that *you* and your ruthless roving sweetheart saw fit to eliminate Smrt!"

"You what?" I stagger backward, breathless.

"You heard me. The whole bitter operation. Smrt left it all to me. Every deed, every title—it's all mine now."

"So that means you're—"

"That's right. The new Ruler of Brethren." She grits her teeth. "In flesh, bone, and *blood*."

The words shoot through my veins like ice. I cannot feel my legs.

"Guards!" She flits her hand, and he tightens his grip on my arm. "Take her away."

"No." I squirm. "You can't do this! I've done nothing!"

"That's where you're wrong." Penelope juts her chin toward me. "I can do anything I want." Her stone-coloured eyes burrow through me, and a quick memory of Flossie buckles my knees.

"Take her away." She tips her head and I tense, forcing back on my heels, struggling.

"Deliver her along with the rest of the inmates," she smirks, dragging the whip through her hands. "Let them know she's to be added to their permanent collection."

"*What*? What do you mean?" I twist, wrenching my head to the side, the veins on my neck straining. "Where am I going?" I shout first at her, and then back to Masheck. "Where is she taking me?"

"Welcome to your greatest nightmare," Penelope whispers through bared teeth, as she turns to leave. "To the castle," she instructs quick-stepping over the stones toward her carriage, and climbing in. The door shuts behind her and the horses clomp away, and my heart balls in my throat.

*What does she mean, my greatest nightmare?*

She's already robbed me of Urlick, is that not enough?

*Urlick.* Who will save him now?

"*No!*" I struggle and fight, kick and scream, as Brigsmen yank me across the yard. Looking back over my shoulders, I scan the woods for a way to escape, when my eyes catch on Wanda, nose pressed through the bars of the freak train, watching the Brigsman haul me away. She's crying, reaching out for me. I shake my head, willing her not to scream, my lips tightly pursed to keep them from trembling.

The Brigsmen track my gaze, so I avert it quickly. Faintly, I hear Wanda whimpering.

We round the corner, and a carriage shimmers into view through the waffling cloud cover. My heart blooms with panic. "*No*, for the love of God, no. *No, please*!" I dig in my heels and writhe back from the black box on wheels with a cage mounted on top. The Loony Bin wagon. They're taking me to the Brink. MadHouse Brink.

"No!" I scramble, twisting, trying to claw my way around the Brigsman that holds my arms, but he hurls me back under his control. With a quick thrust, he whirls me around and smashes me to his chest, knocking the wind out of my lungs. "Settle down," he hisses in my ear. "Or I'll break something." He pushes me toward the howling faces trapped behind the bars. "Back, you animals!" he shouts, swinging at them with his baton, turbines clunking as another Brigsman undoes the lock. A buzzer sounds and the door blows open. Steam scorches the faces of the inmates, driving them back. They howl and fall away as I'm hauled up over his shoulder and shoved into the cage. I kick and bite and scream, but it's no use, he tosses me anyway.

"*Noooooooo*, please!" My head hits the steel back wall of the wagon and my vision blurs. I scramble to my feet and rush blind at the barred door. The guard slams it shut before I can reach it. "Please . . ." I press my face between the bars, sobbing quietly. "For the love of God, let me go."

"Shut up," the guard snaps and trips the lock. "Ain't listening to this all the way."

The other guards disperse as he rounds the front of the wagon and takes the mount. The inmates behind me howl. I look back at their harrowing faces and I fall to my knees. This can't be happening. This can't be real. This can't be the end of my life.

The carriage lunges forward and I loose my balance. My eyes find C.L. through the bars. He's crouched in the doorway of the factory, his face wet, tears pouring. My mind fills with images of Urlick locked in his own cage, kilometers away.

I've no way to save him now.

# Part Two

# Seventeen

***C.L.***

*Save him for me.* Eyelet mouths to me and I'm overcome with 'elplessness. They've taken 'er and there was nothin' I could do. *I will, I promise,* I mouth back to her, and sink to my knees, me 'eart squeezing in me chest so tightly, I swear I'm suffocating.

'Ow am I ever gonna free Urlick now? Me of all people. A simple-minded, armless bloke. And 'is band of broken idiots. Let alone find a way to rescue poor Eyelet.

I reach up and blot the tears from me cheek with me toe, cords pullin' in me chest, as something lands hard on me shoulder. I turn me eyes up. "Pan! Yer 'ere." And just in the nick! We sent 'er on a'ead to check on Urlick. She must 'ave doubled back when we were late.

"What's wrong?" she caws, half in human, half in bird. She tilts 'er 'ead to and fro.

"I'm afraid a terrible thing 'as 'appened." I drop me chin and roll me toes. Worry fills 'er eyes. I look up and blurt, "They've taken Eyelet."

*"Whaaaaaaat?"* Pan lifts from my shoulder.

"There! Up the road." I point. "They took 'er away in the Loony Bin wagon."

Pan's eyes flit between the horizon and me. She circles me 'ead, frantic.

"Just loaded 'er up in the wagon and drove away, before I could think to do anythin'. I shoulda tried to stop 'em, I know I should, but I couldn't. Not wifout givin' up the rest." I turn me 'ead toward the freak train, 'idden in the woods. "I shoulda done more, I know I shoulda—" I turn back to see Pan wingin' off over the trees, a mere dot in the sky already. "That's it, Pan!" I jump up and down, cuppin' me 'ands to me mouth, shouting. "You go after 'er! We'll be along as soon as we can!" I lower me voice. "As soon as I figure out what to do without 'er." I grasp at breath, closing me eyes. "Oh, good Lord, please, watch over our Eyelet."

I open them again, seeing Masheck still cowering in the corner of the factory, dipped in shadows. "That's it!" I power back through the doors.

"I'm sorry," he mutters, seein' me stormin' toward 'im, eyes brimmin' with frightened tears.

"Never mind all that now." I eye 'im sharp. "We've more important things to attend to. And quick. Does that thing work?" I flick my gaze toward the golden beast that lured Eyelet into the factory in the first place.

"The elephant?" Masheck says. "I believe so, why?"

I train me eyes back on 'im, me stomach sparkling with a plan. A wry smile creeps over me lips. I hunker closer and stick out me chin. "I doubt them bolts 'olding yuh to that wall will be a match for 'im." I tip my 'ead toward the elephant. "Do you?"

Masheck looks first to me and then to the elephant. "No, no, they won't!" His eyes shine with promise.

"All right, then," I say. "Supposin' me and me friends was able to free yuh with the 'elp of the elephant there, you be game then to 'elp us go and get Eyelet back?"

"Absolutely, sir!" The boy rattles to the end of his chains. "What friends?" he asks, moving his head around.

I give a whistle and the freaks come running—Martin first, then Wanda, followed by a tottering and stunned-looking Sadar.

Masheck gasps as each new face appears in the shadowy, weak light of the doors at the back of the factory.

"We 'ave your word, then?" I strong-eye Masheck.

"Mine and the word of the Lord, sir." 'E crosses 'is 'eart, tremblin'.

"Very well, then." I tip me 'ead. "Group. Masheck. Masheck. Group." They nod. "Good. Let's get on this, we 'aven't time to waste." I start off toward the elephant, then double back. "One more thing," I say, staring into Masheck's eyes. "'Ow do you feel about a little prison break?"

"They's my favourite." Masheck smiles wide enough to show a mouthful of less-than-stellar teeth.

"Good!" I leap into action.

*

"Just a little more tension, sir!" Martin yells. The elephant's gears slip and strain, and Martin changes them on the fly. With me feet, I work the three rubber-handled levers at the controls inside the chest of the massive elephant, yanking the levers forward and backward, unsure of which moves what. The oil has worked, but the age of the flywheels 'as rendered their teeth dull. They're not gripping as they should. Slipping every second. We needs to find some new ones that aren't so chipped and rusty. And we needs to find 'em quick.

"Flywheels? Where will we find flywheels?" I say to Masheck, jumping down from the elephant.

"In the workshop in the back. There should be some in a box on the top shelf. Careful, though, they're pretty ancient."

"Not as ancient as the ones inside 'im, I 'ope," I say back over my shoulder, slinking into the other room. I gulp at the sight of the massive steam-elephant brigade lined up before me, shuddering at the thought of the damage they could do. It's a good job they've just been left standing there.

For now.

I walk past them into the workshop, get a wrench, then sneak over and filch a flywheel or two . . . or three . . . make that five . . . from the hearts of the killing machines. *I'll get 'em back to yuh.*

*

"Again, sir!" Martin hollers above the noise of the straining gears inside the beast. The elephant falls back. I yank on another throttle. The elephant lunges forward again. Masheck's chains ring, metallically singing, as they pull taut and stiff. The bolts in the walls creak and jitter.

"That's it, sir, press him onward!" Martin cups his hands and shouts.

"Masheck, are you all right?" I look back, seeing a frightened, gulping boy inside a young man's shaky skin. 'Is eyes are wide as washbasins, fixed on the giant, wobbling bolts above his head. "I'm all right, sir!" he shouts back, cringing, gnashing his teeth tightly together.

I yank the throttle back as far as possible. Flywheels whirl as the beast thrusts, attempting to raise a leg. The bolts on the wall wail and pop. The elephant's weight shifts abruptly as the first bolt gives way. It leaves the wall like a Chinese firecracker, tearing past me 'ead, lodging into the wall on the opposite side of the room like a bullet. "Down! Everybody down!" I scream as the others give way.

Masheck ducks. Wanda, Martin, and Sadar fall to their knees. I press myself as far back inside the chest cavity of the elephant as possible, so as not to get stung. Bolt after bolt snaps loose from its fittings with deafening *thrwops*, sailing the length of the room at ferocious speeds, clamps and all. I flinch as each one whirs past me, jumping when each meets its target. Others clank off the buttocks of the great elephant, spraying like shrapnel in every direction, pinging off other objects, and burying deep into the dirt floor. When the dust finally clears, it's like the Brigsmen have held shooting practice. Bolts pierce every wall.

"You all right?" I turn back to Masheck, standing spread-eagled, still attached to the wall by 'is chains.

"I believe so," 'e says. 'Is eyes are full moons. 'E lowers 'is 'ands, and 'is shackles tumble from the wall to the ground around 'im, landing with a spine-jerking *thunk*. 'E moves forward and the chains move with 'im. "I'm free!" 'E smiles.

Wanda jumps to 'er feet, clapping.

The rest follow, applauding like fools. I grin back at 'im, 'eart beating warmly in me chest.

Masheck raises his arms, cuffs still round 'is wrists. "What are we gonna do 'bout these?" 'e says. "Please don't say the elephant."

I laugh; so does Sadar. "Of course not." Sadar waddles off toward the freak train. "That'll just take a bit of butter magic."

"I'm afraid butter won't do it," I holler after Sadar. "Bring the steam-powered ripsaw, you'll find it in me pack."

Masheck's eyes flash. 'E stares at me stubs.

"Not to worry," I say. "That's not 'ow I lost 'em."

# *Eighteen*

***Eyelet***

The Loony Bin wagon weaves up a path of the escarpment at the back of the city. I stare out through the bars at Brethren's dissipating oily streets. I wish I could walk them again. This time I wouldn't complain. I wipe a tear from my eye, remembering my last walk to school, as we rumble round a corner and through a set of iron-spear gates. A Madhouse Brink sign laughs at me from overhead, and I shiver. *What's to become of me?* My fellow wagon-mates writhe and cry out when they realize what's happening. I shudder at the thought of being locked up with them forever.

Clutching the bars of the cage, I press my face between them, watching the last of civilization fade away. I sob.

The Brigsman at the helm laughs. "Say good-bye to it all, little missy."

I push back from the bars, catching my face in my hands. I've got to pull myself together. I cannot give up now. I have one last chance to escape this reality, when he opens the bars of this cage. I need to be ready.

I sling myself back at the bars and survey the grounds for any possible means of escape. The cloud cover up here rolls so dauntingly thick it's almost impossible to see anything. But at last there's a break in the mist through which I see . . . something very strange. The trees around the Brink appear to shift in position. Huge, towering, *leafless* skeletons dart here and there like ghostly apparitions, planted first in one place and then another, their movement concealed behind a wafting, foggy veil. I blink, watching it happen again and again. "What's going on here? Why is this happening?"

"You needn't concern yourself." The Brigsman's voice haunts me from the mount. It's then I realize I've spoken my thoughts aloud. "You'll never be outside again," he cackles, and a cold, clawing chill chatters up my spine.

"What's that? Over there!" An old woman behind me points at the sky through the bars.

I look up, squinting. A tiny blotch of black appears in the mist, just a dot at first, and then . . .

"Feathers," I gasp. "Pan!" I lurch forward, angling my face through the cold bars. "Over here!" I reach out, waving my arms. Pan's eyes glint red. She lowers her head and drops in on us, moving fast like a bullet toward the wagon, then cuts away. "Hold on!" she shouts as she circles up and around the guard, gaining speed and swooping down again.

I lean out, seeing feathers flying, her maw wide open. She caws, slamming into the side of the driver's head.

*"'Ey!"* he shouts and swings, defending himself. The whole wagon wobbles under his weight. *"Wha' the . . . ?"* the driver shouts as Pan cuts around again, clipping him hard. "Bloody 'ell!" The driver falls back, yanking the reins. The horses slow to a near-staggering stop. "You've drawn blood, you bloody bugger!" The guard shoots up to his feet. "What's the matter with you, you nutty bird!" He shakes his fists in the air.

"That's it, Mum, give it to him!" I risk it all, pushing my face out between the bars.

Mother comes round again, a black, bombing, shrieking streak. My heart flies along with hers.

The guard throws up an arm, whip in his hand. Slowly he draws the whip back.

"NO!" I scream, climbing the bars. "*No!* Don't! *Don't, please . . .*"

The guard follows through. The lash snakes through the sky, cutting Pan right out of it. She tumbles, twisted up in the whip, and falls to the ground.

*"Mother!"* I scream.

"Stupid bird," the guard curses, then spits. He brings the reins down over the horses' backs. The wagon lunges forward. I hold my breath as we roll overtop of her, wheels carving through the mud, narrowly missing her, nearly crushing her skull.

"Oh, Mother!" I fall to my knees, seeing her lying there in the mud, sliced and bleeding, her body unmoving. "No, Mother, *please . . . pleeeeease get up*!"

I cling to the cold bars of the wagon as we rattle away. I am soft-kneed and swaying, tears trailing down my face, watching for signs of life in her body, until at last the fog grows so thick I can no longer make out her shape on the road.

I think my mother is dead.

*

The wagon pulls to a jagged stop, knocking me off balance.

I brush the tears from my eyes and peer out, through the bars, at the door to my future—a massive black beast of a thing. It must be twelve or fourteen feet high. It towers over both the gates and the carriage, made of wood one moment and cast iron the next. I blink, not understanding how that's possible. The surface of the door changes again, from dull to glistening. It shines like an oil slick atop a pond one moment . . . then solidifies to black ebony the next. Steel arches round its top and reinforce the bottom, which appears to sink below the building's foundation line.

I shudder, my eyes fixed on the strange iron handle bolted to the middle of the door, as it lifts from its position and divides into slithering tentacles. One by one the octopus-like arms stretch out from the face of the door, tentacles splayed and groping, as if in search of something. As if it's sensed we're here.

Below the handle is carved a message, incised deep into the face of the shifting oily wood. The letters are indiscernible—in another language, perhaps? Or from another world.

I rub my arms, trying to calm my prickling skin, struggling to keep my head together, my mind floundering between Urlick's fate and my own.

What will become of us? Of me? Of him?

*Of my mother, back on the road.*

I need a plan and I need one quick. *What on earth am I to do?*

Frantically, I scan the premises as the guard moves in, his face a white flash of moon against the dark, steaming sky. The prisoners behind me shudder and scream, pasting themselves to the back wall of the wagon in a feeble attempt to escape him as he works open the bars.

"All right, 'oo's first?"

There's a shunt of an engine. Grey mist purges up from the building's footings. Beyond it, faces emerge from the door. Silhouettes, in human form. Cheeks and noses, chins and foreheads, shrieking, howling, desperate hands clawing—pressing in and out of the door's oily surface, as if there were humans trapped within the door itself.

I gasp and fall back. My heart a drum in a cage.

"It only gets better from here," the Brigsman laughs. He drifts forward, undoing the locks, swinging the cage door open. "Ain't no use strugglin' now," he warns in a low growl, reaching for us.

The other prisoners scream. I wait to see a space between the door and his shoulder, then leap out and over his head, stretching my legs as far as I can, but it's no use—he catches me midair. He reels me in. "Guess this means you've volunteered to be first."

"Let go of me!" I struggle, falling into his arms.

He laughs and smacks the cage door shut and drives down the pin, locking the rest of the screaming inmates in again.

"No!" I punch and kick as he drags me toward the ominous black door. My heel strikes him hard in the shins.

"Ain't gonna do yuh no good to struggle," his bitter voice *thwangs* in my ear. "Only gonna make yer journey worse."

"You have no right to put me here!" I slam my fists against his chest. "I've done nothing wrong!"

"That's what they all say." He laughs and flips me up over his shoulder, hanging me upside down by the feet. "'Ere's 'oping yuh 'ave a pleasant stay."

"No!" I squirm. The door handle's tentacles reach out for me. "No, *please*!" I bat away their suction-cupped arms.

The guard trips a lever and the door starts to spin, revealing a giant black hole. I fling myself upward, bending away from it, but it's no use . . . the guard stuffs me through anyway . . . I'm swallowed whole. Razor-sharp fangs bear down on me. I squeeze shut my eyes and scream.

"Tuck your 'ead," the guard shouts, letting go of my legs. "Yuh dun't want the pins to hit yuh anywhere but in the back, trust me!"

I fall, screaming, spiraling, into the building, falling, falling, through some sort of wall-less chute. Everything is dark and hot and hideously loud. Voices shriek in agony as I tumble past them. I bring my hands to my ears, trying to shut out the noise. But I can't. It's as if their screams are inside of me, have become a part of me—or maybe, *just maybe* . . . it's not them.

It's me.

I pull my knees to my chest and tumble head over heels now, out of control, praying the end is near and quick. I land with a *thunk* on what feels like an unforgiving bed of needles. Pain pierces through me, up my neck from my back. My arms go limp and numb at my sides. I can no longer feel my legs, my toes, my fingers, my lips.

It's as if I've been injected with some sort of anesthetic.

The thoughts in my mind grow dizzy and blur . . . and then wipe away altogether. I struggle to hold on to what little fragments I have left.

"Welcome," a woman's voice says over me. Fractured lines of a face wobble into view.

"I'm not supposed to be here," I whisper. "There's been a mistake."

"You and the other eight hundred and fifty inmates," she says.

# *Nineteen*

***Eyelet***

"Not to *wor-ry*," a cheery voice says. Cool hands pet my head. "It'll wear off in a minute, or twen-ty . . . maybe a day." A licked thumb scrubs at my forehead, erasing something from my skin.

I blink, stunned, squinting up at the guilty party, helpless to defend myself. For some reason I cannot move.

Swimming features assemble into a female face before me: blonde shoulder-length hair; white skin; saucer-sized, *striking* violet eyes. A nose, as tiny as a pixie's, puddles in the middle of a pixie-sized face, with a doll's dimpled chin below it. A glowing rim of white surrounds her head.

"Have I died?" I ask her.

"Don't be *sil-ly*," she laughs, a high-pitched, snorting cackle that pierces my ears. I struggle to raise my hands to cover them, but I can't.

"They'd never let any of us off that *eeea-sy*!" she continues. Her voice spoils the picture of her face—spilling out all edges and sharp corners and harsh letters, as if she were a caricature of herself. Such a great beauty, to have never been educated properly. Her voice is in literal contrast to her white, flawless, socialite skin.

"What brings you 'ere?" She grins, sits back, and slaps me hard, snorting—apparently thinking herself quite funny. Then her perfect brows crinkle. "Wha—? You the type tha' don't fancy *'umour*?"

"Humour, you mean?" I manage the words, though they pop out rather distorted.

"That's wha' I said." She looks at me crossly, her voice pitching in an insistent way. Then her brows lift and her mood falls back into childlike temper. "I'm in for promiscuity," she whispers to me. "What's your gig?"

"Promise what?" I slur my words.

"Promiscuity," she repeats proudly as if she's excited about it. "Hysterical, that's wha' they call me." She laughs, leaning closer, and the scents of lye and rose hip overpower me. Her face smears, then pulls into a wicked turn, before at last anchoring in place. What on earth is wrong with me? Why is everything blurry, moving? "I likes me men," she continues, whispering low and sultry. "A little too much, apparently." She giggles. "Imagine, being guilty o' likin' men too much. Idn'it silly?" She cackles and smacks me again, and I feel like my head's going to blow off.

She leans back, and I'm thankful for it, but then she starts filing her nails. The scratching chews at my spine like the mantle of a giant bug. I feel as though I may be sick. Why is everything so vibrant here? Why is everything so pronounced?

"Truth be known, I likes me women, too." She cocks her head and whispers to me, "I'm not fussy. I just likes people." She shrugs her shoulders and folds her hands, tipping her head as if to say . . . *oh my* . . . What is she saying?

I blink at her, bewildered. I've never heard of a girl liking a girl before. Not like this. My mind is dizzy with the thought.

"Oh, not to *wor-ry*, though." She pats my chest. "I don't like anybody who doesn't like me back." Her face melts into concern. "Not tha' I don't like you. I like you *plen-ty.*" She smiles. "Just not tha' way." She reaches out, twisting the curl next to my cheek. "Unless, of course, you'd like me to."

My heart takes a fluttering turn in my chest. I don't know what to say.

"But we can leave that to later," she goes on. "Seeing as yuh's no longer able to form words."

She's right: even if I could think of something to say, I couldn't. I suddenly have balloons for lips.

"Oh, look at you. You poor dear. You're droolin'." She dips over to one side, comes up with a handkerchief, and dabs the side of my mouth. "They should take you off these pins soon. Though they's never really done druggin' us round 'ere—"

"*P-ppp-pins.*" I force the wobbly word from my mouth.

"Yeah. Sorta like the bed of nails. You're lyin' on it." My gaze drops. "Only the pins, they's not designed to drill through yer back. They's fulla drugs. To demobilize yuh. Makes it easier for them to drag us round like tha'." She laughs. "They likes to keep us all hopped up and *stupid.* That way, we's less likely to try to ex-cape. Can't go far if yuh can't move yer legs." She smiles. "But not to *wor-ry*, pet." She gets all serious again, runs her hands over my hair. "They'll be in soon to take yuh off 'em. Too many pins and you'll never move again."

A shudder of cold terror charges through me. Where am I? What's happening to me?

"It's all right," she says, reading my expression. "They don't fancy killing us. We's too much fun to torture." She snorts.

I try to scream, but nothing comes. Not even the slightest sound. My throat feels dry and fat. I no longer have fingers or toes, or the sensation of a neck. I have no idea how I'm swallowing, breathing. Somehow I can still cough.

"I should let you rest." She pats me lightly on the chest. "I remember wha' it was like my first time, yuh poor thing."

First? I drop back, and she tucks the sheet in around my neck.

"Don't you *wor-ry*." She grins at me, all sloppily. "I'll be right 'ere when you wake back up. We's roommates for life now, you know!"

Panicked thoughts crash in my brain as the drugs overtake me. Her face swirls away, replaced by an image of Urlick thrashing, strung up between posts in the gallows, *screaming* . . . as slowly, he's lowered into a steaming vat of wax.

# Twenty

***Urlick***

I shiver, curled in the corner of my cell. I can't get warm. Sweat glistens on my skin. I think I've caught the fever, being left for so long without so much as a blanket in this cold, dark, dank, underground pen.

Something is playing a trick on my brain. Lately, I've been thinking I'm not alone. Perhaps it's the darkness, or the fever. Or perhaps it's the result of starvation. I haven't eaten since the boy came with the potatoes. I don't know how long ago.

It was to be my last supper. Yet here I wait.

What could possibly be delaying their plans to kill me?

Dark spirits spool before my eyes again, dancing and swooping in and out of the bars. I blink, trying make them go away, but I can't. They laugh and cajole, taunting me with their freedom. I know they're not real. But they seem so real . . . I draw in a breath. Perhaps they are. Perhaps I've died and I don't know it, and I'm a spirit now, too.

*No!* I shake off the thought.

I close my eyes and look for Eyelet. She is always just behind my lids.

Through the darkness, her fresh smiling face appears, dancing toward me through the trolling brume of Brethren, out of a world I once hated but now love, because she's in it.

*A world I'd give anything to return to.*

Her gleaming agate eyes sparkle like the sheen of finely loomed velvet. Traces of chocolate and caramel drink me in. *"Eyelet!"* I whisper, I can't help myself—she looks so real. And all at once she's gone. "EYELET!"

*"Sir!"* a voice shouts over mine.

My eyes pop open. It's the boy, Sebastian.

"You's 'avin' a bad dream, sir?" His voice is shaky. I've frightened him.

"Yes," I say.

"You's all right, sir?"

"Yes, I'm fine. What are you doing here? Has there been word?"

"No, sir. But I've brought you this." He shoves a bowl full of soup through the slat in the bars. "I couldn't stand the thought of yuh down 'ere without food any longer, sos I poached it for yuh."

The aroma of potatoes and leeks stimulates my senses. "Where did you get this?" I say, diving forward. It's too hot, but I slurp it anyway, not caring if I burn my tongue.

"From the kitchen," the boy says. "I drained the pot when sculleries weren't lookin'." The boy pushes in a nub of bread. "I also brought you this. And these. Though I've got to get them back." Something metallic glints in his hands. It catches my eye and I sit up, potato cream drooling down my face.

"What's that?" I say.

"The keys—" the boy says.

"To my cuffs or the cell?" I interrupt him.

"Cuffs." He lowers his voice. "I couldn't get 'old of the cell keys, sir, I'm sorry."

"Sorry?" I breathe. "This is wonderful! *Wonderful!*" If I could I'd pat the lad on the head. "How did you manage this?" I say, lurching up onto my knees and turning my back, pushing my hands out through the bars in the cell so he can reach them.

The boy gropes in the dark until at last he finds my hands, his fingers nimble and quick as he unlocks first my wrist cuffs and then my ankle shackles, making sure not to let them clank on the floor as they drop.

"I was able to lift 'em from the guard's pocket as 'e lay back in 'is chair asleep. 'E's got a drinkin' problem, that one." His voice falls. "I waited until 'e was on duty, after I was done with the grub run, then I pinched the key from 'im and come down 'ere."

"So where do they think you are?"

"In the manse of the church, cleanin'."

"Won't you get caught?"

"Not if we 'urry. 'Sides, I did a bit of 'omework. And I knows now 'oo you are."

"Pardon?" A strange streak of terror rolls through me, thinking the boy's found out about my specimen status and has made plans to trade me for his freedom.

"Ain't right, you being locked up 'ere," the boy goes on. "What with you being royalty, and all."

"Royalty?" He unfastens the last clamp around my ankles and lowers it to the floor, and I twist around.

"That's right!" His voice lilts.

"Don't get me wrong." I struggle to move my stiff arms, rubbing my tender wrists. "I'm thankful for this, truly thankful, but . . . I'm afraid you've got me mixed up with someone else."

"No mix-up, sir. You's the one. The last living heir to the throne. Says so right in the official book in the church. I checked."

"What are you talking about? What book?"

"Brethren's official birth registry. I 'eard the officials all goin' on about it. So the next time I was in there cleanin', I thought I'd check for meself. And there yuh was, right on the page she said you would be."

I stare into the darkness, blinking.

*Heir. Throne. Registry. Church. That's not possible. It can't be.*

*Can it?*

"I overheard the Ruler talking 'bout what theys was gonna do with yuh because of it," the boy continues. "That's why all the delay. The Ruler's all in a fix 'bout how she's gonna 'ide yer body from the Clergy. That's why she 'ad yuh stuck down 'ere. It all makes sense now—"

"My name . . . you saw my name, in a register?"

"Yes, sir, and yer description."

"What?"

"The registry mentions the purple mark of royalty on the baby's face." I hear him drop his head. "Beggin' your pardon, sir, but I couldn't 'elp to notice yuh've got some interesting marks on yuh—" He stops himself.

I raise a hand to the open-mouthed-snake scar on the side of my cheek. "So they've known all along. That's why they've been trying to capture me. To lock me away, where I'll never be seen again."

"That's 'ow you ended up down 'ere in the 'ole. It was the Ruler 'oo gave the orders."

"Where is the book now?" I cling to the bars.

"The Ruler 'ad the guards lock it up in a cage and 'ide it in the crypt of the church, so's nobody will ever find it."

"How do you know this, then?"

"I was there when they did it. It was me they sent down into the crypt. Small boy. Small body, yuh know?"

"Is there any way you can steal the book out of there?"

"I dunno, sir. It's pretty risky. I ain't got no business over there in the crypt no more."

"I need that page," I tell the ceiling.

"I'll see what I can do, sir—"

"No. You can lead me there once we're free. Right now, you'd better get out of here." I pass him the bowl through the bars.

"Right, sir. You're sure—"

"Positive. Now get going."

The boy stoops for the keys and rushes off in the opposite direction of the stairs.

"Where are you going?" I holler to him through the darkness.

"Back through the cavern to the manse of the church. I'm not finished cleanin'," he hisses.

"There's an underground passageway?"

"Yes, sir. But it only leads from here to the manse and back. The walls are fortified with steel."

"Who knows of this passage?"

"Only the guards and meself, why?"

My mind bursts with an idea. "Is there *any* way you could filch the keys to my cell?" I lunge at the bars.

"No, sir." The boy is adamant. "The guard 'oo carries that lot ain't no slacker. 'E ain't never gone to sleep on the job. I could never lift from 'im." He swallows. "And if'n I don't get these ones back soon, and the drunk wakes up—" He holds up the keys and they jangle.

"No, no, of course, it's too risky."

"Thank yuh, sir." The boy turns and bolts away.

"Don't forget to keep an eye on my old cell."

"Don't forget to act like yer shackles is still on if anyone comes!" he calls quietly to me over his shoulder, then races on through a door, padding off through the darkness of the passageway.

"I will," I tell the walls.

I slink down to sit on the floor of my cell, rubbing the stiffness from my limbs, thankful to at last be partially free. *Royalty, eh?*

Has everything I've ever known been a lie?

The story of my birth—did my father not step in to help because he was *not* my father?

*The purple mark of royalty. What does that mean?*
I reach up and touch the welt on my face.
Could it be this is not the horror it seems?

# Twenty-One

***Eyelet***

My eyes flutter open to the sound of the same high-pitched voice as before. It takes the room a moment to stop spinning. I hope it's a dream. But it isn't a dream. My greatest nightmare has come true.

I'm trapped within the walls of Madhouse Brink.

"Hi, I'm Livinea." A stuck-out hand dances before my blurry eyes. "Dunce of me not to introduce myself before now. Livinea. Livinea Mae Langtry." The girl takes hold of my hand and shakes it vigorously. My shoulder aches. My limbs feel tired and heavy. I feel heavy all over—and her perky voice is not helping. "Pleased to meet yuh." She smiles full-on. Her teeth are bone straight and lily white. A rarity here in Brethren unless you're from royalty. Or another country's royalty.

She can't be royalty. Can she?

"Langtry?" I squint, fighting hard to dredge up the memory. I know I've heard that name before. It finally registers. "As in the famous Lyla Langtry? The moving-picture star?" I sit up, and my eyes whirl a bit. I'm amazed at how long it took me to wrangle that thought to the front of my brain. What has happened to me? Why can't I remember?

"Yeah." The girl's disposition brightens, then she suddenly scowls. "Only I don't think we's 'ad any relations."

"You mean, you don't think you're related."

"Yeah. That." She nods her head. "Though I wish I were." Her voice turns singsong. She rolls her eyes dreamily toward the ceiling. "Fancy 'er being yer muvver, eh?"

"Mother, you mean?"

"Yeah. *You's smaaaart.*" She playfully cuffs me on the arm. "I didn't 'urt yuh, did I?" She looks worried.

"No." I launch up onto my elbows, overcome by wooziness, amazed by how blurry everything still is.

"You feeling all right? Not gaseous, are yuh?"

"You mean nauseous?"

"Yeah, that."

"No." I dab my brow. "I'll be fine."

"Yuh sure? 'Cause if'n yer not, I can ring the guard—"

"No! Don't do that." I swipe a thick hand through the air, stopping her from lunging up.

"How 'bout some cinnamon tea? That'll fix yuh up!" She turns, and from under her cot she slides a wooden box the size of a trunk. She opens the lid and starts rummaging through clothing, shoes, household goods. "It 'elps to chase away the aftereffects of the pins."

"Pins?" I vaguely remember having this discussion. Or did we?

"Yeah, they gives them to everybody on the way in. Sort of an initiation. Yuh live through tha', yuh can live through anythin' 'ere." She turns to face me. "Yuh landed on a bed of 'em on yer way in. That's why yer 'ead feels like a marshmallow. There it tis!" She turns back, pulling a pouch and a tin cup out of the box. "Tea?" She grins.

"No, thank you."

She frowns.

"All right, maybe just one cup." I feel the need to appease her. Maybe then she'll stop talking. Her voice is rattling my burned-out gas-bulb brain.

She stands and slinks toward the back wall of our cell, checking over her shoulder as she goes.

"How are you going to get the water?" I squint, wishing things were clearer.

"Shhhhh," she hisses and removes a brick from the wall, exposing the pipe that runs behind it. "But you mustn't tell." She brings a finger to her lips.

"I won't," I say, astonished.

She spins a wheel connected to a tap, and the pipe behind jitters, then purges steam. Hot water streams out of a handmade spout constructed from a bootlace and a bamboo shoot. She fills the cup, shuts off the tap, and replaces the brick with the ease of an engine. "Here," she says, turning back to me. "Drink this." She sprinkles in some leaves and passes me the cup. "Remember, it's our little secret," she says.

"Not to worry, your secrets are safe with me." I mimic her, stooping to sniff the brew. The smell of Christmas morning floods my nostrils. I tip up the cup.

"It should 'elp to lighten up the effects of the pins much quicker." She scratches her head. "You got a name?"

"Eyelet." I slurp. "Eyelet Elsworth."

"Eyelet." She ponders the word for a moment. "I like tha'. Sounds like music, it does. Somethin' classical." She looks dreamily at the ceiling again.

"Thank you," I say.

I lower my head, my heart cinching at the memory of my father, his choice of my name, and my mother—God rest her soul.

"That's *one* thing about me mum," the girl continues, wagging a jaunty finger. "Say what you want about 'er running off on me. At least she left me with a *stunning* name."

"Your mother ran off and left you?"

"Sort of." The girl's expression sours. "She passed me on to me auntie and didn't come back." She wrings her hands.

"Oh." I take a sip of tea. "I see."

My mind shifts to Urlick, another abandoned soul. I struggle hard to see his face before me, but he's not there. What's wrong? What's happened to me? I push hard at the thought and he finally appears, but in faint detail—and then he's gone. Why can I remember certain things from the past so clearly, and not others? Why can't I remember why I came?

"Me auntie Octavia's done 'er best by me, don't get me wrong," the girl rambles on. "I got nobody to blame but meself for me trouble."

"What trouble? What did you do?" I realize by the look on her face after I ask it, I shouldn't have.

"It was just that I was so lonely, you know?" She lowers her voice and bends her neck toward me. "Growing up in that old spinster house, all alone. With only me auntie—and 'er 'aving all that trouble, she did, with the *laudanum*."

"The laudanum? Your auntie, she was—"

"Addicted." She finishes my sentence and folds her hands, soft and pretty over the lap of her dress. "As such, she wasn't much company to me." She lowers her voice even quieter then, and her eyes flash. "So's I started sneaking out at night and going down to the pub to chat with the men." She looks back over her shoulders, then adds quietly, "Apparently, that's not wise."

"No, I suspect it isn't."

"You ever touch yourself?"

*"What?"*

"You know." She goes to show me.

"I know what you mean," I snap, horrified.

She squints her eyes into delighted slits. "Oh, you should," she hisses, leaning closer. "It's delightful. Just don't ever get caught." She shakes her head. "Doesn't go over well in some circles."

I get a sudden start in my heart. "I don't think we should be talking about this, Livinea." My eyes dart left and right.

"We shouldn't," she affirms, smiling. "That's what makes it so *delicious*!"

"No, it's not."

"You ever think about touching men?"

*"No!"* I gasp. I pull the blanket up tight around my chin, as if to keep her thoughts out. I've never met such a creature before, so beautiful, yet so bold. So linguistically *daring*, with a far-too-promiscuous mind. I've had a thought or two of my own about men, but I'd never air them in public.

"Oh, you really should." She pulls back, her lashes blinking, smiling all cheeky. "It's wonderful."

"Enough already." I catch my breath, my cheeks reddening. "Let's talk about something else. How long have you been in here?" I'm desperate to change the conversation—the one I can't believe we're having—to something more conventional.

"I'm not sure." She falls back and stares at the ceiling. "Hard to tell time without a window. Hard to tell night from day. But according to me scratch over there"—she points to rows of crossed-out scratches on the wall—"near as I can figure, it's been 'bout a year."

"A year?" It seeps out of me breathlessly.

"Yeah, that." She breaks out into a snorting smile. "I put a fresh mark up every time they serves me supper. I figure that's the pass of a day."

"And no one's said when you're getting out of here?"

The girl laughs. "Never, I 'xpect. Ain't nobody ever gets outta 'ere. 'Less they escape." Her eyes grow fearful and lose their warmth. "Which I wouldn't try doin', if I was you."

"They can hold you here, forever, just for indecent thinking?"

"They can 'old you 'ere for whatever they want, miss," the girl says, passing me a hanky when she sees me tearing up. "Come on now." She dabs my eyes. "The tortures aren't so bad."

"The *what* aren't so bad?" Thoughts collide in my brain.

Livinea scooches closer, throwing an arm around my shoulders. "As long as yuh don't cause them any trouble, they ain't gonna really 'urt cha. 'Sides, we 'ave each other now." She snaps my rigid body toward hers, slapping my ribs to her side, and I fall apart.

A clang at the bars has both our heads shooting up. "What's going on 'ere?" A guard stands peering in at us over a lock. He is tall and thin, the wiry sort. His fingers shake, not like he's nervous, but like he abuses drink—which is clear by the stink of him. He wears a moustache waxed into curls at the end. A tiny piece of dried snot bobs atop the hairs. His eyes, dark and pebble-small, find me behind the bars. "I'd watch that one if I were you," he says to me, leering. "She's been known to fancy anything—"

"Except you," Livinea says, tossing him a cool jilted look.

The guard runs a sinister eye down Livinea's front, sticking on her plentiful breasts.

Livinea leans back and spreads her legs at him.

I turn my head, aghast at her antics. Petticoats aside, she still shouldn't act that way. Then again, we are in the Brink.

"You." I feel the press of the guard's eyes on me. "Get up."

"Me?" I touch my chest, trembling inside, feeling doused with the coldest water.

"That's right. Get up. Yer comin' wif me." He turns the lock and swings open the door.

"She can't." Livinea springs to her feet and dives between us. "She's already 'ad 'er treatment today. One a day. You know the rules." She gets up in the guard's face.

"She ain't 'ad the kind I'm gonna give 'er." He grins, revealing one golden incisor. "Now get outta me way."

He reaches past her and hauls me out of bed, his dark pebble eyes ogling me. My chest tightens. My limbs are still weak and rubbery; I can barely stand.

"Where are you taking her?" Livinea shouts.

"That's none of your business." The guard strong-arms Livinea aside. She falls with a thump to her cot.

"Take me instead." She struggles back up.

"Get out of the way." The guard pitches her aside.

Tearing open the front of her corset, she stuffs his hand down inside, rolling his palm over her nipples, and I pull my eyes away. "There, you see," she rasps in a trembling voice. "You'd rather have that, wouldn't you?"

The guard smiles and closes his fist, hard. Livinea lets out a sharp scream.

"What's going on here?" A woman in a mourning gown sweeps up to the bars of our cell. Her boots snap together when she stops. She's dressed all in black, layer upon layer. A heavy, sheer black veil hangs over her face. The guard jolts back when he realizes what's happened, leaving Livinea standing with her tit flopped out.

I turn away, embarrassed for her.

The woman's eyes squint to slits. "You little whore," she says and grits her teeth.

"It's not what it—"

*"Quiet!"*

I spin around. I know that voice, or at least I think I do. I strain to make out her identity, still dizzy from the aftereffects of the pins. She's tucked in the shadows, wearing a veil over her face, making it near impossible to discern her features, yet . . . those eyes, those cold, grey eyes behind that sheer veil, look so familiar. She purses her thick, red-painted lips.

"I didn't mean—" Livinea says.

"I said to *shut up*!" The woman reaches out and slaps her. Livinea moves her hands to her face. "Take her away," the woman barks to the guard and turns to leave.

"No, please!" I leap to my feet.

The woman whirls back.

"She didn't do anything."

She steps into the cell, studying me long and slow, a ring of keys on her hip.

"You are the new one, aren't you?" she says in a low voice, a curly black hair dancing on her lip.

"I guess I am," I say bravely.

"Consider yourself lucky. She's taking on Black Bart in your place. Most newcomers don't have that luxury." The woman's almond-shaped eyes shrink to slats. With the flick of her head, the guard drags Livinea away, pleading.

I fall to the bars as the woman backs out of the cell, yanking the door shut behind her with a heavy clang. She turns her back and walks away, keys jangling on her hips, ignoring Livinea's screams.

"Livinea!"

Livinea turns, her violet eyes full of tears, as the guard forces her through a set of black, howling dark doors at the end of the hallway.

# Twenty-Two

***C.L.***

We meander through the woods toward the 'eart of Brethren, Masheck at the 'elm, makin' a dapper new freakmaster, if I must say so meself. Then again, that lad would make a dapper anythin'.

I should be so blessed in the attractiveness department.

Unlike Eyelet, 'e fits well in the jacket and britches, and the top 'at sinks down almost over 'is ears. 'E agreed to allow Wanda to shave 'is 'ead so's to be less recognizable. Shame to ditch all those tawny curls, but necessary, I'm afraid. Now if we's ambushed, theys won't recognize 'im. Least not at first.

'E carries off the moustache better, too. Seems 'aving some 'air there for the spirit gum to stick to is key.

With Masheck's 'elp, we made it straight into the 'eart of the city. People are flockin' out into the streets to greet us now, just as we planned.

A small boy points, jumps up and down, at the side of the road, clapping 'is 'ands. "Look at that elephant, Mommy! Look at it! Look inside there!"

Wanda shrinks deeper into the straw bed of 'er cage as the boy glares in through the bars at 'er. Poor Wanda. This mission's quite the sacrifice for 'er.

The cloud cover thickens in the street just ahead of us. The crowd bemoans the presence of it, complaining they can't see. I wait until the crowd is satisfyingly large. "Now!" I shout to Sadar, executing my 'alf of the plan.

Sadar reaches through the back bars of 'is cage and cranks the music box attached to the calliope car in front of 'im. 'E winds it tight as it'll go without stripping its gears, then lets go of the large metal crank and it unwinds, slowly spinning the large brass drum peppered with raised golden nubs, 'idden inside the front quarter section of the calliope train. Sadar tilts the roll forward, so the picks fall against the golden nubs, then scratches a match to light the boiler below. Steam plies the pipes and starts the music flowin', swellin' up, shootin' through the thirty-two gleamin' golden whistles mounted along the gilded calliope car's sides.

The whistles huff and cry shrill at first. Wanda covers 'er ears. Then the magic finally starts, as the steam flows more consistently and the carnival tunes tweet and twitter out of the whistle's puffin' pipe-mouths. Sweet, snappy sequences play on a chromatic scale, like church-organ music. The best part is the eighty-seven small, twinklin', golden bulbs, strung along the exterior frame of the cart, that wildly flicker once the cart 'as built up enough steam.

People flock into the streets, their mouths flung open, toes tappin', mesmerized by its presence, all eyes glued to the magical machine.

The perfect cover. That and the clouds. "Time for me to fade away," I whisper.

Masheck looks back nervously and I nod me 'ead, givin' 'im the sign.

"'Ear yeh! 'Ear yeh!" he shouts, creatin' further distraction, strugglin' to combat 'is very noticeable cockney accent. "Freaks abound!" 'E stands and waves an arm out over the train cars behind 'im, and the crowd sucks in sharp breaths sprinkled with *aaaaawwwwwhhhhs.*

Masheck continues 'ollerin' and readin' from the freakmaster's old script, calliope car beltin' out its best, Masheck showcasin' each of the anomalies aboard the train, townspeople flockin' after it as they roll through the streets of Brethren toward the city-centre square, without me.

I've sneakily veered off down a cloud-covered side street to the left.

"Just a mere twenty-five jewelets gets you a peek!" Masheck cries. "Thirty-five more gets you into the show!"

Sadar and Martin rise to the occasion, standin' and playin' out their parts, keepin' the crowd busy, entertainin' 'em—Martin extendin' his arms through the bars and moanin' like a mummy, Sadar flickin' 'is tongue in and out of 'is tethered mouth like a snake. I cringe, watchin' Wanda duck 'er 'ead through a slip in the clouds. An old shiver runs through my body, a reminder of the pain and shame of me performin' days. A knot tightens in me stomach for us both.

They 'ead into a particularly large swath of fog, and I tuck up tighter inside the chest of the elephant and plunder onward—makin' me way across the open park, the centre square, known as Piglingham, then across town toward the stone jug to free Urlick. And from there to the Brink, to rescue Eyelet.

Afterward, Urlick and I are to meet the rest back at the square in time to 'elp perform the final act, then exit town the way we came in, real organized and gentle-like—no one'll ever be the wiser.

That is the plan.

With the freak show in town, the authorities will 'ave no choice but to postpone all planned executions and dippings scheduled for the square, buying us just enough time to rescue Urlick before his— I freeze that thought, not allowin' it power.

That is, if 'e's not already 'angin' in the gallows when I get there. I swallow 'ard, pull back on the lever inside the elephant chest, and bolt ahead deeper into the fog.

A little boy sees me, trundles out into the road, and shouts.

Me 'ead swings around, no breath left in me body.

Sadar quickly flips the switch on the calliope car again, providin' me the cover I need to get away. I jog the elephant into the park and wipe me brow, sidlin' up next to some foliage near the back gates. Brigsmen patrol the streets on the other side. They look flustered and frustrated, scratchin' their 'eads.

"Did yuh know 'bout this?"

"Are we ever told anything?"

"I thought we was dippin' someone today."

"Well, we's just gonna 'ave to run with it, now they's 'ere, don't yuh think? Better send word ahead to the Clergy the carnival's in town."

"The Ruler ain't gonna be none too 'appy 'bout this."

"Right yuh are. Best make sure we's doin' our duties, or we'll be the next with a rope round our necks. You take the south entrance. I'll take the north. Ain't nobody comin' in from the east or west, not with that great big rumblin' distraction luring them along."

"True. If anythin' we should be thankful it showed up. It'll be an easier day for all of us."

They laugh and disperse, boots clapping along the cobblestone road.

I forge on ahead when it's clear, taking a quick look across at the gallows as I pass, relieved to see nothin' 'anging there but some bum's laundry. Preparations are well under way, though. Clean ropes 'ave been 'ung from the posts in anticipation of the big event. A fresh vat of wax bubbles over the freshly stoked fire beneath. The Brigsmen weren't there over crowd control at all. I gulp. Looks like we got 'ere just in time.

I squint, tracking the Brigsmen's movements, making sure to avoid detection. Somehow I've got to cross the whole park without being found out. Quite the feat, tucked up inside this giant glimmerin' beast.

I 'ole up under the trees at one side to think, waitin' for one lazy bloke to move on. The foliage rustles behind me and I swing me 'ead round, 'alf expecting, completely 'oping it's only a bird. Me 'eart bounces in me throat as I flick me eyes back and forth, scanning. Out the corner of one, I catch a glimpse of something shiny pressed back against a tree. The tip of a wing sticks out beyond the bushes, just a few metres from me.

They's not made of feathers, they's metal.

"Clementine?" I whisper quietly. "Clem, is that you?"

I'd sent 'er back to the Compound to Iris, back at the warehouse when Eyelet got taken away. Did she not go?

I lean out. "Clementine? Clementine!"

Somethin' stomps, then whinnies.

A 'orse's armoured muzzle dips out between two trees.

"Clementine, whatchu doin' 'ere? I specifically told yuh to return to the Compound to Iris—*Iris*?" I gulp, blinking, as Iris's round brown eyes gawk back at me through a part in the leaves. I shuffle over under cover of fog. "What're yuh doin' 'ere? I told yuh to stay 'ome. Oh, good Lord, and yuh've brought Cordelia." I nearly faint.

Iris's eyes are wide, 'er lips're quiverin'. *I couldn't stay away*, she signs. *Knowing they took Eyelet.*

"Me neither," Cordelia chirps.

"Well." I move me eyes from them to the Brigsmen and back again. "Isn't this a pickle?"

Iris grins.

"I suppose yer 'ere now, aren'tchu?" I wipe my brows. "Now all we's got to do is find a way to smuggle both a beastly brass elephant and a winged 'orse across the park."

*Why would we need to do that?* Iris signs.

"'Cause the jug is on the other side." I flick me 'ead.

*What if I'm not planning to come with you?*

"What are yuh talkin' about?" I crinkle me brows.

"Iris and I are going to fly up to Madhouse Brink," Cordelia announces. "To keep an eye on Eyelet, until you're finished saving Urlick. Then you can all come and help us spring her." She rubs her tiny hands together.

"Is this true?" I turn to Iris.

*That was my plan.*

I must admit it's a good idea. "Yer right. There's nothin' like a bird's-eye view when it comes to disaster."

Cordelia smiles.

"All right, then, I'll go as planned and bust Urlick out. Yuhs two fly up to Madhouse Brink and see what yuh can find about Eyelet. We'll meet yuh up there after we connect back with the freak train later."

Iris nods and turns Clementine round.

"Iris"—my voice stops her—"don't try to do anything on yer own."

Iris nods, then jams Clementine's sides with 'er 'eels. They gallop away and take flight inside the cover of trolling clouds.

The calliope train nears closer, its whistles slicing through the air. The Brigsmen's 'eads sprint in that direction. I take advantage of the moment, boltin' across the field under sparse cloud cover and out onto a back road, whilst the front carriage of the freak train swings off the main street, onto the pathway leadin' to the entrance gates of Piglingham Square.

# Twenty-Three

***Eyelet***

I spring to my feet when, at last, Livinea is returned to our cell, the toes of her boots scraping over the stone floor. Two guards drag her in, her head hanging limp below her arms. A third guard watches from the hallway, billy club in hand, tapping it to his palm.

They toss her onto her cot. Her head collides with the wall.

"Must you!" I shout, rushing to her side.

The whip, resting in the hand of one of the guards, finds its way under my chin. "Watch your mouth or you'll be next." he says. His eyes are slithery. His breath is worse than old cheese.

He drops the whip from my chin and pulls back from the cell, closing the iron-barred door behind him. It clanks up against the frame, drowning out the snickers of the guards as they trigger the lock and saunter away. The lock grinds and falls into place with a *clunk*.

"I'll be watchin' you," the one guard whispers and tips his hat with a laugh as he turns, tossing a leering glance my way.

I shudder as he ogles my better bits, boots slowly clomping backward.

"Oh, sweet Lord." I turn away from him and scramble to Livinea's side. "Are you all right?" I pet her head.

Livinea moans and folds in half, turning away from me, hugging her knees to her chest.

"Oh, Livinea." I stroke her back. "I'm so sorry." Her corset is ripped, her chemise torn. She is battered and bruised. Both her breasts are exposed.

I grab for a blanket and cover her, trying to restore her dignity.

"I like me men," she says softly through fat, purpled lips. "But not that man. That man's a monster."

She falls asleep, her head in my arms, me rocking. It's the least I can do, after the sacrifice she's made. "Oh, Livinea," I whisper softly. "How will I ever repay you?"

*

*"GET UP!"* A metal cup clangs the bars of our cell, drilling through my head and driving me forward. I launch up in bed, staring at the culprit holding the cup: a near-toothless, grimy old urchin of a woman with stand-up white hair. No more than four feet tall, she is dressed in a green hospital uniform and wears a hat made of a strainer with a set of old medical coils as antennae. Her eyes are manic.

"That's Trudie," Livinea says, rising slowly. She wipes the sleep from her eyes. "Don't wor-ry, she's 'armless," she says to me, waving Trudie onward. "Mornin', Trudie," she says to her, then back to me, "she's a li'il bit off." The urchin drifts away, eyeing us stiffly.

In a flash, Livinea is out of bed, pulling her blanket up, racing round the cot, tucking in the edges, and smoothing her sheets as if this were home and everything were normal.

I blink at her, wondering if she's in pain, but I daren't ask. I'm not sure I really want to know the details.

"Ready?" She pats her pillow and turns to me with a smile.

I can't believe the change in her mood.

"Ready for what?" I say, a little afraid of the answer.

"Well, first there's brekkie—which we eats in the common—then a moment to stretch our legs, before we's lined up to choose our torture of the day." She grins. "But only some of us gets one. They select a new batch every day."

"What do you mean, stretch our legs?" My mind skips right over the torture part, reasoning that if we get to go outside, perhaps I'll get away, and the torture part won't happen. "Do we get to go outside?"

"Don't be *sil-ly*," she laughs and cuffs my shoulder, waving her hands and snorting. "Yuh's got a real sense o' 'umour, don'tchu?" She threads her arm through mine and pulls me toward the door.

It's amazing how much more tolerable her laugh is today. Even her voice sounds more lyrical, less shrill and squeaky. Perhaps I'm adjusting to this place.

*Please, no.*

Or perhaps the pins are wearing off. Though I'm still not feeling quite all connected. It's hard to explain, but thoughts elude me, then swing back in again, some slowly . . . some not at all. I seem to remember bits and pieces of things, and nothing of others . . . slivers of this and that, but not everything. It's like there're holes in me memories now. Like someone's used a punch and stamped away parts of my mind.

I move with Livinea's help to the front of the bars.

"We gets to walk round the common ground, down there." She points past the caged-in catwalk that travels the length of our cellblock, to the giant open room below.

I push my face between the bars and look down at the large, open, metal-walled space. Everything here is made of steel, with chipping paint in various shades of grey. Iron gates surround the exterior of the room. Wooden benches and tables make up the eating area off the rear of it, beyond another set of iron gates.

"I thought you said we eat in the common."

"Some days. Others we have to make a run for it."

"I don't understand."

"Yuh will." She slides a trunk out from under her cot and goes about choosing a new ensemble. A wooden box of goodies, and now a trunk? I can't help but wonder where it's all come from.

My head swings back, giving her privacy as she changes, taking in more details of the main room below. A plethora of doors lead off the centre square in every direction, from every wall. None of them is marked. All of them seem to be made of liquid. Black in colour, like the mysterious door I was shoved through when I entered—the one I've just now remembered. The doors shift and ooze like a windblown slick of oil on top of a pond. How is that possible?

I half turn. "Why are the doors—"

"Black?"

"No. Liquid looking." I push my face through the bars to get a better view, then turn to her.

Livinea is dressed in an incredibly fashionable frock made of navy-blue-and-cream pinstriped fabric—garment colours unheard of in Brethren. It looks to be spun of the finest silk, with lavish blue-velvet draperies trimmed in tiny navy pom-poms that line her hips. She wears her inner skirt short, like me, with sheer navy thigh-high stockings. A scattered bouquet of pink, blue, and yellow embroidered flowers edges the tops of her stockings, tumbling down her legs, spackling the fronts of her lily-white thighs. Her short inner skirt is striped blue and cream—like her jacket, which is cut in the daring bolero style. Its elbow-length, exaggeratedly puffed sleeves are lined in wide blue-and-white-striped ruffles to match the jacket. White lace inserts protrude dramatically from the edges of the sleeves like scalloped shells. On her hands she wears a pair of cream-coloured fingerless laced-up gloves that extend all the way past her elbows. Her corset is risqué—barely covering what ought to be covered—and made of blue silk satin, bearing a unique Eastern pattern woven into the cloth, depicting playful teacups among fallen leaves. Fake-jewel fasteners run up the centre of it. She does not wear a chemise nor lace-line the top of her corset to help hide her ample cleavage.

No wonder the guards all want to have their way with her.

I glance down at her ankles—covered by boots, at least, though the heels are daringly high. On her head she wears a blue pillbox hat with matching lace veil that falls in a half-moon just above her lips. The top left side of the hat is garnished with jewels to match the front of her corset. A large feather plume extends from the right, also dyed navy.

Where could she possibly have got such sophisticated clothing in a place like this, I can only imagine. Her mother, maybe? Or worse, a gift for services well rendered?

I gulp down the thought and turn back to the bars, poised to repeat my question. "About the doors," I say.

Livinea darts forward, her hands on my arm. "Yuh mustn't touch the doors." She shakes me. "Not *ever*! *Yuh understand?*" Her eyes are wide. Her chest is heaving.

"Why not?" I say, falling back.

"Because"—she swallows—"them there doors will take yuh in and never spit yuh back out! Only the guards can pass through 'em safely. Promise me yuh'll never touch one, *please*." She looks deep into my eyes.

Her hands clutch mine. They are cold and peppered with sweat. Her quizzical brows bend. She passed through a set of doors last night, didn't she? Then again, she was with a guard. Why do I think she knows more than she's saying? "I won't," I whisper. "I promise." I feel bad the second I utter it, because I know it's a lie.

The tension releases from Livinea's face. She takes a breath and dusts off her skirts. "Good." She twirls, shifting her attention to her clothing. "Not bad for being in storage, eh?"

"I'd say not." I smile and she smiles, and her eyes squint.

"They serves *sausages* on Sundays," she tells me brightly. "Perhaps it's Sunday. D'yuh think?"

"Perhaps," I say, rather stunned by her eternal ability to extinguish dark moods in favour of lighter ones. The thought of Urlick passes through my head. How I used to marvel at his ever-changing mood barometer. What I wouldn't give for one of his testy sessions right now.

A loud horn goes off, bursting my dream. I throw my hands to my ears and jump. Turbines clatter and tug at the teeth of gears. Locks release in simultaneous symphony. I gasp as the doors of our cellblock all slowly squeak open, rolling up into the ceiling like curtains at a theatre.

"Come on." Livinea grabs me by the hand and tugs me forward, leaping over the threshold as soon as our bars are up. We race at top speed along the length of the caged-in catwalk that runs outside the cells, toward the spiral tin stairs at the end. Inmates pour from their cages all around us, running, pushing, shoving. "'Urry up!" Livinea calls over her back to me. "They'll beat us!"

"To what?" I pick up speed. Forcing myself ahead of several others, I struggle to keep up to her, matching Livinea step for step. She giggles, tossing satisfied looks back at me over her shoulder, running and darting down the staircase, off toward the finish line, closing in on the kitchen.

"What is this all about?" I yell, breathlessly catching up at last.

"Yuh wanna eat, don't yuh?" She sprints away from me. "Only the first fifty get fed."

"The first fifty?"

"Yep, every day! Twice a day! Only the first fifty!"

"What happens to the rest?"

"They starve. Or worse!"

I break after her, pushing my limits. I'm not a runner. Never have been, but I need to be now. I pump my arms, digging into the chase, bursting past half the pack, in below the prongs of the iron gates, up to the serving rail adjacent to the kitchen at the back of the room. Livinea laughs as she comes to a skittering stop beside me. "Yuh's just about as good as me." She grabs her knees and breathes heavy. "Good do. We has to run a lot in 'ere." Her hand snaps out, snatching me by the sleeve, dragging me closer. "Watch out!" She snatches a metal tray from the pile at the end of the railing and thumps an inmate over the head with it. The inmate coils to the ground, lifeless.

"What are you doing?" I shout at her.

"It's either us or them. 'Ere!" She tosses me a tray. "Bat away a few."

"You're not serious?" I catch the tray.

"Well, I ain't talkin' no fimble-famble!" She swings her tray, thunks a man in the head. I turn, swinging mine, connecting regretfully with another inmate's face. The man groans and puddles in a heap on the floor. I feel sick to my stomach.

"Yuh's a fast learner," Livinea says. "That's good! I knew yuh would be!"

She turns and socks another inmate in the face, grunting furiously when her tray connects.

I can't believe what I'm seeing, people beating people. Inmates crumbling.

At last a buzzer sounds, and the gates to the kitchen fall. The fifty fighting inmates with trays pile into the room. Those who don't get out of the way are speared straight through, literally impaled, by the gate's sharp ends on the way down. Blood spurts up from pierced chests and backs. Punctured inmates scream. My heart stops in my chest.

I shriek at the horror, bringing trembling fingers to my mouth.

"Phew, that was close," Livinea shouts over the commotion. She shrugs her shoulders like nothing's just happened, turns her back, and marches on.

I stand frozen in the middle of the mayhem, my mind racing, splattered in another's blood.

"Oh, let me get that," Livinea says, licking her thumb and scrubbing the streaks from my face. "Bit of guts, tha's all," she laughs. "A little extra protein with brekkie. Shall we?" She loops arms and tugs me toward the food display.

"Shall we what?" I pull back, trembling.

"Why, eat, of course." She slaps her tray down on the metal rails and heads toward the servers.

"Are you out of your mind!"

"No, are you?" She grins. "Now come on, let's go. Before it's all cold." She launches me forward, but I can't do it—my feet are stuck. I gasp and break into a cough. "My goodness." Livinea rubs my back until at last I've caught my breath. "There's that nasty cough of yours again. You really outta get that looked at." She shifts her attention to the food again. "Oooooh, looks like they might 'ave sausage!" She trails away.

"Wait!" I gasp, my ribs throbbing from all the coughing. "What about them?" I stare back at the floor strewn with punctured people, some still alive and screaming, others dead, the guards already busy clearing bodies.

"They'll go off to the science labs. To be used in experiments," Livinea says matter-of-factly. "We all will, eventually . . . that's why we're 'ere." Her voice lilts up, punctuated at the end in giggles. I feel awash with sudden fever.

"They can't do that," I say.

Livinea pulls her face in tight to my own, resting her forehead against mine. "Theys can do whatever they wants with us." She stares into my eyes. "We's their lab rats. Every last one of us. *Oooooh.*" She launches back, rubbing her hands together. "Look! I was right! Sausages! It must be Sunday!" She breaks into a gallop.

It hits me, and I freeze. *Sunday.* If this is truly Sunday, Urlick will go to the gallows first thing in the morning. I've little time left to save him. I reach out, catching Livinea by the sleeve, and whirl her back around. "Are you sure they serve sausages only on Sundays?" I look deep in her eyes.

"Pretty sure, why?" She wrangles a bite of her sausage. Casing and guts squish between her teeth.

"Think, Livinea! It's very important!" I shake her.

She sucks in her bruised, swollen lip. "I dunno." She swallows the sausage. "Could be Mondays."

# Twenty-Four

***C.L.***

*Second window from the left. Second window from the left.* I chant in me 'ead, remembering Pan's original instructions. She'd flown over'ead checking out the premises, back when she delivered Eyelet's original Ladybird message. Then made sure to mark the ledge of 'is sill, so's the rest of us could find 'im later. Guidin' the elephant up onto the grass at the back of the building, where we's less likely to be seen, I squint me eyes and search for 'er sign through the 'azy mornin' fog as we idle. The soup's particularly thick today in Brethren. I ain't seen it this thick in years. The trollin' clouds part slightly, and I nearly jump from my seat, pointin' and shoutin' to the elephant as if 'e was real. "There! There it tis! Lower set of windows, second from the left, just as she said." I spot the torn flag Pan said would be flyin' above it. "That's got to be it!"

All the windows 'ave flags. But Pan tore the one above Urlick's window before she left, to 'elp us locate exactly where 'e is. There it tis, flappin' wild in the wind. And there's the splotch on the sill she left as extra precaution.

Now, to rescue Urlick.

"All right, big boy." I swallow, popping the elephant in gear. "We've only got one chance to get this right. Can't afford to make hash of it."

I shift the lever to engage the beast in motion, then run me toes through me 'air, me nerves clatterin' like windswept kettles as we launch forward. I lift me eyes, focused on the target, and push the throttle full steam—torn flag flappin', trollin' cloud cover swirlin', giant animal approachin' a lumberin' jog. I pounce on the controls as we near the window, workin' the gears, coaxin' the beast up into a barrelin' run. I lower 'is 'ead. "This is it!" I shout. "Give it all yuh *got*, boy!"

I lean forward, pushin' the elephant to 'is limits, the two of us stompin' up the back lawn. Flywheels whir inside the elephant's 'ead, stripped teeth occasionally slippin'. I should 'ave taken time to replace those gears when I 'ad the chance. Too late now.

The animal missteps, and I fall forward. My stomach takes a violent turn. "Don't die on me now, big fella!" I shout, yankin' his 'ead back up, and throw the throttle full-on forward again. The elephant strains to keep up the speed, 'is ears smokin' as we close in on the window bars.

"Come on, come on, just a little bit farther!" The elephant bows 'is 'ead and steams forward, rammin' the stone wall hard. Bars bend, blocks crumble as we bounce back, jarred by the impact. Rubble falls all around us like a landslide. *"Boulderdash!"* I scream, then cough and fan away dust.

A tattooed brute the size of the window gapes at me out the 'ole in the wall I've just made. 'E has but one eye, a glob of flesh for another, and the sharpest teeth I've ever seen. 'E blinks at me through the clearin' debris and smiles.

"Yer not Urlick," I mutter, shocked.

"No, I ain't! But I's glad to see yuh anyway!" 'E grabs 'old of the damaged metal-bar window, tosses it aside, and in one fluid motion 'oists 'imself up and out of the ground. A split second later 'e's away, 'oofing it across the lawn.

In the background I 'ear a guard's whistle blow. It rings shrill in my panickin' ears. I throw the elephant into reverse, thinkin' only of escapin'.

"Wait!" I 'ear a voice. Eyes flicker through the settling dust of the broke-open cell. A young boy's 'ead pops up out of the rubble. "You're looking for the heir to the Commonwealth, right?"

"Not exactly," I say.

"Yuh 'ere for Urlick Babbit, aren'tchu?" The boy blinks.

"Yeah, 'im!" I say.

"Come wif me." The boy waves me in. "I'm supposed to take you to 'im!"

I 'ide the elephant among the trees at the back drive and 'ustle through the window.

"And 'urry," the boy says. "Whilst they're chasing the other runaway prisoner!"

'E turns and I follow him into the belly of the jug.

*

The boy throws open a door at the end of the cavern 'allway. Beyond is nothin' but darkness. I slow to a stop, 'esitatin' over the jamb. "Come on." The boy motions to me. "'E's inside 'ere. The cage to the left."

I swing the lantern through ahead of me, but it's not much 'elp. I've never seen darkness like this before, so thick and seamless—'ell's own porridge. "Urlick?" I whisper. "Yuh in there?"

"C.L.?" Urlick calls out. 'Is voice is gravelly and weak. "C.L., is that you?" I 'ear feet shuffle in the dark.

"Urlick!" I shout, runnin' toward the sound, swingin' the lantern in 'is direction. The boy chases after me. "Urlick?" The light pierces the darkness just long enough for me to make out a gaunt, white face behind the bars—wearin' 'is infamous purple scar. "Blinkin' blimeys, look at yuh. Yuh look like yuh 'aven't eaten in a month. What's happened to 'im?" I hiss back at the boy.

"The 'ole will do that to yuh, sir," the boy says.

"Where's Eyelet?" Urlick interrupts. "I thought she'd be with you. Where is she?"

I swallow that answer and save it for later. "One thing at a time, sir," I say. "'Ow do we get 'im out of 'ere?" I ask the boy.

'E grins and pulls a ring of keys nearly the size of 'im from the pocket of 'is pants. "I lifted them in all the confusion." The keys twinkle gold and silver in the limited light. "One of 'em should do the trick."

"Which one?"

"That I dunno, sir."

"Quickly, pass 'em to me." I try the first three keys—all unsuccessful—and I'm bathed in relief when the fourth falls snug into the slot. I turn the copper key and the lock churns. I grab 'old of the bars with me foot and yank the cell open. "Good to see yuh, ol' man," I tease, slapping Urlick on the back.

"You're a sight for sorry eyes, yourself," Urlick says, stepping over the threshold, free. "Now where is she?" 'E presses me with sorrowful eyes. "Where's Eyelet?"

"All in due time, sir. First we need to get outta 'ere." I steer 'im back toward the cavern entrance.

The door at the top of the stairs creaks ajar. Light spills into the darkness, spiralin' down the staircase, seepin' in under the bottom of the giant door. The boy's 'ead whips round and back. "'Urry, sirs!" 'E leans over and blows out me lantern. "I'll distract 'em, while yuhs two get outta 'ere." 'E pushes us toward the cavern door.

"Wait!" Urlick turns back for 'im, but in a flash of 'is buttons the boy is gone, already through the giant door and riflin' up the spiral staircase, 'is bare feet strummin' 'ard against the metal treads.

"Come on." I grab Urlick by the arm. I 'ave to force 'im to move. Urlick stops partway. "No," 'e says. "We can't just leave him here! They'll kill him."

"We can't go back for 'im now," I breathe. "I accidently sprung your ex-cellmate loose from the jug trying to save yuh. It's 'im they're lookin' for, not the kid. If we don't get outta 'ere whilst the guards are distracted, we's won't be gettin' outta 'ere!"

Urlick purses his lips. Boots thunder overhead. He looks up, dismayed.

"We'll 'ave to come back for 'im, sir, please . . . Time's runnin' out 'ere."

A gunshot rings out overhead. "No!" Urlick turns and sprints backwards. 'E's through the doors before I can move.

"Don't do this, sir!" I shout after him. "It will be your end!"

But he doesn't return.

"Oh, *shake a flannin!*" I turn and race after 'im.

# Twenty-Five

***Urlick***

I gallop up the winding metal staircase I was once led down. I curl my fists, prepared for a brawl at the top. C.L. appears behind me on the landing, and I fling out an arm, knocking the wind out of his chest, throwing him back against the stone wall beside me. I raise a finger to my mouth, cautioning him not to speak, signalling there's someone on the other side of the short partition wall that hides us.

I whisper near his chin, "On the count of three, we rush 'em. I'll distract whoever it is. You retrieve the boy. Ready?"

C.L. nods, eyes wide, objection on the tip of his tongue.

A show of three fingers and I pounce out from behind the wall, C.L. on my heels.

A body lies in the hallway, bleeding, below a trail of steamrifle smoke. The boy holds the gun.

"I've killed 'im, sir," he says in a small voice. "I din't mean to. But I 'ad to, sir. 'E was comin' for yuh. 'E was gonna kill yuh." The boy's lips quiver.

My heart sinks like a boulder in a river. I ache from the look in his eyes. "It's all right, boy," I say, reaching for the gun. "Hand me the rifle, son. Hand it over."

He lifts the gun in my direction, but it's too late—guards converge on us from behind. They pop out at every angle, from every crevice of the hallway. Their steamrifles cocked and already firing.

Bullets jump off the walls and shatter the windows.

C.L. and I dance between them, lunging behind the small partition for cover. I reach out, swooping the boy up in one arm as we fly off around the corner and down the stairs. "Go! Go! Go!" I shout, pushing a stumbling C.L., leaping to the landing from the stairs. I shove him through the wooden blocker door between the stairs and my cell and slam it shut behind us, temporarily locking the guards out.

They butt the door with their shoulders, shouting.

"This way!" C.L. shouts, leading me again to the cavern passageway through the dark. We race through to the other end and up another staircase, back into the hallway leading to my old cell.

"Shhhhh." I bring a shaky finger to his lips, falling behind a jut out in the stone wall, and flick my eyes in the direction of three Brigsmen bent over in my old cell, rooting through things found in the rubble on the floor.

My coat. I spy it in the hands of a Brigsman. I'll need that coat. I need it now.

A wide-eyed woman in a mourning dress paces in front of them, twisting her red-gloved hands into knots. "How is this possible?" She spins around, dress whirling. Her brow is winched, her eyes small yet still an ungodly size behind her bottle-bottom glasses. "Who sprung him?" She is enraged, her already fiercely sharp voice pitching to a squeal. *"How did they do this!"*

She doesn't wait for the Brigsmen to answer. "How didn't any of you *bobbleheads NOTICE*!" she shouts at them. Her voice rockets around the room, reverberating off the walls like dynamite. I have a notion to protect my ears, she's so loud.

"Never mind." She snaps a levelling look in the direction of the Brigsmen as one's about to answer. "Just find him!" she shouts. "And when you do, deliver him up to Madhouse Brink!" She whip-turns, her dress swooshing. "We'll see if he can escape from *there*!"

Her shoes clap the length of the hallway, snapping violently against stone, crunching down dust and debris as she leaves.

Two Brigsmen scramble after her, while the last crawls up through the hole in the cell and races across the prison lawn, gun drawn, chasing after the criminal.

"Follow me," C.L. whispers once we're sure the way is clear. He zigzags through the crumbled remains of my cell, hoisting himself up on the wall. He pokes his head out and scans the yard before continuing. "All clear," he whispers and rises out of the hole.

I swoop down, collect my jacket from the rubble, then turn and scale the wall after him.

"This way!" C.L. waves me toward a brink of trees at the back of the yard.

I chase after him, grinding to a startled stop at the edge of the leaves. "My God," I gasp, stunned at the sight of the elephant.

"Our chariot awaits, sir." C.L. grins.

He steps up into the chest of the animal as I look down at the face of the child in my arms. "No." Sebastian's skin is ashen. Blood seeps through the fingers of my left hand that holds him. "No, no, no, no." I work to pull back his shirt, revealing the boy's chest. Blood bubbles up between his ribs like a fountain. I look up at C.L., tears threatening my eyes. "He's been hit," I say.

"Sir?" The boy's eyelids flutter slowly open, his eyes searching for mine. "I stole the registry for yuh," he says in a whisper, his voice thinning. He coughs and gulps down a bloody breath. "It's 'idden beneath the porch of the manse of the church. Yer gonna get it and get outta 'ere, right, sir?" He stares up at me, his eyes penetrating.

"Of course," I say. "With your help."

His eyes waver. They roll back in his head.

"Listen to me." I take his hand and squeeze it. "We are going to retrieve that registry together. Do you hear me? *Sebastian?*" I shake him.

"I don't feel so well," the boy says. His eyes lose their focus.

"Sebastian?" I shake him.

The tension in his body slackens. His head drops limp over the side of my arm. "No!" I curl over him, checking for breath. "No! No, no, no, no, no . . ."

I melt to the ground, softly sobbing, pressing the lifeless child to my chest.

C.L. lets out a tattered sigh.

"He did this for me, all of this was for me," I whisper, staring off in the distance.

"Whatchu doin', sir?" C.L. chases after me as I stand and stalk the final few steps to the elephant, the bloody child in my arms.

"We've got one more stop to make before we leave town," I say, hoisting myself up into the passenger seat. "Take us to the churchyard."

# Twenty-Six

***Urlick***

"Pull up here." I instruct C.L. to stop the elephant behind a group of tall bushes at the base of the graveyard, halfway between the churchyard and the manse.

"But sir—" C.L. looks over at me, frantic. I can tell by his eyes he thinks I'm crazy to risk this.

"Well, he can't come with us," I say. I jump down from the breastplate of the elephant, carrying the child, my arms and hands bloodied.

"What are yuh doin', sir?"

"Giving the kid a proper burial," I answer, and stalk off across the yard, my steps heavy.

"Wait! I'll come with you." C.L. jumps to his feet.

"No. You stay here. If anything happens, you make the charge and come get me. I won't be long," I say, and lower my head.

"Will do, sir." C.L. salutes me with his foot and sits down again.

I adjust Sebastian in my arms and head off across the open span of grass, dashing in and out of the wisps of trolling fog for cover. It feels so good to be free again, to be walking without chains. I only wish poor

Sebastian could have experienced this. I'm stiff and achy, though the child weighs nothing. My heart is heavy as a hundred stone.

Silly little shit. Risking his life like that. I swallow back the tears that come. I think about what he last said. About the register and my link to royalty. The hopeful exasperation in his voice as he said it, and how with his dying breath he insisted I know where he left it for me. I can't believe how brave he was.

I only hope that what he's said is true, and the child has not died in vain. I steer away the tear that escapes my eye.

If it is the truth, what will it mean?

I haven't time to think of this now. I need to lay this child to rest. I trudge on, knowing the officials keep an open grave dug in case of casualties over at the jug. I need to find it, lay him to rest, and get on my way, before things get worse.

I dash up the hill and spot it immediately. It's shallow, ten inches deep at best, but it'll have to do, I haven't time to improve it. Besides, it's far more decent than what the authorities would do if they were to find his body.

I reach the grave, bend at the knees, and the child flops forward. I roll him from my arms to the dirt and fall back on my haunches. I'm covered in his blood. It's as though I were his murderer.

In a matter of speaking, I guess I am.

His body falls limp as I arrange him in the dirt—thin bones, a meatless middle, his tiny, gaunt face staring up at me. It occurs to me I never really saw him in the light, only that one time for a few seconds. I was right. He can't be more than eight or ten years of age. What a tragic end to such a short life.

"Good-bye, my friend," I say, swallowing back more tears. I reach forward, closing his eyes. Placing his hand over his wounded heart, I stand, chin wobbling, and reach for the shovel next to the grave, filling it with dirt. I wince at the sound of the blade as it cuts through the earth, thinking about my own eventual demise. Who will be there to see over me? To send me off? To say a prayer? Eyelet? Where is she?

I drop my head and say a small prayer, though I'm as far from religion as one could be—*Eyelet would be so proud*—then sprinkle the first shovelful of dirt over Sebastian's face.

Poor child.

I mutter something more that I think Eyelet would appreciate, shake off my emotions, and get to work. I do my best to cover him evenly, with what little time I can afford, so the animals won't get to him.

I'm nearly finished when—

"You there!" I turn into the eyes of the vicar squinting my way, struggling to make out who I am through the cloud cover. He's not close, but he's not far away, either. The clouds break and he spots me; his face is drawn in horror. I must look a sight. My usual repulsiveness, plus all the blood. I look down at my shirt, realizing what he must think.

"Put that shovel down!" the vicar shouts.

My heart picks up speed. "Please," I say, starting toward him. "It's not as it appears—"

"Help!" the vicar shouts, backing up.

"Please, sir, give me the chance to explain . . ."

The vicar stumbles into the mist, his head colliding with a gravestone. A twig cracks at the opposite end of the property, and my eyes shoot in that direction. Through a tear in the meandering fog I spot them—Brigsmen searching deep in the forest for the runaway criminal, their heads now turned my direction.

*"Heeeeelp!"* the vicar shouts from his post on the ground.

The Brigsmen's attention snaps toward the voice. Their steps halt. One more cry and the vicar will have given me away. I can't let that happen.

I pick up the shovel and run at him. "Please forgive me," I pray to the sky and bring the shovel down over the vicar's head. The shocked vicar collapses in the dirt.

I drop the shovel, turn, and race for the manse, dipping in and out of the cloud cover. *Please, Lord, don't let me roast in Hell for that.*

When I reach the porch, I dive beneath it, shattering the delicate latticework that surrounds the edges. Barreling through, wood splinters flying, bouncing off my back, I skid to a stop just outside the front steps. I launch up on hand and knee and scabber about like a squirrel, in search of the register. *Come on . . . come on . . .where can it be?*

I refuse to leave without it.

I can't. *I owe that much to Sebastian.*

Boots thunder down the hillside toward the vicar. Shrill whistles spike the air. I see their boots through the broken latticework, rushing toward me.

Soon, the Brigsmen will be here.

I lunge forward, spotting a scrap of cloth lying in the dirt, tucked under the last porch step.

"Urlick!" I hear a voice behind me. I swing around to see C.L.'s feet and the glistening jeweled toes of the elephant standing next to the hole I punched through the latticework. "Urlick, we've got to go!"

Boots thunder again. Closing in.

"Urlick!"

I throw myself at the cloth, clawing it loose from its hiding place. It rolls open, revealing the registry bound in black leather, tied up in a purple ribbon. A goose feather marks a particular page. I yank loose the ribbon and flip open the book. "Good God," I gasp, running my fingers over the entry.

"Sebastian was right, it *is* me."

# Twenty-Seven

***Eyelet***

We stand swaying in lines in the centre of the common room. Livinea, in the row next to me, still holds my hand. There are hundreds of us, maybe even a thousand—inmates as far as the eye can see, an ocean of silent, dark, waving clothing. It's haunting, really.

The room smells of blood, sweat, and sausage grease, infused with the odd waft of defecation. Someone near us has soiled his or her trousers, too afraid to leave the line. I curl up my nose, shaking inside, and pull an arm to my face, hoping to deaden the scent as I gag. I look up at the ceiling. It's covered in thorns. Even there, escape would be treacherous.

"It's almost time." Livinea leans over, whispering. Her eyes squash behind the wrinkles of her smile. She bounces on the pads of her feet as if she's a child waiting for candy, not a chance at daily torture. What is the matter with her?

They've packed us in so closely Livinea's wild blonde tresses brush the collar of my chemise on the left. I'm sweating and feel like I might pass out. My neck itches. Lights beat down on us from all directions. It's like one giant interrogation room.

I raise a hand to my eyes to try to see what's going on ahead of us, but all I see are backs. Livinea is just that much taller than me that she can see over everyone's heads, including a lot of the men. She's also that much closer to the lights—she's perspiring heavily, her face glistening.

Music seeps out from massive gramophone-horn-shaped speakers near the raised stage in front of us; someone or something is playing Chopin's Etudes no. 12, op. 25. The graceful tickling of the keys produces a fluttering, light, buoyant, whimsical sound, in direct opposition to the moment we're trapped in. Lab rats, every one of us. Livinea's right.

My heart races, speared with panic. My eyes won't stop searching for a way out.

Livinea clasps her hands. She seems overjoyed by all the strange little goings-on around us.

I'm afraid I don't share her enthusiasm.

Curtains part over the stage, revealing a door, and my breath skips. The door has a black, oily surface just like the one I entered the building through. It begins to ripple as if disrupted by a wind that does not exist. I look around, trying to make sense of it.

"What's happening?" I hiss to Livinea above the music.

"The choosing?" Her lips part over teeth strewn with sausage guts. "It's about to begin!"

She claps her hands as the music crescendos, changing abruptly to something more ominous, pulling my eyes to the front.

A guard stands next to the rippling door. His dark eyes cast out over the crowd. It's the same guard from the night before, the one who took Livinea and— I swallow down the thought. In his left hand, he holds a horsewhip. He waves to the crowd with his right. I look over to see Livinea's reaction, feeling mine burning deep in my gut, but she has none.

Again, it's like nothing bad has happened. I wonder if she doesn't remember.

Slowly the guard surveys the room. His squinted eyes stop to rake over Livinea, and light up. A farcical smile teeters on the edges of his lips. He licks them and twists the ends of his vile moustache upward, and it's all I can do not to vomit.

Livinea quickly lowers her head. Her hand trembles inside my own. Something tender pulls apart inside me. She does remember. I shudder at the thought of his lips on hers, his hands where they shouldn't have been. I squeeze her fingers tightly. "It's all right," I say. "I'm here."

I look up to see that the guard's eyes have shifted onto me. I drop my chin to escape his arrogant leer.

"It's all right," Livinea echoes, her eyes darting from him to me. "I'll never let 'im touch yuh. I swear."

I squeeze her hand again twice as if to say *thank you*.

A sudden rushed and hollow feeling comes over me. My mind goes from full to blank. I push at my temple, unable to recall anything, not even my own name. Why can't I remember anything? I look up and gasp for breath.

"You all right?" Livinea whispers.

"No." I shake my head. "I can't seem to remember anything suddenly."

"Don't *wor-ry*," she says. "It'll pass. Or it won't." She straightens. "It's always like this."

"What do you mean?" When she doesn't answer, I pinch my eyes shut and concentrate as hard as possible. Was there something in the food this morning? All at once, bits and pieces start to come back to me, shuffling like cards through my head. "The freak train," I say aloud before I realize it.

*"Shhhhh!"* Livinea scolds me. "We aren't to talk in line."

*The spot in the woods. The hidden factory . . . C.L.* C.L.? What's happened to him?

Why haven't I thought of him before just now? Where has that memory been? What have they done to me? I clasp my forehead in my hand and close my eyes, and more images come flooding back: *the Brigsmen, the professor, the Loony Bin wagon—the look on C.L.'s face as I pulled away.* The wagon, that's how I got here. Penelope. She's the one who sent me. I mustn't forget this. I've got to hold on to it.

Urlick! His name finally surfaces. I'm here to save Urlick.

I look around.

I've got to get out of here.

"What day is it?" I ask Livinea.

*"Shhhhh!"* she hisses.

My memory. What's happened to my memory? It seems to come and go. Perhaps that's what's happened to Livinea. Perhaps that's why she's so inappropriately cheery. Perhaps they've sucked all the depth of her memories away with all their tortures and left her— I've got to get out of here.

A trumpet sounds, causing me to jump, belting out long, sharp notes over our heads. My chin snaps up, as does every other chin in the building. Inmates click their heels together, shoulders back, spines ramrod straight. I look around and follow protocol, my skin prickling.

The trumpeter finally ends his wail and dismounts the soapbox, and the door behind the stage begins to shimmer. The image of a woman appears, a silhouette of black behind the liquid doors, as if someone were almost but not quite there. A pair of hands presses on the opposite side of the door, pushing their way through to our side. The skin of the door begins to slosh and jiggle. The figure leans and the membrane stretches out toward us, growing lighter in colour and ever thinner, like an expanding balloon about to pop. I wince—everyone winces—waiting for the explosion, trying to figure out what's going on, when all at once the hands push through. The murky membrane snaps. It coils back around the figure; it looks like a person emerging face-first from a stream. The woman, dressed in the black mourning gown, steps from the illusion onto the stage, flicking bits of sticky residue from her fingertips. She turns, yanking her veil in behind her, as the door globs shut.

She steps up onto a soapbox, faces the crowd, and, shockingly, lifts her veil. Her features are for the first time clearly revealed. *"Rapture,"* I breathe. Only she's not wearing any glasses.

"How do you know her name?" Livinea whispers.

"Penelope? Her name is Penelope Rapture."

"No." Livinea's brows twist. "Parthena. Parthena Rapture."

*Parthena?* I turn my attention back to the front, focusing on the mole on her lip. Livinea's right, the Rapture I know doesn't have a mole—but someone else I knew did. My mind shifts to Flossie.

The mole. The hair. Her torn mouth. Her pink, pudgy lip.

Parthena waves her hands, and the music abruptly stops.

"Good morning, inmates." She grins. Her tone is harsh and slightly lower pitched than I remember Penelope's to be, and not half as frantic. She's also more graceful than Penelope is, and her cheek doesn't twitch when she speaks. Other than that, and the absence of bottle-bottom glasses, this woman could be Penelope's . . . "Twin," I say under my breath.

"What?" Livinea turns her head.

"Nothing." I shake my own.

"Welcome to your daily torture choosing." Parthena's voice crackles over the gramophone speakers. She brings her hands into a reverent fold across her chest. "May you all choose well." She pulls her lips into a tight, smug smile. "As always, when you hear your name, step forward into the shower chamber to my left." She tilts her head. "From there, you will sign up for the torture of your choice." She flits a hand behind her, and a massive, sawtooth steel door separates. Its jaws pull apart from the top to the bottom of the room, revealing a large shower facility behind it. Lilac steam pours out from the bottom set of teeth in hurried, whirling puffs. The cloying bouquet of smells is both sweet and noxious, and cool to the tongue.

Camphor. Methanol. A mild anesthetic. *Benzene.* Is that benzene I'm tasting?

They're dousing us in benzene.

I suck in a breath and hold it tight, motioning for Livinea to do the same.

"Oh, it's not 'armful." Livinea waves my efforts off. "It just makes the mind a bit sleepy, that's all."

"The rest of you will go immediately to the exercise room," Parthena continues, and that's when I notice Parthena and the guards are protected inside boxes made of glass that couldn't be seen before. Individual boxes; one for each staff member. They move and the boxes float along with them, on a thick, roiling cushion of white steam. The steam curls outward, repelling the purple haze away from their airspace, sparing them from breathing it in.

I reach down and tear a piece of the hem off my inner skirts and wrap it around my face, leaving only my eyes exposed. "Here!" I say, quickly passing a piece to Livinea. "Tie this around you, quickly!"

Livinea laughs. She raises her nose to the air and breathes deeply, chokes a little, then smiles.

"Livinea, no!" I slap a hand over her mouth.

I look around at the other inmates all breathing deeply, as if they've been trained. They cough and choke, then heave in again. "That's right, my pets," Parthena sings. "Drink it in. Drink it all in . . ." She rolls her hands in the air as if conducting a symphony.

"No, stop, please! Livinea, you have to listen to me—" I tug her arm.

"*Shhhhh*, or we'll miss our names." She scowls.

Parthena turns her almond eyes toward the crowd and holds out a list. It unfurls to the floor. She starts reading out names, lilting her voice enthusiastically as if they were recipients of a grand prize. "Anthony Stocking. Harland Hertz. Eleanor Gillow . . ." The music returns, a soft but crescendoing background. "Esther Islington, Gladys Jefferys, Mahala Machester . . ."

One by one the inmates break from their lines and race toward the front. Some of them shriek and wave. I hold my breath, my heart pounding outside of me as Parthena nears . . . "Livinea Langtry . . ."

My heart stops. Livinea pulls her hand from me.

"No!" I grab at her. "Don't go in there!"

"Don't be sil-ly." Livinea leaps to her toes, clapping her hands. "We has to go in there when our names are called. It's the rule. 'Sides, I've been in there a million times before."

She moves forward, and a streak of terror bolts through me.

I clutch at her sleeve. "No, Livinea, you don't understand."

"Not to wor-ry." She smiles and tugs her arm from me. "I just go in, pick out me torture, sign me name on the paper, and then I'm free to go to the common room for walkabout."

*"Livinea Langtry!"* Parthena repeats, forcefully this time. Her almond eyes scan the crowd. The guard next to her reaches for a strange-looking steam-powered bow.

"I've got to go." Livinea tugs away from me. "If I don't, they'll shoot me dead."

She hikes up her skirts and she's away before I have the chance to stop her, shouting back to me over her shoulder.

"I'll meet you in the common room la-ter."

Inside my head, the terror that's bitten me is screaming.

"Eyelet Elsworth . . ." I hear my name faintly in the distance.

A seizing coil of horror burrows through my chest. *Was that? Did she? She called my name . . .* My throat numbs, my tongue, my legs. I couldn't move if I wanted to. All at once I realize, perhaps there's another reason I can't. Perhaps the silver's got me.

Parthena Rapture's eyes lock onto me in the crowd. I struggle to find my breath. Her penetrating stare courses through my frozen veins. "Eyelet. *Elsworth*," she says again, this time with harrowing conviction.

The guard at her side raises his steam arrow.

Gasping for breath, I somehow find my legs and will them to move forward, catapulting myself reluctantly toward the front. It's not the silver, after all. My shoulders rivet with every step. I look around for a way to escape, but there doesn't seem to be one. Guards stand with steam arrows aimed at me from every mount—staircases, stage, widow's walks.

I slow my step as I reach the bottom of the door that juts up out of the floor like teeth. I look back over my shoulder one last time and bite my lip, my heart heavy with desperation, then step into the steam-filled shower room.

Thoughts of destruction whirl in my head.

Is this how I'm going to die? Willingly, like this?

I think of Urlick about to be dipped in wax and hanged, or perhaps it's already been done. Perhaps I'm too late, for both of us. Tears blur my sight.

Inside the shower room, amid the frolicking purple mist, inmates fall into rows, lined up behind wooden tables manned by clerks dressed in full gas-masked hazard gear—rubber-and-canvas suits that cover them head to toe, held together at the joints with brass clamps—like the costumes deep-sea divers wear. Tiny hoses protrude from the tanks on their backs, leading to the giant fishbowl helmets they wear on their heads.

From behind their glass visors, guards bark directions at the inmates, passing out papers with white rubber-gloved hands. Behind the guard tables sits an assortment of torturous devices. Things I've never seen before, except as drawings in books.

Among the assortment are some medieval apparatuses that we were taught about in our obedience classes back at the Academy. Forms of torture the Commonwealth leaders adapted from the Middle Ages, used commonly nowadays to reform criminals—or murder them.

In school, the headmaster forced all in attendance to study these tortures, as a means of deterring any of us from engaging in the practice of anti-state behaviour.

My heart punches the sides of my chest as my eyes drink the devices in, one by one. A mechanical set of cat-o'-nine-tails hangs over the back of a heavily spiked Judas chair. Against its legs leans a knee splitter, and a set of thumbscrews, and next to that a heretic's fork. Beyond that lies a metal scold's bridle and, atop a wired chair, a head crusher. I swallow, my blood running arctic in my veins.

Livinea was right. This is not just an institution where they hold the Mad. This is a scientific torture chamber. And we are their specimens.

I turn my back, with thoughts to run, and the sterling blades of a Spanish donkey glisten. Tucked in behind them, at the very back of the room, stands a heavily rusted garrote. I know enough to know no one returns from that.

The tortures today are designed to eliminate.

I shudder, my eyes catching on a square wooden bed filled with water. Young bamboo shoots float inside. A set of four posts line the bed on either side, equipped with shackles to chain the victim to. Slowly, the bamboo grows through the body, eventually killing its victim. *The bamboo sleep.*

I gasp, bringing a trembling hand to my chest.

It's not. I shake my head. It cannot be.

That's an Eastern torture.

I've got to find Livinea. We've got to get out of here. Right *now*!

"Eyelet!" Livinea waves to me through the purple haze, smiling. "Over here!" She signals for me to join her in line. "They've got so many new things!"

Her eyes are big, her pupils dilated, her movements slow and sloppy.

"Back away from there!" I shout, clawing my way through the line toward her. "Livinea, back away!"

The clerk offers her something—some sort of device that looks like a pear sitting atop a set of four steel prongs. At the base of the pear, there is a crank that controls a threaded screw that turns up through the middle of it. The clerk activates the crank, and the steel petals of the pear peel slowly open.

Livinea's eyes spring open, too.

I stare at the apparatus and my mind suddenly connects.

*The pear of anguish. Oh, God, NO!* "Livinea!" I shout. "Livinea, *don't sign that paper*!"

She turns to me, her eyes dancing, pencil in her hand. "But it's special, just for me. The clerk said so."

"*No!* Livinea! *No!*" I dive for her, but a guard hauls me back.

"Let go of me!" I shout into his glass-bubbled face.

"Get back in line!" He whirls me around. "And get this off your face." He tears the cloth from around my mouth. Immediately, my head starts to spin. My eyes grow weary, the lids heavy, my vision blurred.

"Livinea!" I scream. I struggle against him, pounding his back, trying to break away. I finally thrust free, only to crash into a wall of glass.

A hand rises up from inside, swiping the condensation from inside the floating box. Through it I see Parthena's gaze narrow in on me, dark and fierce. "Is there a problem?"

"No, miss—" The guard jumps in front of me, snatching me by the arm, and starts to lead me away.

"It's all right." Parthena raises her hand to stop him. "This one doesn't need to get back in line." She smiles smugly. "Her torture has been predetermined."

"What?"

"Take her away."

"*No.*" I shake my head. "You can't do this! I've done nothing!"

Parthena laughs. "You always say that." She leans toward the glass and tsks. "How very naïve. Looking for justice, in a place where there is no law." She jerks her head to the right, and the guards drag me away backward over the floor.

"Livinea!" I shout, twisting and kicking. "Livinea! Don't sign that paper! Don't put your name on it! Livinea!"

She waves as though nothing at all is happening.

# Twenty-Eight

***Eyelet***

The guard drags me, staggering and stopping, through the common room into a smaller, cold, dark room off to one side. I writhe and scream, but it does nothing; no one I pass reaches out to help me. All fixed in their zombie states, they rock in their lines, waiting to hear their names, to choose their tortures—the way they're possibly going to die.

I close my eyes, unable to stand the sudden weight of them. My blood jerks in my veins. Something is wrong, very wrong with me. I feel like I'm coming out of my skin. Metallic spittle curdles in the back of my throat. There's a hint of burned toast.

All at once I know.

The room spins. The silver's rising.

*No.* I shake my head. *Not an episode. Not NOW . . .*

I feel myself begin to shake, not from fear but from forces beyond my control. The world around me has begun to dim. Soon I'll be left drooling and riveting about the floor, an uncontrolled animal. I can't let anyone know.

In a quick move, I bite the hand of the guard to make him let go. He tosses me up against a wall. My head spins from the thud. I shrink dizzily down to the floor. Reaching into my pocket, I frantically search for the small syringe of serum I tucked into the seam before I left the Compound. The same serum that saved Cordelia's life, pulling her from an episode, in case I needed it to save my own.

"You little dolt!" The guard lunges at me, shaking the pain from his bit hand.

I pull the syringe from my pocket, trying my best to conceal it in my fingers, but my brain is sloppy, I'm woozy and slow.

"I'll take that." The guard leans in, snatching the serum away. "What *is* this?" He holds up the syringe, examining it closely in the light, his eyes beaming through the tiny glass vial. "Thought you were gonna stick me with this, did you?"

I shake my head, shivering, trembling, trying to hold on, the silver coursing toward my brain.

"Sorry for you, I ain't that dumb!" The guard swings around. He fists the syringe and stabs me with it, sinking the needle deep into the muscle of my arm. He launches the plunger, pushing the serum into my veins, and I fall back, relieved, onto the ground.

His wide-eyed, pockmarked face wobbles close to me. "You just lost thirty of your sixty minutes in the common today," he says, tossing the needle aside. "We'll see how you like that." The room goes black, save for a set of crooked teeth laughing over me.

But really, I'm the one who's had the last laugh.

# Twenty-Nine

***Urlick***

We rumble through a thicket of leafless birch saplings. Branches crunch and crackle under the weight of the elephant. I look back, checking frequently to see if the authorities are still following us, astonished to see they're not. It appears they've given up on us after crossing through that gurgling bog. Since then, there's been no sign of anyone. Not a single Brigsman attempted to enter it. In fact, they retreated from its edge. C.L., however, crashed the elephant headlong through its steamy, smelly guts, as if he knew what the outcome would be. Then again, what other choice did two fugitives have? I'm only thankful the elephant made it through.

"Where are we?" I say.

"Almost there," C.L. answers.

"How do you know?"

He says nothing, which I take as strange, but not as strange as the atmosphere, which has grown gradually darker and darker with every step. The cloud cover is thicker up here too, than it was below. If I didn't know better, I'd swear we've entered the area of unprotected forest that runs between Gears and Ramshackle Follies by mistake—only we haven't crossed a fence line, have we?

I reach out to clear a path through the thick mist in front of us, and it moves along in a chunk. *That doesn't even happen at home*, I think to myself, shuddering. Perhaps instead of a fence it was a bog.

"There it tis!" C.L. jumps forward in his seat, pointing a wobbly toe toward the top of the escarpment. "There she is, there, you see. We've almost made it." He sighs, sounding relieved.

I wave a hand through the soupy cloud cover. Madhouse Brink comes into view. A great beast of a building, ominously black in colour—a grand, Gothic-looking, windowless, whipped-meringue sort of castle—dressing the farthest peaks of Brethren in a frothy half-halo ring. Around it, giant rolls of candlelit barbed-wire fencing dance forward, backward, taunting all who dare to come near. I tremble, thinking of Eyelet stored inside the belly of that beast.

How will we ever get her out of there?

C.L.'s breath becomes quick and tattered. He starts to shake. I've never seen him like this in my life. Something is wrong. His eyes grow wide and glassy. He blinks often, as if trying to blink something away.

"What is it?" I say.

"Nothin'."

He answers too quickly. He doesn't look at me. I don't believe him—for the first time in my life. I look ahead of us at the building, seeing something shift in the mist.

"Did that wall just move?"

"Yes, sir, it did." I stare at C.L. "That's the puzzle of the Brink. The walls are ever changin', ever growin', ever increasin' in number. That's why it appears to take up the entire landscape, when really only a portion of the walls you see are real. The rest are just an illusion."

"An illusion?"

"Yes, sir. Not real."

"How do you know all this?"

C.L. clamps up, stares ahead. The muscles at the sides of his jaws start churning.

"You were in here, weren't you?"

He sucks in his upper lip. When he turns to me, his eyes are watery. "I did nothin' wrong, sir. I assure you that. It was all just a wicked mistake. You see, me muvver died when I was seven"—he hangs his head—"and me father gave me up for seven pike."

"A pike wouldn't buy you a flake of soap."

"I know, sir." C.L. lifts his chin. "Me father, 'e just wanted me gone. 'E 'ated me. After me muvver passed, there was no one left to protect me. That's 'ow I ended up 'ere."

"But you escaped. That's how you knew we could do it."

"Yes, sir." C.L. slowly nods his head. "But that was a long time ago. Things may have changed—"

"But still, you're Eyelet's best bet."

"I suppose so, yes, sir. When yuh put it that way."

"How did you end up with the freakmaster, then?"

C.L. sniffs. "He captured me that same day, not far off of the bog. 'E constantly threatened 'e'd return me 'ere if I ever tried to escape. That's why when you took me in, I insisted you keep me secret." He looks at me like a beaten puppy.

"Why didn't you ever tell me this before?"

"Because I was afraid to, sir. I was afraid you'd start to fearin' me, if you knew the truth." His lips wobble, delivering the words.

I pat his back. "Never, C.L. Never." I look away, up at the stretch of black moving wall that lurks ahead of us. C.L. wipes a tear and shifts the elephant back into gear.

"So how are we going to know which walls are the real ones going in?"

C.L. turns to me. "I'm afraid we don't, sir."

"There must be a way. How else does anyone enter?"

"There's only one way in that I know of, sir, and it ain't pretty." He shivers. He veers off to the left.

"Where are you going?"

"Manoeuvrin' round the back side of that hill, to come up on the 'ouse from behind. That's where I told the others we'd meet them," C.L. says. "They should be there by now. From there we'll concoct a plan."

He shifts the elephant into the next gear, and its framework stutters. Then, finally, the beast bursts forward, sure of one step, then not the next—tripping and stumbling, then surging forward, an unsteady mess.

"What's wrong?" I clutch the sides of the breastplate seat as the elephant teeters off balance, nearly throwing us from our perch.

"I dunno." C.L. shifts the gears backward, bringing the beast to a halt. He leaps from his seat, disappearing into a coil of cloud cover.

"What is it?" I shout.

C.L.'s brow furrows. "I'm afraid the bog back there may 'ave been too much for the ol' thing." He looks up at me.

"What do you mean?" Spirals of tinny-smelling steam billow up from the elephant's legs. I jump down, dropping through the hissing yellow clouds to the mucky ground below. "Bloody hell." I falter.

"What is it? What's the matter?"

The brass outer coating of the elephant's legs has melted away, leaving the inner workings of his metal mechanics exposed. Half-melted gears now thread through eroded teeth, their iron tips slowly drizzling in a line of hot metallic drool to the ground. Gaping pockmarks glare up from where effervescent jewels once lined the creature's toes and ankle dressings. The shiny brass exterior is now a corroded shell of tin. The once-glistening, golden, majestic beast, reduced to a heartless heap of utilitarian steel.

My heart takes a bitter turn in my chest. Is nothing out of the reach of destruction in this world?

I pull my gloves from my pocket and bend down to explore the situation further.

"Don't touch it!" C.L. shouts from above.

"Why not?" I jerk my hand away.

"It'll do to yer 'and what it's done to the steel," he says, slowly crawling down. "Lost me friend to the bog, years ago, when she and I, we—" He stops himself. His eyes are swollen and red and caught on a memory, I can tell, but he offers nothing further. "It'll melt the skin from yer bones. That's all you need to know."

"So what are we going to do, then?" My eyes shift in the direction of Madhouse Brink, my heart thrumming at the thought of Eyelet penned up in there. "We're still some seventy metres away." I turn to C.L. "The woods are too unpredictable up here."

"Perhaps we can limp the beast there?" C.L. offers. He circles the elephant, surveying the damage on the rest of its legs. "These three aren't as bad." He pokes at one with a stick, and the stick dissolves. He looks up, gulps. "We'll have to 'urry before the 'ole thing collapses onto its carriage."

"Well, we'd better get going, then." I grab the undamaged ear of the elephant and hoist myself back up into the passenger seat.

C.L. plops down hard in the seat next to me and starts pushing and pulling levers. The elephant bounces, careening this way and that. I hold on as C.L. recalibrates for balance. The elephant jerks sloppily forward, but it's moving the gears of its left front leg, whirling and then sticking, as we pulse and bob our way up the road.

*

We arrive at the rear of the Brink in our bobbing caravan. C.L. pulls the elephant to a stop behind a bush and whistles into the trees. One by one the freaks emerge, and my heart does a full wrench round in my chest. I'm not proud of it, but it does. No amount of verbal coaching could have prepared me for seeing them in the flesh, though C.L. did try to warn me on the way up.

"Martin, this is Urlick. Urlick, Martin." C.L. jumps cautiously down from the elephant in front of a very dry-skinned man.

"So good to meet you." Martin sticks out a weathered hand for me to shake.

"The pleasure is all mine." I accept his hand, a little worried I might be left with some of it.

"This is Sadar." A man with a dastardly crooked spine bows to me, and I wince for the pain he must feel. I return the favour and he nods his head, bringing his hands to his chin in prayer.

"Reeke," says a squat, round man with numerous tumours. He smiles, and a bit of drool seeps from between his rows of staggered teeth.

"Pleased to meet you, Reeke," I say, stooping to meet his eyes.

"And this is Wanda," C.L. announces as the last, a haired woman who looks much like an ape, dips shyly out of the bushes. She does not look me in the eye but instead stands and studies her feet, blinking, long lashes waving in the breeze.

"Hello," I say gently. The woman rolls her shoulders.

"Wanda takes a bit to warm up to strangers," C.L. says. "Idn't that right, Wanda?"

She lifts her gaze.

"Been about eight years since she's said a word to anybody, so don't be offended," Martin adds.

Wings flap behind our heads. I whirl around defensively, prepared to fight. "Clementine?" I squint as she hits the ground. She bounds to a stop in front of us, pawing the earth in her shimmering armour, extending a gilded wing toward my hand. The rider reaches for her face mask to throw it back. Eyelet? My heartbeat quickens. Could it be?

*"Iris?"* I sound both shocked and disappointed.

Iris frowns. *Nice to see you, too,* she signs.

Clementine whinnies and snorts, as if laughing.

Iris dismounts, annoyed.

"Where's Cordelia?" C.L. says.

"Right here!" Cordelia pops out from behind Wanda's girth. "Iris and I have already made the freaks' acquaintance. They let me stay with them while Iris did another pass over the building."

"I see." I stare hard at C.L.

"It was Iris's decision to bring her, not mine, sir." He raises his toes in defence.

Next a tall, stocky but well-built young man slips out from the trees onto the road. I suck in a quick breath. "Who's this?" I say, onceing him over. He wears a pair of tattered trousers and a sleeveless vest. His skin is bronze and his head is shaved. He holds his fists tight at his sides, arm muscles tensed and bulging. Piercing navy eyes level me.

"Oh, that's Masheck," C.L. laughs.

"Where did he come from?" I say, still staring at him.

"Eyelet found him," C.L. says.

"She what?" I feel my eyes pop. What does he mean, *found*? A prickly new emotion gnaws at my gut, an emotion I've never felt before now.

"In a warehouse on the outskirts of town. 'E 'elped us save you, in exchange for 'is freedom," C.L. says, noting the heat in my eyes.

"Really," I say.

The young man loosens the grip on his fists.

"Masheck, Urlick. Urlick, Masheck," C.L. tries again.

He puts out a hand, and I tug at the points of my waistcoat before offering my hand to the stocky young man with the rippling, muscled chest.

"He was chained to the wall of a factory when we found him, poor bastard," C.L. goes on.

Yes. Poor bastard.

"Forced to make killing machines, 'e was," C.L. rambles.

"Make what?"

"Elephants like that one, only with guns for trunks."

"Why?"

"Near as I could figure, they was plannin' a war." Masheck drops my hand.

"Who?" My brows cross again. "Over what?"

"Smrt and his lady friend. The one 'oo inherrited the factory. Over resources, I aspect," Masheck says.

I ignore the mispronunciation, because the question's burning in my mind, "What resources?"

"The skies and the water."

"But the air and the waterways are contaminated. Everyone knows that—"

"Yeah, because o' them," Masheck snorts.

"What are you talking about?"

Masheck shifts on his feet. "It was them 'oo did it. They was the ones manufacturing all the bad 'ealth round 'ere. Toxifying the clouds and the water. Treating the 'ealth of only those 'oo'd pay the biggest purse. Leaving all the rest to suffer."

"How do you know all this?"

"I over'eard 'em. Talkin' 'bout their plan to weed out the weakness. And take only prized ones with 'em into the new world."

"What new world?"

"I dunno. Suppose they were cookin' that up, too."

"How does someone toxify the clouds and the water?" I squint at Masheck, not quite believing him.

"They 'ad these pellets they dropped in the stream this side of Brethren. Made everything within a kilometre unfit to drink. Little round pills of death, they called 'em. Little purple things that smell like skunk. Manufactured out in Gears at another of their factories. They ruined the skies with the *cloudsower*. An engine they made to inject poison into clouds. It's a giant bastard of a thing. I saws it once, guns and all. 'Oses comin' out either end. One set to suck up the clouds, the other to spit 'em back out."

"You mean to tell me *they're* the ones controlling our atmosphere?" I look around at the foul-smelling, soupy brine we've been forced to live in. "It's not the result of—" I stop myself before I say it. My mind traipses back to the journals we found. To Eyelet and me, standing next to the Illuminator at the Core, the guilt we felt over our fathers' connections.

"As sure as I know they 'eld me captive," Masheck says.

"So, the sun, it could be up there, still. Hidden beyond the clouds." *Still intact, as Eyelet always thought.*

"Could be." Masheck tilts his head.

I look hard into his eyes. "If we could somehow stop them from sowing the clouds, do you think there's a chance we could reverse the damage they've done to our universe?"

Masheck thinks. "We could do, I suppose . . . maybe . . ."

"Than we shall." My mouth teeters up into a crooked smile. "First, though, we need to save Eyelet." I clap Masheck on the back. "Welcome to the mission, my friend."

# Thirty

***Eyelet***

"You've got to get up! The march is starting!" Livinea shakes me.

I wake confused, disoriented, completely unaware of where I am. Livinea's striking violet eyes blink down at me. Then it all comes crashing back—the shower room, the tortures, falling into seizure, the serum, the guard . . . that silly guard. A smile comes to me when I think of him. Thank God the shot worked.

Slowly, shadows of bright colours move in front of my eyes. An alarm bell bleats in the distance. "We've got to go!" Livinea yanks at my arm. "The walls are shifting!"

"They're what?" I sit up. The whole room is moving.

Livinea loops an elbow through mine and hauls me to my feet with a grunt. "Come on!" She jerks me forward. *"Run!"*

I stumble along behind her, my feet sloppy beneath me. There hasn't been enough time for the passing episode to let go of my brain. There's still a thread of silver in me.

"Just move your feet!" Livinea drags me along.

"I'm trying." I fight hard to make my legs follow my mind's command. My eyes, too, are refusing to completely register. Everything's a blur.

"We've got to make it through the doors before they liquefy!" Livinea shouts.

I don't know what she's talking about, but I keep running the best I can. The clap of my shoes fills my ears. I look ahead. Why is everything echoing? Inmates stand in lines on the opposite side of a looking-glass-type wall. Where did that come from? It wasn't there before. Was it? I squint. Another alarm bell sounds.

*"'Urry!"* Livinea wrenches me forward.

The world around me grows more solid, more colourful—more familiar, less tainted by the silver. I'm finally feeling the ground beneath my feet. I let go of Livinea's arm and double my speed, racing after a bolting Livinea toward a set of smooth black doors at the end of the room, in a now-shifting wall. A whistle shrieks, and the doors shiver—a wobbly, black-ink, disturbed-puddle-like movement. I slow down and stare.

"Don't stop now!" Livinea hollers back at me, sprinting into the rippling ink.

I watch as she leaps through the shimmering liquid door. She flutters strangely over the threshold, her form disintegrating into tiny cube-shaped fragments before reintegrating into herself again once she's landed on the other side.

"It's all right!" she shouts back to me, her mouth vibrating, moving in tiny jerky squares ahead of her words. "Once you get across, it'll be all right. Come on!" She waves me over. Her hand does the same thing, disintegrating inside puffs of steam and reintegrating again.

A flashing light goes off above the door. The alarm bleats faster. *"Now!"* Livinea screams. "You're running out of time!"

The door wobbles harder. I suck in a breath, knees trembling, work up the courage, and leap over the threshold. As I pass through the membrane, a strange current-like sensation snakes through me. I look down, seeing my hands break into tiny unattached squares, then re-form back into hands again.

"Pretty fancy, ain't it?" Livinea says when I land beside her.

"More like perplexing, I'd say." I stare at my hands. "How did we get on the wrong side of that?" I glance back at the wall.

"Yuh tell me. Yer the one who took a nap," Livinea says. "Come on, we need to get in line." She grabs my sleeve and launches me forward. I stumble, not quite all together yet. The air in this room feels stale and static. All around us stand leafless tree-skeletons. "Where are we?" I ask, turning my head.

"Yuh ask a lot of questions for a girl in the Brink," Livinea snaps. "Yuh shouldn't do tha', yuh know?" She tugs on me harder, wrangling me through the lines of inmates, her eyes glued to the floor as if searching for something.

"What are you looking for?" I trot along behind her, bouncing off other inmates' shoulders.

"We've got to find our mark on the floor."

"Our what?"

She flings me round onto a lit-up square, arranging my feet so they cover the light from heel to toe, shoving me around by the shoulders and propping me up straight. "Now stay there," she says and slips over onto her own square, adjusting her feet.

The trees in the centre of the room shift, creating a clearing. A platform rises from the clearing's middle. I squint, trying to figure how it's all happening. It's like an illusion—all seamless and mysterious, without end or beginning. Like an ongoing, liquid dream.

The guard from the night before, the one who hurt Livinea, steps into the centre of the platform, horsewhip in his hand. He wears a sardonic look. Twisting the ends of his moustache, he nods at the ceiling. A twinkling of lights begins. One by one, the squares beneath each inmate burst into flame. Inmates jump but stay fixed in place.

"Don't move," Livinea hisses. "They're counting us." When it nears me, I wince, bracing against a pain that doesn't come. *What is this place?*

When finally, the last light is illuminated, music thunders down through the trees from a pair of cornucopia-shaped gramophone speakers, just like in the other room. They hang on wires suspended from the ceiling among the limbs. There must be twenty of them. The stark beginnings of *Preussens Gloria* crackle forth. Snare drums and trombones blare. The guard draws back his hand and cracks the whip. It licks the heels of the inmates in the row closest to him. "March!" he hollers, and the inmates whimper, leaping into action, jogging laps around the fake-forested stage.

"What is this? What's happening?" I look to Livinea.

"Exercise." She leaps forward. "Stay to the outside," she shouts, steering me away from the middle. "Keep movin' and avoid the lash! Not to wor-ry, though." She grins, giggling. "It'll be over in a loop or two. They've only gots one song."

"Then what happens?" I jog beside her.

"Then we's free to mingle for five or ten, before they takes us off to be tortured."

*Tortured.* My heart jerks in my chest. "We have to get out of here, Livinea!" I grab on to her arm, my eyes searching the walls. "We have to leave, right away!"

"Was it the sausage?" she asks, ignoring what I've said.

"What?" I look over at her strangely.

"Is that what knocked yuh out back there? Was it the sausage, do yuh suspect? I swear sometimes they give us stuff that's gone skunk already."

"No," I shout. "It wasn't the sausage. Livinea, are you listening to me?"

"What was it then, caused yuh to fall down like that?" She blinks at me.

As much as I've come to adore this silly girl, I don't know if I can trust her. She can't know my secret. No one can know it. "You ask a lot of questions for a girl in the Brink, you know that?" I say.

Livinea laughs her hearty, squealing laugh and folds her arm inside mine as we run. "Yuh's quite the little minx, yuh is, Miss Elsworth." She drops a finger on my nose. "I'm so glad we's met."

"Livinea, listen to me." I pull her to a stop. "Did you sign that torture paper?" When she doesn't answer me, I shake her by the shoulders. "Livinea, answer me!" Her expression tells me she did. "You do know what the pear of anguish is, right? What they do with it? Where it goes?" I drop my gaze to my lady parts.

Livinea's brows jump. "Really?" she gasps.

"Yes, really," I say.

"Oh . . . well, it can't be any worse than electrocution." She brings a finger to her lips.

"Electrocution? They've electrocuted you?"

"Oh, yes, many times, miss." She smiles.

No wonder she makes so little sense.

"I was told it would 'elp take away me impure thoughts. The guard said if I signed the papers and the treatment worked, I'd be leavin' 'ere forever, and I'd never 'ave to come back."

"You won't be coming back, all right. They're planning to kill you, Livinea."

"What?" The music falls silent. The inmates slow to a walk.

The guard sinks down through the platform on the stage, leaving nothing but a landscape of trees behind.

"Come on, Livinea." I yank her forward. "We have to find a way to get out of here. Both of us. Right now. Before they come to take us away—"

"We can't." She pulls me back. "There's no time."

"Sure there is," I say. "You said we had five or ten on our own before . . ." I look around. "What about the doors? Lady Rapture passed through them this morning, so there has to be a way—"

"No, miss." Livinea's voice falters. "We'll never get past . . ." She pulls her hands from mine.

"Don't tell me you're more afraid of the doors than the pear of anguish! What's wrong with you? *I don't understand!*"

"I don't expect yuh to understand me, miss." Livinea grits her teeth. Her brows crouch over her violet eyes. "I've tried escapin' through them doors once before," she says in a low voice, checking over her shoulder as she speaks. "Them doors, they steal yer memories. They've taken every last one I 'ad. Memories is all you got when yer packed away in a place like this. Without 'em, you ain't got nothin'." She sucks in her quivering lip.

A buzzer sounds above our heads. Bars rise at the room's far end.

"Livinea, listen to me, before it's too late—"

"I can't." She shakes her head. "It took me a full year to remember me own name, and another to remember why I'm 'ere. I still don't even know if the story of me mum is true or not. Or just some made-up piece o' rubbish the guards fed me. But it's all I've got, don't yuh see! If I go near those doors again, I'll 'ave nothin' left. Nothin'."

"What about your auntie?"

"What about 'er." She clenches her teeth. "She's the one 'oo put me 'ere. Traded me off for money for 'er drugs. I ain't like yuh. I ain't got nowheres else to go."

She breaks away from me and bolts for the bars.

"Livinea!" I shout after her. "Wait!" I chase after her and hurl her round by the shoulders. "It's not true. Think about it. You knew the way here and what to do in the shower room, and about the tea and the aftereffects of the pins. You haven't lost use of your memory. It's there when you want it. You just have to concentrate. Don't you see, it's the tortures you should be afraid of. That's what's damaging you. They've done far worse to you than the doors."

Her eyes grow wet. Her pupils dart over my face. Confusion floods their centres. "I'm going to take me torture today," she says. "You can try to run if you like. I won't stop yuh. But I'm not comin' with yuh."

"But they're going to kill you."

She stares.

"No. I won't let you do this. You've got to come—" I yank.

"I won't." She stands firmly. Tears spring to my eyes as she backs up from me. "Go," she says. "I'll cover for yuh. But I'm not coming, it's not meant to be—"

"Livinea, please . . ."

*"One minute to caging!"* The cornucopia gramophone speakers blare.

"'Urry, before yuh run outta time." She turns me around and pushes me.

I sprint away, then dive back, kissing both her cheeks. "I'll never forget you!" I say.

Her violet eyes fill with tears. "Go," she says. "Head for the door. The horned one. Always the horned one. It's the only way out. Go, *now*!"

She shoves me and I race toward the door at the opposite end of the room, working my way through the stream of inmates headed for the raised bars, a voice over the gramophone speakers barking orders for them to fall in behind. I look up when I reach the door, seeing a faint set of oxen horns waffling in and out of view, inlaid within the liquid black. Horns. Just as she said.

I push on the door.

*"Hey!"* A guard's voice breaks out above me on the widow's walk. I look to him, then Livinea. He reaches for his whistle, and she screams, collapsing dramatically to the floor, a limp hand draped over her forehead. She writhes around as if in abdominal pain and spits foam from

her mouth. Inmates scramble away from her as she starts to scream. "Scarlet fever, it's the fever! Me stomach—it's churnin'! Me eyes! Me eyes, is burnin'! I's burnin' up with *fever*!"

In between flipping and flopping, she winks at me.

I smile, close my eyes, and think only of freedom, of falling into Urlick's arms when at last I reach him, and lunge at the door. I slam my palms against it hard. The surface laps like water against my hands—a great angry black ocean. Driving forward, I throw my palms into the membrane again and it pushes back, as if inviting me to just try and cross it. I push harder and the sloshing door snags me up by the wrists and snaps me forward, until I'm half outside and half in its jamb. I struggle against the sticky grip of the door, trying to either go through or break free of it, but neither motion works. It's seized me and I can't get away.

"Guards!" I hear a voice cry out behind me. The door clenches its jaws, tightening its grip on my arms. I swing my head around, hearing Livinea's screams.

Her eyes bulge, seeing guards surge toward me.

I dig my heels in, struggling to break free of the door, as Livinea lets out a hair-raising scream.

The door startles, ejecting my arms. I fall on my bottom to the floor. Scrambling to my knees, I jump up and snap a limb from the fake forest using it to level the first guard who approaches me. He folds over, holding his gut. I chop a second in the knees, haul up my skirts, and run.

There's a zing and a thwack, then a sharp *ping* registers in me. Something's burrowed itself into the middle of my back. Whatever it is dulls my brain and stalls my feet. My muscles become jelly. Sloppily, I fall to the floor, a set of metal prongs embedded deep in my skin. I reach up to pull them out, but I can't. I'm virtually tethered, like a chained dog, to a set of wires leading back to the nozzle of a smoking gun, feeding live current into the nerves of my back.

The room around me turns to blur. Tears spring to my eyes. I lay paralyzed, in a gyrating heap on the floor, guards swooping in all around me. Parthena Rapture joins them, her distorted face shuffling slowly into place—her eyes like black demons in a white, white nest. "Did you honestly think it'd be that easy?" She blows smoke from the end of a gun. "My sister was right. You are more trouble than you're worth."

"Your sister?" I wince, my head a growing ball of drug-soaked cotton.

*I was right. I knew I'd seen those eyes before.*

"Guards take her away."

"What about 'er cellmate?"

"Drag that dolt back to their cell, we'll deal with her tomorrow. Take this one straight to the operating theatre and call Dr. Melnick. Tell him the procedure can't wait."

# Thirty-One

***Urlick***

"All right, so what's the plan?" Sadar rubs his hands together. His eyes indicate he's eager to get moving. And fearless. Completely fearless.

I like that in a fellow *crazed-about-to-bust-into-an-asylum* comrade.

"I'm not sure we 'ave a plan." C.L. turns to me, forlorn looking. He seems nervous, completely thrown. *This* worries me.

I snap the Dyechrometer shut. I've been measuring heartbeats. Happy with the reading, I tuck it in my pocket. No one out here but us. "Tell me about the moving walls," I say to C.L., not caring if I've exposed his secret. We haven't time for that now, anyway. "How much do you know about them? Do they ever cease?"

"Not as far as I know." C.L. hangs his head. His cheeks turn red.

"Is there a pattern? Do they shift in a certain sequence?"

"Yes." Martin steps up. "They do." He pulls out a small notebook and pencil and shows me some figurings. "I've been watching them, tirelessly, as we've sat up here waiting for your arrival. Near as I can figure, it's a six-sequence movement, repeated half-hourly. See, I've recorded it here."

"How? How are they doing that?"

"Well, of that part, I'm not sure." Martin scratches his head. "You see, the walls appear to shift from this side, here"—he points at the building through the murky fog—"clean over to there." He points to the other side. "Then they switch back, alternating forward and backward the entire way. The movement gives the illusion that the building is in constant movement—"

"But you think it isn't."

"That's right. I think it's a trick. Some sort of moving picture."

My suspicions are confirmed. I've thought, since I first noticed them moving across the horizon line, that it all seems too perfect. There is no possible way a foundation could shift, especially under a building of that magnitude. I thought it had to be some sort of grand sleight of hand. Some magical illusion.

"I think they're moving, sir," C.L. interjects. "In fact, I know they're moving."

I wave him away with my hand.

"What's most interesting about this," Martin continues, "is that the fence moves opposite the building, in exactly the reverse pattern."

"Let me see that." I take his book and study the drawing. I break loose from the group and parade toward the structure, squinting, a thought burning in my mind. The dancing fence line that surrounds Gears operates on heat sensors, as did the gates at the Academy. Perhaps this one does, too. I swing around and stare at Martin. "You're sure this is an illusion."

"Yes, sir. The walls seem to be responding to the lights."

"What lights?"

"Watch closely"—Martin places his hand on my shoulder—"and you'll see them pass over the moving parts of the building, and back again, the lens always trolling, the movement always occurring after a puff of steam. Try to concentrate only on the light shadows, not the actual image of the building, and you'll see what I mean."

I squint, observing the building closely—as closely as I can through rents in the thick, black, rolling fog. Sadar and Reeke step up with us, also squinting. At first I don't see it; then I keep my eyes focused, and it is as Martin says. The trolling light creeps ever slowly across the front façade of the stones, followed by a rippling shift in the building after a giant pulse of steam. When I concentrate hard enough, I think I even detect the split in the frames of the photos they've used to create the images. But where are they coming from? I whirl around, tracking the lens's haze. "It's smoke and mirrors," I say, flying off toward the bushes. "Literally smoke and mirrors!" I pick up a stick and start to beat the bushes. "The projector must be up here somewhere."

"No, it's not, sir." C.L. bolts forward. "Trust me, that building is moving! The walls, they do shift."

Iris stares at us, bewildered.

I ignore them both, pick up a bigger limb, and move deeper into the woods.

"Where are you going?" C.L. shouts after me.

"To find the mirrors and smash them!" I say.

"Wait!" Martin chases after me. "Do you think that's wise?"

"It'll be much easier to ambush a stationary building."

"Yes, but it will also spark a lot of attention, don't you think?" Martin narrows his gaze.

I run my eyes over the skeptical crew before me: Martin, C.L., Iris, Masheck, the rest of the freaks—it seems they all agree. C.L.'s quivering bottom lip gives me pause, but I turn and continue the quest anyway, chopping at underbrush with the branch as I go. We're running out of time to save Eyelet. I have to find out.

*

A sharp, short whistle draws my head up. I turn to see Cordelia pulling her fingers from the corners of her mouth. Iris stands beside her.

By the looks on their faces I can tell they've found something. I drop the branch in my hand and gallop through the mist. "What is it?" I say, bounding. "Did you find the"—I stop short, my mouth dangling open—"*mirrors*." The word lingers on my steamy breath as I raise my chin, my mind drinking in the sight of them.

As tall as the trees, protected by a rolling hillside of bramble bushes, perched in a semicircle on the highest point of the ridge, sit six massive, six-paneled, horizontal mirrors, each clamped into a metal stand. Below them, the nozzles of six giant guns poke out from the earth, purging great wafts of steam. They alternate every few minutes in a pattern from left to right. Martin was correct.

Each suspended segment of mirror is positioned on a slightly different tilt, covering an array of angles up to 180 degrees. A cog-and-wheel assembly built behind the mirrors controls their movement, constantly switching their angles. The whole contraption runs on steam, the force of which twists and tilts the mirrors, causing an illusion of movement. Much like the old game I played as a kid, rendering etchings on the edges of the paper of a book, each one slightly different from the last, so that the image appeared to move when you riffled the pages quickly. Only this projection is on the grandest scale.

C.L. stumbles up beside me. "Blustering blimey." He lets out a breath. His eyes bug from his head.

*What do we do now?* Iris signals.

"We smash them, that's what." I pick up a stout branch.

"No, no, no!" Sadar shouts, grabbing me by the arm. "You can't!"

"Why not?"

"Because of these." Martin pokes a stick through the thorny protection of the brambles, revealing a blinking light under mossy cover at the base of each mirror. "They're equipped with alarms. You smash one and you'll give the whole mission away. Then we'll never get to Eyelet."

I stare at the blinking light he's exposed, not unlike that of our own Guardian system. He's right, we can't risk triggering them off. "Blast it!" I pull a hand through my hair.

I lower my head, defeated. How will we get to Eyelet now? By morning, they'll be searching for us. We only have tonight to get in there. My mind spins through a jumble of clocks and Brigsmen and ticking time—and Eyelet trapped in an asylum with God knows what going on. "What do we do?" I turn back to Martin. "How do we leave the mirrors alone and still find the building?"

"We could try to disable the alarm," he says.

"But that'll take time." Reeke steps up.

"Time we don't have," I say.

"What if we only damage them enough to disrupt the pattern, without actually settin' off the alarms?" C.L. says.

"What are you thinking?" I say as he ducks behind the mirrors.

"Once, when I was a kid, I accidently scraped the silverin' off the back of me muvver's mirror, and wrecked it. She was mad as a wet hen at me. Perhaps if we did the same thing, only on a larger scale—not touch 'em, but just scratch 'em enough to disrupt the sequence, send the 'ole thing 'aywire, without triggerin' the alarm."

"I'm afraid I don't follow." I shake my head.

"Mirrors need a clean slate of silvering in order to project an image," Martin explains. He scurries up the hillside, joining C.L., stone tip in his hand. "Smashing the mirrors will draw too much attention. But if we were just to carve some the silvering off the back . . ." He raises the stone, pantomiming the action in the air.

"Then the full image won't project," I say. "I've got it." I clap my hands together. *I've finally got it.* "It's a brilliant plan. We'll scrape just enough to disrupt the process and let us find the real building, buying us time before the authorities clue in." I turn. "Iris, do you have a hairpin?"

"I think it's gonna take more than an 'airpin, sir," C.L. says. "Them's big mirrors."

Iris jumps into action, hauling up her modest skirts, pulling a needle-nose knife with a serrated edge from out of her high-topped boots.

"Iris!" I avert my eyes, shocked by her behaviour. "Learn that from Eyelet, did you?" I say. Iris grins maniacally. *Among other things*, she signs.

"Here, give me that." I swipe away the knife. "Before someone's missing an eye."

Iris laughs as I trudge up the hillside, joining C.L. and Martin in the brambles. "Now." I stare up at the massive mirrors towering over our heads. "How are we going get up there?"

# Thirty-Two

***Eyelet***

"Please." I struggle. "I've done nothing wrong. Honestly. I'm being held here against my will."

"If I 'ad a jewelet for every inmate told me that in 'ere . . ." The guard's laugh claps off the walls of the asylum's basement corridor as he pushes me onward down the hall. It's cold and dark in the basement, and my legs don't work quite right yet. Lit by only a single flame above our heads, it resembles a crypt. I half expect to see graves.

"It's true!" I dig in my heels as he yanks me round another corner. "I've done nothing! Absolutely nothing! You have to listen to me! I shouldn't be here! I'm not even crazy!"

"I dun' 'ave to listen to nuthin'." The guard reels me in and barks in my ear. My ribs slam hard against his. "I only 'ave to make sure I deliver yuh to the butcher!"

He slings me forward into a small, whitewashed room. I stumble and fall to the stone floor. "No, please." I scramble to my knees, but it's too late, he's already slammed the door.

"Don't worry." The guard sticks his face against a tiny iron screen in the door. "By mornin' yuh won't remember nothin' 'bout nothin'." He grins. "Yuh won't even know 'oo you are."

"What are you saying?" I fling myself toward him.

"You'll see." He breaks into a cackling laugh, triggers the lock, and turns his back, and suddenly I'm alone.

An inmate across the hall from me lets out a spine-bending shriek, and I shrink down the back of the door, hands over my ears, my heart trembling.

*Oh, Urlick . . . if by the grace of God, C.L.'s somehow managed to save you . . . please find a way to save me.*

# Thirty-Three

***Urlick***

"Over. Over. That's it . . . that's *iiiit.* That's *iiiit.*" I guide C.L. as he yanks on the levers. Gears grind, the giant golden mastodon's head below my arse, swinging right and left.

"Just a little more," I urge him.

C.L. shifts gears again, and I claw at the elephant, holding on to his ears, fighting to stay straddling the beast's rounded head.

"Sorry," C.L. shouts, trying again, slower this time, raising the elephant's head up as high as he can and snugging it in close to the back of the mirror.

"Perfect!" I slip down the front of the elephant's skull onto his trunk and pull the knife from my boot. "Now, as I carve, swing its head and lower it as quickly as possible, all in one motion. That way, the damage will appear erratic and not planned."

"But won't you—"

"With any luck I'll be able to ride it out." I tug at my waistcoat. "Ye of little faith." I scowl. "Believe it or not, I've wrangled a bull or two in my day."

"You 'ave, sir?" C.L. pops his head out from the controls inside the elephant's chest.

"Well, in a dream state, yes." I blink down at him. "But this can't be very different, can it?"

C.L. laughs and returns to his perch. "Right, sir." He grabs hold of the throttle. "Ready?"

"One can only hope." I cross my chest.

"On three." C.L. yanks back on the controls. I grab the elephant's ear. The elephant bobbles. "One. Two."

"Steady," I shout, slipping down.

C.L. strips another gear, and I'm flung up in the air a good three metres, leaving the elephant's trunk altogether. Clinging to his ear as I swing back down, clamping my legs around a tusk.

"Sorry," C.L. mutters, looking up at my swinging bottom.

I put the knife between my teeth and crawl back up. Standing, I reach out as far as possible, knife poised in the air. "Now!" I shout and lean forward, driving the tip of the knife into the mirror's backing. C.L. springs into action and the elephant descends, head flopping this way and that down to the ground, snapping and snaking in every direction. My shoes slip and slide over the elephant's shiny metal-skin trunk, erratically scarring the mirror down to the glass.

Flakes of silvering fall as we drop. I wince, half expecting sirens.

"It worked!" Martin hollers as I tumble off into the brambles. "The lights! They're shorting out!"

I look up through the thorns, seeing the image of the Brink faltering, my lost knife slicing torpedo-like through the air over my head. I close my eyes, and the knife comes to rest with the *thwack* of a hatchet, point side down, between my legs.

"That was close," C.L. says.

"Yes, it was." I sit up, prickled in thorns. "Again."

*

C.L. swoops down with the elephant's trunk and plucks me out of the brambles, dropping me to the ground in front of the others.

"All right, everyone, listen up." I stagger on my feet. "We have very little time before they figure out they've been ambushed."

"Urlick's right," Martin says. "They'll know something's gone awry very soon, if not already." He looks down at my pocket watch. "Within the hour, I assume—"

"How did you get hold of that?"

"Sorry, sir." He sheepishly hands it over. "Old habits die hard, I'm afraid."

"Right." I scowl and snatch it from him. "C.L., you're coming with me. Martin, Reeke, Wanda, Cordelia, and Sadar, you wait up the road a stretch, hidden in those bushes there"—I point—"and prepare yourselves for our getaway."

"Yes, sir!" Sadar clacks his heels and salutes me.

"What say you, Masheck?" I turn my eyes to the brawny brute. "You up for a little challenge?"

"Always." He tightens his fists.

"Good!" I slap him on the back. "Iris, we'll need you to run interference. In case we run into guards."

Iris nods and takes her mount on Clementine.

"Not on her, on him." I turn and point at the elephant. "C.L., give her a quick lesson on how to operate him, will you?"

C.L. scurries over, helping Iris up by way of the elephant's leg.

"Let me do it, sir." Martin steps up, standing solider-straight in front of me. "I'll take the elephant up. Battle's no place for a woman."

Iris snaps around, her eyes looking furious.

"I'd never say that again, if I were you." I pat Martin on the shoulder. "Besides, out of all of you, I'd least like to tangle with Iris." I smile, swooping down to collect C.L.'s pack off the ground. "Did you bring the Dyechrometer?" I ask him.

"Yes, sir. I brought everything I could think of."

"That you did," I say, squinting and looking in the pack. "Ahhh, the candlesnuffer-mace-ejector, wonderful choice . . . with the whip-adapted morning stars. Oh, and the miniature fire-poker serrated *shuriken*—very good. Steam-powered ripsaw. Nail blaster. Can opener." I take inventory one by one. "Doorstopper. Eggbeater. A set of injectable reed darts." I look up and wink. "I see Iris has been busy again." I turn to Martin. "Here. This is for you." I pull out four miniature cans of what appears to be harmless tinned fish and pass them over. "Should things get out of hand up here on the hill, pull back the tabs."

Martin stares hard at the tins of fish. He smiles at me warily.

"Ready?" I nod at Masheck.

"I'm already gone," he says, rubbing his palms together.

"All right, then." I swing up onto Clementine, feeling the buzz of fearful anticipation in my stomach. My heart brims with hope at the thought of seeing Eyelet again. *Please let me see Eyelet again.* "Let's get on with this, shall we?" I reach down for C.L., giving him a hoist up. He drops into the saddle seat behind me as I take up the reins. "Until then." I tip my head at the rest.

Clementine dances around in a circle as Masheck climbs aboard behind us, facing backward on the horse's bum behind the saddle, steam bow and arrow raised just in case.

"It's nine now," I say to Iris. "If you don't hear from us by ten, you'll know it's time for more drastic measures." I toss her a serious look. "All right, we're off!" I drag the reins over the side of Clementine's neck, turning her. "Remember," I say to Martin before spurring the horse's sides. "If things go hairy the rest of you just get out of here. Don't worry about us."

*

We circle twice before landing. Clementine settles down on the rooftop as softly as her hooves will allow. Her armour clanks slightly against the slate shingles as she lowers her wings to her sides. "Good girl." I lean forward and pat her neck.

Masheck kicks up his heels and dismounts off the back. He lands catlike, not even a rustle. It's clear he's had experience at this. C.L. pitches off next, landing not-so-gracefully. Slate shingles tremble under his feet.

The air fills with the rickety crank of poorly oiled gears. A searchlight, mounted on the widow's peak of the roof next to us, swings, scanning the premises. I dive off Clementine's back and hide behind a nearby chimney, dragging Clem along to cover her as well. If they didn't hear us before, they know we're here now.

The other two follow suit, scrambling to hide, their backs pressed up against another chimney. The roof seems to be covered in them. There must be a least five.

Fragmented light sputters across the lawn of the massive stone building, whipping back around and over our heads, taking repeat passes over the property.

"What do we do now?" C.L. calls to me softly.

*"Whhhhtttt!"* Masheck whistles. Slivers of him slink in and out of view around the searchlight's beam. His head bobs up and down out of the mouth of the biggest chimney in the centre of the roof, avoiding the light's sweep. "I think I may have solved it." He pats the side of the bricks. "Come on. This chute leads to the laundry, I think."

I glare over at Masheck. "You're not serious?"

"You got a better idea?" Masheck squints.

"But what if it doesn't?"

"Well then, I guess we end up in the soup."

"But—" I don't know how I imagined us getting in, but whatever it was, it didn't involve tumbling freely down a chimney.

"You comin' or not?" Masheck says, ducking the next pass of the light.

I do the same, my heart squeezing in my chest. Time's running out.

"All right," I say and slap Clementine on the rear, sending her flying off the side of the roof, then I leap into action, shinnying up to the top of the chimney's stack. "What now?" I ask Masheck, teetering on its edge.

"Follow me," he says, unfastening the belt on his trousers.

My eyes grow wide. "We've got to do this in the buff?"

"No." Masheck shakes his head, laughing. "We need to use our belts as leverage."

"Oh."

He makes a loop round his shoulder, then lowers himself into the chimney's hole, just his bottom, bicep muscles straining to hold the rest of him up. "Like this." He grins, and I feel every bit of my manhood being challenged as he lowers himself gracefully below the brick. Back to one wall, feet pressed tight to the other, quick as lightning he begins his controlled descent, walking his feet down one side of the bricks, his backside sliding down the other, travelling the inside of the chimney to the hearth like a pro.

Clearly it isn't the first time he's done this. Or so I convince myself. I imagine him dropping into rich people's houses all over Brethren, pinching their expensives, though no one mentioned he was a thief.

Elsewise, how would someone gain such a skill? He's not Saint Nicholas, for blimey's sake.

I follow, much less gracefully, crumpling at the neck when my feet get behind my bottom, my head clapping hard off the brick. Growing fearful I may fold completely over and fall headfirst, I stop the progression by throwing my hands out to the chimney's greasy sides, giving my feet time to catch up and try again, still sliding. C.L. snickers overhead.

"Wait till it's your turn!" I whisper-shout back at him.

He only laughs and pulls away.

I make it to the bottom with a bit of a crash, my arse significantly higher upon landing than it should have been, my head ringing off the prongs of the iron cradle in the hearth. I buckle and roll out onto the carpet, stung, a slick, gasping, creosote-coated ball. "First time?" Masheck kids, giving me a hand up.

I smirk at him, then cough, sputter, wipe the soot from my eyes, and take in the surroundings—a true laundress's haven. Masheck was right. The room is filled with wash buckets and fold tables; a coal bin and shovels stand next to the giant hot-water stove. Bicycle-powered drying racks shunt and swing with train-wheel precision through the centre of the room, over a furrow dug into the floor, teeming with hot coals.

C.L. lands with a bit of a boom, his legs tangled in the grate. Extricating himself, he bangs his head on the metal prongs and whacks his backbone.

"Better make ourselves scarce, fast." He jumps up, surprisingly agile after such a crash. "Laundry duty starts at ten."

"How do you know that?" Masheck says.

"Long story." I slap him in the chest as I pass.

C.L. leads the way, springing out the doors at the north end of the room.

Masheck and I follow.

C.L. tiptoes out into the main hall, first checking right and left. He flattens his back to the wall, motioning for us to do the same, drawing a nervous toe up over his lips to shush us.

Voices fill the corridor a short distance away—giggling voices, one high, one low.

C.L. moves quickly, slipping in between two juts of wall, down a narrow—*too narrow for humans*—hallway. I dart after him, then signal for Masheck. He barely makes it before the voices start up again.

"What is that?" A voice comes from the end of the hallway.

I press back against the stone wall and suck in my stomach.

"This way," C.L. whispers, racing to the end of the passageway. There, he activates a turnstile of bricks that throws us into a sort of alternate dimension. We spin inside a fugue of steam, and a seam in the bricks mysteriously parts. C.L. yanks us through the cranny.

"Where are we?" I say, waving away the trolling black mist that engulfs us, baffled by the nothingness that appears. No floor. No walls. Just dark nothingness.

"We're in the world between the walls," C.L. answers.

"We're what?" Masheck makes a grim face.

"Don't worry, we won't be 'ere long. We can't afford to be."

C.L. reaches out, groping the air, tapping invisible bricks with his toes until at last we hear a solid clunk. "Follow me," he says quickly, pushing at the spot. The air warps around him.

Masheck and I do the same, sucked into some sort of semispinning vortex. There is more blackness, then light, then blackness again. Then an unexplained, mind-crushing pressure has me throwing my hands to my temples. "What *is* that?" I gasp. "What's happening?"

C.L. reaches for me, hurling me through the edge of a dark membrane. I trip out into the same corridor where we were before. Or at least it seems to be. The pressure from my head finally lifts. My ears pop, and I swallow. "We've lost Masheck," I say, whirling around. "Masheck, he's not here."

Just as my heart ramps up speed, C.L. reaches in between the seam of the bricks and retrieves him, pulling him out through the dark seal in the wall with a pop.

"What just happened?" Masheck says, rubbing his head.

"I dunno," C.L. says. "All I know is if yuh get trapped between there, yer a goner."

He turns his attention back to the hallway, looking left and right before dashing out.

Masheck and I scramble to catch up with him, flying past flickering candlelit sconces.

The floors are made of stone, but the walls have now changed to smooth steel. I've never in my life seen anything like it. Another sound erupts at the other end of the corridor, and our heads swing around.

Boots drum their way toward us.

"Let's go," C.L. shouts, heading off in the opposite direction.

"Where are we going?" I hiss after him.

"To the barracks," C.L. says, swiping a flaming sconce from the wall. His eyes are a brilliant shade of silver in the light. "They keep the women on the uppermost floors, which is sort of an illusion considering you come in through the basement. But, anyway, by my calculations, we should find Eyelet there!"

"We should, or we will?"

"I dunno."

# Thirty-Four

***Eyelet***

I struggle against the restraints, strapped to a hard operating-theatre chair in the centre of a white windowless room. Shiny metal objects cover a smooth-surfaced table next to me. My breath lopes in my chest as I stare at them, the edges of scalpels peeking out from under a blanket of gauze. "You don't have to do this," I gasp, squirming.

"Don't I?" The guard's woolly brow jumps upward. He flicks bubbles from the sharp-needled syringe in his hand and places it on the metal table next to me.

I look around, desperate for a way to escape, but there is none. Only one door and it's been sturdily locked. My legs are shackled to the bottom of the chair, my wrists belted down to the armrests. Even my neck has been harnessed to the headrest in back. I'll never be able to get out of this.

I look up, blinded by the interrogation-style light shining directly into my eyes. "Please, you can't do this! I've done nothing . . ."

"I'll take it from here." A voice drifts into the room. The guard leaps to unlock the door. A cool swish of dragging silk scrapes over the stones, then Parthena's veiled face appears over me. Her grey, almond-shaped eyes are narrowed and fierce. "Leave us," she says in a low, calculating tone.

The guard lowers his head and scrambles from the room, locking the door behind him. Parthena picks up the needle on the table next to me.

"Why are you doing this?" I struggle. "What have I done?"

She ignores me, picking up the loaded syringe and test-plunging it into the air.

"Please, don't do this. I've done nothing to you."

"That's right. You've done something far worse." She leans closer. "You've wronged my *sister*."

I shudder as the corners of her lips curl into a wicked smile. There's a strange light in her eyes.

"Penelope is your sister, isn't she? You are her twin?"

Something cold flashes in Parthena's eyes, and I have my answer. She turns her back to me and engages a machine. Electricity crackles in the air as she twists the knobs.

"Why do you listen to her? Why do you carry out her requests?" I gasp. "What power does she hold over you?"

*"Shut up!"* Parthena whirls around. The skirt of her mourning gown binds at her knees.

"She does, doesn't she? She holds power over you. Her very word is your command—"

"Our arrangement is none of your business!" Parthena hisses.

"What arrangement?" I heave.

"I told you to close your mouth." She pinches my chin. Unkempt brows crouch over her vengeful eyes. She stares at me long and hard. "Tell me, while you still can. How did you kill him?"

"What?"

"Smrt. How did you do him *in*?" Her lips are quivering, but not out of fear or anger—it's something else.

"What do you care how your sister's lover died?"

She strikes me, her hand rapping hard across my cheek.

"Answer the question!" she shouts through her teeth.

"I—I . . ."

*"You killed him with your bare hands, didn't you?"* Her voice is shaking, her eyes strangely filling with tears. "Or did you have your little boyfriend do it for you? Tell me"—she leans in—"did it happen instantly, or do you still have nightmares of him gasping in his last breaths?" Her voice fills the room. "Answer me. How did it happen?"

I stare into her hardened eyes. "He wasn't your sister's lover, was he?" I finally say.

She falters backward, as if I've just electrocuted her with my words.

"It was you, wasn't it? *You* were Smrt's lover, not your sister. That's why you want to know—"

*"Lies."* Parthena's voice trembles. *"All LIES!"* she shouts.

"That's why they put you in here. She had you put away. Just like she has all the others."

*"GUARD!"* Parthena turns, grabs up her skirts, and pitches herself at the door.

A photograph tumbles from her pocket as she turns. It comes to a rest near my feet at the leg of the chair. The gaze of a child stares up at me: the image of a babe, not more than a year, with bright grey eyes and a head of dark curls—and a harrowingly damaged lip.

The story Urlick shared with me in the woods comes flooding back, of Flossie's presumed and unplanned entry into the world. The product of Smrt and his supposed Academy-colleague lover . . . "It *was* you," I say breathlessly. "You bore the child, not Penelope."

Parthena lunges, snatching the photo from the floor. She stuffs it in her pocket, and pounds at the door.

"That's why you're here! You disgraced your family, so they put you away!"

*"Guard!"* she shouts.

"They took her from you, didn't they?"

She whirls back around, her brows fiercely knit.

"The child. They took her from you and hid her in the woods."

"What are you talking about?" Parthena's voice cracks.

"You don't know, do you?"

Parthena's eyes grow small and heavy. "The child is dead," she seethes. "Died many years ago."

The guard appears behind her. He throws open the door, and Parthena launches through it.

"No, wait!" I shout after her. "It's not true!"

An ether-doused cloth drops over my face, and the room begins to turn.

# *Thirty-Five*

***Urlick***

Masheck and I follow C.L. to a metal spiral staircase and wind along behind him toward the top. The stairs grow narrower and narrower as we ascend, and I stumble, my feet too big for the systematically shrinking treads.

"How much farther?" I say.

"Not much," C.L. answers, twining around the stairs' centre post. "When we get to the top, we'll need to get past the dorm-warden's office before we can get into the coop," he whispers.

"The coop?" I say.

"The henhouse. Where they keep the dingy dames. The guards call it the coop."

"I see," I reply, taken back by the cruelty of the Madhouse slang. To think poor Eyelet has been stuck between these walls and treated like a madwoman. I look round at all the fencing and chains. I pray no harm has come to her.

C.L. creeps up the final step, heaves in a breath, and presses his back to the wall. Masheck and I follow, squishing in shoulder to shoulder.

"There's the guard hut there." C.L. points to a tiny, fenced-in box next to a gate, leading down a fully fenced corridor. Even the roof of the corridor is covered by cage. This is serious lockup. "I'll keep 'im busy, whilst yuh two muscle yer way through the gate." C.L. turns to me.

I glance back at Masheck, thinking how much more suitable he is to muscle his way in than me.

"They's a pair o' tin snips 'angin' on the back wall of every guard's post, just in case the inmates ever riot and lock them up in their own cages," C.L. explains. "Nip in there and steal 'em and use 'em to cut the locks."

"You really do know this place, don't you?" I turn my head.

"Aye, sir. I am a bit of an expert on the subject, I'm ashamed to say."

"And then what do we do?"

"What do you mean, then what do we do? We go and save Eyelet."

"What about the guard?" I whisper loudly.

"Don't worry about 'im." Masheck steps up, rolling his fist in his hand.

"What's that supposed to mean?" I twist around.

"Ready?" C.L. hisses. With the speed of a mink, he dives out from behind the jut in the wall. He dances round in front of the guard's post, jabbering gibberish, tongue flicking in and out of his mouth like a lunatic. "Oi!" C.L. shouts, jumping up and down on the metal-grate catwalk like a monkey. "'Ey, you! That's right, you!" He jams a toe through the wires of the warden's cage. "You big ugly bear, you!"

The warden's eyes pop open, and his arms unfold from what appears to be a position of sleep. He drops the newspaper under which he's been concealing his nap and scowls hard at C.L., his underbitten jaw showing angry teeth.

"Yeah, that's right, I've woken you up! Whatchu gonna do 'bout it, big boy?" C.L. continues dancing, his head tottering side to side.

A monster of a man rises, and I flinch. His discarded stool rings the metal cage behind him as he stands. He growls, busting open the hut door with such whiplike speed, I don't even see him unlock it.

"You wanna go, *Crazy*?" He grits his teeth, launching in C.L.'s direction.

"'Urry, quick!" C.L. shouts.

The monster licks his lips as if he's about to devour C.L. for breakfast. He curls his mitt-sized fist and takes a swing. C.L. ducks the punch, relieving the guard of his key ring in the process and tossing it to me with a flick of his toes.

I capture the key ring midair and bounce toward the gate, fumbling through the *billion* choices, as the warden launches another punch—cut short by Masheck's wild right hook.

The warden's jaw rocks side to side as he falls in a blacked-out heap to the ground. His melon rings loudly off the metal floor of the catwalk.

"Well, that's the end of 'im," C.L. grins.

Masheck smiles as he shakes out his hand.

"Come on!" I say, snagging the tin snips from the post and snapping the gate open. "As good as that was, it's not gonna last."

"Yuh underestimate me?" Masheck says as the three of us spring through the door.

"She should be somewheres in this section 'ere," C.L. pants, racing to the end block. Frantically, we check each cell as we go, ducking our heads in and out of the bars. Women shout and scream, clutching their belongings. I dash round a skinny corner to the next set of cages, amid the cacophony of female shrieks.

It's bad enough with C.L. peering in at them, but quite another range of terror when I stick my face in. I've forgotten how horrifying I look.

*The sheer volume of their screeching may give us away.*

"Let me go first." C.L. dashes out in front of me.

"No." I clap his shoulder and drag him back. "I need to find her. She's *my* Eyelet. I don't care what happens here." I push past both him and Masheck and continue my search. *"Eyelet!"* I cling to the cages, scanning their occupants. "Eyelet? Eyelet, where *are* you?"

"Does anyone know of an Eyelet Elsworth?" C.L. cups a foot to his mouth and shouts over the screaming. "Brownish hair. Amber eyes. She'd be fairly new 'ere."

"Anyone?" Masheck shouts, following. "Anyone at all?"

"There!" A grimy old urchin of a woman shouts out, her stand-up white hair peeking through a strainer hat. "Over there!" She points a gnarled finger. "They's a new one bunked in with ol' blondie there! Three cells from the end!"

"Thank you," I say and burst into a run, my boots slamming hard against the metal catwalk grates. C.L. follows. Masheck hangs back, trying to quiet the crowd, now rattling their bars and chirping like wild chimpanzees.

I wheel myself up in front of the cell the woman indicated. My eyes fall on the girl resting on a cot. Her back is to me, her face pressed against a stone partition, her hair twisted up in a ratty bun. "Eyelet?" I say breathlessly, clinging to the iron bars that separate us. "Eyelet, is that you?"

The girl flings around. Her shoulder-length blonde locks spill around her face. She nearly falls off of the cot.

"You're not Eyelet." I deflate, disappointment exuding from me.

"I sure as *'ell* am not," the girl scoffs. She sits up, stares at me. "'Oo are yuh to be askin', anyway?" Her pixie-like smile dampens into something more sinister.

"I've come for Eyelet. I'm here to save her. Where is she?"

The girl tosses back her blanket and pops to her feet. Her eyes rake over me suspiciously. "Yer assumin' I know 'er." She pinches her hips. "Maybe I don't."

"You're her roommate, aren't you?"

"I might be. Who's asking?" She struts cautiously toward me.

"The name's Urlick, Urlick Babbit."

"And who's that?" She narrows her already-narrow eyes.

Shouldn't she know me? Wouldn't Eyelet have mentioned me to her?

"Give me one good reason I should be tellin' yuh anything," the girl continues, her chin snapped up cockily.

"Because I've risked my life to come and save hers, that's why!" I blurt. "Now, please, tell me where she is!" I bang a hand on the bars.

The girl jumps. "Yer not gonna 'arm 'er, are yuh?"

"Never." I shake my head.

Alarm bells clamour overhead. The lights begin to flash.

"Please," I say. "If you know where she is, for the love of God, tell me."

"Gotta go, chief." Masheck races up beside me. "The guards, they's on their way up the stairs at the other end."

I look down the corridor, seeing a swarm of guard-uniform blue winding up the staircase.

*"Oooooh!"* the girl purrs, her eyes flashing at the sight of Masheck. "Look at *yuh*!" She primps her hair and bats her eyes at him. "Quite the specimen, aren'tchu."

C.L. scoots up next, panting and breathless. The girl's head swings in his direction.

"Oh. *My.* Goodness . . ." she gasps, bringing a fluttering hand to her more-than-ample chest. "Aren't *yuh* an interesting one?" She bats her eyes at him. "'Ave I died and gone to 'eaven?" She drapes a dramatic hand over her forehead.

"Can we focus here?" I shout and her head snaps back down. "Eyelet." I repeat. "Where is *she*!"

"Locked up behind the torture gates." The girl coos, licking her lips, never taking her eyes off C.L. "I can take yuh to 'er, if yuh'd like." She smiles at me.

"I'd like."

"Quickly," Masheck says, grabbing the keys and tossing them off to C.L, guards gaining at our backs.

"C.L.?" I nudge him, he and the girl still caught in a stargaze. "Open her cell door, please!"

"Oh . . . yeah," he stammers, drops his head, and fumbles through the ring until at last he finds the right key.

"Come with me," the girl says, threading her arm around C.L.'s waist as she slinks from her cell. "I knows a way the guards knows nothin' about."

*

The girl moves with incredible stealth and speed, weaving in and out of the shadows of the dimly lit, cobwebbed basement corridors of this building between the walls. She is truly finessed in finagling her way around this establishment—even better than C.L.—leaving a dead-stopped, buzzing hive of baffled guards in her wake.

"This way," she hisses behind a curved hand, shoving us through another tiny passageway in the stone corridor. We have to duck our heads to enter, reduced to crawling on our hands and knees as the space becomes narrower and narrower.

"How did you know this was here?" I ask.

"I know all the tangled webs the ol' Brink weaves." The girl grins back at me over her shoulder.

"How long 'ave you been in 'ere?" Masheck asks, crawling along behind me.

"Dunno," the girl answers. "Don't remember." She makes a troubled face. "I might 'ave been eleven, maybe twelve when I come 'ere?" She poses it like a question, like we might know better than her. "The guards'll know. They's the ones that remember for me. God knows I can't do it for meself." She crawls on, then stops.

"I'm Livinea, by the way." She sticks a hand back at me. "Livinea Langtry." She winks at C.L., who nearly crawls right into Masheck.

"Langtry, as in the moving-picture star?" C.L. trips on his knees.

"You know 'er?" Livinea's head swings around, her eyes delighted.

"Well, no . . . not personally." C.L. drops his chin.

"Oh," Livinea says.

I shake her hand.

"Livinea," C.L. offers quickly. "That's a purdy name."

"Thank you!" Livinea perks up again. "What do they call you?" She pushes her gaze past me exaggeratedly, making sure I don't mistakenly answer.

"C.L." He grins like a fool. "Stands for Crazy Legs," he adds. "That's me performing name."

"Yer a performer, too?"

"Of sorts." He blushes. "Me real name's Ernest. But ain't nobody but me mum use that name, though."

"Ernest." The girl breathes the word slowly. "It's got a real earnest sound to it." She smiles.

C.L. smiles, too.

I flash a look back at C.L., trying to tell him to stop acting like an idiot, but it's too late—I can tell by the goony grin on his lips he's too far gone already.

The girl crawls on, then stops abruptly, swinging open a trapdoor in the floor at the end of the tunnel. The lid creaks up into the air. "'Ere we are," she says, dropping through the hole without warning. She whoops as she falls, disappearing like Alice through the rabbit hole, skirts flying up around her ears. Candlelight shoots up all around her from the room beneath, cloaking her image in golden rays. It's like she has no care in the world—or no sense at all.

"Just drop your feet over the edge, then thrust your hips forward. It's easy." She demonstrates. My eyes pop as she thrusts her hips forward. I don't know what to make of this girl. "And prepare for a jolt when you land," she adds, giggling. "It'll put 'air on your chest, it will."

I sit and hang my legs over the side of the hole, cautiously, following her instructions, feeling a little uncomfortable about the thrust in mixed company. My heart lurches up into my throat as my hips drop through the hole. The sudden light blinds me. I land—she was right—with a knee-crushing jolt. C.L. and Masheck follow, nearly landing on top of me.

Livinea giggles as we peel out of our heap.

C.L. giggles with her.

My eyes finally focus on the room. It is filled with unthinkable things. A miniature guillotine blade shudders in its mount in the darkened corner; whips and shackles *tink* together over the form of an iron maiden. Stretcher racks, lining the walls, rattle under the pouncing weight of Masheck and C.L. landing. "What is this place?"

"This 'ere's the torture storeroom," Livinea answers matter-of-factly.

"Is that a Spanish donkey?" I stumble toward it, pointing, then gulp and step away. The apparatus is displayed like a prize in the centre of the room.

"I think that's what they calls it."

I remember reading about this and other torture devices in the *Mandatory Civil Deterrent Handbook* Flossie brought from the Academy. I'd half hoped those manuals were a joke. Every potential graduate had to study them. I remember lying long nights in my bed, shuddering at the sight of the drawings, nearly retching over their descriptions. All the while worrying in the back of my head: which would be used on me if I were ever discovered? The Spanish donkey gave me the greatest nightmares. And now here it is, in the place where Eyelet's being kept.

"I'm much more familiar with shock therapy, meself." Livinea grins, flashing her perfect white teeth. I can't help but think the most prejudiced thought. How did someone so strikingly beautiful end up in a place like this? Like anyone deserves to be here—as if *this* were only reserved for the ugly of the world. But still . . .

"What's shock therapy?" I turn and say.

Livinea points to a bed with many straps and a metal helmet attached to the end of it. Squiggly wires stretch from the helmet to a nearby machine with dials and screens.

"You mean to tell me they've electrocuted you?"

"Yes. Many times." She says it so matter-of-factly, like it's yesterday's postscript. My mind crashes like water over stones. I want to scream, *Not Eyelet, though, right? This hasn't happened to her.* "They electrocute people around here all the time," Livinea adds with a smile, and I feel my stomach curdle.

But before I have the chance to say another word, she's gone, pushing down the hallway through another set of doors.

"Livinea?" I dart after her. She moves so swiftly, it's hard to keep up. Masheck and C.L. sprint after me. We follow Livinea up a set of cast-iron stairs, then down another hall, where she comes to an abrupt stop in front of a windowless metal door. I slam into her back, excusing myself as Masheck does the same.

Livinea giggles, then something crashes on the other side of the wall, and she pulls a quick finger to her mouth. *"Shhhhh!"* she hisses, then throws out a hand, plastering all our backs to the wall.

My chest heaves under her grasp as we wait. I cringe, expecting to hear footsteps. Instead, a rumbling noise starts up behind us, faint at first and then steadily growing louder until I can feel its movement in my organs. Livinea's eyes pop open wider. "Oh, no!" she gasps. "We's too late!"

"What do you mean, too late? What is it? What's the matter?" I feel the floor begin to shimmy beneath our feet.

"It's a shift!" Livinea says, darting forward as the walls behind us tremble.

"A what?"

"Come *on*!" she shouts, clutching her skirts up high in white knuckles, breaking into a spirited run. Masheck and I move, him driving ahead of me just as the wall at our back rotates, batting C.L. from his feet before he has the chance to react.

"C.L.!" I shout, turning.

"Get up!" Livinea yells. "Get up and run!"

I reach for C.L., but it's too late. The wall turns, sweeping him away with it, C.L. caught in the churn.

"NO!" Livinea shouts and bolts back for him, slipping her arm behind the wall, grabbing C.L. by the shirt. With a grunt she hauls him out from behind it. He gasps and sputters, as the turning wall melts.

I burst into a run to try and escape what's happening, but I'm pulled down into the melting riptide current. C.L. loses his balance and falls in with me, too. Livinea turns back and lunges in after us, but her fingers don't quite reach. C.L. and I are pulled from her grasp by some strange centrifugal force I can't explain, and sent spiraling backward into the goop as the wall becomes a giant, grey ocean. The liquid is strangely cool, not hot as expected, more like vapour coming from a block of melting ice. My teeth crash together as my legs are heaved out from under me and I'm forced to swim.

"We've got to reach them or they're dead!" Livinea shouts to Masheck.

Masheck throws down his pack and punts forward, rushing into the ebbing, churning ocean of wall. Livinea throws her hands to her mouth to stifle her screams as metal gears grind and wheels screech.

I look up, seeing the other steel walls around us shifting, being slowly dragged over the stone floors, twisting, turning, melting, dropping, the whole building dissolving.

"C.L!" I shout, looking back. "Where are you?"

He surfaces, blinking molten metal from his eyes. It cools, and steely icicles cling to his lashes. "'Ere!" he says, pedaling his feet, trying to stay afloat. He lunges forward close enough for me to reach him, and I pull him to my chest. My arm around his middle, I continue to swim.

"My hand!" Masheck shouts, reaching out to us. "Grab my hand!"

The wall of water rushes now around his waist, knocking his feet from under him. He staggers back up and reaches again.

"I can't," I say, trying to keep my hold on C.L. "If I do, I'll lose him!"

"Then lose me!" C.L. shouts above the violent roar. "Go on ahead, sir." He turns to me, thick silvery-black water swelling around his neck. "Go on, save Eyelet—"

"No. I'm not going without you," I say, heaving him up into the silvery-grey solution. I lunge forward, digging a hand into the thick waters, kicking hard with my feet, launching C.L. ahead into Masheck's waiting grip.

Another wave of melted wall crashes, slamming against the tide I'm swimming in. Masheck turns, hurling C.L. to the shore of the floor just in time, then turns back for me. I dig into the current, sidestroking furiously against the silvery-grey waters, kicking as hard and as fast as I can. I make no progress. In fact, I lose ground. I don't understand this.

I look up to see yet another wall beginning to shift.

"'Urry!" Livinea's voice screeches out over the shifting gears. "If another wall turns, yuh'll be stuck 'ere forever!"

I look around. If I don't make it to the shore soon, I'll be closed in behind the second wall—or drown in it, if it, too, suddenly melts.

"Come on!" Masheck yells.

I suck in a breath and dip my head beneath the silver-grey line of liquid, point my fingers, and drive my arms through its metallic surface, hand over hand, violently thrashing my feet—but still, I go nowhere. It's as though the principles of physics have all been thrown out the window. I don't know what to do.

My heart lodges in my throat. I close my eyes and see Eyelet again. Alone in a cell, awaiting God knows what. I cannot fail her now.

I burst forward again as Masheck lunges out. Livinea screeches for him to come back. He doesn't listen and I thunder toward him, and finally my strokes are starting to stick, digging into the thick edges of the now-cooling, hardening metal sea. The tide has reversed and is pulling me slowly toward Masheck and the safety of the floor. I swim harder, digging my shoes into solidifying river.

"Reach!" Masheck throws out his arm.

All at once I'm inexplicably yanked forward inside a monstrous guttural groan. *Rrrrrrrrrrrrrrhhhh!*

Livinea claps her hands to my shoulders. Somehow she has waded in and reached me, sunk her fingers into the back of my coat collar, and hauled me to safety, up onto the stone floor. "Get up!" she shouts. "We've got to run! The walls are not finished!" She scrambles to her feet, yanking me with her. Globs of wall drain from our clothing as we bolt back to the opposite side of the room, Masheck following close behind us.

The last wall dissolves around us as we leap for solid floor, landing in tumbling heaps at C.L.'s shaky feet. I cough and sputter as a fully formed wall shoots up on the left of us and shifts into place, forming a new corridor. I stare at the activity, astonished, my heart a racing dog in my chest. C.L. swoops in, helping first Livinea back onto her feet and then Masheck and me.

"I told you the walls in 'ere moved, sir," he pants.

"So you did," I say, finding my footing and slapping him on the back.

"We'd better go!" Livinea says, spitting fragments of melted wall. "Before another shift."

"Another?" I say, struggling to collect my wits. "Wait!" I say, chasing after her. I grab her by the arm. "I owe you my life."

"Don't be sil-ly," Livinea chirps in her singsong voice. "Yuh don't owes me nothin'. The pleasure was all me."

*

"Eyelet should be somewheres in 'ere." Livinea comes to a stop in front of a block of cells. Smooth surgical-steel doors line the hall. Eight in total.

"What are these?"

"Holding cells." She launches up onto her toes, spying through the tiny wire-grid window at the top of one of the doors, checking inside one after another, her hopeful expression dissolving to a frown as she reaches the last in the block.

"What is it? What's the matter?"

"She ain't in 'ere," she says.

"What do you mean?" I throw myself at the doors, instinctively rechecking the windows, feeling the void of each room hit my stomach as I search.

"They must have already taken her to the laboratories," Livinea says quietly, wringing her hands.

*"Laboratories?"* I storm toward her. "Where? Where is that?"

"I dunno," she says, and my stomach flips. "I don't know 'ow to get there." She shakes her head. "I'm always drugged by that point. I can't remember the way."

"Think, Livinea!" I can't help myself; I shake her by the shoulders. "Think!"

"Look!" Masheck points to a trickle of dried, splattered blood on the floor. It forms a trail from one of the holding cells down a dimly lit corridor to the right.

I'm already running by the time Masheck takes another breath. I grab hold of the stone wall at the end of the corridor and hurtle myself around the corner, following the trail of the spattered blood. Masheck, Livinea, and C.L. thunder along behind me. I push through a set of swing doors and end up in front of an operating theatre.

Livinea races to catch up with me "Wait!" she hisses. "You can't just barge in there!"

"The *hell* I can't!"

I throw up a leg and *boot* down the door. It snaps back against the wall inside, wailing out a colossal, spine-jerking clash. Three faces in medical masks snap around, gasping at the sight of us—*me* in particular, my usual fate.

Beyond them, Eyelet lies strapped to an operating chair. Her arms and legs are tied down. Another belt secures her middle. Her head is cranked back at a neck-wrenching angle, her skull held in place by a halo of metal and leather straps. The lid of one of her eyes has been drawn forcibly open, held there by steel metal clamps.

A surgeon hovers over her, holding an ice pick in one hand, a hammer in the other.

All the breath seeps from my chest.

*"No . . ."* I lunge toward Eyelet. She gazes aimlessly at the ceiling. Something glass-like inside me breaks. I'm too late. I've come too late. They've already destroyed her. "Eyelet!" I shout.

"Urlick?" she says weakly. Her pupils flicker, and I draw in the hugest breath.

The surgeon whirls around. His gaze ripens at the sight of me. He scrambles backward like a frightened child as I close in on him, teeth clenched.

"That's right"—I lean toward him, bringing my anomaly of a face uncomfortably close, glaring at him through blazing pink eyes—"I am your greatest nightmare!"

# Thirty-Six

***Eyelet***

"Oh, Eyelet, what have they done to you?" Urlick leaps toward me, stroking my head and kissing my brow.

"Nothing yet, thankfully." A river of happiness surges through me, just seeing his face. My heart roars in my chest. "Though my eye . . ." I flit a glance toward the metal clamps still stretching my eyelid wide, trying not to blink.

"*Oh, yes!* Yes, of course." Urlick snaps forward, clumsily releasing the tension on the clamp, and my lid snaps back into place. "I've been so very worried about you . . ." He races to undo the rest of my straps, releasing first my head, then fervently working his way down my body, his voice as shaky as his hands. "When I got your message about you coming to free me at the stone jug . . . why, I nearly—" He yanks loose my wrist straps, and I leap from the chair, my lips upon his, my hands at his jaw. I devour him in kisses. The deepest, most *blood-warming* kisses I can affect, over and over again, until we're both left gasping and breathless.

"Oh, Eyelet," he whispers into my mouth between kisses. "I was so afraid I'd never—"

"Just shut up and kiss me, will you, please?"

He grins that luscious grin of his, boysenberry lips arced up at the corners, and draws me to him, crimson eyes dancing as he lifts me from the theatre chair, our arms intertwined, our mouths pressed. I melt into the warmth of his broad shoulders as he squeezes me tight inside muscular arms. I feel his heart beat against mine, and a small sigh of contentment escapes me.

"Oh, Eyelet," he whispers into my mouth. "I was so afraid—"

"Not half as afraid as I."

I pull him to me, fusing my breasts to his ribs, my hands stroking his face. Every fiber of me is aflame with arousal. His hands press into the small of my back, bringing my waist flush with his, and I can feel his arousal, too. I tilt my chin and fall onto his mouth again, kissing him hard and heavy.

"I guess 'e wasn't kidding when 'e said yuh two know each other." Livinea giggles, standing behind us.

Urlick kisses me harder, pulling me closer, and I throw my legs up to straddle him.

"Oh, my goodness," Livinea gasps and turns her face away. "Perhaps we should leave the room." She peers back through her fingers.

# Thirty-Seven

***Eyelet***

"Eh-hem." Masheck clears his throat. "I hate to break up the party, but—" He jerks a thumb toward the doctor and assistants, bound and gagged on the ground.

"Oh, yeah," Urlick says, releasing me and fixing his hair. His breath is as heavy as my own. The look in his eyes tells me he's sorry to stop. It's sinful, I know, but I don't want to stop, either.

Reluctantly he backs away from me, leaving me cold and yearning. He tugs at the points of his waistcoat. I smooth my skirts, as well. "Masheck's right," Urlick says. "We'd better get out of here." He drags his gaze from my eyes. "We haven't much time."

"Right." I breathe, rolling my tongue over my lips, savoring the taste of him that lingers there.

"I'll go first." Livinea steps between us on her way to the door, giggling. "The rest of yuh follow." She waves her hand as she exits the room.

Urlick threads his fingers through mine and yanks me out into the corridor. His grasp is so tight on my hand it nearly cuts off the circulation to my fingers, yet I feel the same way: that I must never, *ever* again, let go of him.

We run, the clap of our boots bouncing off the walls of the open corridor. I worry we'll be caught, and look back over my shoulder. Nothing but the light of flickering wall-sconces as far as the eye can see. My heart settles down in my chest.

Livinea stops below a cut in the plaster at the far end of the hall. "Up 'ere!" she shouts, pointing. "We'll 'ave to travel the rafters, elsewise they'll catch us." She signals for Masheck to give her a boost up. Masheck cups his hands together and she springboards off them, hoisting herself up into the ceiling.

"Come on!" Livinea signals for the rest of us to join her, her head hanging down through the hole in the ceiling. One by one, we vault up through the hole—Urlick boosting me, followed by Masheck boosting C.L., then Urlick boosting Masheck, who reaches down to clasp Urlick by the elbows and haul him up last.

We've no sooner disappeared than jackboots *thrump* the stone floors below us. *Guards.* We've made it in the nick.

"Holy bejeezus!" one of the guards shouts. "They've knocked 'em all out!" Their voices stream down the hallway, coming from the operating theatre.

"They're onto us," Urlick says, wide-eyed.

"They must have found the doctor," C.L. gasps.

Livinea claps a hand to his mouth. "Shhhhh!" she hisses. "Follow me." She turns, walking catlike along the upper beams of the ceiling, her arms outstretched for balance. The guards below us scatter. Boots stomp everywhere. We all freeze in place.

When at last again the hall below us grows quiet, the group carries on. "Watch your step and tread lightly," Livinea whispers back at me as I teeter slightly, nearly falling off the beam my first few steps. "Look straight on ahead, like yuh's just walking down the street," she encourages me. "Chin up, eyes forward, back ramrod straight," she parrots her instructions to me from earlier in the day.

I take a breath and do as she says, but it takes a great deal of concentration for me to stay square on the beam, shaking as I am. Livinea seems like she's done this a million times before. Perhaps she has. Perhaps she's attempted escape in the past.

I bite my lip to keep it from trembling, fighting against the rising coil of fear that stirs in my belly. Guards' feet thunder up the walls from the floors underneath as they rush through again. I suck in a startled breath. They're searching for us. The jolt of each of their steps passes up my legs. I don't think I can do this.

Livinea pauses as the boots grow nearer, hand to her heart, back pressed up against the pipe which threads along through the ceiling beside us. I press back up against it as well and close my eyes, listening to the guards' angry voices calling out in all directions.

"You take the north hall. I'll take the west."

How will we ever get past them all?

"Not to worry," Livinea whispers to me, as if she's read my mind. "They ain't travelling where we's going. Now come on." She signals for me to move, taking me by the hand. "We've got about fifteen more ticks of the clock before they figure us out."

We push on through the darkness, taking our lead from the soft tap of Livinea's shoes. I reach up to catch my balance now and again, fingers groping through spiderwebs. I shudder, flicking them from my fingertips. All at once, alarm bells ring, bleating down the corridor below us.

My heart nearly breaks loose from my chest. Panic slithers through my veins.

The soles of my boots slip on the smooth edges of our metal escape route, and I fall. Urlick catches me. I suck in a frightened breath. The girders have changed now from square beams to round metal pipes, making the passage just that much riskier. "How much farther?" I whisper, trembling.

"Not long now." Livinea grins, turning her head. Bright violet eyes shine through the darkness, followed by a flash of white teeth. How can she be so calm?

"Where are we going, exactly?" C.L. asks.

"Yuh wanted out, didn't yuh?" Livinea turns to face him.

"And yuh know the way?"

"Of course I do. I've always known." She winks back at me. She slinks along the pipe a little farther. We follow, bending our heads as the roofline declines. The compartment gets smaller and smaller until soon we're on hands and knees, crawling, and then on our bellies for a spell. There's a distinct odour of lichen.

"There!" Livinea points. "There it is!" She slides up to a crouched sit, finally again able to. Flickering candlelight floods up from a hole in the ceiling just beyond. Livinea scurries ahead, straddling the pipe until she's reached it.

Through the opening in the ceiling I spot a door. Its surface is black and oily. It's wobbling, just like all the others, only this one has a window in it. I've not seen outside since I've entered the Brink. Tears form in my eyes. Brethren's beloved soupy brume drifts past the window, whirling and spiraling through distant trees. My heart pumps warmly, reveling in its nostalgia. Imagine me longing to experience Brethren's never-ending gloom again!

"This is it," Livinea says, slipping along the pipe past the hole. She swings her legs around and faces us. "The only known way out."

Masheck leans forward, then pulls back. "How do you know?" He sounds nervous.

"Do you see the sheen on the door?" Livinea answers. Masheck leans in again. "See how it shimmers blue-black from time to time, like the coat of a raven?"

"Yeah."

"And the horns. Can you see the horns?"

"Faintly."

"That means the door is passable. They's the only doors people can pass through around 'ere unharmed," Livinea adds. "Well, sort of." She scratches her head. "This one is the only one with a window. Which means it's the only one that leads outside. But it takes some doin' to figure 'em out. They changes the route every day."

"What do you mean, they change the route?" Urlick asks.

"That's what makes leavin' 'ere such a puzzle." Livinea grins. "The door outta 'ere is never the same. Well, it tis . . . every six days." She taps her chin and squints her eyes. "Or is that seven?"

"What are you talking about?" Urlick snaps.

"The doors. They's on a rotation. Some days, the door out is this one. Some days, it tisn't. They switches the route so's none of us'll get wise to it and try to escape. Only I figured 'em out."

"When, Livinea?"

"Years ago." She slides back on her haunches as if she's said too much. "I figured out, when they serves bacon, it's the southeast corner door. When they serves porridge, it's the southwest."

"And today they served sausage," I say.

"Yeah! Now yer gettin' it!" Livinea smiles.

A new alarm siren cuts in. Jackboots thunder along the halls beneath us again. I suck in a tight breath and hold it as they pass. The alarm triggers a light over the door below us.

"What's that mean?" Masheck asks.

"It means we've gotta 'urry." Livinea's tone shifts. "Quickly. We've got to get yuhs through the door before it solids up." Livinea whirls me around, stuffing my legs down through the hole in the ceiling. She all but shoves me over the edge.

"Wait! What are you doing?"

"They know someone's trying to break out, so they's changing the door sequence. Yuhs got to get outta this place *now*, before they discover yuhs."

"What about you, Livinea?" I look back. "Aren't you coming?"

"I've already told yuh, miss. I've got nowheres to go if I leave 'ere. This is me home now. I 'aven't another."

"That's not true." C.L. sweeps in. "You 'ave a 'ome with us. Idn't that right, Urlick?" He tips his head.

I elbow Urlick in the ribs. "Right," he says.

Livinea's concerned expression melts. She drops through the hole, signaling for the rest of us to follow, her skirts up about her ears.

Urlick drops down next, a back pocket of his britches tearing on a loose screw as he falls. His shoes slap like a couple of gunshots when they hit the stone floor. He cranks his head this way and that, checking the corridor for guards, then smiles at me, reaching up. "Let's go," he says.

I drop from the pipe into his arms, my front grazing the length of his muscled chest. His hands grip my waist, encircling me almost completely in a band of strength, lowering me slowly to the floor. I gaze up into his eyes—*his gloriously brilliant pink rabbit eyes*—remembering what Livinea said about the treatments and the doors in this place, how they whittle away at your memories: the more times you're exposed, the more you lose. How for days after passing through, I struggled to remember anybody. Not to mention the aftereffects of being on the pins.

A searing thought jags through me. What if I pass through these doors and I lose my memories again? What if I can't remember Urlick, or why we're here? How long will it take for him to come back to me this time? What if this round I lose him for good?

What about Livinea? What will happen when she passes through? She's endured far more treatments here, than me. My heart rushes like water in a melted stream.

Masheck drops next to me, then C.L.

"Ready?" Livinea says.

Urlick turns me toward the door. "I can't do this," I say, pulling back.

"What?" Urlick scowls.

An alarm bell clangs over our heads. Panic jerks through my veins.

"The doors in this place, they strip you of your memories. Especially if you've had treatments. Isn't that right, Livinea?"

She nods.

"So, what if I pass these doors now, and I can't remember you?" I say to Urlick. "I can't bear to *lose* you again!"

Urlick reaches out, cradling my face in his hands. "What makes you think you could ever lose me?"

"Because I lost you once, Urlick, when I was exposed to the pins on the way in here. The pins steal pieces of your mind away. I had to fight so hard to get you back. What if we go through this door and it erases you completely from my memory?"

"Then *I* will remember *you* and never stop insisting that you remember me, until I draw my last breath."

"And what if I can't? What if I *can't* remember you?" My voice wobbles.

Urlick's gaze grows intense. "Then I will court you again, as a stranger, never giving up until at last I've won your heart." He brushes his thumb along the side of my cheek, erasing the tear that falls.

"But—"

He brings his finger to rest over my lips. "How much do you trust me?" he says.

I stare up into his eyes. "As much as the stars and the moon and the pesky ol' sun." I grin, kissing him, hard.

"Now, shall we do this?"

I nod and he thrusts himself toward the door, yanking me along behind, alarm bells screaming, Livinea, C.L., and Masheck dropping into line behind. Jackboots crash over stone flooring to the rear of us, guards' voices closing in.

"Hands out!" Livinea screams. "Stiffen yer elbows, and *push*!"

We rock forward, pressing our palms against the jellylike substance. The wobbling membrane buckles. The door thrashes against our weight. "It's fighting back," I say.

"PUSH HARDER!" Livinea shouts. All of us drive the heels of our palms against the goop-like gel, leaning into it with all our force. "HARDER!" Livinea yells.

The gel stretches thin at the centre, then thick again. With the force of a tide it throws us back.

Boots clatter closer. Masheck's head whirls about. "We're running out of time!"

"AGAIN!" Livinea shouts as the boots round the corner. We lean in again, a united force.

Livinea's violet eyes double in size as the membrane stretches and strains thin, bulging, encasing us in a brightly lit bubble of white light before at last it snaps, peeling back around the edges of our fingers like skin, rolling back over our arms.

"PUSH!" Livinea shouts again. We do, and the membrane gyrates past our ears, over our faces, expelling us like we've been shot from a cannon. The pressure is incredible, like two spikes being driven into my head. I close my eyes and rail against the pain, fighting hard to hold on to my image of Urlick as I'm slung from the Brink to the outside world—

Free at last.

I land and tumble down a mucky hillside. Bits of membrane cling to me, hanging in sharp severed bits from my fingers, nose, and mouth. They grow hot and sticky, and I spit them away and shake them from my fingertips, shrieking.

"Are you all right?" someone asks, hovering over me. I look up into a face I don't recognize. A face marred with scars. Bits of membrane hang from a frightening purple welt. It takes my breath away.

He reaches for me, and I pull back, staring up into his bloodred eyes, shaking.

"How much do you trust me?" he says, and my mind fills with moving pictures. Bits of film splice and splinter away. What remains, spirals to the front of my brain: A house on a hill in a remote destination. Tea. Hands. Conversation. A face. A badly marred face.

*His* face.

A man at a carnival. A promise. The words "How much do you trust me?"

All at once I'm flying. On a bat-winged bike. There's a bottle of steam.

The boy's there again.

He kisses me.

We're running in the woods. I fall. He's there.

We're in a room with a bed.

We open a door. There's a machine. Sparks fly.

I lose sight of him . . .

I'm devastated.

*I'm devastated* . . . I shake my head. Why am I devastated?

I turn and gaze into the stranger's eyes—and then it comes to me.

His words surface in my head, as if being resurrected from the bottom of a deep, deep sea: "Then *I* will remember *you* and never stop insisting that you remember me, until I've drawn my last breath . . ."

"Urlick!" I say. My eyes spring open. "It's you, isn't it?"

"Yes!" He falls on my mouth in the heaviest kiss, and every nerve in my body shouts. I feel everything in that moment, every sense, every touch, every smell . . . every second we've ever spent together rushes over me, wrapping me up in a warm, sparkling breeze.

"How is she?" Another breathless boy appears above us. Half the buttons on his shirt are missing. His bronze skin is wet with sweat. He has no sleeves, just a vest and a shiny bald head. In his eyes I see elephants.

A beautiful brass elephant . . .

"She's here, she knows me," Urlick says with a smile. "How are the others?"

"I'm not so sure." The boy casts a weary gaze over his shoulder. "See for yourself."

Urlick swings around and I look to see . . . *"Livinea?"* She's tangled up in a shameless embrace, straddling C.L.'s middle. She has him pinned to the ground, her mouth pressed over his.

"I've only just met 'im." She comes up for air. "But I likes 'im already."

# Part Three

# Thirty-Eight

***Flossie***

I lower my arms and the Infirmed bow to me, bent in the middle, hands outstretched.

I *can* get used to this.

A noise in the woods, moments later, has them perched on their haunches and sniffing the air like blood-thirsting wolves catching a scent. They rise into the mist, mingling bodies, chattering and shouting and screaming. Drool drains from their torn lips.

"Shhhhh," I hiss at them. "Silence!" I raise a hand, and they descend to the earth again. "Keep your hungry mouths shut and your howling to yourselves!"

They cower under the weight of my voice and float in silence—hundreds of wild-eyed, ghoulish dogs, awaiting my command.

"Stay here," I instruct them, jutting myself forward, floating out past their husk-like bodies to the edge of the clearing, following the noise. My heart is aflutter with the thought that it might be Urlick returning. Perhaps he recognized my face as the Brigsman hauled him away, and he's come back to save me. I press my hands together . . .

I blink into the clearing through the trees. No such luck—just some old *biddy* in a too-tight dress with buggy eyes and bottle-bottom glasses. She's arrived in a coach with a couple of warty-looking Brigsmen at her sides.

Like they can protect her from the likes of me. I fold my arms and watch them. People are so silly.

"I want you to search every inch of this forest. Do you understand me?" she shouts through the visor of her gas mask.

The Brigsmen cower and lower their heads. "Yes, mum," the closest one says.

"And don't come back until you can hand them over!" She turns and stalks away.

"But we've already searched every inch of these woods," one Brigsman calls after her. Big mistake.

*"Then search them again!"* The woman darts up in his face.

The Brigsman jerks back, and I laugh. *A woman after my own heart.*

I fold my arms, entertained by their escapades, wondering what it is she has them out here searching for. What could be so important they'd risk the Vapours? Why would a woman of her stature travel these dangerous woods?

"I can't believe my sister, letting her escape like that." The woman mutters, pacing, slapping the dust from her skirts. "Did she think, when I sent her a prisoner, it was a joke? I specifically told her to *destroy* that girl, not to see her set free again!" She turns. "See, Father? I was right." She wrings her gloves, looking at the sky. "Parthena *is* the one who's thick in the head. She never deserved that appointment anyway. The Academy is better off without her." She flits a hand and grins. "As am I."

"What's that, ma'am?"

"Was I *talking* to *you*?" She snaps on the Brigsman like an assaulted twig.

"No, ma'am, I just—" he stammers and shifts away, digging again in the dirt.

"I didn't think so," the woman snorts, tossing him a levelling look.

She turns and stomps away in the opposite direction, toward the burned-out heap that used to be the Core. Picking up a stick, she pokes at the ashes, muttering on again. "There probably wasn't even any truth to what the girl said. My sister's patients will say anything on the pins." She cups a hand to her eyes and stares up through the cloud cover. "Though it would be amazing." She squints. "Limpidious, my arse." She drops her hand. "There's nothing out here but Vapourous cloud. No secret entrance to an alternate world. No stairway to Heaven through the clouds. My sister's likely just been tipping back absinthe again. And I was stupid enough to believe her."

She circles the remnants of the building and heads back to her carriage, her shoes crunching over glass. "Oh, and one more thing." She turns back to the Brigsmen, the venomous snake now a dripping comb of honey. "There's an extra five hundred jewelets in it for any one of you *imbeciles* who can come back with the girl *and* the vial."

*"The vial,"* I whisper to myself. My eyes narrow. So that's what she has them looking for.

"And if you see any strange light transpiring up in the clouds"—she points over her head, her eyes shooting skyward—"I want to hear about that, too."

"Yes, ma'am." The Brigsman gulps, looks up, a fearful twist in his smile. "You're sure the vial is out 'ere somewhere?"

"As sure as you breathe air," the woman snaps, her eyes reducing to slits. "I have it on good authority that the vial I seek was dropped in his struggle with Smrt the day you lugheads arrested him. Our little scar-faced prisoner's cellmate overheard him, in his post-pummeled state, pining over the loss of it. Apparently, he was going on about having lost the miracle cure for the miracle machine. How devastating for him." She slaps her hand with her glove *"I want that vial."* She lashes out, hauling the Brigsman in by the scruff. "*And* the girl. Before her inkstain-faced lover catches up with her! Do you understand me?"

"Yes, ma'am." The Brigsman trembles. She shoves him away.

"Very well, then." She dusts off her hands and waddles toward her awaiting carriage, heels crushing leaves into paste beneath her weight.

I mistakenly stir, and the woman's head wrenches around. "Do you hear something?" Her eyes flash in my direction, behind their magnified lenses.

"Hear what, ma'am?" her dolt of a Brigsman answers.

"I thought I heard a noise out in the forest." The woman trembles, the hem of her oversized dress jiggling in the dirt.

"No, ma'am. I didn't 'ear nothing. Did yuh?" He turns to the other Brigsman.

"Can't say I did."

"You're sure?" She presses, scanning the forest, nostrils flaring, sniffing the air like a dog.

I slide a hand to my mouth, trying not to laugh and give myself away.

"Footman!" she squeals and bolts for the carriage, jumping aboard, springs hollering. She slams the coach door shut and the carriage is away, bobbling out onto the road.

I wait for the buggy to completely disappear, then remove the vial from its hiding place between my breasts. "What a wonderful piece of leverage I've stumbled upon." I cackle, twirling it in my hand. "Even more useful than before.

I swirl around and jut back toward my tribe of worshipping dimwits, still cowering in the trees where I left them. They fall on bended knees when again they see me. "Get up!" I shout. "For goodness' sake. We have work to do and no time to waste. I need your help to stop that carriage."

# Thirty-Nine

***Eyelet***

I spend the better part of the next twenty minutes convincing Livinea she agreed to come with us, we are not kidnapping her, and that, in fact, she was being held captive elsewhere, from which we saved her. But as soon as I convince her of that truth, she loses it, and the arguing starts up again. That final trip through the doors of the Brink, I fear, has destroyed her memory for good. Thankfully, I've regained everything. Every memory—even the unpleasant ones.

C.L. had a few blank moments that scared us all, during which time Urlick filled us in on C.L.'s past—his brief stay in the Brink, the damage that was done to him—I can't believe the life that poor man has led. Then C.L. snapped back into himself and accused Urlick of personal treason for sharing his secrets. He's still bitter, but slowly getting over it. "Where are we going?" He purses his lips and scowls up at Urlick. We've been driving for almost an hour now.

"To the bog," Urlick says from the driver's mount inside the elephant. The rest of us follow in the train.

"Masheck, you all right back there?" Masheck tips the ringmaster's hat. He's driving the train, same arrangement as before.

"Why the bog?" C.L. asks. He looks confused, as if he doesn't remember what it is.

"Because you know as well as I do that's the only place the Brigsmen are too afraid to go."

"Shouldn't we be heading for the border?"

"In the dark of night?"

"It won't be much better in the day." C.L. is bordering on belligerent now, his upset with Urlick affecting his judgment. Livinea moves in, petting his shoulder.

"We need time to regroup," Urlick says firmly. "And think of a plan. We won't be getting out of this mess without a crafty one. You know yourself we'll never get this caravan back across that checkpoint without being discovered."

C.L. hangs his head. "But what other way is there, sir?"

"I don't know. But we'll have to think of something."

"I know where there's a hole in the dancing fence line, between Brethren and Gears," I offer. "It'll at least get us that far."

"Big enough to drive the elephant and the freak train through?"

"No," I sigh. "We'd have to abandon them and go on foot."

"Then what? 'Ow would we get 'ome from there?" C.L. lifts his head. He looks worried. A spike of anxiety rises up in me, too.

"We'll find a way," Urlick says, staring off into the nothingness ahead of us. I can tell he has no idea.

*

"Do you think that's wise?" I hover over Urlick as he lights a small campfire alongside of the bog. The stench is enough to knock you down. We've purposely parked as close as possible to stay out of the reach of the Brigsmen, but C.L.'s right, the bog smells like the spray of a billion skunks.

"Do you fancy freezing to death?" Urlick scowls, rolling two sticks.

"No. It's just that—" The campfire lights. I lift a hand to my nose to block out the stench, and Urlick takes offense. He thinks it's because of the smoke.

"Is this going to be like that other day with the tire in the woods?"

"No."

*"Then!"* He jerks his head to one side and presses me with his eyes to move on. I kick a stone and don't. "I've arranged the logs so the east wind carries the smoke out into the forest, away from the city. Have you any better idea?"

"Well, no, but—"

"Good," he snaps.

"Might I suggest somethin'?" C.L. steps between us, a swaggering look to his eyes. In his hands he holds an odd-looking set of mechanized fireplace bellows."

Urlick's face relaxes. "Brilliant!" he says, accepting them. "You really did think to bring everything, didn't you?"

"I tried, sir." C.L. puffs out his chest.

Men. They are so silly sometimes.

Urlick sets the strange apparatus up on its handles next to the campfire, in the dirt, revealing a secret compartment in the handle, and snaps together a crank. Out of another compartment he pulls the makings of a stand and assembles it, steadying the bellows inside it.

"What is that thing?" I finally ask. I can't stand their smug silence any longer.

"A smoke-sucker," Urlick says. "I designed it in case of emergency, should I ever get stopped in the woods. It draws in the smoke to hide your whereabouts."

"Clever. You're always thinking, aren't you?" I smile.

"If you're not, you're dead." Urlick tips his brows at me playfully. He attaches the handle and gives it a crank. It fails. He ditches his overcoat and tears open the seam, retrieving a quick-assembly lug-nut wrench from inside the hem.

"Are you always packing?" I say.

"Usually." He grins. He assembles the wrench and tries the apparatus again. Nothing.

It's clear to me the lug nut is on upside down, but clearly Urlick doesn't see it. Do I risk all by letting him know? He sighs, adjusts the nut, and tries again. I think not. I take a seat on a log behind him and try to ignore what's happening. But can't.

"Here, let me." I finally jump to my feet, reaching across him. My arm brushes his arm, and the hairs on my arm stand. I set to work jimmying off the lug nut, careful not to strip the threads, trying desperately to ignore the growing chemistry between us.

The heat is debilitating.

"There," I say eventually, rethreading the lug nut after three missed tries, and return the wrench to his hand, letting my fingers linger there a little too leisurely. "Thanks," he says. He folds his fingers over mine.

His steamy pink eyes weaken my knees, and in the worst way, faced with danger or not, I want to stop everything and kiss him.

The wind shifts. Smoke charges up between us and we're divided, coughing and sputtering, waving it away. Urlick props up the bellows in their stand and wrenches the crank around. When he lets go, the accordion-sleeved apparatus pumps *in, out, in, out*, lapping up the campfire emissions, keeping our identity hidden within it. I can't help but smile at Urlick's achievements. He has quite the superior mind.

We settle in, all of us, on rocks and logs around the edge of the campfire. A well-deserved break from a heart-pounding day. I plop down in front of Urlick and nestle back against his chest, delighting in the strength of his arms as I wrap them around me.

"What are we going to do about her?" I say. I look across the campfire at a babbling Livinea, still questioning who we are and why she's here. "She doesn't even seem to remember me."

Urlick reins me in closer, his heart beating at my back through his clothes, strumming sweetly against my spine. "Does it matter?" he says.

I scowl up at him.

"I mean, seriously, does it really matter if she remembers anything at all, as long as she's happy, free of persecution in the Brink?"

He's got a point. I never thought of it that way. What does it matter if she remembers anything? In fact, it's probably better she doesn't. What other option did she have? Death by pear of anguish, or life with loss of memory. Confusion with us has got to be better. I stare at her violet eyes playing in the light of the flames. She's curled up against C.L.'s chest, stroking his rib cage like the keys of a fine piano. She looks up at him and coos his name as if learning it for the first time—hoping for an invitation to snuggle even closer, knowing her. Her face is glowing—porcelain-white skin, pink lips, blushed cheeks. She looks positively enamored with C.L. He stares down at her adoringly, as well.

"I suppose you're right," I say to Urlick, a small laugh escaping my lips. "What more can anyone ask for in life than what's going on over there?"

"Well . . . perhaps what's about to go on over here." He swoops me backward off the log into a kiss. A small, surprised shriek escapes me on the fall back, which turns to giggles after he's finished kissing me in the crunchy leaves. He looks down from overtop of me, collects me up into his arms, and kisses me again, long and hard, threading his hot tongue through my eager lips—setting my brain and body afire. I never wanted anyone so badly.

I lean into the kiss, roll him over, and climb on top, shocking him to the point he's lost his breath. "What's the matter? Am I too much for you?" I sit up, laughing, feeling the answer ripening between my legs. "Oh, Mr. Babbit," I say.

He blushes. "I—I dare say . . ." he stutters. "W—we might pick a better time . . ." He twists his head toward the googly-eyed crowd we left on the other side of the log, whom I'd momentarily forgotten about. All staring.

"Oh, yes," I say, glancing back over my shoulder, feeling the passionate rush drain from my body. I brush the leaves from my disheveled upsweep, and I slip off of him. "We'll continue this later." I wink and pat him on the chest, driving forward for one more quick, take-his-breath-away kiss. Dusting my hands on my skirts as if nothing's happened, I crawl back over the log into my previous position and cross my legs daintily.

"What?" I say.

Wanda giggles. I raise my tea to her and smile.

Just then, Masheck returns to camp, his arms stacked high with kindling for the fire, and the whole camp goes silent. "What 'ave I missed?" he says.

"Nothing," Martin snorts and slurps his tea. The whole group starts to giggle.

Masheck's eyes move to Urlick placing himself awkwardly back in position on the log next to me, waistcoat rumpled, his hair full of crumpled leaves, his normally white cheeks glowing a lovely shade of crimson. "Oh, that," Masheck says with a laugh. "Everything all right, sir?"

"Tea?" Sadar breaks the tension. He rises to his feet, pot in hand, steam chugging happily from its spout.

"I'll 'ave some," Livinea accepts right away, holding her tin teacup high.

"What about you, Eyelet? Up for some boysenberry?"

"Boysenberry tea?" I say, making a face, thinking of how I've used that word many a time in my mind to describe the colour of Urlick's lips. There's a tea to match?

"Yes. It's a forest specialty," Sadar says.

My mouth falls open.

"We drank it all the time on the freak train," Sadar adds.

I hold out a cup, and Sadar slowly fills it. The brew circles in.

"Whatchu think?" C.L. asks after I've taken a sip.

"I think . . ." I hesitate, sloshing a second swallow around in my mouth before answering. "If one were to drink the colour purple, this would be it."

The campfire crew laughs.

"Not that that's a bad thing," I quickly add and flick my brows at Urlick. He laughs even harder, as if he knows my secret use of the word, his purple cheek turning raspberry, his white one still blushing hot pink.

"Let's move on to a plan, shall we?" Urlick stammers, tugging at his waistcoat points, trying to look authoritative with crushed leaves in his hair. "First of all, we need to get through this evening. I say we all take a turn on watch duty. Everyone agree?"

Heads nod.

"Eyelet and I will cover first . . . Watch, that is." He stumbles over the sentence and everyone snickers. "Masheck, will you take second watch?" He nods. "C.L., you're up after that."

"Will do," C.L. agrees, still snuggling close with Livinea.

"I suggest anyone who's not on watch try to get some sleep in the train cars. That way we'll be able to get away quickly, should anything happen."

"Good idea," Sadar agrees, scurrying along after Martin. "I'd love some rest."

"C.L., I trust we can count on you to look after Miss Livinea?"

Livinea grins at the sound of her name.

"Absolutely, sir." C.L. stands.

Martin opens his mouth as if to object, and Urlick says, "Martin, can I trust you to watch over the rest of them?"

"Certainly, sir." His sour face brightens. He clicks his heels, salutes, and marches away.

One by one, the freaks trade the comfort of the fire for a bunk in the train. Only Iris hangs back. She rolls her fingers inside her palms, frowning. Cordelia stands glued to her skirt, pouting.

"Go on." Urlick nudges Iris with a look, as if urging her just to cooperate. *Please?* He mouths. "It'll be all right. I promise," Urlick assures them. "We will never be separated again. Now go on, do as you're told, please."

Iris bites her lip, then turns her back slowly, pressing Cordelia hard against her leg as they walk away.

An unsettling cloud of worry settles over me. My bones shake under my skin.

I lean back against Urlick's chest, looking for comfort.

"What is it?" He looks down on me.

"It's just that—" I start, then stop myself. The stench of the bog shudders through me, reminding me of the Vapours in the forest. "I'd be better with your arms around me," I say instead of what I'm thinking: *I wonder if we should be letting them that far out of our sight.*

Urlick drops more wood on the fire, then settles down in the leaves, back up against the log, and pulls me to him. Sparks hiss and spray from the flames before getting inhaled by the smoke-swallowing bellows. He wraps me up tight in his arms, then adds a blanket overtop. "Everything is going to be fine," he says.

The fire crackles over the backdrop of creaking iron train-car doors. Opening, closing, locks dropping into place over hammers, our friends settling down in their beds—then the stillness of the eerie forest.

I take in a breath and snuggle as close to Urlick as I possibly can, trying to relax, but the baritone belch of the bog gurgles up my spine. All at once, I feel my lungs seize as if being gripped from the inside. I cough, trying to loosen them, but I can't. I can't stop coughing. Pain shoots through me like a spear, and I tense.

"What is it? What's the matter? Why are you coughing so hard?" Urlick holds me out at arm's length. He stares into my eyes.

I can't answer. I can't get my breath. The pain is too fierce, too deep. It has my tongue. The pain has been increasing every time. Growing worse with every session of coughing. It sticks hard between the ribs, harder than ever before. I look to Urlick, feeling panicked, trying to get my words out, but they're jammed in my throat.

"Eyelet?" He holds me.

I gasp again, not exhaling, and he knows I'm in trouble. "Iris!" he screams, and she materializes instantly. "There's a gas mask in the back of the caboose! Go get it!" Iris and Cordelia run.

"There are no Vapours here. This shouldn't be happening," I hear him say, though he sounds oddly distant. His face is rumpled. It starts to fade.

I want to shout to him, *It's not the Vapours*. Or at least I don't think so. Perhaps it is. Perhaps their effect has stayed with me; I did start coughing after I was exposed so long at the Core. But still, why would I be coughing here, now—and before, in the asylum, where there were no Vapours at all?

Blood rushes from my cheeks. My fingertips grow cold and numb. I feel as though my extremities are slowly disappearing. My thoughts jump to the idea I might be having an episode. But it's not an episode. There's no smell of toast. Besides, they've never affected my breathing before.

I try to work through other scenarios in my mind, but my thoughts grow thick and muddy.

"Eyelet?" Urlick's features blur before me. "Eyelet, stay with me, please . . ."

He strokes my head, but I don't feel his hand. He's too far away.

Laying me back, he drops his mouth over mine, like he did before in the forest in the Vapours—but there are no Vapours here, are there? He forces air into my lungs, and they burn. I feel the push and then a sharp pain, and then fire, as though he's lit a match inside of me. I will him to stop, smacking at his face, but I'm not sure I'm connecting.

Something is wrong. Very wrong. It's as if I'm floating away, leaving my own body.

Folding his hands over my chest, he pumps up and down, and I wince from the pain. I see him doing this, going through the motions, shouting words . . . but I cannot hear nor understand him. I'm leaving the ground. Hovering overtop of him, overtop of me. I fight to say something, but the words don't come. I struggle, trying to lower myself back down in my skin, but I continue levitating.

I don't fully understand how I can be here and yet there at the same time. I watch Urlick at work, desperate to revive me, feeling the rise of something cold in my veins. I think it's the silver, then I realize it's not silver at all, it's something else, something strange and much more foreboding—a suffocating, intoxicating moroseness. It consumes me, drawing me higher and higher up into the trees, further and further away from Urlick.

*Wait!* I yell at it. *I want to go back. I won't go with you. I want to stay with him!*

Urlick's brows grow distraught. He dives forward, frantic with attempts to revive me on the ground.

*Let go of me!* I shout at the sensation. *Let go of me, now!*

I writhe and thrash, searching for my breath, struggling . . . and then all at once, I break loose and fall from the trees back into myself, sucking in a huge gulp of air.

I gag and sputter, anchoring back into my skin, and brace for an impact that never comes.

"Eyelet!" Urlick shrieks, pulling me to his chest. "Oh, Eyelet!"

I push away from him, wide-eyed, gasping, my flesh stinging as if it's not my own.

"You have to stop doing this. My heart can't take it." His eyes are frantic.

"Nor mine." I manage a smile.

He collapses over me, tears in his eyes. "Oh, Eyelet, I thought you'd decided to leave me for good this time."

I stroke his face with my hands. "That's just it, I did."

"You what?" He draws back.

"But I demanded to come back to you, and it released me—"

"What did?" Urlick frowns.

"I don't know. Whatever it was that took me. But it doesn't matter anymore, because I'm here now, with you, and I'm never going away again." I reach up, clinging to him, pulling him into the deepest hug I can manage. I tremble, hoping I'm right.

"The Vapours," he says to Iris over my back. "They must be getting to her."

"But there are no Vapours here, are there?" Cordelia says.

"Doesn't matter." Urlick's breath heaves in and out. "They've done what they needed to do. Either that or—" He stops himself short and pushes me back, staring into my eyes. The look in his own is alarming. "Your father. The exposure—"

"It's nothing." I cut him off.

"It's not nothing," Urlick says firmly, and I follow his train of thought. To the journal, the entry about the ray and Father's warning about its effects. About the serum my father left for me, and my need to drink it before . . . "It's as your father warned. You need to drink what's in that vial."

"What vial?" Cordelia scowls.

My eyes flick to her and an equally worried-looking Iris. "It'll be all right," I say, knowing it's a lie, knowing something is wrong, *very* wrong—never before have I felt so unwell, so unmoored. "I'll just drink the vial and I'll be fine—"

"No, you won't." Urlick cuts me short. He turns, pulling a trembling white hand through his hair. He scrambles to his feet and starts to pace.

"What do you mean?" I say, crawling to my knees.

He looks at me, an empty slate, as if his heart is dissolving. "I lost the vial," he says, white-faced.

"You what?" I try not to gape.

"In the struggle with Smrt back at the Core. *I-i-i-it* fell"—he stammers and holds out his palms—"from my pocket as we struggled and rolled over the side of the . . ." His eyes dart left and right.

"The side of what, Urlick?" I say.

He swallows hard. "The escarpment." He looks at me, fear and sadness for eyes. "I tried to grab it, but . . . it rolled over the edge and disappeared into Embers."

I suck in a breath and grab for my heart, the weight of his words registering—my one true salvation, the only known sample of the cure, the one my father insisted I require, has been lost . . . *to Embers.*

"I have to go back"—Urlick paces, hands clapped to his head—"I've got to find the cure." His voice shoots up. Tears brim his lids. "I lost the one thing you need most in the world. I've got to go back and find it—"

"No," I say, grabbing his arm, pulling myself to a stand. "*We* will go back and find it, together."

# Forty

***Flossie***

"For the love of God, will you shut up!" I shout at the Infirmed, hands raised.

Their howling alone is enough to deafen the entire Commonwealth, voices ranging between freshly boiled lobster and skinned-alive bunny.

I undulate up to the side of the stagecoach carriage as the last of the Infirmed fall silent. They waggle in the air behind me, cool streams of white, wispy apparitions, silver faces gaunt and drawn, bobbling and twisting amid the dark, trolling cloud cover that smothers this part of the forest. The air around us is tinged with just a *hint* of deadly Vapours. A perfect addition to the scene.

I suck in a breath, unafraid. After all, I have nothing to fear any longer but the merciless drag of time. The state I'm in, not much else affects me.

The footman at the mount glances back at me over his shoulder, petrified. He snaps his head forward, gas mask on, back jerked straight. He mutters what sounds like a prayer beneath his breath. Poor soul, he thinks I'm after him.

"Don't worry," I whisper in his ear, levitating. "I won't let them eat you. This time." I grin, stripping the glove from my still-intact hand. I leave the other glove on. "Unless, of course, I don't get what I've come for." I spin around, facing the carriage. I laugh and my whole body short-circuits again, twitching and faltering from stem to stern. I need to get on with this, and I need to get on with this quick.

"Get out!" I say, lowering myself to the ground and flinging open the coach's door. The bug-eyed beauty inside the carriage shriek-gasps. It's really quite entertaining. The size of her gaze behind those unnaturally magnified lenses alone is a source of comedy. She must be blind as a bat.

She blubbers and moans like a child in need of her mother. "Oh, save it for later," I say, hauling her out by the hair.

She shrieks and stumbles, eventually righting herself in a twisted-ankle circle, in a botched attempt to get away.

"Are you quite finished?" I stare. Just for fun I shake the bun in my hand that's attached to her head, and she yowls like a wet cat. Something about her has the hairs on the back of my neck standing. It's something about the eyes. Those vast wells of stone-grey, save for the glasses' exaggeration, could be the very reflection of my own. Even her voice, though higher-pitched and more strained than mine, has a quality I find oddly comforting.

"Yes!" she screeches when I shake her again. "Yes! Yes! I'm finished!"

Her eyes fill with magnified tears. She swallows hard and clutches the crucifix at her chest.

"Do you promise not to run if I let you go? Not that running will do you any good at this point." I motion to the ghouls in the trees, who swoop and laugh. One of the ghouls adds to the drama by dragging his bony finger across the back of the woman's neck. The woman screeches and curls into me, her jaw a vibrating instrument.

"Yes, yes, I promise!" Her gaze darts left to right.

I flit a hand at the ghoul, and it backs away.

Slowly, I let go of the woman's hair.

She hesitates, then attempts to bolt. *Fool that she is.* With *this* I seek a partnership? *Perhaps I'm the fool.* "Surround her," I tell the Infirmed, and they drop from the trees. They form a tight circle around the woman and press in. "I see your promises are worth nothing," I say. "Pity, really." I examine my nail beds. "I had *so* hoped you could be spared." I raise my hand, and Infirmed start yowling.

"Wait!" the woman shrieks. "You can! You can trust me!"

"Good," I continue. "Because you know, at any time, I could just as easily eat you." I examine my nail beds again. The Infirmed sniff.

"What do you want from me?" The woman recoils.

"Well, first of all, you can start by mending that tone of yours." I drag a pointed fingernail under the woman's chin, grazing it.

The woman shudders. What little fight left in her all but extinguished. She trembles, her already-bugging eyes jumping triple their magnified size. My father was right. There is nothing else like having ultimate power over another. The feeling is, in a word, *exhilarating.*

I lean in closer, and her shaking increases. Blubber wobbles like pudding beneath her generous clothing. "I've come to make a deal," I say in a low, commanding voice. "I wish to enter into a business agreement with you."

"With me?" The woman looks up at me, astonished.

A twinge of Vapours passes through the trees. The woman gags and turns her face away.

"You see," I continue, twisting her chin back to face me, "I have something you want. And you have something I need. Thus, I'm here to propose a simple exchange of goods. Sounds simple, doesn't it?" I grin.

The woman gulps heavily. "I'm afraid I don't know what you're talking about."

"The *girl,*" I snap, jutting her way. "I want the *girl!*"

"What girl?" She shakes.

"The one you ordered your Brigsmen to search for, back there in the woods near the ravine." My temper shortens.

"You heard that?" The woman's eyes pop. "You heard what I was saying?"

"*Hell horses*, woman, the whole forest did." I lean back on my tentacles. "Shouting is not the way to go if you want to keep something a secret round here."

Her gaze shifts side to side, as if stupid enough to be planning another escape—*foolhardy, nearsighted gulk that she is!* Vapours tickle her nose and she sneezes.

"So, that's it, then." Her voice totters, struggling to convey composure. "I give you the girl . . . and you'll let me go?"

"No," I say. "I want the boy, too."

"The boy?"

"Don't play stupid." I narrow my eyes. "I heard all that was said, remember."

"Yes, yes, of course." She nods her head. "The boy." She gulps. "Certainly you can have the boy. There's just one small problem."

"What's that?"

"I'm not exactly sure where he is." She cowers.

"What are you talking about?" I bark. "I thought you *had* the boy. He was dragged away by your Brigsmen—I saw them."

"*Had* is the operative word there." She bites her nail.

"You mean to tell me, you stood back there cursing your *sister* in the woods, calling her a *dolt* for losing her inmate, when you yourself have lost your own?"

Her plump, jowly cheeks redden.

"What's that called, again?" I wrinkle up an eye. "Pot calling the kettle black?"

"How dare you!" The woman snaps toward me. "You can't talk to me like that! Do you know who I am?" It appears she's taken leave of her senses for the moment. She's forgotten that her head could be my lunch. "I mean—" Her eyes flash, a sign she's suddenly remembered.

*"Where is he?"* I scream, my voice blowing her clothes back.

She stumbles backward, blinking. "It appears he has bobbled away on the back of an elephant!" she offers, thrusting her hands up in front of her face in defence.

"An elephant?" I snort. How creative. "One would think it rather easy to spot an elephant in these woods," I say.

"Yes, well . . . apparently *not*." She glares at me sternly.

How like Urlick to concoct a grand-enough scheme to leave the authorities bamboozled and gobsmacked—oh, how I *love* that boy! "So"—I creep toward her—"you need my help more than ever, then, don't you?"

She startles. "I don't know what you're talking about."

Her gaze drops to my hand, which is growing more and more translucent with every wasted second. I've only three and a half fingers left. I need to make this deal and fast.

"Tell you what," I say, hiding my hand behind my back. "How's about I'll sweeten the pot a little."

The woman's brows furrow.

"What if I were to loan you, say, the services of my friends, over here." I tip my head toward the swooping Infirmed. "I suspect your search could benefit from their observant eyes and ears above the forest, no? Who better to spot your runaway convict?"

I flicker again. My entire body short-circuits, fritzing in and out. The ends of my hair plume and fizzle, stinking like fricasseed skunk. Smoke chugs out of my ears.

The woman's eyes bloom into two buckets of fright. She draws back as if she's just been struck by voltage. I swear I see the panic thicken in her blood.

"Well"—I lean back on my tentacles, recovering—"what do you say? Do we have a deal, or not?" I can't wait forever for this dolt to make up her mind. Clearly I'm running out of time.

Her gaze falls to the flashing light in the vial, concealed inside my corset between my breasts. Her wary brows rise. "Surely you don't expect *me* to make a deal with *your* kind," she says, "without some extra measure of assurance."

Pause.

I glance down at the light, then back up into her face. I can't believe this woman. A woman I could, at my whim, lunge out and infect—she thinks she can bargain with me. Another surge comes over my delicate circuit system, causing me to sputter and smoke. "How's this for assurance?" I say, pulling the flashing green pendant out from its intimate hiding place.

The woman's mouth falls agape. "Where did you get that?" She attempts to snatch the pendant from me but I swing it away.

"Does it really matter?" I tuck it back down between my breasts. "Now, are we negotiating, or aren't we?" I lean her way.

"Fine." She huffs, trying to appear invincible, swiping a rogue hair from her eyes. "What is it that you want?"

"The boy. Delivered to me. *Unharmed.*"

"But—"

I raise my hand. "Either that or the deal is off, and I turn you over to my friends for dinner."

The woman looks over my shoulder and gulps. "All right, all right, is there anything else?"

"Yes." I turn. "I want unfettered access to the Academy's top medical laboratories, as well as their finest medicines—"

"But that's impossible," the woman guffaws. "You're Infirmed. You can't come into the city."

I crawl toward her on spiked tentacles. "I can if you let me in."

She recoils.

"Not only me, but all my colleagues here." I flick my gaze toward the hovering Infirmed.

"But I can't possibly—"

"You can and you will," I snap. "Once we're there, they'll stand guard as the boy works on a cure for me—"

"A cure? But there's no cure for—" I glower at her and she stops, gulping down her next thought. "Is that it, then, or is there more?" She winces.

"As a matter of fact, there is." I smooth down my ruffled corset. "I want *your word* that once the boy cures me of my condition, *no one* will ever know that this has happened to me."

"Of course—"

"Oh, and one more thing." I drift intimidatingly closer, my breath hot at her neck. "Once the girl is found, I get to kill her."

"You *what*?"

"You heard me!"

"But she—"

"Do we have a deal or *don't we*?"

The woman falls back, shivering. The Infirmed around me hiss and moan and stretch their jaws.

"Very well, then." She swallows. "The boy, access to the Academy's laboratory, medicine, and my silence . . . as well as the chance to end the girl's life. All that, in exchange for my freedom and the vial, is that correct?"

"And passage to wherever it is you think you're going."

Her eyes grow wider. "Whatever are you talking about?"

"Oh, don't play coy with me, I overheard that part, too. Something about a sighting of Limpidious? I take it that's what you meant, all that drivel about finding a stairway to Heaven." I take out the vial and twirl it in my remaining fingers. "If it's found, I'm on the voyage with you?"

"Very well. One ticket to the promised land—but passage only for you, not them." She flicks her eyes contemptuously at the Infirmed.

"So we have a deal, then." I extend my good hand for the shaking.

The woman waffles at the knees. "Yes. But I'll need to interrogate the girl before she dies," she says, muttering, *"Or we'll never find our way to the new land."*

"Done," I say.

Hesitantly, the woman reaches out and sticks her hand straight through mine.

# Forty-One

***Urlick***

I stumble to the edge of the ravine at the back of the Core, ashes kicking up beneath my boots. Embers belches its own brand of filth into the sky, adding to the toxic cocktail that looms above our heads. I kneel, thinking I see something, which turns out to be nothing, just like the eighteen other times I thought I spotted something since we got here. I stand, holding a hand to my eyes, and look around. The whole area is burned out, blackened, charred. Pools of melted, cooled, now-hardened metal shine up from the ground like futuristic lakes. It's as though Eyelet and I have entered another dimension altogether.

"Pretty horrible, isn't it, ol' girl?" I stroke Clementine's withers, and she whinnies.

"Did you find something?" Eyelet murmurs through her gas mask, approaching.

"No." I turn.

She falls apart coughing, and my heart picks up speed. "You all right?" I step toward her. She waves me off and straightens. "I don't think we should stay out here too much longer," I say, haunted by the incident at the campfire.

"Nonsense. We're here to find the necklace, and find the necklace we will. Besides, we've come all this way. There's no going back now." She scowls. "What's the matter with you?"

"You're right," I concede, seeing the worry in her eyes. She *needs* the necklace. More than ever now. Secretly I decide I'll give it an hour—then we fly back, and I'll return alone tomorrow if I have to. Whatever it takes. She can't go on like this.

I lower my head and resume combing the edges of the ravine along the side where Smrt and I last struggled. Where I'm sure I lost the vial. Visions of Smrt's last breaths shiver through me. The look in his eyes. His desperate gaze. I swallow down the guilt that purges into my throat and shake away the cold, murderous feeling that crawls my skin.

"It was here," I say, batting at the undergrowth, making a third pass over the same trek of ravine. "I know it was here. Right here!" I point, stamping. *Think. For the love of all that is good in this world, Urlick, think!*

"It's all right." Eyelet looks up from the pit where she's digging. "We'll find it, eventually." Her eyes tell me she thinks I'm overreacting. I'm not overreacting. She's treading into dangerous territory again with that cough, I can tell.

"I mean, how hard can it be?" She makes light of the moment, swaggering toward me, all bright-eyed and silly-faced. "To find a shiny glowing object, when everything else around here is"—she holds up a burnt stick—"well . . . not shiny." She coughs and my nerves flare.

"Here," I say, offering her a canteen of water.

She takes down her gas mask and drinks in a sip, coughing.

"It's nothing, really." She reads my expression. "Just water down the wrong way." She pats her chest. I know she's lying. I can hear it in her breath. It's become raspy and hard since we arrived in the forest.

There's a new rattle in her lungs. I don't care what she says. That cough of hers has gotten worse. And it's happening more frequently.

We've got to find that necklace.

I turn and poke the bushes again.

Perhaps it isn't the previous exposure to the light that's causing it. Perhaps she picked up something in the Brink. I only pray the vial is the answer. I couldn't bear life without Eyelet in it.

"You've got a little . . ." I motion for her to wipe the smut from her nose. She reaches up and smears it further, blinking at me like a prizefighter, a dash of smut under each eye.

"Where?" she says, making it worse.

"Here, let me." I remove my ascot and dunk it into the canteen, then charge over to where she is. I tip her chin back, feeling my breath ball in my chest at her beauty. I could look at Eyelet forever and never tire of her. Her eyes shine like they did that day in the cupboard of the kitchen when I first kissed her. That seems a lifetime away.

I think back to how just the thought of her kept my heart beating as I faced the gallows. How her image, behind my eyes, gave me the will to live on in the jug. Gives me the will to continue today.

She bats her lashes, her body rippling in gooseflesh, and I long to just throw her down and have my way with her. But then I remember where we are and how crazy that would be, and I force myself to return the mask to her face.

"We'd better get back to it," I say.

"I guess." She smiles at me through her visor and starts poking about the earth again.

We search for another good hour, producing nothing, Eyelet intermittently coughing behind me. The sound of her uneven breathing whittles away at my spine. We've got to give up on this. I've got to get her back.

"We were struggling right here," I say, pulling a frustrated hand through my hair. "Right here." I pace over to the point at the edge of the ridge where I tossed Smrt in. "The vial should be here, but it isn't."

"Maybe you're wrong. Maybe it's a little bit that way."

"No, it's gone." I feel my features grow stern. "We've got to give up on this."

"Give up!" Her nostrils flare. "I refuse to give up. It's got to be here somewhere." She turns, searching frantically.

"Look." I clutch her hard by the shoulders, and spin her round to face me. "We have the formula. I can make it again. Let's just return to the Compound. I'll make it there. Please, Eyelet, let me try—"

"No," she says, backing away from me. "We've got to find the vial."

The ground wrinkles beneath our feet. We both collapse to our knees.

"What was that?" Eyelet looks to me, her eyes screaming. "Are the Vapours on the move again?"

"No, they can't be." I look around. "It's too soon. The moons haven't changed. It must just be an aftershock."

"That strong?" she asks as the earth ripples beneath our feet again.

"Come on, we need to take cover." I grab her hand.

"Where?"

"I don't know. Clementine!"

The earth buckles, spooking Clementine. She tears off into a haphazard gallop toward the road. "Clem!" I scream after her. "No! Clem! Come back!"

A tree crashes down between us, driving us back.

"What now?" Eyelet gasps, fogging up her gas mask. The ground continues to pitch and jolt crazily.

I pull her to me, catching sight of something through the cloud cover, something poking up from the ground off in the distance, to the left of what used to be the Core. I've never seen it before. "Run!" I press my hand into the small of her back and push her toward it. "Over there! Do you see it? That wooden structure!"

"Yes!" She stumbles forward.

The earth revolts again and I race past her, grab her by the hand, and bolt for the structure, dragging Eyelet along behind me.

"What is this thing?" she shouts when we reach it, clinging to the broken beams.

"An abandoned mine shaft, I think." I pant. "Left over from the coal-excavation years. They're all over the place out here in the woods." I fall to my knees, scraping the earth below the rickety structure, searching for a door, some way in. At last I find it and yank the door up by its latch.

"We're not going inside it." Eyelet shakes her head.

"We've no other choice. There's nowhere else."

"But the ground, it's unstable."

"We'll be safe below ground, trust me."

"Unless it fills in. We'll never get out of there."

"These shafts have been around for a hundred years. They've survived many cycles of Vapours. It's our best bet, Eyelet. There's nowhere to go."

"What about Clem?"

"She has wings, we don't. She's not stupid—"

The earth rolls at our backs.

"I'll go first." Eyelet nods.

I help her down inside, her feet searching for the metal rungs of a long, descending ladder. At last they connect. When her head dips below the earth, I follow, hauling the broken door down over our heads.

"It's too dark," she says. "I can't tell where my feet are going." I sense the panic of her voice inside my ribs. "I can't tell what we might be climbing into."

I pull out my pocket watch, snap it open, and depress a button on its back. Up from the lens pops a miniature metal anemometer—a pinwheel of cones—and with it comes light, in the form of a flame. It shoots up frighteningly high, driving Eyelet back, then dulls to a cool, blue glow, thank goodness. The pinwheel starts to spin, sniffing the air as it turns.

"What *is* that?"

"I call it a Quantum Tunneler."

"A quantum what?"

"It's an electronic nose. It can sniff out the presence of various chemicals, even in their slightest odour. It's so accurate it even measures the acetone in your breath and the sugar in your blood."

"Oh, now you're just making things up." She purses her lips at me.

I wave the device past her mouth and a beep goes off, a number registering on the gauge immediately. "One forty-two." I grin like a cat fat on a canary as Eyelet's mouth falls open. "Must have been that peppermint sweet you ate back there."

"Show-off," she says.

"If there's anything down the hole we shouldn't be into, it'll let us know immediately, and we'll have to come up with another plan."

Eyelet drinks in our surroundings, as I swing the device in all directions. "Here's hoping it finds nothing." She gulps.

"Here, you hold it." I hand her the watch. "I'll go in first." I slide past her on the rungs. "If anything flashes, let me know right away. Keep it steady," I tell her. "Don't tip the face. It won't work."

She stabilizes herself on the ladder and starts her descent. I steady her from below, in a halo of dim light, my hand on her knee, trying not to look up her skirts. With my other hand, I lower myself into what appears to be a cavern. Or a cave.

"We okay?" I say about halfway down.

"Yes." She lifts her chin from reading the watch face.

The earth balks again above our heads, shaking the ladder beneath our feet. I dig my fingers into Eyelet's boot. "You all right?"

"Yes." She sounds breathy, worried, though in a million lifetimes she'd never admit it. Sometimes she's too tough for her own good.

"We're almost there." I look below me, seeing the bleed of light. Just a tiny glimpse, but still, it's there . . . mysteriously. I drop down from the last rung, amazed at what spreads out before me. Not only light, but more . . .

"Good God in Heaven," Eyelet gasps as she steps from the ladder, her eyes wide as beams.

In the hollowed-out entrance of a lavish cave hangs a dazzling display of colourful stalactites. The ceiling above them twinkles in shards of amethyst and corundum. "This is not an abandoned coal mine at all," I say.

"I'd say not." Eyelet laughs. "What is it, I wonder?"

"A gem mine?" I guess, checking the watch in her hand. "It's safe. We're safe. Incredibly safe." I can't believe the reading. The air down here contains fewer toxins than on the streets of Brethren. It's the purest air I've ever recorded. I snap the watch face shut and pocket the contraption. "We don't need these gas masks anymore."

Eyelet peels off her mask and dashes away. "Look at this!" she shouts travelling deeper into the cavern.

I shed my mask and follow her, a little worried at her overzealous pace. "Wait, I'm not sure we should be—" My jaw drops at the sight of a small blue pool at the centre of the cavern. Its shimmering waters lap at my feet.

"It's a dream." Eyelet turns to me. "It can't be real." She runs her hands along the side of a stalactite. "Are you seeing what I'm seeing?"

"I am."

"It's unbelievable. Like a fairy tale." She walks around, touching everything, every formation, every rock, dipping her hands into the water.

"Don't tell me you believe in those, too."

She scowls at me, then suddenly looks up, her face all at once illuminated as if standing in a ray of sunshine. "Look!" She draws in a childlike breath and stands, enveloped in a capsule of light. "Where is it coming from?"

I rush to her side, my heart racing, entering the beam of shining light that pours in through the centre of the hole above our heads. "I don't know," I say slowly. "I don't even know how it's possible."

She squints. "But it's definitely here, right? I've not imagined it."

"No, it's definitely here."

"There!" she shouts. "It's coming from there!" Her eyes register on something and she darts forward, leaping haphazardly rock to rock across the pond.

"What are you doing? Be careful!" I bolt after her, not as agile of step. I slip at one point, arms backpedaling in a fight to regain my composure, bringing a cheeky smile to her lips. At last I land next to her on the island where she stands, staring up at the same hole as she, neatly carved in the cavern's roof, just a few rock jumps ahead of us. It's not a large hole—they're more like slats, several of them, cut next to each other to form one big hole. "They must be part of the old mine-shaft construction."

"But what about the light? Where is it coming from?"

"I don't know." I squint. "I don't understand it. There's nothing up there. We've just come from on top. Or, at least I think we have."

The earth rocks again, very slightly this time, and I rush forward, collecting Eyelet up in my arms. I crush her to my chest, harder than I mean to. She feels warm and soft against my ribs. Our hearts beat together until the rumble passes. I'm reluctant to let her go.

"I have to know where it leads." She pushes off from me.

"No." I reel her back in. "You can't go in there. We've no idea how deep the water is!"

"But I have to know." She pushes off again, and continues jumping rock to rock, until she's directly under it. My heart thunders in my chest.

"Well?" I say, as she tips her head.

She raises a hand to her eyes and squints. "I don't know. It's blinding."

"It's likely just a reaction from the minerals."

"Minerals?" She lowers her chin.

"Yes, minerals and oxidization and all that sort of thing." I tug at my waistcoat.

"You haven't a clue what you're talking about, have you?" She stares at me.

"I suppose you have a better explanation?"

She looks up again. "It appears to have no end to it. The light, I mean."

"Well, that's not possible, we know what's above this. We've just come from there."

"But what if . . ."

"What if what?"

Her eyes have that same gleam in them they did the day we stood at the edge of the smoky black ravine, watching the workers dump factory scraps into Embers—where she made mention of a fantastical floating world. "You don't think you're seeing—"

"It's likely nothing," she says weakly, as if she's afraid to spill her thoughts aloud. Or is it that she's afraid of what she's seeing? Funny, her cheeks have suddenly flushed. "It's like you said, we don't know how deep the water is, I'd better get back."

I'm about to protest when she starts jumping toward me over the slippery stones. My heart lodges in my throat when she catches a heel and shoots forward, arms floundering. At last, to my relief, she reaches the shoreline opposite me.

"Come over here," she signals, grinning. As if I'm about to retrace *her* steps. "There's more room than over there, and it's drier." She insists. "Come *onnnnn*, Urlick."

"Very well, then . . ." I swallow down the glob of fright that clogs my throat, and I start the tedious journey over. I slip on some craggy moss and taste my heart, I swear, before my boots right themselves and I catch my balance again. Eyelet finds this deliciously amusing, apparently. She's so much better at this stuff than me. I really should just stay in the laboratory.

I start hopping again and stop halfway.

"What is it?" Eyelet gasps.

"The earth." I look up. "It's no longer moving. It hasn't moved in a while now. Whatever was happening, it must be over." *And her breathing has gotten much better, too.*

"You're right," Eyelet says, staring up at the ceiling. "Must be."

"We could probably go back up, if you want." I leap the final stone, landing awkwardly on the shore next to her. "What?"

Her eyes slink over the outline of my body, quantifying my every movement.

"What are you looking at?" I say.

"Nothing." She grins, and all at once I'm incapacitated, unable to think or move . . . or breathe. Am I breathing? What is that look in her eyes?

"If it's nothing, why the funny face?" I say.

"What face?" The corner of her sweet mouth lifts as she speaks, and I know something's afoot. Standing there in that ray of light, she's never looked so beautiful—so intoxicatingly beautiful. I shift my weight, and I swear her eyes snap up from my groin.

She folds her arms, and her breasts bubble up against the lace of her chemise. They scream for attention—not that I'm giving them any.

*All right, maybe a little.*

*Oh, good Lord in Heaven, girl, have mercy, do not* hug *yourself.*

I avert my eyes in an attempt to calm things down, but it's no use; things have begun to sprout. I fidget, trying to conceal my hidden yet obviously growing interest in her.

Praying it stays hidden.

"Do I look funny to you?" She slinks toward me, thrusting her hips out in front of her, breasts again *titillating* . . . I mean, tussling. "What's the matter? Don't you like my affections?" She clutches the lapels of my suit coat and pulls me to her.

"I would *not* say that is the reaction. No." I gasp in some badly needed air.

She snuggles even closer.

"It's hot down here, isn't it?" I tug at my shirt collar. "Are you warm?"

"Very." She moves her hands to my face.

"If it is a rise you're trying to get out of me, you're succeeding." I swallow.

"Good," she says, dragging her fingernail down and around the side of my chin. "I was hoping that would be your reaction."

All at once, every molecule in my body heats up, then screams, then turns to burning ice within seconds. An exhilarating, yet excruciatingly painful experience, I must say—especially in my brain . . . and my lower half.

She presses in even closer against the development. "Is there something troubling you I should know about?" She frowns up at me.

"I should think if you keep on this way, you shall know about it very soon."

She giggles.

Then, like a minx, she drops her eyes to my groin again, slowly, dragging her steamy gaze up my front, tugging upward along with it the apparatus I've been so desperately trying to keep hidden in my britches. "Are you having fun?" I ask, my heart a stumbling machine in my chest.

"Yes, very much so." She darts forward, sucking my bottom lip into her mouth, and I nearly break apart at the seams. "I should think I could be having more fun, though," she purrs, walking her fingers provocatively up the front of my chest.

"Miss Elsworth." I pull back, astonished. "If I didn't know better, I'd swear you've learned a thing or two from your roommate back in the Brink."

"Maybe I have." She grins. "Is that a problem?"

She arcs her brows in a provocative way, and my heart trips in my chest.

"You are suddenly full of surprises, aren't you?"

"You've not even discovered the half of them."

She takes my lips into her mouth before I can object . . . not that I would, *ever* . . . unbuttoning my shirt and loosening my ascot at whip speed, her cool fingers slipping in underneath. "What is all this?" I gasp through her kisses.

"If you have to ask, I fear it's not going to be very fun, now is it?"

*Did she? Is she? That was a proposal . . .*

"You mean you want—?" I blush.

She pulls away. "Can you think of a more beautiful place for it to happen?"

She touches me again and my skin pulses alive. *I am coals, she is fire.*

Launching up on her toes, she kisses me hard before I have the chance to properly answer. Her warm cinnamon tongue darts in and out of my mouth, and something primal inside me takes over.

The next thing I know, I'm bending her backward, almost throwing her to the ground, lowering myself down overtop. Eyelet reaches up, stripping the drawstring from my britches, fervently kissing me. My heart convulses like gunfire in my chest.

I pull back, gaining my wits about me. "Are you sure about this?" My arms tremble.

"*Why?* Don't you want me?" Her bosoms heave. There's hurt in her eyes.

"Of course I want you, it's just . . . don't you want to wait, until, say . . . we can properly marry?"

She furrows her brows, snapping up onto her elbows beneath me so quickly we nearly clash heads. "Who will marry us, Urlick?" Her voice falters. "Where will we ever be married? In what universe would that ever be possible? You, the way you are, and me, the way I . . ." She swallows down the end of her sentence. Tears fill her eyes.

A piece of my heart shatters, knowing she's right. There will be no church wedding for us. No celebration of sacrament. We have no choice but to live our lives out as sinners. Any children we bear will be born bastards. Unrecognized, unaccepted . . .

If we manage to live through all of this.

"Don't you see?" She cups my face in her hands, her fingers cold and shaking. "All we have—*all we'll ever have*, you and I, is the moment we live in. This very moment. Nothing more. For us, nothing else is guaranteed.

"I want this moment, Urlick, please don't take it from me . . .

I want to experience this.

To experience you.

To experience real love. Just this once.

I may never have another chance.

*We* may never have another chance.

Please, Urlick, give me this moment."

I stare down at her, staring up at me, the forlorn, loving look in her eyes. I've never wanted anything more in my life than this moment.

"Of course, Eyelet," I whisper, dropping down and kissing her tears away. "I give you this moment, along with my heart."

She pulls me closer, guiding me between her legs, boldly stroking my back. I clasp her thigh, coating her face and neck in a tender trail of affectionate kisses, as I drive her skirts upward and work her stockings down.

# Forty-Two

***Eyelet***

I wake, groggy from sleep, the most blissful sleep I've ever enjoyed, my heart still racing, blood rushing through me, tingling delicate parts of me. A warm campfire burns deep in my belly.

Urlick lies asleep beside me, peacefully sleeping, a garden of temptation. The muscles of his stomach drift gracefully up and down between his ribs, calling my fingers to touch them. *Oh,* how I love this man, from his artistically marred face, to his boysenberry lips, down to his ghostly white toes. I close my eyes, remembering last evening, how cautious a lover he was with me, gentle and considerate, yet at the same time voraciously hungry—as desperate to experience me as I was him.

And now that I have done so, I don't believe I'll ever be able to get enough.

I sigh, lying back against the cool earth, staring dreamily up at the stalactites, listening to the placid *drip, drip, drip* of their ongoing creation—hoping to stave off the unholy thoughts of wanting Urlick that will not leave my head—to quash the pang of throbbing desire still pulsing between my legs.

I understand, now, Livinea's line of thinking. How she can be so obsessed with such unthinkable things. A taste of this could drive anyone to hysteria.

Oh, good Lord, stop thinking.

I roll over and back.

He stirs and sighs a gentle sigh, and I reach over, running a finger over first his scar and then his lips, giggling when he flinches but does not wake. From there I trace the thick muscles of his shoulder, watching them shudder at my touch, feeling the heat of him rise through his skin. The veins of his forearms stand taut and raised. Such power this body holds. Such magic and mystery.

I lean forward, pressing a kiss to his lips, no longer able to stop myself. I want him. I want him again. He moans, softly objecting before his eyes flutter open and he realizes it's me who's pestering him.

"Thought you could tease me while I slept, did you?" He pulls me into his arms and rolls, me shrieking and laughing, until we've switched positions and he's on top of me.

"Don't be silly, what fun would that be?"

He kisses the end of my nose. Then he scoops me up, pressing me tight to his chest, and envelops me in a long, hard, passionate kiss.

A flurry of moths beat lustful wings inside my chest.

Is this going to happen every time now?

He threads his fingers through mine, our hands pressed to the ground. My body is charged by his touch.

"What time is it?" He flips my wrist over to check my chrono-cuff. "Half past ten." His eyes lift, streaked in a blaze of panic. "The others are going to wonder what happened to us. We'd better get going."

I nod and lurch to get up, but he catches me, my face in his hands, and kisses me again. This time, it's as if all that is sweet in the world is my lips and he can't get enough of them. I join in his quest, thirsty for more—the roll of his breath, the touch of his skin, the essences of him again, inside me.

"Yeah, now we'd *really* better get going." He pulls himself away from me, swiping his brow. His cheeks red as passionate apples.

I lower my gaze, afraid he'll read the shameful spark of desire still burning in *my* eyes.

"Everything all right?" he asks.

"Yeah." I smile at him over my shoulder. "A little *too* all right."

He laughs.

I reach for my cast-off corset and duck my head inside the light fabric of my chemise. Its cool fibers rake over the ends of my nipples, sending a chill down my spine. I bite my lip, remembering things. Urlick's hands all over me.

One by one, I fasten the buckles down the front of my corset and tug the drawstrings in back.

"Need help?" Urlick asks hesitantly, watching me struggle.

"It's all right." I smile. "I can get it." I'm afraid to let him touch me again, for fear we never leave this place. If I had my way, we never would.

I look around at the blue-green waters, at the light shimmering off the tapering stalactites, and I want to stay in this place, inside this moment, forever.

A tear warms my eye, and I push it away.

"You're sure you're all right?" Urlick turns to me.

"I'm fine, really." I launch to my feet, donning the gas mask to hide my emotions. "As you said, we'd better get going."

Urlick stands and strides toward me, a lean, agile panther. He lifts my chin, slides the gas mask down, and brings his forehead to rest on mine. "No matter what happens." He stares into my eyes. "We will always have this moment. No one can ever take that away from us."

I smile and press my head harder against his. "You're right," I say. "It'll be ours forever."

He kisses me, leaving me breathless.

"How about I go first." He leans back, still clutching my arms. "Seems to have worked out nicely last time."

"Oh, I don't know." I smirk and pull away. "I'm sure I could have handled it."

I roll my eyes and he cuffs me on the bottom, causing me to yelp, then reaches for the rusty rungs and hoists himself up on the ladder, taking slow stock of me one last time before he starts to climb.

I suck in a breath, etching the beauty of the cavern and our moments here together deep into my memory—then follow.

# Forty-Three

***Eyelet***

Urlick throws back the door at the top of the shaft and gives me a hand up out of the hole. I jump to my feet, blinking at the dull, grey hideousness of the forest, all draped in fog. How I long to go back to the beauty beneath. I look down at it over my shoulder with longing.

"Clementine!" Urlick shouts. She stands in the clearing, gas mask half-on, half-off, hoses unhooked, her wings wildly off-kilter. "You've come back."

Clementine paws the ground.

Urlick strides firmly toward her. "You'd think she had a night like we had." He looks slyly back at me over his shoulder and winks.

I laugh. "Not quite so lucky, I'm sure." I smile, and something wild stirs in my belly.

A black blotch appears through the trees, driving toward us, cutting through the air like a blade. My heart takes a tumble at my ribs. Urlick goes for the knife in his boot and throws himself in front of me.

"No, wait." I push him aside, squinting. "I think I know what it is." The black smudge dips down below the cloud cover, swooping through the trees. "Pan!" I shout. "Is that you?" I race toward her, my eyes welling with tears. Her beak cuts a bloodred seam through the murky forest, drawing closer. "Mother!" I call to her.

"Mother?" Urlick frowns, shooting me a confused look.

Pan flutters past, cawing. Tears flood from my eyes as she circles my head. "I thought you were dead. I thought that guard had killed you." I reach out to her, trembling.

She lands on my shoulder and nuzzles my chin. "I was only stunned, thankfully," she jabbers in broken speech.

Urlick falls back on his heels.

"I tried, but I couldn't find you when I came around. You were nowhere to be found." She flaps.

"It's all right. You're here now." I cuddle closer to her. "We're here! Together!"

"Mother?" Urlick repeats again.

"It's a long story," I turn and say to him.

"Go on." Urlick moves his hand in a circle, urging me to elaborate.

"Well, I guess eventually you'll have to know, so . . ." I swallow. "Urlick, Pan is actually my mother."

"She's wha—?" The news nearly knocks him from his feet.

"Rather, my mother is actually Pan, or whichever way you want to take it."

Urlick's mouth falls open. He gasps for air. "How is that possible?"

"You remember that thing called magic you didn't believe in? Well . . ." I jerk my head. "Suffice it to say . . . it is as I tried to tell you, back when she first appeared at the Academy: sometimes magic trumps logic. Especially when love is involved." I look at Mother, and she flashes her eyes at me.

Urlick looks to me, then to Mother, confusion in his eyes.

"You see . . . as Mother lay dying, Pan made a choice to die in her place, so that Mother could live on, to be with me. It was a selfless act on Pan's part—made possible because she was a—"

"Valkyrie?" Urlick fills in the blank. "Pan was a Valkyrie . . . your mother is now . . ."

"A Valkyrie. That's right," Pan says. "Now you're getting it."

She lifts off, circling me, then lands gently on Urlick's shoulder. "But that's not why I've come." She caws, loudly. "There is another reason."

"What is it?" I say. "Is something wrong?"

"I'm afraid so, yes."

"What's happened?" Urlick turns.

"It's Iris." She caws. "C.L. sent me. They've taken her."

# Forty-Four

***Eyelet***

We land aboard Clementine under the cover of the clouds, near the edge of the woods, just outside the walls of the Piglingham Square. Abandoning her, we scramble the last thirty metres and take refuge behind some taller shrubbery to the left of the stage. The Ruler stands in the centre of it.

I look around. The whole of the Commonwealth is here. Man. Woman. Child.

"Burn the heretic!" The crowd shouts.

"Dip her first!" a lone woman screams.

My heart kicks at my throat.

The woman launches onto her toes above the rest of the heads in the crowd to get a better look. Others stir and push toward the front.

"We've got to get closer," Urlick says, looking out of the collar of his overcoat. He's stood the collar on end and pinned it up high around his face, donned the freakmaster's top hat and pulled it down as far as he can, and tied his ascot like a scarf around the bottom half of his chin to hide his face.

I, too, have done my best to conceal my identity, pinning my hair high up under Livinea's borrowed top hat, tilting it at a severe angle down over my eyes. I swapped her clothing for my own, in the hope of better disguising myself—but so far, her flashy fashion is proving to do just the opposite. It seems the bold navy-and-ivory-striped fabric, and the unusual cut of the sleeves of her jacket, are drawing unwanted attention from the women in the crowd. Eyes track and stare at me.

A woman reaches out and touches my arm as we pass. "Did you see that?" she whispers to her friend. "That woman wears real silk."

A sick feeling invades my stomach.

I lower my head and stumble after Urlick. He yanks me through the hating crowd. We tuck in behind a couple of overgrown boxwood evergreens at the far side of the stage, where we can hear but we can't be seen. Rain threatens overhead.

I raise my chin, daring to take a peek. "Oh, good Lord in Heaven," I gasp, seeing a squirming, screaming Iris, gagged and bound, tied to a post atop a mound of kindling, behind centre stage, big enough to torch the entire city.

Urlick stares up at her, speechless. A tear rolls down his cheek.

Her darting eyes lock onto mine.

*Oh, Iris, I love you so . . . Hold on, please.*

Hot, angry rocks burn in the pit of my stomach. I feel so helpless.

To the right of Iris stands Penelope Rapture, all dressed in black, her vengeful eyes scanning the crowd.

I avert my gaze, gasping as my eyes register a second horror. Something I never thought I'd see again.

A second woman appears, also dressed in black. She moves in swiftly next to Penelope. Her face is the most unnatural shade of peach. She wears a matching mourning gown, as if in a show of sympathy. A sheer black veil covers her beady grey eyes.

"Flossie," I breathe.

"What?" Urlick's head whips around.

"It's Flossie. Look," I say.

His eyes are like moons. "How can that be?" he hisses. "I thought you said she was dead? I thought you said you killed her."

"As good as, when I left her!" I gasp. "I don't understand this, either."

Behind the two women, Iris struggles against her gags and ties. The haunted look in her eyes stops and starts my heart. "This can't be happening." I blink away tears. "It can't be real."

It's then I note that Flossie doesn't seem to be quite riveted to the floorboards of the stage. Rather, she keeps levitating, just slightly, each time she raises her elbows at her sides. She flaps her arms to combat the movement, grounding herself again, her gloved hands clasped in front of her. "She's floating," I say. "It must be an illusion."

Urlick turns.

"Flossie." I point. "She's floating."

Urlick jerks his head around and stares through narrowed eyes.

Flossie floats up again. There are no feet under the hem of her dress. Instead, I swear I see the glimpse of tentacles. "She's been infected by the Infirmed," I say. "She must have been. When I left her, she was about to be eaten."

"Why on earth would Penelope risk being near her, then?" Urlick cranks around, surveying the huge fields of rubber-screened filtration devices that line the boundaries of Brethren, designed to suck up all Vapourous entities that attempt to breach the city's borders. "How did Flossie circumvent the scrubbers and screens?"

"Penelope must have let her in."

"Why would she do that?"

"I don't know," I say, my eyes still fixed on the stage where Penelope and Flossie stand, holding hands. "Something is very wrong."

Beneath the folds of Flossie's clothing, something glows an eerie shade of green. As though a light were pulsing rhythmically at her chest. Is that? *The necklace* . . . Could it be?

"Urlick—" I start.

"Your attention, please!" Penelope hollers, gramophone crackling. She lifts her arms, and the crowd instantly quiets. Urlick wrenches me back behind the cover of the trees. "We have gathered you here today," she continues, "to assist us in ridding our community of a *wretched evil.*"

The crowd goes up as if it's been lit on fire.

Iris lets out a jagged wail.

"As you know," Penelope rasps over the amplification, "we here in Brethren have had our first prison break." The crowd roars, and fists pump in the air. "As well, I've received word that a highly dangerous mental patient has escaped from the Brink." The crowd gasps.

"What?" I falter.

Urlick claps his hand over my mouth, pulling me up tight to his chest.

"We have every reason to believe they are on the run together! And this heretic here"—Penelope swings awkwardly around and points to Iris—"is the one responsible for their FREEDOM!"

The crowd goes wild, shouting, chanting, calling for her death. "Burn the traitor! Make her pay!"

Iris's eyes pop with panic. A metallic ball of fear chokes my throat. I've never been so afraid.

Penelope's vengeful eyes narrow. She addresses the group again. Flossie stands next to her, scanning the faces of the crowd. "In an attempt to reclaim peace and effect justice for all who dwell in Brethren, I have decided this heretic must be burned at the stake!"

The crowd cheers in loud agreement. Penelope encourages them with a smile.

"It is my hope that, by slow-roasting their accomplice, we will smoke the offenders out. At which time they, too, will be dealt with accordingly! To the fullest extent of our laws!"

The crowd screams. "They cannot hide *forever*!"

"Burn 'er!" an elderly woman shouts.

"Light the torch! Roast the heretic!" others yell.

Penelope signals something to Flossie, who turns her back to the crowd, then whirls her floating self back around, holding a device in her hands.

Penelope flaps her arms, quieting the crowd. "As you all know," she begins again, "the air here in Brethren has become unbearably thin, the water is disturbed, our resources are dwindling."

Urlick and I share a quick, confused look.

"It has been my plan for quite some time, as it was Smrt's before me, God rest his soul"—she bows her head as if in prayer—"to go forth and conquer the East, so that we may secure a more suitable place to raise our future generations!" She throws out her arms, punctuating her sentence, and the crowd lets out a shout of approval.

"The East?" Urlick whispers to me.

"I know nothing of this." I shake my head. "There's never been a plan to leave Brethren."

"It's heretics like this"—Penelope points to Iris—"who stand in the way of our progress! Like the two fugitives at large, they threaten our plan for success, by undermining my *authority*!"

The crowd ignites again. Fists punch and voices rail.

"Off with their bloody 'eads!" a man behind us shouts.

Urlick looks back at me, wide-eyed. "This is madness."

Flossie squints her right eye and places it behind the viewer of the device in her hand. She cranks the handle, and a reel begins turning. A beam of purple light shoots out over the heads of the crowd, scanning its members, projecting their likenesses back onto the giant slate screen behind her.

"Duck!" I shout, throwing a hand over Urlick's head as the beam sweeps past us.

"What is it? What's happening?" he whispers as I haul him down.

"She's taking a viteogram." I suck in a tight breath. "Flossie's recording all the faces in the crowd. They'll have a record of every person here."

The beam sweeps past our heads again. Urlick yanks me toward him. I land with a thud against his chest. He throws his body over me like a shield behind the boxwood tree, pinning us as close as possible to the ground as the beam keeps searching, sweeping our area of the grounds.

"We've got to get out of here." He launches up after it passes, dragging me to my feet.

"But what about Iris?" I pull back. "We can't just leave her here."

"We're not!" Urlick hauls me forward. "We just need a plan."

I look back over my shoulder. Flossie's eyes connect with me briefly.

My limbs grow weak.

Urlick tugs at my arm, and I duck my head and race forward amid Iris's screaming, my heart pulling from my chest. A lightning-like shiver pulls like rope through my veins. I gasp. *No. Not the silver. Not now . . . please . . . NO!*

"This way!" Urlick hurls me to one side, out of the path of the oncoming beam. I slip in the muck and I ditch in behind the trolling curls of cloud cover, slinking along inside them after Urlick, toward the forest at the park's end. The thoughts in my mind are growing progressively muddy.

I reach into my pocket as I run, feeling myself slipping, the silver rising, and grab for the last leaf from the plant room at the Compound. Stuffing it into my mouth, I chew wildly—thankful when its venom spreads quickly. The bolt of silver lightning inside me softens. The fog that threatens my mind dissipates.

"You may have heard a rumour that a prince has been found," Penelope's voice blares out over the gramophone speakers above our heads. I turn to see her shaking a fist in the air. "Well, I am here to tell you, *there is no truth to it*! There is no such prince! There never has been. I am your rightful ruler!"

"Long live our RULER!" The crowd bellows.

"Now we've really got to go." Urlick reaches out to me, his brow wet with sweat.

"What? Why?" He yanks me forward.

"Eyelet." He races on, his breath heaving. "There's something I really need to tell you." He looks back at me, his lips twitching. "And I will, I promise . . . just not now."

Spying a break in the cloud cover, he dashes through it. I stumble, falling after him.

The viteogram beam scurries again over our heads, tracking us like an autoscope on a sniper's steamrifle.

"I am your *ruler*!" Penelope's voice rings out. "There is no other! I, and I alone, will lead you to the promised land!"

*"Rapture! Rapture! Rapture!"* The crowd chants.

Thunder claps. My chin shoots up as the skies split open.

Rain falls, bouncing off the backs of the people, who shriek and moan and race for cover. They swell from the park like a school of frightened fish. Urlick and I race among them, hands over our heads, slipping on the wet ground. The viteogram beam of light falls away.

I look back over my shoulder. Flossie stands centre stage—the rain-doused candle of the viteogram smouldering in her hand. Her black dress is dissolving, draining down the front of her like washed-away ink, along with her overly peachy complexion. The colour seeps through the slats in the floorboards as if it were paint, leaving behind a hauntingly translucent-looking Flossie.

# Forty-Five

***Urlick***

"We can't just leave her there," Eyelet sobs as we run.

"We can't go back for her now." I clear a stump. "Thankfully, the rain has bought us a little time. We'll have to figure something else out." I pant, tracking Pan in the air, making sure we're on course, headed back to the freak train.

"Like what?" Eyelet stumbles to keep upright beside me.

"I don't know," I say, squeezing her hand. "All I know is"—I look back—"this isn't going to be your *run-of-the-mill* rescue mission, that's for sure!"

"Because all of them have been up until now!"

We pull to a stop in the clearing. I drop my hands to my knees, sucking in big gulps of air. Eyelet does the same, pinching the stitch in her side and pacing in a circle, then she falls into another horrid fit of coughing.

"You all right?" I rush to her.

"Fine," she coughs, waving me away. "I'll be fine. I will."

But she's not, and I hold her hand as she gasps to catch her breath.

"What did you mean when you said you had something you really needed to tell me back there?" She looks up at me, changing the subject.

I hang my head, swallowing air. *No time like the present, I suppose.* I let go of her hand and tighten the grip on my knees. I speak without looking at her. "It seems," I start, a little shaky—but then again, who wouldn't be with what I have to divulge—"there's been a bit of a mix-up regarding my identity."

"Your what?"

I raise my head. "It appears I'm not who I thought I was."

She scowls.

"I mean . . . I am who I am . . . It's just"—I bite my lip—"it appears I'm a bit more than I thought I once was."

"More what?" She looks afraid to even pose the question.

I let out a laboured breath. "What would you say if I were to tell you . . ." I squirrel up an eye and hesitate, biting my lip. "I'm royalty." I rush out the rest of the sentence. I keep my eyes pinched, bracing, as if expecting to be hit.

"You're *what*?" Eyelet staggers.

"A prince . . . it appears." I tug down my waistcoat.

Eyelet's eyes bloom twice their size. Her expression is of unbridled disbelief. *I think.* Either that or she's about to laugh.

"The only living heir to the throne of Brethren," I stammer on quickly, filling the awkward air. "The Ruler's rightful successor. That's me." I poke my chest.

"You're joking, right?" Eyelet grins sheepishly.

"'Fraid not."

Eyelet launches backward, holding her own chest. She must think me suffering from madness.

"Apparently, though, I'm not a bastard." I lilt my voice and flit my eyes playfully. "That's a good thing, right?" I swoop my brows.

Eyelet stares at me, an O for a mouth. What does one say, when one's lover announces such a thing? She springs forward and tests my head for fever. "What did they do to you in that jail?"

"Nothing." I pull away. "It's all right here in this register from the church." I produce a wrinkled, folded piece of paper from my pocket.

"You pulled out the page!" She scowls at me. "From the formal church register?"

"Just a couple of them."

Eyelet gasps.

"See, there's my name, right there." I stab at the paper. "My birth date. My birth weight. And above all else, the markings match." I point to the corresponding line on the ledger. "Can't argue with that, now, can they?"

"Let me see." She pulls at the edge of the paper.

"And see what it says after that?" I point to the next line.

Her eyes dash over the explanation of my birth, at the formal script, the words declaring my true heritage . . . certified at the end by the press of the royal wax seal. Eyelet looks up at me, flabbergasted eyes round as dessert plates. Her mouth hangs open, questions teetering on the tip of her tongue.

"So your mother—?"

"Had a child for the Ruler, yes, in exchange for an appointment for my father at the Academy. We were poor and my mother was a great beauty, it says here, which was also confirmed by Smrt." I shake out the papers in my hand. "Smrt may have even been the one to arrange their meeting, I'm not sure. At any rate, apparently the Ruler took notice of my mother at some event, and a deal was struck between all parties involved."

"So she was used. Bargained with . . . like chattel."

"I suppose you could say that." I squirrel up my mouth. "The Ruler was fearful that his wife—who, at that point, had given birth to three dead sons—would never be able to produce the male heir so badly needed to succeed him, so he commissioned my mother to produce a spare. Just in case, you know, his real wife could never produce one."

Eyelet swallows. "And what if she, too, had failed? What if the child had been a girl?"

"I don't know. I suppose she'd have suffered the consequences." I drop my gaze to the paper again, feeling a pang of hurt for my mother in my heart. "It says here, no one outside the Royal House knew about the arrangement, except, of course, for Smrt, who was sent to attend and verify my birth. But when I was born . . . as I am"—I trip over the words—"the deal was apparently dashed." I look Eyelet in the eyes. "The Ruler reneged, and I was to be destroyed, but then . . . apparently, the Ruler—my father—came to view me and couldn't bring himself to go through with his orders. So he had me stowed away in the woods—his only living heir—never to be seen again unless necessary." I fold the papers in my hand. "The orders to destroy me were reversed. He may have even paid for my education."

"How do you know all that?"

"It's right here in print." I pull out another rumpled page—a handwritten letter from the Ruler to his son, a sort of plea for forgiveness from the Ruler's deathbed, left for me. The words explain not only the circumstances, but the Ruler's regrets—one of which is that he didn't raise me himself, but rather had me banished. His *only* son.

Eyelet reaches up and strokes my arm, comforting me.

"That's why the father I knew never loved me," I say soberly. "How could he? I was an experiment gone terribly wrong. An experiment that took the love of his life from him, after she'd agreed to do something this atrocious to improve his position." Saying it out loud makes me feel sick. I swallow down the spittle that rises in my throat. "The guilt must have driven him mad," I say. "Then I showed up on his doorstep. A terrible reminder—"

"You can't think of it that way." Eyelet moves in, touching my shoulder. "None of this was your fault—*is* your fault. *You* were not consulted on the matter. *He* should have been man enough to embrace the half of you that was his love's. You are, after all, also the product of your mother. And a damn good one at that, if I must say."

"Eyelet?" I gasp, shocked that she's sworn.

She smiles and takes my hand. "That must have been why Smrt had your specimen card." She looks past me, off into the trees. "Obviously he must have been ordered to destroy you, then do away with it, but didn't do either." She returns her eyes to me. "Perhaps he was planning a coup on the Ruler way back then?"

"I wonder what else he didn't destroy?" I look down at the explanation in the letter, wondering if, somewhere, there's more.

Eyelet chews her nail. "I knew you cut your meat too well."

"What?"

Her eyes flash as she snuggles up to my arm. "At the Compound, with the quail. The way you held your silver. You manoeuvred your fork and knife around your plate in such a refined way. It was all too graceful for a commoner, I knew it."

I stare down at her, perplexed.

"Never mind." She flips me a flirty grin. "Your Highness." She curtsies, and I swat at her playfully. "Where did you find all this, anyway?" She pokes at the papers in my hands.

"I didn't. A friend found them for me." I look up, feeling the press of hot tears at the backs of my eyes. "God rest his battered soul. He found the register hidden in the crypt of the church, so he stole it for me and left it under the porch of the manse next door. Along with these." I pull out a pair of royal footprints: a baby's feet pressed into ink and then to a page.

Eyelet touches them and a smile comes to her face. "No two prints in the world are alike, you know. Do you know what this means?" She takes them from me. "Above all else, this is your ticket. Your solid proof. No one else in the world can match these footprints. Only you."

Eyelet's gaze falls to the letter in my hand. "Your poor mother," she sighs. "She was used as a pawn."

"Like mother, like son," I snap rather harshly.

Eyelet looks up at me longingly. "You are going to claim it, aren't you? Your rightful throne, I mean. You're going to do your mother that honour."

"Yes." I tug a hand through my hair. "But I have no idea how."

"You'll figure something out." Eyelet smiles. She takes my hand, then flits away, sort of skipping, and then she turns around. "You realize what this means, don't you?" She scowls at me rather provocatively, slinking slowly back my way. "You are an outlaw"—she walks her fingers up my chest—"a prince on the run, and I'm your latest conquest." She punches me in the arm and lowers her voice. "Rather debonair of us, don't you think?"

"*Only* conquest," I correct her, blushing.

"Really?" She giggles. "Sounds so much more mysterious the way I put it." She links my arm.

I grow serious. A lump of emotion balls in my throat. Taking her chin in my hands, I look deep into her eyes, stammering before I say, "We shall be married. Properly. I promise. As soon as I take the throne. That is"—I swallow—"if you'll have me."

*"Hmmmm . . ."* Eyelet taps her chin and tilts her head. Pursing her lips, she ponders the question, her eyes at the top of her lids. My heart leap-pounds.

"You're kidding, right?"

"Of course I'm kidding." She throws her arms out and reels me into the biggest hug she's ever given me. "Your Royal Highness." Her breath in my ear. "I would love nothing more than to be your queen."

Her face is a radiant ball of light. Closing her eyes, she engages me in the most fiery, blood-rushing kiss that ever existed—*I'm quite convinced*—and then closes it off with three short, lip-nibbling, darting, swallow-like kisses that leave me wanton.

*I swear this woman can undo me in an instant.*

"We'd better go," I say breathlessly, pulling away. "We've got an awful lot to accomplish all of a sudden. First we free Iris, then overthrow the Ruler and dispose of Flossie once and for all, then perhaps before sundown we can take back the Commonwealth. What do you say?"

Eyelet laughs.

"It's really too bad we don't have any connections on the inside." I stroke my chin, look dreamily past her head. "It would be so much easier if only we had some sort of in."

"Wait a minute!" Eyelet draws back.

"What is it?" I scowl.

"Come with me!" She grabs me by the arm and breaks into a run.

"Where are we going?" I stumble to catch up with her.

"To see another banished princess about a dethroning."

# *Forty-Six*

***Eyelet***

"I can't believe you're trying to break back into the very place we've just broken you out of!" Urlick paces, a jumpy bundle of nerves. Not that I blame him, Madhouse Brink is as intimidating from the outside as it is from within. And we barely made it out the last time. He strides along the stone pebble driveway—so lanky and so lissome—wringing his shaky gloved hands.

"Can *you* think of any better way to have an audience with the keeper?" I place my hands on my hips and stare at him. "It's not like we can just ring her up."

He turns, crinkling his eyes at me, pink burning irises flickering through the heavy wisps of fog. Sweaty curls cling to his troubled forehead. He's as annoyed with me as he has ever been. I know I shouldn't, but I grin at him, just slightly. I can't help it. Every time I look at him now I fall more and more in love.

"Seriously, you've gone mad!" He flips angry hands into the air, cancelling me out. "You've utterly lost your mind."

"And you haven't, Prince . . . what was that again?" I cock my head.

"Fine. We'll break back in through the chimney." Urlick juts out his chin, scraping his top teeth over his lower lip. "But if you lose your mind on the way out, I'm not retrieving it this time."

"Nor I for you." I cross my arms.

Urlick reaches out, forgetting himself, and leans against the smooth stone surface of the Brink's outer wall, setting off the alarm.

"Or we could do that!" I flash my eyes at him.

He strikes the starfish pose, arms out, legs out, hands clawed in the air, his eyes darting.

"It's too late for panic now!"

Lucky for us, the walls have remained stationary since our little heist. The authorities haven't managed to figure out how to repair the damage to the program, though they have constructed some sort of archaic warning system, looping wires over the premises, which Urlick has also managed to trip.

Like a steamzapper that's just caught a bug inside it, the wires go off, crackling and sizzling, slowly frying, igniting a fuse that travels down another wire to a makeshift hammer made of a stick and a rock that repeatedly strikes a bell.

"Good Lord." Urlick looks to me. "Where are they, for God's sake? We could have gotten away eight times by now."

I laugh at him amid the bonging siren's pathetic wail. A searchlight at last leaps into motion, and Urlick and I dash about, trying to get caught up in its stream. "Bloody hell," Urlick shouts, sliding in the muck. "When we didn't want to be caught we were nearly caught, and now that we want to, we can't. This is madness!"

I laugh so hard my stomach hurts. I fling myself at the searchlight and miss.

Urlick dives for the light and slips in the muck. "Oh, for the sake of Pete!" he cusses, his hard shoes skirting ahead. He's rendered tail over teakettle, falling hard on his arse on the ground, his backside now as generously painted with mud as his face.

"Perhaps if we just stand still," I say.

"Stop!" a voice shouts through the darkness.

"At last," Urlick sighs as the guard's light finds him—blinding him momentarily with its aggressive beam. He raises a hand to his eyes.

I pull him up to his feet beside me, and the beam spots us both.

"Hands up!" the startled guard shouts, his voice trembling. The wagging nose of a weapon comes into view as we comply. The guard steps from the shadows. He's a shaking mess, steam arrow stuck out in front of him in his white-knuckled hands.

"We come in peace," Urlick jests, and I elbow his ribs. "What? We do."

I frown. "Not exactly."

"Shut up!" the guard shouts, trying to sound tough despite his lisp.

"Thuttup?" Urlick mocks him, and I elbow his ribs again.

"Move out of the way, you idiot." Parthena overtakes the guard. She emerges from the darkness, steamrifle in hand. She's the picture of sorrowful authority in her sheer black veil and mourning attire. A peacock-plumed pillbox hat sits askew atop her head as if hastily plopped there. "Well, well, well, what have we caught here?" She tsks. "It's not often we get returns." She grins and raises her brows. Her gaze rakes over my frame. "And you've brought me an extra. How nice of you." She narrows her almond eyes at Urlick. "What *is* that you have on?" She scowls back at me. "Don't tell me. You're letting your little inmate girlfriend dress you now?" Her eyes shift back to Urlick. "And I suppose she's doing your makeup."

He stutters.

"Save it." She steps toward us, circling, her heels squelching in the muck. "Half of Brethren is out looking for you, and yet you return to the very place you worked so hard to break out of. Why?"

"Do you see how absurd that sounds now?" Urlick says to me.

"Quiet!" Parthena snaps.

Two more guards totter in, gasping and panting, slipping in the muck, flanking Parthena's sides. They gulp and stare at me in amazement. "It's about bloody time," she seethes their way, then returns her venomous look to me. "I've asked you a question."

I gulp and sway. "I know what your sister's done to you. I know why you're here," I spit, holding my hands together to keep them from trembling.

"*This* is the big news you've come to share?" Parthena wobbles her head. "A revelation—you think I don't *already* know?"

"No, of course not, it's just that—"

"Guards, take her away." Parthena picks up her skirts and struts off.

"No, wait!" I shout as the guardsmen move in. "I know about the child! I know where she is!"

My final words catch Parthena's step. She whirls around and stares at me. Panic dances in her eyes. She charges back toward us, lips quivering. The side of her cheek twitches uncomfortably. "What are you talking about?"

"I've seen her. She lives."

"She was my tutor," Urlick says with a flick of his head.

Parthena's eyes dart between us. Confusion threads her brows. "That's not possible. My child is dead. She died shortly after birth—"

"It's not true," I say. "That's just what they wanted you to believe."

"You don't know what you're talking about, either of you."

"I think we do. And I think you know it."

Parthena rocks unsteadily back on her heels.

"Your sister told your father about you and Smrt and the baby, didn't she?" I say bravely. "Highlighting your shame so that she could steal your appointment at the Academy from you."

"How do you know all this? Where have you been?"

"Like I told you, your daughter, Flossie, was my tutor." Urlick steps forward.

"Flossie? Her name was *Florence*—Flo. She was to be *Flo* . . . not Flossie . . ." Parthena falls back, clutching her heart. Her eyes look far away. "It's not possible. They took her from me. They told me she was dead."

"They lied to you." I take a step closer. "Smrt and Penelope. They took your child, and they raised her as their own."

"No. The night the child was born, they came to take her from me. But then she was born deformed, not expected to live the night, so they left us here alone. But she did live, and then one day Penelope returned, and she stole the child away from me. Tore her right from my arms. She said she had to do it . . ." Her voice slows and her eyes drift away. "In order to save Smrt's position in society." Suddenly she returns from her dream. "I'd agreed to be hidden here until such time as I gave birth, but I never agreed to become prisoner of this place. He was a married man, you see." Her gaze blurs. "Smrt's wife lives within the walls of this institution. A victim of an illness that robbed her of her mind." Parthena gazes away to nothing in particular again. "My sister, she double-crossed me and arranged to have me locked up in here for good, citing my interest in absinthe as a habitual problem. I had no *habitual* problem—I drank a little absinthe, that was it! But my sister had other aspirations." Parthena purses her lips. "In return for her silence regarding Smrt and my delicate little matter, my dear sister was awarded the position Smrt had promised me at the Academy, while I was left forgotten and rotting here in a cell. Eventually, I'm not sure why, my father took pity on me and forced my sister to arrange for me to become warden of this place. I've held the post ever since." Her eyes narrow. "So tell me, why should I believe you? How do I know what you're telling me is true? Why should I trust you, when my own flesh and blood has betrayed me?"

"Because," Urlick speaks up, "it is the truth. Flossie and I sometimes shared personal stories, including the stories of our births. She told me of her rudimentary entry into this world. Of how she was born the illegitimate love child of two prominent professors at the Academy—and that it had to be kept a secret."

Parthena claps a hand to her heart. "But that's not possible." She breathes. "You have no proof that this Flossie is my child!"

"She bears the same mark as you," I say. "A mole on the side of her face that matches the one on your wrist." Parthena's eyes shoot downward. "I noticed it as you tightened the straps on my arms in the theatre chair. It was then I was certain she must be yours. Along with your eyes. She has your exact eyes—"

*"Stop!"* Parthena's chin wobbles.

"I'm sorry," I whisper to her. "But it's the truth."

Parthena looks away and twists her hands tightly together. In a strange way, my heart breaks for her—a victim of circumstance just like all the rest of us.

"You mean to tell me, not only did my sister take away my freedom, my dignity, my position, and the affections of the only man I ever loved, but she stole my only child away from me, too?"

"I'm afraid so," I say weakly.

Parthena turns. "Until his death I held out hope that one day Smrt would come back for me. That one day, this nightmare would be over."

"What if I were to tell you that it is?" Urlick bolts forward. "That I have the power to exonerate you from this hellhole once and for all." Parthena scowls. "What if I were to promise we could get your life back?"

"Urlick—" I say.

"What if I were to tell you, we've come here for the sole purpose of helping you effect revenge on your sister for all she's done to you, in return for a little help?"

Parthena's eyes dart over the two of us, confused. "How on earth could the likes of you do that?"

Urlick pulls another page of the church register from his breast pocket and holds it out for Parthena to read. "What if I were to tell you your sister threatened your lover and extorted money from him in order to further her position and pay off your father's business debts?"

"My father?"

"His business was failing, then suddenly it wasn't; isn't that true?" Parthena's eyes widen to twice their size. "It's all in there. All the paperwork needed to prove the crimes she committed against you. Every detail of her dirty dealings, including the one that pegs Penelope as the rightful guardian of your daughter, Flossie."

"Let me see that." With shaky fingers, Parthena snatches the page from his hand. She slowly reads. *"Born, one twenty-ninth of December in the year of our Lord, eighteen hundred and eighty-four . . . a baby girl six pounds, five ounces, to Parthena Pearl Rapture, a known local whore . . . Father, unknown. Markings: Child was born with a harelip, deemed grotesquely disfigured and not expected to live the night . . . died January two in the year of our Lord, eighteen hundred and eighty-six . . ."*

"But then you see here"—Urlick leans in, pointing to the paper—"there's been an amendment . . ."

"In my sister's hand." Parthena eyes fill with tears. "Where did you find this?"

"In a locked box in the manse of the church, where Penelope was hiding it."

"Those are my father's initials, as witness," Parthena says. "He was in on it?"

"We can't be sure. According to the ledger, he did stand to profit, some two hundred thousand and fifty jewelets to keep the birth a secret—put up by Smrt."

Parthena reroutes a tear from her cheek. "I've spent a lifetime mourning a child who's still alive." She looks up. "And the loss of a man who never really loved me."

"It's not too late to make things right," Urlick says. "That's why we've come, to ask for your help in dethroning your sister. In return, I promise you, you will see her punished to the fullest degree."

Parthena's teary eyes reduce to angry slits. "What is the plan?" she says, handing back the pages of the register.

# Forty-Seven

***Urlick***

"Parthena's guards will meet us here . . ." I draw a map with a stick in the dirt. "We'll enter the city from the east." I draw a semicircle. "While C.L., Livinea, Masheck, and the rest of you enter from the west. Hopefully creating a big-enough distraction to give us time to ambush Penelope at the castle and meet you back over here . . ." I stroke an X in the middle of the dirt map where we last saw poor Iris, tied to a stake.

"What if we're stopped?" C.L. asks, wide-eyed and trembling.

"You can't be."

"Does that mean . . . ?"

"That's right." I turn to Masheck. "You have my permission to do anything necessary to get there." C.L. lowers his head. "We only have one chance to get this right. It must go off as seamless and painless as possible—but if need be, we *will* destroy whoever gets in our way." I add, matter-of-factly, "We have no other choice. I'm not prepared to lose any of you." I glance at each in succession around the circle. "And not Iris either."

All nod.

"We'll take the city tonight, under cover of darkness. And if all goes well . . . I'll be Ruler by morn." *That sounds so foreign still, coming from my lips. Though it sounds wonderful, just the same.*

"Everybody ready?" I pull back my shoulders.

"Ready, sir." C.L. springs up. Martin, Reeke, Sadar, and Masheck follow with equal enthusiasm.

I turn, grab Eyelet by the hand, and tug her forward. "We'll see you all in the city centre, then." I toss a hand in the air behind me. "Godspeed, everyone."

"Wait!" Parthena claps a hand on my shoulder and pulls me back. "How do you and Eyelet propose to get into the city unnoticed?" Her eyes flick nervously between us. "My sister will have a Brigsman at every post. You'll never make it anywhere *near* the outskirts without being arrested—if she hasn't already sent troops up here to find you."

"She's right." A shaky Eyelet turns to me. "We can't possibly just expect to storm our way into the centre of town, after all that's happened. They know every trick we've played."

"Maybe not." Parthena's lips pull up into a wry smile. She shifts her eyes in the direction of the driveway. Parked on the gravel lane next to the entrance to the Brink is the Loony Bin wagon, hooked to four strong horses. "There is one way into the city they'd never think to check."

Eyelet swallows. "You can't be serious."

*

Eyelet sucks air sharply into her lungs and moves her feet jerkily forward. Her hand trembles in my own. I climb up into the cage. It smells of foul breath, dried blood, and urine. My knees wobble beneath me. I turn and face the outside quickly and hold out a hand to Eyelet. "You all right?" I say, giving her a hand up.

"I will be, as long as you're with me."

But I know it's a lie, despite the faltering smile. Eyelet has never shaken like this before, no matter the situation. She is truly terrified, looking around. I can't blame her.

We crawl to the back and take a seat on the bench. Parthena closes the door. The iron bars squawk, falling shut with a clang behind us, and both of us are elevated from our seats, every nerve in my body sparking as Parthena's fingers work to secure the lock.

"Stay quiet until we get there, no matter what happens," Parthena cautions, pulling the drawstring on the carpets in back. They fall, encapsulating the cage in darkness. My heart clenches into a tight, hurtling ball in my chest.

Eyelet squeezes my hand and whimpers. I pull her closer as Parthena fastens the last of the locks on the Loony Bin wagon door.

A sharp *shwing* of a knife blade exiting its sheath. Parthena gasps, as whoever's holding it places it to her neck. "I'd better see them both at the palace when we meet up again," Masheck says, in a low voice. "Yuh wouldn't want to lose that pretty head of yours, would yuh now?"

"You have my word, sir," Parthena mutters.

"Make sure it's better than your sister's."

*

We're barely away, and Eyelet begins to cough again. Another hard cough she cannot seem to stop. She leans forward, coughing something into her hand she will not let me see. Not that I could through this infernal darkness. I pitch forward, about to move the carpets up, and Eyelet stops me.

"It's nothing, really!" She hides her hand behind her back. "It's just because we're in this cage."

"Boulders." I swing around. "You were coughing earlier, even when we weren't in this cage—"

"Can we please just keep focused on the mission at hand?" Eyelet averts her eyes. There's something she's not telling me. I know there is. Why else would her chin be wobbling?

I take her face in my hands and pull it to me, cart rattling beneath us as we bounce over the road. "You are not fooling me, Miss Elsworth. I know something is wrong. If you don't want to tell me this moment, that's fine. But as soon as we have Iris completely secured, I'm going to locate that necklace, and when I do, you'll drink the contents of that vial—no ifs, ands, or buts about it. Do you hear me?"

Eyelet slowly nods her head.

I turn her around, intending to roll her into my arms, but she reaches back and takes my face in her hands, kissing me slowly. "How did I ever get lucky enough as to find someone like you?" she whispers into my mouth.

"How did I ever get lucky enough for you to pay attention?"

# *Forty-Eight*

***C.L.***

I stuff me pockets full of sticks of dynamite flares, and round the back of the train. "Masheck, yuh lead us along with Parthena's guard." I haul myself up into position on the widow's walk at the caboose. "I'll take up the post in the rear."

"I'd prefer the guard go in the cage." Masheck gives the Brigsman a stiff look. "Don't fancy ridin' up 'ere with no peeler."

Can't say that I blame 'im. Who's to trust 'em now, without Parthena present?

"'Ave it your way," I say. "But 'urry on . . . we ain't got no time to waste."

Masheck nods, races round, and stuffs the hollering Brigsman in through the bars of the train car. "Hey!" he says as Masheck turns the lock. "I didn't sign up for this!"

"Stop yer blubberin'," Masheck says. "We'll let yuh out once we're into the city. Unless, of course, yuh screw somethin' up for us." 'E leans in. "Remember, yuh ain't got nothin' to say, until we gets there. That clear?" Masheck makes a tight fist.

The frightened Brigsman nods 'is 'ead.

"Good." Masheck races back around and plops down on the driver's mount, quite the spectacle in his white gloves, top hat, and tails. A regular gentleman, give or take a threat or two.

"What about me? What shall I do?" Livinea teeters after me on her toes. She looks up at me, wearin' a goony grin. Even half out of 'er mind, she has me 'eart poundin'.

"You, my dear, will try your best to stay out of 'arm's way." I pop a kiss on her head. "Wanda? Take Livinea into your cage and keep her safe, will yuh, please?"

Wanda nods reluctantly and drags 'er off.

"Whose 'arm?" Livinea looks back at me, confused.

"Never mind." I wave the thought away. "Later, my sweet!" Livinea blows me a kiss.

I close me eyes and thank the spirit for blessing me with such an interesting creature.

Who'd've believed such a lovely would ever go for the likes of me?

"Look what I found." Reeke's low, hollow voice pulls me back from me dream. I turn to find him standing in front of me, cherry puff bombs in 'and. And not just any cherry puff bombs: heat-sensing ones, the kind that seek out the heated hearts of their victims.

"Where on earth did yuh scare those up?"

"Under the master's driving seat."

"That dirty bugger." I smile and toss one in the air with my foot. "'E was 'olding out on us all those years, wasn't he?"

"And I found these." Martin saunters up, his thick proper accent laced with excitement. In his hand he holds a high-powered crank-and-gear crossbow and a quiver full of rocket-powered arrows.

"Don't tell me the master 'ad a set of those 'idden, too!"

"No, sir." Sadar dips his head in a sheepish grin. "Urlick did. I found them in that pack you brought for him from home."

"Really?" I take one and twirl it around. "I don't seem to remember packing them." I scowl. My mind calculates they are far too big for the satchel.

"That's because they came inside these." He holds up two empty tins of mustard sardines, not much bigger than his 'and. "They were like prizes inside," he tells me, wagging the curled-lip tins in the air. "See? They collapse." He demonstrates, bending both arrows and the bow. The crossbow folds in equal eighths. The arrows do the same. "One tin held a crossbow, the other held its arrows."

"Good job, I brought one of each." I examine them, marveling at the compartmental construction. "That Urlick. 'Is mind never ceases to amaze me."

"I think I've got a problem." Martin appears out of the darkness. "Not much I can do with this!" He swirls the end of an eggbeater around on the end of his thumb, and I duck, screaming at him. "Watch it, will you? That thing is bloody lethal!"

"This?" Martin blinks, holding up the beater, like I'm telling a tale.

"Don't *crank it!*" I shout. "And whatever yuh do, don't push that lever there." I point, then yank my toes away, wincing.

"Not until you've seen the whites of their eyes, at least," Cordelia sings proudly, popping up onto the railing of the caboose beside me.

"What are you doing running around loose?" I snag the apparatus away from Martin and scoot a giggling Cordelia off into the caboose. "'ere, and take this. Yuh little expert sharpshooter." I pass off the egg-beater with a wink. "Careful now. Yuh know what it can do. Places, people!" I hike myself up into the rumble seat on the back of the plat-form, steamrifle at the ready across my knees. A symphony of barred doors clanks into place, and I give Masheck the high sign for the train to pull away. "We've a city to surprise tonight!"

*

"What are you doing passing this animal train through the city streets at night?" A Brigsman calls up to Masheck at the top of Market Street, at the junction of Middlesex and Blythe. We haven't done too badly. Almost made it past the market section of the city before being detained. Lucky us, the Brigsmen are slow tonight.

"We've been instructed to set up camp for the night, . . ." Masheck lies, flipping through fake papers he finds under the seat next to him, trying to look official, "at a Piglingham Square?"

The Brigsman looks up, scowls. "Have you?" He shifts his weight to the other foot and sneers up his nose. "And where's your permit?"

"What permit?"

"The one granting you permission to camp for the night."

"Oh, that one," Masheck says, all calm and cool-like, as if 'e's done this a million times before. At of the corner of 'is eyes I see a devilish glint spawnin', and I bite my lip. "It's in 'ere." Masheck points to 'is trouser pocket. "Do yuh mind?"

"No." The Brigsman signals, leaning on the carriage. "Go a'ead."

Masheck smiles all nice-like, reaches into 'is pocket, and comes out with a right punch to the Brigsman's face. The officer's jaw rocks to one side as his nose goes splat! All of it waggling through the air in slow perpetuated motion. 'E falls, 'is 'ead meeting the ground with a sleep-inducing thud. The burly beast doesn't move.

"Oh, my girders," Livinea cheers. "That was *brilliant*!" She bobs up and down and claps her hands. "Wasn't it, Wanda?" She elbows 'er.

"Yes, until he wakes up and tells 'is friends what's happened to 'im," I say, crawling to the top of the caboose, looking over at 'is sleepin' carcass.

Masheck twists around from his post and grins. "Not to wor-ry," he teases, mimicking Livinea. "He won't be wakin' up any time soon."

"But they's awake . . ." I divert my eyes to the top of the street, where two more Brigsmen draw their batons. They rush toward us, shoutin' and screamin' for us to stand down or they'll bang us about.

One blows 'is whistle. And like dogs, several more appear on the 'orizons of adjoining streets. *'Ere we go.*

I'd rather 'oped this would 'appen a little closer to our final destination, but—I draw a tattered breath—ambushers can't be choosers, now can they?

"Consider the *allow-Urlick-and-Eyelet-enough-time-to-enter-the-palace diversion* officially launched!" I stand and 'url the first hissing cherry puff bomb the Brigsmen's way.

# Forty-Nine

***Eyelet***

Parthena throws back the carpets, and the weak greyish light of first twilight floods in. She unhitches the lock on the Loony Bin wagon door, and it groans slowly open. The tension releases from my spine. I suck in a deep breath of trusting relief and stand to exit.

"Thank you," I say, jumping past her to freedom on the ground.

"This way," Parthena hisses, traipsing up a path between two buildings toward some steps, soft on the balls of her feet, her shoes like hushed children being herded into church. Urlick jumps down from the wagon and we follow.

"Where are we?" It's dark, but still I should know, I lived here for years—yet I don't recognize the surroundings. I stop in the middle of the stone walk. "This is not the way into the palace." I turn.

"Of course not." Parthena swings around, looking annoyed. "Did you think they'd allow me to bring the wagon right up to the front palace steps?" I look back at the wagon's shabby grey tin cover and rusting bars, wooden wheels caked with mud. "This is the laundresses' entrance. The palace is on the other side of the wall." Parthena huffs and turns back around. "Come on." She starts away and signals us to follow.

I feel the flush of embarrassment rush to my cheeks. Of course this isn't the palace. What was I thinking? Even I used the servants' entrance when I lived here. I look up at the sign over the door, and my mind finally registers our whereabouts. Have I really been gone that long? I'm struck with a sudden pang of remorse for all that's been lost to me. My mother. My father. My heritage. My home.

Urlick grabs my hand and yanks me forward. "No," I say, hooking my head left. "This way's better."

Parthena purses her lips. "Trust me," I say, heading off in the opposite direction, down a narrow corridor between two towers.

"She should know." Urlick turns and follows me, leaving a confused, unasked question hanging from Parthena's lips. She swallows it down and leaps after us, but I'm sure that's not the last I'll hear of this.

"In here," I whisper and slip through the stable pass to the servants' entrance, where I jerk open the heavy wooden double-gate door.

Parthena gasps at my actions, then clutches her heart.

"Don't worry." I wink. "There are no alarms on these doors. They shut them off to accommodate the servants. In the mornings, they go from here to there, fetching hot water from the laundresses' room back to the kitchen to cook. Alarms would only slow down the process, so the Ruler ordered that they be removed. A major design flaw of the castle."

"How do you know all this?" Parthena winces.

"Let's just say I had cause to be on the premises for a while." I turn from her, not willing to offer more, and zigzag my way around the cookery, through the east doors, and out to the hallway. Parthena and Urlick follow, falling into a neat line behind me, backs pressed tight up against the wall. The tick of the clock in the grand ballroom thrums in time with my heart. I look both ways before crossing.

Urlick rushes along behind me, as does Parthena, as I skirt the next corner briskly and break into a slight jog. Running through the open space of the well-furnished parlour and the library, I stop again in the next hall. "How much farther?" Urlick hisses, catching up with me.

"We need to make it to the back stairs," I say. "If we can get that far without running into . . ." I round the next corner and draw back, my boot sliding to a squeaky stop on the freshly waxed floors. "Her!"

Urlick slams into my back. Parthena into his. We stand there, three frozen, gawking, frazzled faces, each holding our breath. *Don't move*, I mouth to them, bringing a quick finger to my lips.

"What was that?" The old woman standing in front of me sniffs the air. Parthena and Urlick look on, confused. "Who are you? What is your business here?" The old woman's heels snap in tight half circles this way and that. I curl to one side, avoiding her spindly fingers—but just barely.

Urlick pulses his eyes at me.

*She's blind*, I mouth. *She can't see.*

He exhales, relieved, letting out a little too much *oh*.

"I may be blind," the old woman scoffs. "But I have other senses. Now identify yourselves before I ring the bell." She pulls a dainty brass tinkler from her pocket.

"It's me, Matriarch Burgess." I drop my head, hoping she remembers me. "It's Lettie."

"Lettie?"

I elbow Urlick in the gut. "And friends." I lift my brow.

The woman pulls back, her jaw feverishly churning. She shivers inside her cone of oversized clothing. "Lettie," she repeats. "But that's not possible. They told me Lettie was dead."

"I know," I say. "It must be strange to hear my voice, but it's true. I'm very much alive and standing before you." She reaches out, running her weathered fingers over my face, stopping at the scar on my forehead. The one I acquired while riding wildly down the palace staircase at the age of three, under Matriarch Burgess's watchful eye.

Her body language softens, her elderly bones settling back into their ninety-year-old droop. "Lettie, what are you doing here, child?" She looks back and forth over her shoulder, futilely. "You know they'll kill you if they see you here?" she whispers, her forehead rumpled with concern.

"I had to come," I say. "There is something we have to do."

"We?" Her head cranks in Urlick and Parthena's direction.

"Can you keep a secret?" I pat her hand.

"Of course I can." She takes in a breath. "You know better than that. Besides, at my age I can barely remember my own name, let alone give away a secret." She turns and sniffs the air, then smiles. Her wrinkled skin gathers into a nest of sunshine at the corners of her eyes. "This one always was my pet," she tells Urlick.

"And you were always mine." I squeeze her hand.

"What can I do for you, child?" she asks, her expression sensing I'm in trouble, the same way it used to when I was small, seeking asylum from a scolding from my mother.

"Perhaps you could help us get to the main bedroom of the house?" My voice lilts up weakly, worried she'll ask why. Matriarch Burgess's eyes flash. "If I promise you nothing bad will happen," I add quickly.

"Well, that won't be any fun." She frowns.

"All right, so some *teensy* bit of bad will happen, mixed in with a whole lot of good. What do you say?" I foolishly pinch my fingers in the air, showing her the measure as if she can see it. Urlick stifles a laugh.

The matriarch ponders my request a moment. "How about some cookies first?"

"No, thank you, Matriarch." I clasp my hands. "We're sort of in a bit of a hurry."

"Well, then . . ." Wiry brows jump over milky eyes. "I suppose it can't be any worse than what's already happened. Things have gone all to *hell* around here since my son died."

"Yes, I know," I say. "I'm sorry for that." I turn to a stunned-looking Urlick and Parthena and explain, "This is the former Ruler's mother."

"Pleased to make your acquaintance, madam." Parthena curtsies awkwardly.

Urlick leans in. "What if we could promise you, if you help us get to the Ruler's room, we'll set everything right again?"

"Then I'd say you're just the bloke I've been waiting for." Matriarch Burgess slips her arm through Urlick's. "Now, if you could be so kind as to point me in the direction of the lift."

*

The lift comes to rest on the lip of the second floor. Urlick secures the crank and sets the levers to automatic. He folds back the cage's accordion door, careful not to make too much noise, and we shuffle out—all but Matriarch Burgess. "I'm afraid this is where we part ways," she whispers, hanging back. "The last thing I need is to get caught up in a pither-pother. Such a commotion at my age could do me in. Then again, so could bad fish." She smirks. "At any rate, since my son's untimely demise and the subsequent change of regime, I fear I'm living here on borrowed time. Don't want to give the new administration any good reasons to cut me short." She raises a wary brow. "God knows there's been talk of that already," she mutters. "Anyway, the room you're looking for is on the left, third door down. You have about a half an hour before her dressing brigade shows up. Good luck, my pet." She blows me a kiss, trips the switch on the elevator, and starts her descent.

"Thank you," I call, her white hair sinking below the floorboards. She looks up through the elevator cage one last time. "Give her *hell!*" She shakes her fist before completely disappearing.

Parthena snorts. "Full of spunk, isn't she?"

"Come on, we'd better get going before someone hears that lift and comes to investigate." I sidestep down the hall toward the room. My eyes catch sight of something, glinting gold in the flickering shards of streetlamp light that seep in through the south windows. The brass doorknob of the conquest room. I've almost reached it when—

"Unhand me at once!" The Matriarch's voice filters up through the elevator shaft. "Good gracious, can't an old woman take a wrong turn without launching a criminal investigation!" She's shouting now, clearly trying to warn us we've been discovered. It'll only be a matter of time before guards head up the stairs. "For goodness sakes, I'm quite capable of opening the door myself! Unhand me, I said! Let me *be*!"

I turn and race the remaining few steps to Penelope's bedroom door—Parthena and Urlick follow in tow—and burst through the door into a lavishly decorated dressing room. Louis XIV pink and blue silk furniture lines every wall. "Through here!" I shout, dashing forward, falling hard on the handle of a second inner door, the door to the bedchamber, bouncing back when my shoulder slams into it. "It's locked," I turn and say.

"Not for long!" Parthena kicks out a boot. Wood chips splinter everywhere.

A pillow-squish-faced Penelope flies up in her bed, looking like a startled dwarf. Royal-purple drapes adorn either side of the massive four-poster. A golden canopy stretches the length of the wood beams overhead. Penelope's hair rises from her crown like a tornado. She strips the night blinders from her eyes, and gasps.

"Good morning, Penelope!" Urlick launches his face out in front of hers. "What's the matter? Not expecting company?"

# *Fifty*

***Eyelet***

Penelope's gaze lopes around the room, questioning the possibility of such a motley crew of ambushers. She gropes for the whistle hanging on a cord next to her bed and blows it—three short, one long.

"Dammit!" Parthena curses and lunges for the whistle, missing.

Jackboots stamp the floor below us, flooding toward the corridor stairs.

"Call them off!" I snap at Penelope. "Call them off, or else!" I pull the knife from the top of my boot and hold it to her throat.

"Eyelet?" Urlick's eyes pop as Penelope gasps.

"Call. Them. Off!" I press the knife against her skin, ignoring Urlick.

Penelope swallows hard, groping the air for the whistle again. She brings it shakily to her mouth. She blows the signal in reverse—one long and three short.

The jackboots below us slow to a staggered stop.

"There," she says. "Now, don't harm me."

"You'd better hope they all turn around."

"Everything all right in there, mum?" a guard calls from the outer door. Penelope lets out a cowardly whimper. "Shall we enter?"

*"No!"* Her voice cracks. "Everything's fine! I'm fine! I called you in error! I just woke from a nightmare, that's all."

"You're sure?" the guard persists. I press the knife a little tighter to her throat.

"Yes! Now, get on your way!"

"Very well then, mum," the guard says, hesitating a long moment before clomping away, boots crashing loud against the treads of the stairwell as he calls off the others and descends.

Breath escapes from all of us. I wait until I'm sure the floor is clear of guards before I remove the knife from Penelope's throat.

"You're going to pay for this," she spits, rubbing her grazed neck. "Every last one of you."

"I believe some of us have been paying for a long time already." Parthena moves in.

"What do you want?" Penelope snaps, turning on her sister with contempt.

"Where shall we start?" Parthena leans, clenching her fists at her sides. "How about we start with my dead child? Or perhaps with your affections for my lover? Or how you lied about my absinthe abuse to have me locked away!"

"I did no such thing."

*"Liar!"*

Urlick steps between the two women.

"You have no proof of anything!" Penelope rakes her sister up and down.

"Oh, don't I?"

Urlick reaches into the vest of his waistcoat, produces the church register, and tosses it onto her lap on the bed. Penelope's pupils quicken. Her breath races.

She dives at the book. "Ah ah ah, not so fast." Urlick swipes the register away. "First, you're going to answer a few of your sister's questions." He tips his head toward Parthena to take the stage.

"Why?" Parthena says, jutting her neck forward. "Why did you do it?"

"Why do you think? You were always the perfect one, the smarter one, the *better-looking* . . . Oh, don't look at me like that, you did this to yourself, opening your legs to that cheat! You *knew* he had a wife! Yet still you couldn't control yourself!"

Parthena slaps her.

"Aaaah!" Penelope gasps, and rubs her cheek. "How dare you, you ill-tempered tart!"

"No wonder Father never loved you," Parthena says under her breath.

"Love *me*?" Penelope chuckles. "You actually think he was capable of love?" She snaps forward. "Who do you think signed Smrt's request to have you thrown away in the Brink?"

Parthena falls back, hand to her chest, gasping.

"That's right," Penelope continues. "Our father would do just about anything for money. And he *did*. At least *I* had the heart to modify his decision and give you a fighting chance—"

"A chance to what? Become warden of that *hellhole*? You expect me to be thankful for that?"

"If Father had his way, you'd have hanged."

Parthena draws in a breath and clenches her teeth. "Tell me, what happened to my child?"

"She died—"

"The *truth*! I want to hear the truth!"

"She's dead! Or she may as well be."

"What are you saying?"

"When Smrt first sent me to murder his bastard child, I thought I could do it, I could kill her. But when I got her out into the woods, I couldn't bring myself to wring her neck. So I knocked on the door of a cabin instead. A woman with very little sight appeared, and I struck up a deal with her. She would care for and raise the child, posing as her aunt, for which she would be compensated handsomely, and no one would ever be the wiser. Over the years, I wrote to the girl a daily letter, through which I became very fond of her."

"You stole my daughter from me. You stole my life away."

"I cleaned up your mistake! Did you really think a professor was going to marry a commoner, whilst he had an upper-class wife in the Brink, you *dolt*? If only you'd gone on with the plan and not fallen in love with him—"

"What plan?"

"The one Smrt and I concocted!" Penelope gasps, drawing a shaky hand to her mouth, as if trying to take back what she hadn't meant to say.

"So it's true, what they say about the business deal." Parthena shakes.

"I know nothing of it—"

"Really?" Urlick cuts in. He pulls a handful of register pages from his vest pocket, holding them out in the air over Penelope's head. "You thought you could bury it, didn't you? Along with the truth about me. In the filthy crypt of the church, in a locked box, where no one would ever find it. You thought you could end the lineage forever, *snuff out* my royal heritage, and erase her child, all so you could improve your own destiny. Only trouble was, you didn't have the guts to make her child go away . . . and I wouldn't die either, would I?" He leans in.

Penelope shrieks and lunges at the papers. Urlick pulls back, handing them off to me. "I thought you might try to destroy the evidence, that's why I did this." He produces a long, slim, silver metal device that looks like a cross between a wizard's wand and a train's silver whistle. He waves the wand-whistle in the air. "I've already photocrank-copied all the pages we need to prove our case and sent them up into the cloud." His eyes flick toward the ceiling.

"The cloud? What cloud?" I whisper to him, turning my back to Penelope.

"It's a new device I was working on before we left the Compound," he whispers. "I've discovered I'm able to break images up into the smallest particles through a means of photocrank-static-electricity, and move those particles to another location for reassembly, like a transportable jigsaw puzzle." He tips the device in his hand. "It works rather well, actually, I'm shocked . . . I mean, I'm *confident*." He tugs on the points of his waistcoat.

"And this cloud thing." Penelope looks at him sceptically. "Where is it?" Her eyes dart all over the ceiling mockingly as she waves her hands in the air.

"That's the beauty of it!" Urlick turns, breaking away from me, poking his nose out at her. "It could be anywhere." He lowers his voice and makes it sound like a ghoul's, throwing his lanky arms out at his sides. Penelope is driven back, a scowl of fright on her face.

"You don't really know where it is, do you?" I whisper to Urlick when he straightens up again.

"No," he whispers back. "But don't worry, the images are all etched right here in the memory of this device." He taps the wand-whistle, and it topples from his hands. He swoops to catch it.

"How about I look after that."

"None of this means anything without the proof of birth!" Penelope rails from the bed, craning her neck out over the covers. "Anyone could enter anything in a church register!"

"Perhaps," I say, unfolding one of the pages. "But not many would have access to a royal seal."

Her brows vex. She's quiet a moment, then stretches her gaze to me. "Do you really think the people are going to award you a kingdom over a piece of pressed wax?"

I lean down, pushing my face closer to hers. "They've awarded *you* more on far less."

A crooked smile comes to Penelope's lips. Her eyes rake over each of us. "Look at you. A more disgruntled band of ex-cons and mental misfits there's never been. Do you really think anyone in their right mind is going to believe any of you?"

"It doesn't matter who believes them, they have me." The door behind us swings open. "A witness who can corroborate all the facts."

The Matriarch appears, tottering on the bent handle of her cane. She teeters forward on aged but nimble knees, bending at the waist when she reaches the head of the bed. "You thought because I'm blind I serve no purpose." She grins. "Well, my son, the Ruler, thought otherwise. In fact, I was not only his mother but his most trusted *confidante*, present at both the dirty business dealings of another high-ranked controversial birth, and the conception of his secret heir." She reaches back, patting Urlick's chest. "Welcome to the family, by the way." She flashes her blind eyes in Penelope's direction. "Now, where were we?"

"But that's not possible." Penelope heaves a nervous breath. Her eyes dart frantically side to side. "No one was present at the birth of my sister's child, not even the Clergy! There wasn't even a doctor present! I saw to that myself. Not even Smrt really knew the truth of what became of her! I lied to everyone about it!"

"*Weeeeell.*" The Matriarch stretches back. "Even better." She smiles, folding accomplished arms across her chest. "Can't argue with self-admitted guilt, now can we?"

I laugh into my hand.

"How could you?" Parthena steps in, touching her chest. "How could you do that to me? All those years, leaving me locked away, letting me believe my child was dead! How could you take her from me and lie about it? We were sisters! Twins, for *God's sake*!"

"It was a business arrangement—get over it!" Penelope curls up her lip. "A way for me to extort money from Smrt's overflowing purse, to save Father's failing business! How else did you think we were going to survive? I never even *loved* that squib."

Parthena gasps and falls back.

"Truth be known, he never loved you, either! I arranged it all! That's right. I did! Every last pathetic detail! You were both so easily tricked. *He*, the aging wealth holder desperate for an heir, *you*, the star-struck dreamer, believer in the impossible love affair. In the end, it all came down to a simple exchange of goods—*a fortune for a broodmare*!"

Parthena steps up and slaps her sister's face again.

The shot rings out across the room.

Parthena drops her face in her hands and starts to weep. I take her by her shoulders and steer her away.

*"Get up,"* Urlick says, dragging Penelope by the scruff from her bed. "Reign over!" He launches her hard at the wall.

Penelope bounces off, spilling to the floor with a thump.

"Get dressed, and hurry up about it." He tosses her clothing at her. "You've got a heretic to set free, and a kingdom to hand over. All before lunch!"

# Fifty-One

***Urlick***

"Where are you taking me?" Penelope wriggles at the end of the rope to which I have her tethered like a fish destined for the fry pan. Her hands are firmly tied behind her back, though I haven't gagged her mouth, and I'm seriously regretting that omission. I push her from the castle down the steps.

"Where do you think?" I say, booting her forward over the slick cobblestones of the courtyard, my knee to her backside. "To end the party you invited everyone to yesterday—the one that got rained out."

"But they'll be expecting to see the burning of a heretic." She cranks her neck around to face me.

"Yes, I know. And they *will.* As soon as you've appointed me Ruler."

"What?" Penelope's eyes pop. "I'll never do that!"

"You will do what I say." I clench my teeth. "Now, get moving!" I whirl her around and knee her in the arse again.

The glint of something red catches my eye. My gaze leaps past Penelope's head to Masheck, standing beside an engine parked to the left of the courtyard, behind a short wall. The engine is mounted on a chassis equipped with hoses and spindles. A giant tank serves as its belly. "What is it?" I shout.

Masheck turns. "It's the cloudsower."

Penelope swallows.

"Are you sure?" I say.

"As sure as I breathe air." Masheck struts alongside it, dragging his hands over the middle of the copper-coloured beast, inspecting the front and then rounding the back. A giant, wide-mouthed spout is corked with a metal plug at one end. At the rear, an array of hoses protrudes like rubbery octopus arms from a silver base. He buckles over, disappearing behind it. "Those are the guns," he says, swinging back to a stand, pointing to the row of ten trigger nozzles attached to the engine's hoses in back. "And the chemicals go 'ere." He rushes to the front, pointing to the neck, patting his hand on the cork.

He takes on a strange look, his gaze drifting off across the courtyard. "And there are the chemicals." He races off toward a stack of wooden barrels marked with a red flag at the far end of the courtyard. Then he turns back. *"Yuh."* He points to Penelope. "Yuh were the one! It was yuh 'oo came to the factory. Dressed as a man. Yuh oversaw this death engine. It was yuh 'oo gave the orders to seed!" He rushes toward her, fists balled at his sides.

"I have no idea what you're talking about." Penelope cowers behind me.

Masheck leans in, his face tight to hers. "I remember the eyes now, those great big eyes, glaring out through the glass-bubble 'elmet. The 'elmet she wore with the suit to protect 'erself from the chemicals." Masheck turns to me.

"He's wrong!" Penelope shouts. "It was Smrt! It was never me!"

"It was *'er* all right. She filled the tank and gave the orders. I saw 'er do it meself. Then she'd slip off to 'ide below the earth in one o' them old abandoned gem mines out in the forest, where she'd be safe until the toxins cleared. I used to 'ear the workmen complainin' 'bout 'avin' to do 'er dirty job for 'er. They was told to dump the fumin' waste over the side of the ravine, into Embers, somewheres way out in the forest, and to keep their mouths shut about it, or she'd 'ave their 'eads."

*"Lies, all lies!"* Penelope spits.

I stare into her eyes.

The ravine. Those trucks. The dumping. The rancid steam . . .

That must have been what those workmen were doing, that day Eyelet and I saw them dumping refuse in the pit.

Masheck jerks toward her again, his temper running high. "Yuh knew what yuh was doin' all along, didn't yuh?" He stabs her chest. "And yuh didn't care what 'appened to any of us because of *it*!"

"How else was I going to get them to follow me to the *promised land*?" Penelope's eyes dart between us. "How else was I to get them to take up arms and fight the East? Smrt had already ruined our world when he detonated the—"

She sucks in a breath. The end of her sentence hangs frozen in the air, but my mind fills in the gap. *He* was there . . . in the Core . . . the day of the catastrophe. *Smrt* was responsible. . . not my father.

"So yuh'd 'of killed us all just to get yer way!"

"All who were expendable, yes!"

Masheck lunges at her, his eyes flashing like burning torches in a winter sky, his fist lined up with her jaw. I stop him short of knocking her head clean off her shoulders. "Hold up," I shout, yanking him back by the arms. "We still need her, sadly. But when we don't, trust me"—I breathe, patting his shoulder—"you'll be the first I call when we don't."

Masheck jerks away from me, pulling a frustrated hand through his hair as he stalks off.

Penelope sucks in a deep breath. "That's right, you don't *dare* kill me!" She juts out a mocking chin.

"I wouldn't be so sure about that." I fling her around and shove her forward.

"You'll never find it, if you do."

"Find what?"

"The promised land, of course. The utopian world that exists above the clouds." She stops and stares up at the sky. "Oh, come on now, don't act like you don't know about it." Her brows thicken as she studies my face. "It was your little sweetheart's magic that produced the hole in the cloud cover, revealing its existence. Or so the ghoul in the forest said."

I stare at her, perplexed.

"Limpidious. The floating world beyond our own."

"Limpidious?"

My mind riffles back to Eyelet standing in the parlour at the Compound, steam map hanging at her back. The broken glass on the hearth. Her questions at dinner. The missing section of the map.

The rumours about a utopian world lingering just above the clouds.

The steam jar.

Its mystery.

The warnings from my father.

Eyelet's refusal to stay out of the room . . .

"You really don't know, do you?" Penelope laughs. "How precious. Your sweetheart's kept it a secret from you. And yet, I bet you've trusted her with all of *your* secrets, haven't you?"

"Shut up!"

"Perhaps her plans don't include you after all—"

"I said to *shut up*!"

She lowers her voice. "You won't last a year down here alone. This world is too far gone."

It's all I can do not to strike her. I whirl her around and push her away.

"We found them!" Eyelet's voice breaks on the horizon. She and Parthena materialize out of the mist, waving papers in their hands. "They were exactly where she said they'd be." They stagger to a breathless stop beside me, pinching stitches from their sides. Eyelet shoots Penelope a contemptuous look. "Two weathered but legible birth certificates, craftily hidden." She hands them over then notes my frown. "What is it? What's the matter?" Her eyes dash from me to Penelope and back.

I say nothing, a bubble of anger and confusion.

"Oh, nothing." Penelope takes the stage. "I was just telling your sweetheart, here, about your little secret."

"What secret?" Eyelet winces, looking dismayed.

"About your plans to flee to the utopian world floating just beyond the cloud cover."

Eyelet's cheeks turn red.

"You knew about this?" I snap.

"Yes—*I mean*, no . . . I mean . . ."

"You didn't tell me. Why didn't you tell me?" My heart pulls.

"I planned to. Honestly, I did. There just wasn't time." The look in Eyelet's eyes tells me she's breaking apart inside. "I didn't know what it was, exactly." She shakes her head. "There are no secrets between us, Urlick, you know that."

I turn on Penelope. "How do you know about all this?"

"A little birdie told me," she smirks. "One I believe she tried to clip the wings of, *but failed.*" She glowers at Eyelet.

"Flossie," Eyelet breathes. She turns to me. "She must have seen it. She was there . . . in the forest, when it happened . . ."

"What are you saying?"

"That day, at the Core. In the middle of the explosion, I saw it, through a tear in the cloud cover, as I fell from the hydrocycle. A whole new world, floating above ours. Flossie must have seen it, too." She swallows. "I would have told you, but there's been so much going on."

"It's all right." I grab her hand.

Behind us, a distant crowd rises into chants. Voices demand a burning.

I jerk around to see smoke billowing above the west end of the building. They've relit the fire.

"Iris!" Eyelet gasps.

"We've got to go!" I say.

"It's too late," Penelope sneers in a low, gloating voice. "I left orders to restart the fire at twilight dawn. Dawn has passed. By the time you make it up the hill, your little freak friend will be engulfed in *flames*."

"Can I smack her now?" Masheck flies forward.

"Not yet," I say. "But soon!"

"Move!" I throw Penelope forward, roped and tied and kicking. "Help me with her, will you?" Masheck single-handedly launches Penelope up and over the backside of Clementine, fastening her tight to the saddle. I step into the stirrup and turn around. "Eyelet, you and Parthena take the wagon and meet me on the hill. Masheck, bring the elephant. C.L. should be there with the freak train by now. We'll all meet up in the square."

"Will do," Eyelet says. The rest nod their heads.

I dig my heels into Clementine's sides and whirl around, stopping short of taking off, seeing Masheck tear across the courtyard.

"Where are you going?" I shout after him.

"I think it's 'igh time the people found out what their Ruler's really all about, don't yuh?" He stops and steps up onto the engine. "Besides"—he pumps the hand crank on the start panel, and the engine whirs to life—"according to this"—he taps a meter on the dashboard—"there should be enough water stored in the belly of this 'ere beast to put out the flames of that fire."

"Good idea," I say. "We'll see you all there, then!"

I whirl Clementine around. She prances, hesitating as if she senses something, her hooves clomping jittery over the cobblestones. Eyelet starts to cough. I wrench around, seeing her clutch her chest. "Eyelet?" She falls to her knees, gagging and gasping.

*"Eyelet?"* Parthena races to her side. "Something's wrong." Parthena looks up at me. "She can't breathe."

I sit back hard on the saddle and yank on the reins, forcing Clementine to a sliding stop, and scramble down from the saddle.

"Eyelet? *Eyelet*, what is it?" I fall to my knees. She coughs and gags and retches. Her face has turned an eerie shade of grey. She's not breathing in. "Eyelet?" I pound at her back. She strains, then gasps for breath. This is the worst coughing fit I've ever seen her have.

"I'm all right!" She finally waves a hand. She looks up at me, her eyes desperate.

"You're not all right," I say.

Eyelet's coughing turns to a spasm. Her back heaves and falls, her lungs crackle. A bolt of panic swells throughout me. I grab for breath myself.

"What do we do?" I turn to Parthena.

"I don't know." She rubs Eyelet's back.

"I'm fine," Eyelet insists. "I'll be fine." She fights for air. "You've got to go." Her eyes plead with me.

At last she recovers a small amount, heaving in a noisy breath, then chokes again before breathing steadily.

My mind leaps back to the time in the balloon, when she went out on me. But when that happened, she wasn't struggling to breathe . . . This is completely different—isn't it?

"Please," she says, looking at the sky. "I'll be fine, honestly. Go."

I turn around, following her eyes. Smoke pours up behind the building, thick.

Eyelet wheezes, clutching her heart. "I'll be all right! Go! Go to Iris, *please*!"

The look in her eyes is pushing me away, but something inside me won't let me go.

*Please*, she mouths. *I'll never forgive myself if she dies . . . Go save Iris . . .please.*

"I'll stay back with her!" Parthena shouts.

*"No!"* Eyelet rasps. "He needs all the help he can get. Parthena, take the elephant. I promise, I'll be fine. Please, Urlick." She turns to me. "How much do you trust me?"

Her words sink into my heart. I search her face for an excuse to stay, to fold her into my arms. Iris's screams rise at my back. Reluctantly I pull my gaze from Eyelet's, facing the smoke on the horizon, jam my heels into Clementine's sides, and gallop away, a burning void in my chest.

Looking back over my shoulder as I lift off, I see Eyelet's head bobbing, hear her coughing, her whole body heaving as she retches into her handkerchief.

# Fifty-Two

***Eyelet***

The last in the group gallops off to save Iris, damaged hindquarters of the elephant glinting gunmetal grey under the fading streetlights. I bow my head and say a prayer for Iris. "Please, Lord, let them make it in time. Please protect her until we meet again."

I cross my heart and crawl to my feet slowly, tucking my soiled handkerchief into my pocket, considering what to do next.

I've got to find out why this is happening. I can think of only one place the answer might be.

Hobbling back through the main doors of the castle, I steady myself, then steal the keys to the Academy and a hooded cloak for disguise. Pulling the hood up over my head, I scurry across town as fast as my lungs will allow me, arriving at the gates winded and wheezing a few moments later.

Everything is spinning. The earth feels rubbery under my feet. I can't believe how weak I am. I bend at the waist, pinching my sides, sucking in shuddering breath after breath. No matter how hard I try to gulp away the shaky sensation it doesn't clear.

I stagger up to the gates. Edgar and Simon raise their heads in query. Their steely beaks tilt to and fro. I throw back my hood and stand in front of them, gasping, letting them get a good, long look, cathode beams scanning. "How much do you trust me?" I push the words out on an exasperated breath, coughing and gagging afterward.

They flap their wings and the gates fold back. I fall to my knees, convulsing, retching hard. The stone walk below me is spattered with blood.

What is this? I touch it. This has never happened before.

It's as if my chest were a runaway criminal and the air the Brigsman's sword.

I raise a hand to my mouth, shocked and trembling. It, too, wears traces of blood. What does this mean? What's happening to me? I rub the blood off on my skirts.

Pulling myself to a weak stand, I stumble forward through the gates, heaving breath in as I go, pitching myself through the doors of the great room and down the hall to my father's old office. Once inside, I drop to my knees next to the magic circle on the floor—the one with the oracle where Urlick and I found my father's hidden, sacred journals. *Please let one of these hold the answer.*

The spiked arms of the crypt remain open. Twelve tiny triangles point toward the ceiling. Red hardbacked volumes lie scattered about the floor, just as we left them; a few remain anchored in their crypts beneath.

I shuffle through them madly, searching for clues, stopping only when my hands cradle a volume marked . . . *Soleil. Soleil*—the French word for sun.

I take in a deep breath and cough it out, then break open the spine. Turning to the page marked by a ribbon, I grow teary at the sight of my father's handwriting, and even tearier at what it says.

*One day, Eyelet, you will understand why I must do what I do today. And why I must risk everything to go there. I hope you will grow to understand it was all for you. You, Eyelet, were my everything.*

I close my eyes and hear his voice, the lyrical sound of his words, the promise he spoke into my ear that last day in the kitchen. His desire for me to go ahead to the carnival and have fun.

I swipe the tear that warms my eye, drop my chin, and continue reading, my fingers trembling as they hold open the page.

*Though the long-term effects of the "ray" are at this point not completely known, what I do know is the following: Every patient I've exposed to the light has become adversely affected. Though their symptoms vary, they have all become irreversibly ill.*

I stop on the words, my lips quivering. I dry my eyes and read on.

*There has been, however, one recurring symptom shared by every patient. Each has developed a violent cough, which slowly but eventually escalates to something more heinous. They struggle to breathe at all and eventually begin to cough up blood, which, in my estimate, indicates a tumour has begun to take hold in their lungs.*

I hesitate, bringing my hand to my mouth.

*If they are not treated immediately with my antidote—prognosis is grim . . .*

I drop the book in my lap, shaking.

What I feared most since we found the machine has come true.

Since the cough began, I've felt myself slowly slipping into the depths of darkness, like I was drowning in my own body. I said nothing, not wanting to worry Urlick, thinking eventually we'd return to Brethren and re-create the potion my father left me, and all would be well again.

But now, I fear we could be too late.

I close my eyes and swallow down the sick feeling that comes.

I must have the antidote.

Urlick is right.

I must drink it, *now.*

I open my eyes and tip my head back toward the ceiling, and a vision of the vial comes into view.

"Flossie!" I say, remembering something pulsing green between the folds of her clothing. "She has it! She has the vial!" I gather my legs beneath me and stand, dropping the book to the floor. "I must find her! And steal it away! My very life depends on it!"

# Fifty-Three

***Urlick***

Clementine drops through the cloud cover, circling the chanting crowd. Their voices lick the sky with bloodthirsty howls. Revenge burns in their eyes.

We land just outside the main stage in the centre of the park. Clementine finds her balance and drops her wings. The startled crowd pulls back.

Behind us, Iris is shrieking. Fire rages at her feet. Thankfully, the flames have not found her yet, but it won't be long before they do. She chokes and coughs and cries aloud. I can't bear to see her like this. "Hold on," I whisper to her. "Hold on."

"Yuh look after them!" Masheck eyes the crowd, as he pulls the engine up behind me. "I'll take care of Iris!"

"You're sure—?"

"I'm sure." Masheck jumps from the engine, hastily unravelling the hoses. "A little 'elp 'ere!" he shouts as C.L. pulls up in the freak train. C.L. yanks the horses to a halt and leaps from the mount. The rest of the freaks spring from the bars of their cages, and race toward them.

"IRIS!" A streak of red curls flies past me. I swoop down, snagging Cordelia about the waist before she makes it to the flames. She writhes and kicks as I haul her up into the air. "NO!" She pounds at my arms and legs. "Let me go! Let me go! *IRIIIIIIIIIIS!*"

"Listen to me!" I shake her, staring deep into her swollen eyes. "I promise you, I *will* save Iris, but this is not helping. You need to stay calm and go and help the others. Promise me you will?"

Cordelia sniffs. "But—"

"How much do you trust me?" I say.

Her arms and legs stop swinging and she nods her head, crying.

"Wanda!" I shout, crowd chanting at my back. "Take Cordelia and don't let her out of your sight."

Wanda reaches out and I pass her the child, then I turn to face the crowd. My gaze floats past Iris in the flames, her mouth pulled awry. Streams of black smoke curdle up from the pile. Ravens circle overhead. "Help is coming," I breathe to her and dig my heels into Clementine's ribs. Clementine rears, shocked, and jumps forward. We ride headlong through the crowd then I coax her into a leap. She clears the heads and fists of the angry protesters and lands with a crash on the floorboards of the stage. Her giant wings cause the crowd to gasp and pull back, giving me a breath of time to collect my thoughts.

Looking out into the faces of the people who stand before me, I see nothing but hatred in their eyes. They spark into a chorus of fearful screams. Their voices rage up to the clouds.

Women turn their faces to their husband's chests at the sight of me. Frightened husbands take up arms. Children cry and run, screeching. It's the first time I've ever allowed myself to be seen in public, and the reaction is horrifying at best. I've got to do something, quickly, or it'll be the end of me. Steamrifles rise.

"You want to burn a heretic!" I shout, leaping from Clem's back to the stage. "Here is your heretic!" I haul Penelope down from the mount and launch her out in front of me, bound and gagged. The crowd draws in a collective breath. They fall back on their heels. They shake their fists and threaten to kill me.

"Tell them," I hiss in Penelope's ear. "Tell them why I'm here." I tear away the gag that binds her mouth.

"Don't believe him!" Penelope shouts. "He *kidnapped me*! Took me against my will!"

I clap a hand over her mouth and yank her to me. "Tell the truth or I swear I'll *wring* your bloody neck!"

I remove my hand from her mouth and shove her to the front of the stage. She stumbles to stay on her feet. "This is who should be burning in those flames!" I shake her. "She is the liar, the cheat, the one who's done you wrong!"

"Kill the monster!" someone shouts. A man trains his bow on me.

*"No! Wait!"* Parthena darts in front of us. "He speaks the truth!" she shouts at the crowd. "You must believe me!"

"Believe the keeper of Madhouse Brink!" Penelope scoffs. "How foolish do you think they are?" The crowd joins Penelope in laughter. Behind us, Iris screams. I twist around, seeing the flames edge ever closer to overtaking her, Masheck frantically pumping water into the machine.

"Tell them the truth!" I shout into Penelope's ears. "Or I swear it'll be you in those flames!"

At last the gauges fill and whistles sound. Water shoots from the hose. Masheck dances backward, struggling to keep control under the force of the surging water, as he douses out the flames. Burned steam billows skyward. The crowd wildly objects. Martin rushes up on the stack of smouldering kindling, and he emerges seconds later with a smudged and choking Iris in his arms. The edges of her dress are singed where they've been stomped out, but otherwise she appears unharmed.

*"Now!"* I shout, shaking Penelope.

An earsplitting howl snakes through the trees.

The crowd erupts in a frightful roar, but they're no longer looking at me. Instead, their heads twist and turn, tracking the movement of something circling toward the stage. A long, low growl coils out of the forest, enveloping us all in its wake.

*I know that sound. I've heard it before.*

It warps from a growl to a moan, and then I know. I know what's happening.

It can't be.

The cloud cover beyond the trees streams black. Curls of grey smoke sidewind toward us. White-flame eyes burn through the skeletal limbs of the forest trees. *The Infirmed.* I suck in a breath. *They're coming for us.*

My skin shudders as my eyes jump to the horizon, spotting ten, twenty, thirty more. *It's not possible. They can't be here. But they are.*

"What's happening?" I turn on Penelope. Her eyes are the size of moons.

The crowd ducks and screams as shimmering silver faces swoop and stalk them from the clouds. Ghastly mouths attached to stealthy, wraithlike bodies dive at them like bats. Others whirl and churn above the crowd's heads, bombarding their minds with demonic chants.

An apparition drops down in front of me, centre stage, its maw hiked open wide, fangs bared at me. C.L. takes aim and sends an arrow through its head. The spirit bursts, splintering into a snowfall of ashes, then just as quickly returns to its form, laughing as it soars away, howling on the wind.

"How did they get here? Who let them in?" I shout, shaking Penelope.

"It was me!" she shrieks. "I let them in!"

"You did what?" Parthena snaps up beside us. C.L. joins her, along with Livinea, Iris, and Cordelia not far behind, all of us staring her down.

"We had a deal," Penelope snivels. "Urlick and the girl in exchange for the vial and my freedom." She gulps. "You don't understand. It was either my life or this."

"With who?" I dig my fingers into her shoulders. "With *who* did you make this deal?"

"With her." The words wobble weakly from Penelope's mouth. She points a shaky finger.

I follow it to the horizon, where a twitching, shorting, Flossie emerges, storming out of the woods toward the stage like an angry cloud. Her once-black dress a deathly shade of grey. Her skin is eerily luminescent—half human skin tone, half translucent blue. The veins in her forehead bulge and shimmer. Her legs are missing, replaced by tentacles. Some of the fingers on her hand are missing, too. Her hair stands straight up from her head.

"What do we do now?" Livinea breathes.

C.L. steps in front of her and takes aim with his crank-crossbow.

"No." I lower his bow. "No amount of firepower is going to get rid of her. She'll only return to her form. Just like the apparitions."

"Then what, sir?" C.L. says. "'Ow do we fight the beast?"

I stare into the panicked faces of the screaming crowd before me, and all at once it registers. "Masheck." I turn to him, still standing by the engine. "That hose you're holding, it works in reverse, correct?"

He looks down at the hose in his hands and then at me, confused.

"The engine! It pumps things both in and out via the hoses, isn't that right? You said yourself you saw the engine used to suck in the clouds and spit them back out filled with chemicals, am I right?"

"Yes, sir. I did."

"So the engine, it must work both ways."

Masheck's eyes brighten. "Yes. It does."

"You get busy changing those hoses. Martin, Sadar, help him out. The rest of you, get ready to take cover. C.L., you and I have to hold things off until they're ready."

"Right, sir." He raises a strong-willed bow.

"Oh, and Masheck"—he turns on his way to the back of the engine—"don't make a move until I give you the signal. We're only going to have one chance at this."

"Right, sir!" He nods his head and disappears, Martin and Sadar running at his side.

"Wanda, go and see if you can find Eyelet." I scan the crowd. "I don't see her anywhere." A sharp spear of panic rises in my heart, as Wanda jumps from the stage and races back toward the castle.

"Parthena, you keep an eye on *her*." I flick a seething look toward Penelope. "Whatever happens, don't let her go!"

Flossie moves in, a dark funnel cloud of arms and tentacles, suction-cupped legs slopping down over the skirt of the stage. She pulls herself up, suction cups *thwacking,* amid the demonic chants of her following, the Infirmed. She slithers closer, and my gut flips.

C.L. leaps out in front of me, crossbow raised. Livinea flanks his side, quiver full of steam arrows at the ready.

"Is this a joke?" Flossie bats them aside.

Parthena gasps, clutching her heart. The Infirmed crowd even closer. They swoop and scream.

*"Silence!"* Flossie shouts and they freeze in the sky, their heads bowed in submission.

"Where is she?" Flossie jerks herself forward on her tentacles, closing in on Penelope, her ghoulish eyes flashing. "We had a deal! You promised me both of them! I only see one! *Where is she?* Where is the girl?"

"He has her." Penelope points past Flossie to me. "He's hidden her away from here!"

I suck in a breath as Flossie churns around. *"Where is she?"* Her voice thunders. The force of her breath throws my hair back.

"Even if I knew, I'd never tell you." I clench my teeth and speak slowly.

"Really?" Flossie slinks closer. "Is that the game you *really* want to play?"

Cordelia whimpers behind me. Iris pulls her close. C.L. jumps to his feet.

My eyes fall to a green pulsing light emanating from the folds of Flossie's clothing at her chest. Through the fading luminescent fabric, the lines of chain link can be seen. A glass vial dangles from its end.

"Look familiar?" She tracks my gaze and yanks the chain from between her breasts. "Oh, I'm sorry, did you need this?" She taunts me, pendant swinging from her flickering fingertips.

"Where did you find that?"

"Right where you left it. Hanging over the cliff of the ravine where you *murdered my father*." She presses her burning eyes at me.

I stare at the vial, not knowing what to do, or how exactly to steal it back from her . . . without . . .

"What's the matter, afraid to come and get it?" She swoops toward me, and I falter back.

I reach for the Quantum Tunneler in my pocket, hoping the light may have some effect on her, and she claps a cold hand on my wrist. "Come now, Urlick. Do you really think I don't know your tricks?" She pinches me until I've released it. "Where is she?"

"I will never tell you."

"All right, then." She flings herself around, the crowd screaming. *"Eat them!"* she shouts to the Infirmed in the sky. They spring to life.

*"No!"* C.L. shouts, training his crank-crossbow on Flossie. "Call them off or I'll shoot!"

"Oh, now, don't make me laugh." She snags the crossbow from C.L.'s hands and turns it on me.

"Maybe this will make you change your mind." Flossie screws her damaged lip.

I stare down the arrow's tip. My breath catches.

"Urlick!" The crowd gasps and falls back, creating an opening through which I see her.

"Eyelet!" She runs toward the stage, a journal pressed to her chest.

Flossie turns, sizing up Eyelet with the arrow instead of me. "I so love it when the drama gets high, don't you?" She wrenches the string back, increasing the tension . . . and slowly, lets it go.

I launch toward her—

"NO!" Cordelia shouts. She bolts from behind Iris's skirts and dives across the stage, taking the arrow meant for Eyelet straight through her tiny heart.

"CORDELIA!" C.L. leaps to the ground, collapsing over her body. "No! My sweet Cordelia, *nooooooo* . . ."

Iris shrieks and races from the stage, cradling Cordelia up into her arms, rocking.

I cannot find my breath. It's as if all the air in the world has evaporated. I clutch the sides of my head and scream.

Flossie stretches back the bow again, training it on Eyelet.

*"NOW!"* I shout at Masheck. *"NOW!"*

Masheck gives the freaks the signal and throws down the hammer on the machine. Martin and the rest of the freaks snap to attention, hoses pointed at the sky. Flywheels flutter. Steam pours from the vents. One by one the hoses spring to life, sucking the howling, fleeing, wraithlike bodies of the Infirmed from the sky, trapping them within the belly of the cloudsowing engine, their harrowing voices reduced to tinny, whispering screams.

The engine backfires, purging a dark, black cloud of smoke into the sky.

"Eyelet?" I shout, waving my hands.

"Urlick!" Her voice streams up through the clearing smoke.

I whirl around to find her fighting her way toward the front of the stage. "The necklace!" she calls.

I turn my eyes to the sky.

But it's too late.
Flossie's already taken flight.

# Fifty-Four

***Urlick***

"What happened to you? Where have you been? Are you all right?" I drop down from the stage, collecting Eyelet up in my arms.

"I will be, as soon as we get that vial back," she whispers, breathless.

"I promise you, that vial will be ours—"

"Urlick!" Parthena calls, struggling to hold on to a squirming Penelope on the stage. "I hate to interrupt but . . . don't you think we should settle this?" She glances at the crowd.

I turn to them and then back to Eyelet. "Go," she says. "I'll explain later."

"Are you sure?" I stroke a lock of soggy hair back from her face. Her eyes are glassy. Her brow is glistening with sweat. "What's going on?" I touch her head. "You're on fire."

"It can wait." The crowd stirs. "They can't."

"But—"

Eyelet places a shaking finger over my mouth. "What power do we have if you're not officially sworn in? Think about it." She cups my cheeks and stares deeply into my eyes. "We need this to happen. *You* need this to happen. Before you can save me." Her eyes plead with me to return to the stage. "Now go, *please.* Take what is rightfully yours—*ours.* Take over your rightful throne."

I hesitate, my gaze darting all over her face. Her lips are trembling, her skin perspiring. I've no idea what's the matter, but I sense the matter's urgent. The sooner I get this over with, the sooner I can help her. "All right," I say, pulling her into the deepest, most ravishing kiss I can effect—hoping she can feel all the love that emanates from my body to hers.

"Nothing means more to me in the world than you, Eyelet," I whisper to the back of her hair, then turn and catapult onto the stage, racing across to where Penelope stands.

"Now, where were we, before we were so rudely interrupted?" I spin her around to face the crowd. "I believe you were about to tell them the truth about me."

Penelope snivels and cries out.

"Go on!" I shake her. "Spit it out!"

She tries hard to assume her former Ruler stance, clears her throat, then begins. "It has recently come to my attention—"

"Louder, so everyone can hear."

"That there has been a grievous oversight"—she drops her head—"regarding the proper heir to the throne . . ."

The impatient crowd mumbles. They shift on their feet.

"Keep going." I nudge her.

*"I am!"* she snaps.

"It appears that a rightful heir to the throne of Brethren is, in fact, not me." Penelope nervously laughs. "Who knew?" she adds, tossing her brows up, her voice squeaking up to an ear-piercingly shrill octave.

No one in the crowd is amused.

Penelope swallows nervously. "It appears there was an heir no one knew anything about." I knee her from behind. "Well, they didn't."

I pinch her.

"All right, maybe some of us knew," she mumbles. "But no one knew where to find him . . ."

Matriarch Burgess climbs the stairs to our left, guided by Livinea. She narrows her useless eyes and taps her cane, nodding in Penelope's direction. Then she clasps her withered hands tight over the hook of the cane.

Penelope's knees knock. I feel the vibration through the floorboards.

"All right, all right, so we did." She lowers her head.

"Go on . . ."

"At any rate, now that the *legitimate* successor to the throne of the Commonwealth has been located"—she trips on her words—"it behooves me to rescind my rights to the throne." She gulps. "Thus, without further ado, it is my duty to introduce to you the rightful Ruler of the Commonwealth of Brethren . . . your new leader . . ." She stops to wince before announcing my name. "Urlick Winston Willam Harland Babbit." *Pause.* "Winslow." She drops her head.

The crowd erupts at the sound of the Ruler's official family name. Their heads twist this way and that. Confusion etches deep into their brows.

"Yuh mean 'im?" one angry patron shouts, pointing at me.

"Yes, him," Penelope confirms.

"Is this some sorta joke?" An old man's eyes wrinkle in the crowd.

"I can assure you, I am as shocked by this revelation as you are," Penelope shouts.

The crowd falls back on their heels, aghast.

Hot nerves ball up in my stomach.

"How do we know you're not lying again?"

"How do we know he's who he says he is?"

"Yeah, how do we know who to believe!"

All eyes stare up at me.

The hairs on the back of my neck lift. I have the urge to run, but I force myself to stick.

"It's all right here, in the birth certificate." Parthena jumps in. "Here, Penelope. Read it." She sticks the certificate in her sister's face.

Penelope jerks a filthy look at her sister. I tighten my grip on her arm. She clears her throat and begins, staring hard at the paper, never once lifting her eyes to the crowd. *"The child in question, born heir to the throne, is distinguishable by the following list of unusual markings,"* she mumbles.

"Louder!" someone yells.

*"A raised purple port-wine stain takes up most of the right side of his face . . . and the markings of a purple hand wring his throat and neck!"*

The crowd inhales sharply.

"There are drawings included, if you'd like to compare them," Parthena shouts over their noise.

Penelope's eyes roll.

"Go on," I prod her, scowling.

"Must I?" Her pleading brows lift.

"*Finish.*" I shake her.

Penelope lets out a whimper then starts to read again, but not first without pausing to bite her lip. "*The child in question can also be recognized by the distinctly white cast to his skin and the unusual pink pigment of his eyes. And finally . . .*" She stalls again. Her mouth trembles. Sweat breaks out on her brow. She sucks in a heavy, quivery breath, cowardice swimming in her eyes.

"Say it." I pinch her and she squawks like a bird. Then in a timid, crackling voice, she continues, "*The rightful child bears the mark of the Commonwealth branded on his skin at birth—*"

"What?" I snatch the paper away from her.

"*—above the hairline at the nape of his neck.*"

I read it then look up at the crowd, astonished, certificate shaking in my hands. I held this very paper less than an hour ago, at the castle, where Eyelet and Parthena delivered it to me. But I never thought to read it. There wasn't time. After all, saving Iris was the priority.

Parthena rushes over, parts my hair, and flings me around for the crowd to see. "It's there!" she declares, stabbing at the spot at the base of my skull. "Right there. There it is! You see?"

A shocked gasp pulses throughout the park.

I stare at the words on the paper, reading them over and over again in my mind.

All this time . . . all this *bloody* time I've borne the mark of royalty without even knowing it. A mark that could have assured my freedom. All our freedoms . . .

*A mark that could have saved us all.*

The crowd coos in disbelief.

I look up into their bewildered faces—more than a little bewildered myself.

"Go on, *declare it*!" Parthena shouts at her sister, whirling her about.

"All right, all right," Penelope sneers. "Don't rush me." She huffs the hair from her face, and at last addresses the crowd. "By the powers vested in me as Ruler"—she takes a breath—"I hereby denounce my right to the Commonwealth throne in favour of its rightful successor." She stops and swallows, as if downing something vile. "Urlick Winston William Babbi—I mean, *Winslow*." She drops her head. "Long. May. He. Rule."

The crowd falls to their knees. They bow their heads and clasp their hands in prayer.

"What are they doing?" I whisper to Parthena.

"Worshipping you." She pats my shoulder, softly.

One by one, the people lift their heads, each peering deep into my eyes. Their faces slowly break into warm, welcoming smiles. A hot swell of happiness blooms in my heart. Cheers rise up like fanciful kites twisting through the cloud cover, dipping and swirling, enchanting my ears. I stand basking in the glory of it, my gaze coming to rest on

Eyelet in the front row. *My Eyelet.* She smiles up at me, and my heart swells even more.

This moment could not be any more perfect.

I nod my head to the people, and their voices rise again like a celebration of firecrackers in a dark night. Their chants and cheers reverberate through me, singing in my heart and bouncing off my ribs. Tears of joy press at the backs of my eyes.

I can't believe this is real.

"What do yuh want us to do wif 'er?" Masheck jerks his head toward Penelope, sniveling at the right of the stage.

I turn, placing a hand on Masheck's shoulder. "As much fun as it would be to let you have a go at her, I think that honour lies with her sister, don't you? What do you say, Parthena?" I turn her way. "Can you think of a place we could put your sister? Where she'll no longer be any trouble?"

Parthena drags an all-knowing look over her sister's trembling carcass. "I think I know just the place." She grins.

"No!" Penelope digs in her heels. I signal for the Brigsmen to haul her away. "No!" Penelope kicks and screams. "*No*, Parthena . . . no, *pleeeeease*!"

A strangled cough rings out in the crowd. All heads turn.

I swing around to see Eyelet bent at the waist. Her back is horrendously heaving. "Eyelet?" I lunge to the edge of the stage. "Eyelet, what is it? What's happening?"

She looks up. A small dab of blood rolls from her lips. Her complexion is strangely grey.

*"Eyelet?"* I leap from the stage and charge through the crowd toward her. "*EEEEEEEEEYELET!*"

She collapses to the ground.

# *Acknowledgments*

*Aaahhh*, where to begin, well, let's see . . . with Rosemary Danielis, of course, who is always there for me, waiting at the end of the phone/Skype line to help me conquer all the daily/hourly obstacles of writing, no matter how big or small. HUG. To Kimberley Griffiths Little, who offers keen writing advice and a sharp critical eye . . . thanks, as always. To Donna Walker, without whom, I'm convinced, I could not survive this. Thank you for always being there for me. To Lorin Oberweger, who helps mold and shape my wild ideas into even wilder ones . . . *no, actually* . . . into sensible, intriguing, and even more exciting ones. There aren't enough words. And, of course, to Veronica Rossi for her continued encouragement and support. And to my other writing friends in my network too vast to name here—you know who you are. I LOVE YOU ALL. I would also like to acknowledge my husband, who is always there to support me through all of my writing endeavors, my first reader, my last reader, my biggest fan. More love than imaginable to you, Sean. And to Seth, who puts up with me at my computer for endless hours . . . I will always break for bowling.

And now to some very special readers who have helped me shape this particular book into a rich and personal read. Special thanks go out to Helen Kubiw, Kimberly Mayberry, Ali Goff, Cody Smith-Candelaria, Carole Milner, and to Victoria Blackman, for helping name Livinea. Also to Natalie Trantham for providing Livinea with her middle name, Mae. I couldn't do any of this without *you*, my treasured readers. Unlimited love and thanks to you ALL!

Jacqueline

# *About the Author*

Jacqueline Garlick loves strong heroines, despises whiny sidekicks, and adores good stories about triumphant underdogs. A teacher in her former life, she's now an author of the very books she loves to read: young adult and women's fiction. *Lumière*, the first novel in her Illumination Paradox series, won the prestigious 2013 LYRA award for Best Young Adult Novel and an Indie B.R.A.G. Medallion. The book also received the title of B.R.A.G. Medallion Honoree. Jacqueline lives in a house with a purple wall or two, and dreams of one day having a hidden passageway that leads to a secret room. Visit her website at www.jacquelinegarlick.com.